DIABLO

DARK VALENTINES COLLECTION

T STEDMAN

ISBN (Print) 978-0-9933098-5-4

Website www.tstedman.com

Cover Art & Graphic Design
By
Freddy Studart

Edited by
Helen Williams &
Nicky Jeans

This edition published: December 2015

ACKNOWLEDGMENTS

For Chay
A special thank you to my children and to my readers, Diane
Burke and Gavin Stedman-Bryce.

PART I
DYLAN

CHAPTER 1

London

It was summer, Friday and six o'clock. Grace shoved her stuff into her bag so she could get the hell out of the office and not waste a minute of pub time. The weekend had been a long time coming.

Fidgeting in the lift along with several others, all intent on the same thing, Grace piled out at the ground floor with the first ping of the lift doors opening. There, as arranged, was her best friend, Janey, waiting for her.

Even though they'd seen each other practically every day since playschool, they still embraced like a couple of dizzy teenagers who hadn't seen one another for a month. "Come on, we've got an hour before the others get here," Grace said, linking arms with her and steering her off in the direction of the Olde English Boozer, not far from where she worked.

With the first creak of the heavy sprung door, their senses were bombarded. Hit with the smell of stale beer and hot food, it was a hive of chatter and laughter. Rammed and getting busier by the minute, filling with people all finishing work and starting their weekend. The air was filled with the clatter of change in cash registers and the clinking of glasses.

Grace managed to worm her way into the smallest sliver of an opening at the polished wood bar. "What ya having?" she said, before she'd fully registered the flustered look on Janey's face. "Like that, is it?" she said, turning back to the barman. "Two large gin and tonics, please."

They arrived quickly and Grace pushed one into her friend's hand. "You look like you need it more than me?" Grace said, clinking glasses with her. And that was saying something after the week she'd had. *It had been shit!*

"Oh my god, Grace… I'm bloody exhausted. You are so lucky working full-time, and in London, in all this," Janey said, gesturing with her hand to encompass the whole of their surroundings.

Grace bobbed her head slightly impatiently. *She really wouldn't want her life, not really*, but she kept quiet and allowed her old friend to continue with her rant.

Janey took a deep gulp of her drink. "By the time I've made Dave's tea early, bathed the kids, got my mum round and showed her what's what … then tried to get myself ready, while the kids are arguing and fighting, I start to kinda wonder why the hell I bother. I'm bloody knackered," she finished with a bubble of laughter.

Grace couldn't help laughing with her. "Once you're out, you're okay." It was all so far out of the realm of her experience that she could only guess at what it must be like. She felt a slight pang of yearning. Janey had it all: the semi-detached house, the devoted husband, two adorable kids, well, *most of the time.*

Janey narrowed her eyes at her. "You wouldn't," she said, shaking her head.

Grace laughed, exasperated. She should know; Janey

could read her like a book. "Wouldn't what?" she said, all innocence.

"You know what… want my life."

Grace made a face like she'd been busted and laughed. "Okay, why then… why wouldn't I?… Doesn't every girl want it all… Someone special?"

Janey laughed while she ordered two more drinks, then, pushing a drink into her hand, she gave her a sardonic look. "Someone special, maybe," she conceded with a bob of her head. "But the kids, whole housewife, homebird bit?" She shook her head, not believing a word of it.

Grace looked dramatically affronted. "Whatever do you mean?" she said, and they both giggled.

They both sobered for a moment when Grace no longer laughed and swirled her drink.

"No, seriously though, girl… You okay?" Janey said with real concern.

Grace nodded and sighed, still clinking her ice cubes around in her drink. "Just a bad week… well, a bad month really."

"Come on, babe… You can tell me?"

"I'm nearly thirty, Janey."

"So… you've got loads of time."

Grace raised her eyebrows, not convinced. The fact was, Janey totally understood her. She was as good as family. In fact, with both her parents dead, she *was* her family. The constant partying, the not sticking with one guy, it was all because life could go in the blink of an eye, and she'd been determined to live every damn minute of it.

Grace shrugged and knocked the rest of her drink back in one. "It's all just getting a bit… You know… old now."

Janey nudged her playfully and knocked back her own drink. "Don't go all boring on me now I've finally managed to get out."

Grace laughed; as usual, Janey had managed to drag her out of the doldrums. "Wouldn't dream of it," and the two women laughed and ordered two more drinks.

"Hey, do you remember when we just started school, and we used to love to play dressing up with Michael White, so we could take turns to marry him?" Janey said.

"Oh yeah, how funny we were," Grace said wistfully, while she visualised their little bodies dressed in oversized clothes, walking down an imaginary aisle, with crowns on their heads.

"Yeah, even then, you couldn't just be an ordinary bride, Grace, you had to be a princess.

Grace laughed at that; it was so true. "And did you know he ended up gay?"

"No!" Janey said, scandalised and they both laughed together again.

They spent the rest of a very pleasant hour chatting, reminiscing, ogling the very rare hot passing male (usually far too young) and Grace accepted the ribbing she always got for being the last remaining one out of their group to get hitched.

The friends all oohed and ahhed and hugged and kissed when they met at the usual place at Charing Cross Station. They remarked on who'd lost weight and who looked fabulous, sporting a great suntan from a recent holiday. They were already raucous and loud when Janey shouted over them to hurry. "Come on, let's go!... Table's booked for eight."

Grace looked on indulgently at her old friend, who'd come alive and let go of the domestic bondage she'd been bemoaning not more than half an hour ago. She shook her head and followed on behind, sighing. She really had to make an effort to liven up and get on everyone's wavelength and shake herself out of this mood she was in.

Covent Garden was alive and buzzing. The six women squealed, giggled and tripped their way up the small staircase into the trendy cocktail bar that looked out over the main drag where it was all happening.

"What's everyone having?" one said loudly, and they all swarmed the bar.

Grace did her best to look enthusiastic. She met up with her oldest mates periodically for girly chit-chat and to catch up on their latest goings on, which in her case were never very much. Oh, she went out enough, and they were all envious of her, but her social life usually revolved around people connected with work – one long round of drinks and nightclubs, but nothing that had any substance, or anything that meant anything, or anyone.

As the dating got less and less, she kidded herself that she was going through a dry patch. *Yeah, right,* one that had lasted several months now.

She studied her oldest friends while they chatted animatedly and compared cocktails. All were married or in serious relationships. Most had at least one kid. Everyone was hitched one way or another. All except her, that is. The only one who truly understood why was Janey; the others simply thought she loved the high life.

"Let's drink 'em quick and get another… table's booked for eight, girls," Janey reminded them.

Grace smiled at her. With two kids under four, Janey had a hall pass tonight and wanted to make the most of it. She could only guess what that was like; the comfort of someone to go home to at the end of the night. Grace could go out and stay out or do whatever she bloody well wanted, and had no one to miss her – ever. Yep, life just seemed to have lost its lustre lately.

Another round of drinks was passed around.

It wasn't that she had consciously chosen a career over a relationship, even. Her friends envied her, but she was only a PA – although the company had a young and lively work-force. She owned her own modest mid-terrace house, drove a small, average car and wore high street clothes, nothing to write home about really.

Life had hit an all-time low when they'd all started referring to her as Bridget Jones. Over the last few months, with the big three O looming, they'd excruciatingly pointed out every geeky bloke they passed, calling out, 'Look, Bridget, there's ya Darcy'. *Shit.* The problem was that even if she liked any of the gormless blokes they picked out for her, she couldn't even be bothered to date any more.

It seemed that all the men at her workplace were boring. They had wildly inflated opinions of themselves. Spoke in fake Cockney accents about football and dumping girlfriends, competed over who had the biggest bonus or had the best company car on the new company perk list. She yawned just thinking about it.

Janey shoved another drink in her hand. "Drink up!" she ordered.

Grace nodded meekly and mouthed "sorry", realising that she was being a killjoy, but she just couldn't help it.

It wasn't that she wanted Brad Pitt, or anyone like that, but she wanted, no, needed, something more. She couldn't even put her finger on what that something extra actually was; all she knew was she hadn't had it yet and she missed it desperately. She wanted some kind of deep connection with someone, on a whole other level. Maybe being completely alone in the world made it so important, she wasn't sure. Or perhaps she wanted to meet "the one"; the old cliché.

"Grace… Grace?" Cindy was shouting at her.

She frowned. "What?" She shook her head, mildly annoyed.

Cindy was bobbing her head to the side like she had some sort of affliction until Grace realised she was trying to indicate where she should be looking.

She quickly scanned the bar area and cast her eyes back at Cindy. "What?" she said again.

"Mind-blowingly drop-dead gorgeous bloke at one o'clock checking *you* out!" Cindy said through gritted teeth, flicking her eyes sideways for her to look again.

Grace tutted and made no attempt to hide her glance. But her gaze planted and froze for god knows how long. It had to be several seconds, or minutes, or whatever. Quickly getting a grip, she looked over her right shoulder to make sure Kate Moss hadn't just come in and was standing right behind her.

Nope, he was definitely looking unashamedly straight at her.

She must have been in shock because her eyes went on a walkabout and did a complete visual sweep. From his dark-brown tousled hair, impossibly blue eyes, down his way over six-feet frame, not muscly but taut and firm.

Grace found herself swallowing, then noticed the tattoos peeping out from the collar and rolled-up cuffs of his shirt that hung loose over the slim waistband of his low-slung jeans that tapered and hugged his long, strong legs, finished off with expensive black boots.

She meandered slowly back up to his eyes. They hadn't moved. In fact, he continued to sip his beer from the bottle as if he were waiting for something. His eyes stayed riveted to hers, intense, inquisitive and enquiring.

Fucking hell. She looked back at her friends for some kind of help, but they were all openly staring at him as well, gobs open, then back at her, amazed at the irregular spectacle before them.

"Who is he?" one of them whispered too loudly.

Grace just shook her head slowly. She hadn't the foggiest, but there was something in those eyes she found vaguely familiar and she couldn't quite place him. Maybe she'd seen him on telly. He was good-looking enough. Didn't explain why he was checking her out, though.

She was pretty, but Grace was under no illusions; she wasn't anything special. Her hair was a light mousy brown, wavy and mid-length. Her eyes were brown, her nose a little too small and her lips a little too thin. Skin wasn't bad, waist was smallish, butt too big, and boobs not big enough.

Grace held her breath when she watched him slowly take his eyes off her and bend his head to whisper something to one of the blokes he was drinking with. He nodded and looked over at her as well. She gulped.

Then the mystery man leaned over, put his beer down on the bar and walked towards her in long, easy steps. She had to concentrate on not looking like a dribbling wreck.

"Shit, Grace… he's coming over," her friend Fern giggled.

"Shh!" She tried to look natural, but was sure she was just coming off looking startled.

Her eyes got wider the nearer he got until all she could do was shut them as he appeared to squeeze behind her, probably to go to the men's room.

Mmm, a waft of him drifted up her nose as he went to pass. It was sublime. He smelled gorgeous.

"Grace?" rumbled next to her ear.

She jumped out of her skin. The last thing she was expecting was for him to speak, let alone know her name.

She turned slowly, heart hammering, looking a little like a deer caught in the headlights. "Yeah… yes?" she stammered.

He smiled the most beautifully affecting smile, showing fabulous, even white teeth. Eyes stuck on his mouth, she eventually dragged them up to his heavenly blue eyes. He was staring down at her, waiting.

Ah fuck, she seemed to have lost her power of speech.

Her friends were no help; not one spoke a word or twitched so much as a muscle and all gawped as gormlessly at the poor guy as she did.

"You don't recognise me, do you?" his fabulously deep voice rumbled again.

She shook her head slowly.

He laughed easily, looked away and back at her again, the loveliest male laugh she had ever heard.

"It's me, Dylan… don't leave me hangin'?"

She continued to stare at him. *Dylan... Dylan...* "Dylan!" she screamed. "My God!"

He laughed again and bent his head slightly so she could throw her arms around his neck.

She managed to find some decorum and let him go with an apologetic look. She didn't know what had come over her. Whether it was the genuine pleasure to see him or the relief that she knew him and where from, she wasn't sure. "You've grown," she spluttered, feeling really foolish at her response.

He smiled and nodded. "So have you… Listen, can I buy you and your friends a drink?"

Panic surged through her for a second and she looked at her friends nervously, desperate to spend a little time with this would-be sex god and knowing their table was booked for eight.

They all shooed her with their hands. "Go!" they all said.

She slowed her hammering heartbeat down from Motorhead to Status Quo, and thought she'd have to work with that. Then she walked slowly with him back towards the bar.

He gave her the only vacant stool and she tried to perch on it as ladylike as she could. He rested on the bar next to her with one arm and rested a foot on the rung of the barstool.

Everything he did looked graceful and effortless, while she felt clumsy and awkward. He had to notice. *Fuck.*

Could he be the same guy?

"What?" he said, smiling, pushing a vodka, soda and lime within reach. Then he swigged a new beer.

"I can't believe it's you… it's been years?" she said, simply. "How did you get so tall?" He had always had a pretty face at school, but he was little and weedy for his age and mainly quiet and morose.

He tipped his beer bottle towards her hand. "You're not married?"

Her heart pounded for a second at the implication in the question and then stalled. "No." *Stupid cow, it was just an observation.*

He cocked his head to the side a little in the most adorable way. "You wish you were?" His expression was one of wonder, like she was something he didn't understand.

She shook her head vigorously; the last thing she wanted was to come across desperate for wedding bells. Like she knew he could never be interested in her in that way, but she had to come across as being cool at all costs. The reminder of her last, clumsy date helped her along no end.

He laughed again, probably at the horrified look on her face.

"No," she said, relaxing slightly, all too aware of how weird she was coming across. "I just haven't met the right one yet," she said, circling the ice around in her glass.

He watched her again while he took another mouthful of his beer.

"What about you?" she asked, with a small smile.

He stood up straighter and grinned while he swigged his beer and shook his head as if the idea was ridiculous.

"Not found 'the one' either?" she added.

He raised his eyebrows and finished his beer. "I wouldn't

subject me on anyone, Grace," he said, smiling, and looked deeply into her eyes as was becoming his habit. *God, he was mesmerising.*

If he hadn't belted her so dumbstruck, she would have analysed those words more deeply, but he had been an odd kid at school and she supposed he couldn't have changed that much.

"Do you work 'round here?" he said, breaking the spell again.

"Victoria… easy by train… You know?"

He nodded. "Career girl."

She shook her head and looked into her drink again. "No… just secretarial… nothing special."

He was studying her again.

"What about you?" she said, to take some of the heat off herself. "Do you work nine to five?" The minute the words left her mouth, she frowned and joined him when he laughed and just shook his head.

"No, I don't suppose you do," she conceded. It was a ridiculous thing to say. She could tell that just by looking at him.

His eyes left her for the first time when a voice called from behind her. "D!"

She moved sideways as his friend passed him a leather jacket and black crash helmet. *Of course he rode a bike.* She could visualise no other way of him getting around. *Public transport? Ludicrous.*

"We're off," his friend said.

She became aware of another two men standing with him, ready to leave as well.

Dylan looked down at her and smiled regretfully. "I have to go."

She smiled up at him. "Short and sweet." *Like most good things in her life.*

Dylan reached over the bar towards the barman and asked him something. He came back with a pen, then he tossed over a beer mat.

"Can I have your number, Grace? I'd like not to have to rush off next time."

She blinked at him a few times, like she hadn't heard properly, then pulled the mat close and bent over it, scribbling wildly; her mobile, her work and her home number. She steeled herself before she gave her email address as well. "I could put it straight in your phone if you like?" she said, passing it to him and not looking him in the eye. *For fuck's sake!*

He grinned and put it in his jacket pocket, then shrugged it on. "I'm an old-fashioned kinda guy."

Grace felt embarrassed. Of course, he probably lived with someone gorgeous and sophisticated and would never want to give her *his* number. *Doh*, that was why he wanted her number written down, so it wouldn't look as suspicious. Girls must pass him their numbers all the time.

He smiled knowingly, as if he'd just read her thoughts and they amused him.

Yeah, stupid plain Grace, and she felt herself blush.

He moved towards her and brushed her cheek with his lips, then stayed there a moment too long. "Later then, Grace Fellows," he said, right next to her ear.

The words tingled on her cheek and went down to her toes. *He remembered her name.* All she could do when he pulled away was to swallow hard and stare at him as if he were a Martian. And for the life of her, she couldn't think of a single word to say. He flashed that charismatic grin of his and stepped away to join his friends loitering near the exit.

Grace watched him idiotically from her bar-stool till he disappeared. She'd completely forgotten her friends until Cindy shouted, "Quick … veranda!" and they all scurried out onto the smokers' balcony overlooking the cobbled stones beneath. After a much-needed moment to come back down to earth, Grace scampered after them.

They were all hanging over the balcony when he emerged from the door underneath them. He raised a hand to his two friends, who, after a brief conversation with him, walked off in opposite directions. Then he walked in his easy, fluid steps to a large bike parked across the way, threw a leg over, flipped it back off its stand and smiled straight up at the balcony, knowing they'd been there the whole time. Well and truly busted, they looked down at him with their mouths open – Grace, the reddest of all.

Completely at ease, he raised a hand to them in goodbye, started his bike and moved off gradually. They didn't hear the roar until he was out of sight.

They watched the space he'd left for quite a few more moments before Janey said, "Fucking hell, Grace, who is he?"

"Dylan O'Shea, Grace said, in a really small voice. "Little Dylan O'Shea."

Janey turned and faced her in all seriousness. "Well, there's nothing fucking little about him now."

And they all dissolved into shrieks of laughter.

CHAPTER 2

Grace was in a daze the whole journey home. The rest of the evening had paled into insignificance after bumping into Dylan.

Lost in old memories, she racked her brains to try to remember some forgotten friendship with him, but the truth was there had been very little. She had felt a bit sorry for the new kid at school and sat with him in some lessons as no one else would, had a go at a few idiots for taking the piss out of him a bit for being quiet – that was about it. He'd hardly spoken a word to her and she'd just shrugged it off and carried on with her school life, with him often hovering nearby. He was so in the background that, despite being there at the time, Janey had had to be reminded of who he was.

Then, at sixteen, she'd left school and hadn't laid eyes on him from that day to this. Just went to show how a person could change.

The days that followed their meeting again were long and slow. Never-ending rounds of work, stables, sleep, work, stables, sleep. With no interest in socialising, the time she spent with her little horse, Jet, was the only relief she had from the torture of waiting for his call.

Janey and the rest of her friends had phoned for an update every day, and she would snatch up the phone, thinking it was him and sag with disappointment when it wasn't. By the tenth day, her friends had stopped asking and even she had given up.

Why would someone like him want to spend time with someone like her? He probably had a stable of women. She laughed at her own silly joke as she closed the door to Jet's stable.

She made the short drive home to the village where she lived and threw her keys down onto the small telephone table next to the front door. The phone was already ringing. "Hello?" She sounded as tired as she felt. It had been a long week.

"Grace?"

She stopped breathing.

"Hello?" the deep male voice said. "Grace?"

"Dylan?" she said, shaking herself out of her shock.

"Hey... I was worried you would have forgotten me."

As if. "Oh no, I could never... *Shit!* You just took me by surprise, that's all."

His lovely laugh permeated the airwaves. "Are you okay to talk?"

Did he think she wasn't alone? "Yes, of course," she said, frowning at how manic she sounded.

"Sorry I haven't been in touch sooner... been working," Dylan said, not elaborating further.

"Oh, that's fine," she lied. "No worries... are you okay?"

"Yeah." The line went quiet for a beat.

He sounded sad or tired or something and the silence felt awkward. Realising she might not get another chance, she bit the bullet, "Dylan, do you want to meet up... for a drink... or just a coffee even?"

The smile returned to his voice. "Yeah, I do."

She was swamped with relief.

"Whereabouts do you live?" he asked.

"I'm only about five miles from where I lived when we were kids."

"Do you want to meet out somewhere? I doubt you'll be into bikes."

"How dare you… I handle half a ton of mad horse, okay, so I think I can cope with being on the back of one little bike."

He laughed, "You ride horses?"

"Yes, I do. You can pick me up from home if you like?"

"Okay," he said, in mock defeat. "You'd better give me the address then?"

She reeled it off and waited while he wrote it down.

"Do you always give your address so easily to strangers, Grace?"

Her heart stalled and she wasn't sure what to say to that. Was he telling her off, or just being the concerned friend? "You're not a stranger, Dylan," she said eventually.

There was an agonising silence on the line. *Had she fucked it up already?*

"I suppose not," he said, eventually. "But you can't be too careful."

GRACE WATCHED HIM PULL UP, peeking round the curtain of the upstairs window of her two-up two-down terrace cottage.

Dylan pulled off his crash helmet and ran his fingers through his hair to bring it back to life after being flattened. He studied the house for a few moments, then slowly got off the bike and approached the door.

Grace scooted downstairs at the sound of the doorknocker and threw open the door. She had forgotten just how big he was. His presence, smile and his wonderful smell all blasted her senses at the same time. *Oh boy, he should carry a health warning.*

"Ready?" he said, grinning wider.

Was he aware of the effect he was having? Shit, he was going to walk all over her.

She took a deep breath and nodded, summoning the courage while he passed her a crash helmet, black like his, and a smaller leather jacket. "You'll need this too."

She closed the door behind her, pulled the jacket on and slung her small bag across her body.

"Biker chick," he said, smiling his approval.

He pulled his helmet on, straddled the bike, started it and indicated with his head for her to climb on behind him. She did it without hesitation.

"Hold on to me," he said. "And lean with the bike."

Her head felt cumbersome as she nodded and she inched closer to him. *Such a hardship!* Gingerly, she put her hands around him.

"Tighter!" he ordered.

Oh god, and she did as she was told when the bike moved off.

The ride was exhilarating and all the more so with the genuine excuse to cuddle into him. The habit of telling herself he was just a friend started from that moment. She just couldn't afford to get carried away. He was heartbreak material. She was just riding pillion on his bike, that's all.

After a ride that was over all too quickly, they pulled into a pretty country pub restaurant. They hung their helmets on the handlebars and she followed Dylan into the bar. He ordered them two beers and took her outside to a garden full of wooden tables that swept down to a river perfectly designed for such an evening. A young waiter was bringing out pub food as well as drinks. There weren't too many people as it was a weeknight; a large group, a few couples and only a handful of kids still wading with fishing nets.

Dylan guided her to a wooden table at the furthest point in the garden and they sat opposite each other.

"Have you come here before?" she asked.

He nodded. "Yeah, it's out of the way… I like it."

She wondered if she was just one of many girls he'd brought there.

They both stayed quiet for a few moments and she realised that he was like that by nature, just as he'd been as a kid. "So what have you been up to for the last thirteen or so years?" she said, breaking the ice with a grin.

He smiled at her and shrugged. "Not much… Work."

He was looking at her with that penetrating gaze again and the silence gaped between them.

Rushing to fill the gap in conversation again, "Where do you live?" she said, blasting red. His reserve made her feel awkward, like she was being nosy with every question. "I mean… did you have far to come?"

He smiled slightly as if he knew he was making her uncomfortable and took a sip of his beer.

"Not much of a talker, are you?"

He laughed. "Yeah, I have to live near central London."

She laughed with him, relieved that the awkwardness had lifted slightly, but he hadn't really answered her question at all. *Why did he have to?* It was as though she had to prise everything out of him. "You never said what you do for a living?" she said, looking him straight in the eyes. *It was a reasonable question.*

He laughed uneasily into his drink and took a large swig.

"What?" she said, laughing as well but more out of confusion. "Did I ask the wrong thing or something?" She waited for him to answer.

He sobered his features as if he knew he would piss her off if he continued in the same vein and pushed his beer bottle away from him. "No, it's just that I kind of hoped it wouldn't come up this quickly?" he said, staring straight at her with his intensely blue eyes again.

She frowned. "How bad can it be?"

He sighed and put his head back to search the sky. Then he looked to either side of him and laid his hands flat on the table like he was trying to find the right words.

Her blood began to pump and a deep feeling of unease crept over her. She already thought he was just too good to be true. *Was he a bank robber, a drug dealer?* They were the worst things she could think of off the top of her head. Then just as she wanted to scream, *for fuck sake, say it.*

He looked her dead in the eye. "I work in the adult entertainment industry." Then studied her face closely.

Adult entertainment? She had to run through all the connotations of what that could actually be. "What… like a Chippendale or something?" she said, flatly.

His expression became pained, then he gave an involuntary blast of laughter. He looked away, then back at her in absolute disbelief. "A Chippendale?… I say adult entertainment and you say Chippendale?"

First, she was really worried she'd offended him, then a wide grin extended across his face, letting her off the hook. He simply couldn't believe what she'd come out with.

"What?… Why are you looking at me like that?" she said, with a nervous giggle. "That's adult, isn't it?"

He raised his eyebrows. "You could see me doing that?" he said, clearly holding in his amusement.

Relieved, she bit her lip at her foolishness and shook her head. "No … come to think of it, I couldn't."

"I don't know whether to have the hump or kiss you?" he said, smiling shyly.

She grinned. He was playing with her, which, along with his quiet reserve, was irresistible. She wasn't going to let him off the hook though. "Okay, so you don't shake your tush in public," she said, laughing. "What then?"

Just when she thought he would answer her, the young waiter came to take their empties.

"Can I get another two beers?" Dylan said.

"Sure." The waiter went off.

He flashed his eyes again. "I work in films."

She continued to stare into them until he averted his. *Films... Films.* "What, porn?" she blurted, frowning. It just sounded too absurd for words.

She hoped he would break into laughter and say, gotcha, but he continued to look at her, face deadpan, eyes angelic and then she knew he wasn't joking. "Behind the camera?" she said, *please!*

"In front," he said, letting her down softly, his eyes studying her intensely.

She instinctively knew that how she dealt with this revelation would affect everything going forward. *But fuck, porn?* She wanted to scream.

So she got a grip on her spiralling thoughts and emotions. *No one had broken any trust. They were just getting to know each other. This was part of the process. There was always going to be a catch with this guy, and this was it.*

Again, they were interrupted when their drinks came. Dylan gave him a note. "Keep the change." Then they were alone again.

She took a deep breath. "It's not like it makes a difference to me," she said, shrugging. "We're just friends." And she picked up her beer and took a big gulp.

He lifted his and watched her as he put the bottle to his lips. The silence was deafening.

Was that a flicker of a flinch in his eyes, as if he'd been wounded? Why did she feel bad? He hid it immediately. "That's right," he said, smiling again and back in control.

She swallowed hard. "So that's what you've been doing since I met you the other day... filming?"

He nodded slowly, but his face got serious. "Yeah... I don't see or speak to anyone."

She had a curious feeling of concern for him that just wasn't logical after what she'd just learnt. She didn't really know him at all, but what was coming across in waves was that he didn't seem to like what he did very much and that wasn't what she would have expected at all. She would have loved to question him further, but felt she didn't really know him enough to pry. He would have to volunteer information when he was ready. *At least he hadn't hidden it from her?* "I don't suppose it's easy having a relationship in your line of work?"

His eyes looked soulful and he smiled regretfully. "Impossible."

A lump came up in her throat. *Shit*, she felt so sorry for him. He seemed so incredibly alone, just like when he was a kid – even more so. A million questions buzzed around her head, but she knew instinctively that if she dwelt on it, it would only make him feel shittier about it. She exhaled loudly, "Look... there's a footpath down there. Shall we see where it leads?"

His expression changed immediately from sadness to surprise, then to a smile of relief. He nodded. "Yeah ..." Then he stood and held out his hand to help her up.

Despite Dylan's revelations, and awkward beginning to their date that wasn't a date, Grace resolved to keep it light and he began to unwind, which seemed absurd. He was the drop-dead gorgeous sex god; she should be the one unable to string a sentence together.

They followed the path that followed the river, smelling

the wonderful summer evening smells, pulling the heads off the long grasses and petting the noses of inquisitive horses reaching over the fences to say hello. Gradually, they both seemed to relax into each other's company—well as much as a girl could walking alone with the sexiest man she'd ever met. When they accidentally bumped arms, or he stood a little too close to look at something with her, she couldn't help blushing from head to toe with an acute awareness of every inch of him. It was an involuntary response.

"You like horses?" she asked, when a velvety muzzle went from sniffing her hand to nipping at Dylan's pocket.

He smiled, nodding and rubbed a hand between the horse's eyes. An act only someone completely at ease and used to horses would do. Out came a pack of mints and he took one out and popped it on his flattened palm for the horse to nibble on. Good-looking, sexy and comfortable around horses – could he get any sexier? She shook herself out of her delusions and they continued along the path. She kept her questions general. "So what do you do in your spare time – any hobbies?"

They seemed to gravitate to each other constantly, with his hand brushing hers for the umpteenth time. Pausing, he looked down into her eyes with that hypnotic gaze of his. In response, her face radiated heat again. "Not really... I like a drink occasionally, I keep fit... I have to, you know?"

God, that unblinking, smouldering stare of his. Instead of letting it get all weird again with the reference to his job, she reached up and pinched his bicep and shrugged, "Could still do with some work."

He laughed out loud, that wonderful deep sound that she decided she'd never get tired of and she turned and walked on before he saw her red cheeks yet again.

"Shh!" she whispered, stopping suddenly and grasping his hand. There on the path in front of them was a duck with a line of ducklings so tiny and cute. His body heat quietly stilled behind her, igniting her nerve endings as if he encased her. She silently breathed through it.

The duck led her little charges into the water and they eventually disappeared along the riverbank. Grace looked up at Dylan and he smiled down at her. "Beautiful," he said simply, and they looked at each other a long while. Her heart thudded in her ears with a moment charged with electricity. But instead of kissing her, he gently touched the base of her spine and they walked on. She swallowed and attempted to get her head together again. *Friends... that's all we are.*

Eventually, they came back to where they started and it was nearly dark.

"You have to be up early?" Dylan asked.

She nodded sadly. "Six."

He flinched.

She bet he hadn't seen that time in the morning for years unless he hadn't gone to bed.

"Come on, I'll take you home."

She sighed. She'd had a wonderful time with him and didn't want it to end. He was such easy company when they both relaxed. "Take the long way?" she said.

He passed her the crash helmet and beamed a smile. "You really like the bike," he said, nodding his approval.

She grinned back. *Let him think that for now.* And not that she couldn't get enough of being up close and personal with him, and wanting her arms around him for as long as possible.

CHAPTER 3

Grace sat in Janey's front room with her friends and they all shrieked with laughter, pinging crotchless knickers and making jokes at the size of the latest Rampant Rabbit.

She'd known most of them from school. A couple were cousins of friends that had come along later, joined the group, and stayed ever since. All girls together, and away from their husbands, they were as spirited and as noisy as a bunch of hyenas.

"Ah come on, Grace, buy one," Janey said. "You need it the most," and they all erupted into laughter.

Grace was used to the joking about her lack of sex life. "Pass me the catalogue," she said, in defeat. It had been several days since her date (if she could call it that) with Dylan. So it didn't look as though she was getting any with a real live man any time soon.

A new bottle of Cava was opened and all their glasses were topped up.

"You're quiet tonight, Grace… What's up?" Fern said. A

plump girl with short, brown, elfin hair, and a little more serious than the others

"Yes, Grace, you've not been yourself in ages," another said.

Grace drank down her drink with all eyes suddenly on her. "What?" she said, palm upturned, all innocence. "I'm fine." But she felt her face tinge with crimson.

The room read her guilt and Janey hitched a breath dramatically. "You've spoken to him," she said, pointing an accusing index finger.

Grace's eyes widened and she looked at her friends' faces, neither confirming nor denying.

The others seized on the juicy gossip and demanded she spill.

"We went out a couple of days ago," Grace admitted cautiously.

The room was momentarily stunned, then erupted in questions.

She held out her hands to calm them all down. "We're just friends. We went out for a drink. That's all, okay?"

"No, babe... blokes don't go out of their way to be just friends," Fern said.

Everyone nodded sagely.

Grace considered it and bobbed her head, conceding that there was some truth in that. But when she thought about Dylan and what she knew of him so far, she had to question that logic. "I think you're wrong, Fern."

They all chimed in again, talking over each other in their general excitement.

"Look, he's different, okay? He's like no one I've ever met."

The room all chorused, "Oh my god, she's got it bad," and, "she's so naive."

It was all starting to make her feel a little exasperated with them. *Could she confide in them totally?*

Janey shut everyone up. Grace wasn't sure whether she was perceptive or just giving her a break. "What makes you think that then, Grace?" she asked. "Men can talk a good talk, you know they can."

Grace felt defeated. All she had was a gut instinct that told her that this one was different. She wasn't even sure how yet. "That's just it, he doesn't tell me much at all."

"Secrets… now there's something new," someone said, and they all laughed.

Grace was getting really irritated with them. It did all sound silly now she was away from him, but when she was with him, walking, talking, riding on his bike, everything seemed right and okay. "Look, nothing's gonna happen. I know it's not."

"Ain't there no chemistry, Grace?"

She raised her eyebrows. There was certainly plenty of that on her part, but she shook her head. "He doesn't see me like that, I know he doesn't."

"What, you've actually had that conversation?"

"More or less."

"More or less?" Janey mimicked. "You mean the bastard actually took you out and gave you the 'I only see you as a friend' convo?"

"Not exactly." Grace wished she hadn't got into it now.

"What then?"

"He told me what he did for a living." There, she was going to drop the bomb to shut them all up.

The room fell silent.

Grace swallowed, took a deep breath and went for it. "Look, you mustn't breathe a word that I've told you, okay?"

They all nodded vigorously. Some made the cross on their chests.

"No, really... because I get the impression that he wouldn't want me to blab about it."

"God, Grace, just flippin' tell us," Janey said.

"Adult films!" Grace blurted and put her hands up to her mouth.

They all repeated the words and looked at each other in case they hadn't understood properly.

"What, porn?" Fern said, for them all.

Grace nodded apprehensively.

The room remained stunned.

"Shit, I wasn't expecting that," someone said.

"There's all kinds, ya know?" Fern continued, a little more kindly.

"Yeah, some are really quite comical," another chimed in.

"Yeah, sick an' all."

They all had an opinion and had all seen at least one. That was one more than Grace.

"What's he do?" Janey asked.

Grace shook her head. "I don't know. All he said was that when he's filming, he doesn't see or speak to anyone."

They all frowned and looked at each other again.

"That don't sound good," Janey said.

"Ah, come on, Janey ... you don't know that?" Fern said.

Grace was grateful for the optimism.

"What do you think, Grace?" another said.

She shook her head, feeling overwhelmed with it all.

"Do you like him?"

She sagged. No point in lying. "What's not to like?"

"He could have AIDS, Grace."

She looked into her friend's eyes and nodded. That was very true; he could be HIV positive, and an angle she hadn't really thought of. Dylan was probably screwing on a large scale and with a high-risk group of people who could be carrying all manner of nasties.

"Are you going to see him again?"

She smiled in defeat. That was the most poignant question of the evening and the one she undoubtedly knew the answer to, no matter how much her friends warned her.

Her mobile phone rang. Saved by the bell. Stunned momentarily, she rummaged in her bag and peeked at the display. Caller: Dylan. "It's him!"

"Answer it!" they all demanded.

The room hushed and she pressed the button. "Hello."

"Grace?… Hey, it's me."

"Oh, hi Dylan, how are you?" she said, trying to sound as unaffected as possible, with all the rapt faces watching her closely.

"I'm good. What are you up to?"

"I'm at my friend Janey's house… at an Ann Summers party," she said, cringing. Why that somehow concerned him, she didn't know?

There was silence for a beat and she prayed he hadn't heard her cringing in her voice. *Fuck!* She closed her eyes.

"Okay, I won't keep you long," he said, eventually. "I just called to say I enjoyed the other night."

"Me too," she said more softly, wishing she were alone.

"What are you up to on Sunday?" he said.

"I have a small Ranch Horse event at my stables."

"Like a horse show?"

"Come down if you want… I'm there all day?"

He laughed as if he knew she was trying to be flippant about it. "Okay … better text me through the address."

"So you're not a stranger now, then?" she said, grinning.

He laughed again. "Too late now, Grace," he said quietly, sending a shiver down her spine. Even his voice held a promise and did wicked things to her.

"I'd better warn you, my friends you met the other night will probably be there?"

"Thanks for the heads up. Maybe I'll come late, wouldn't want to crash the party."

"Okay," she said, not knowing what else to say. "I'll text you later."

"Later then." And he was gone.

She took the phone away from her ear slowly, still reeling from the interaction with him.

"You still think he's not interested, Grace?" Janey said, one eyebrow up.

Grace shrugged. She wanted to believe her and understood what her friends were saying. He certainly made her feel good when she was around him. He didn't act like the big-headed womaniser you would expect him to be, looking like he did, being as cool as he was, and doing the work he did. She was confused. Something just wasn't adding up with him.

DYLAN ROCKED up during the afternoon. Grace's eyes had strayed to the drive all day, waiting for him until she had told herself he probably wouldn't come. But there he was, as bold as brass and just as beautiful, not the slightest bit fazed that all her friends were there, or that she was riding western when she lived in England.

Her father was a keen horseman and loved anything connected with cowboys, so when a chance came to give it a try a year or so after his death, it seemed a great way to stay connected to him, as well as being super fun.

Totally thrown off balance at his arrival, she made a pig's ear of her first attempt at roping the calf, snagging her foot instead. *Shit*, just when she wanted to look like an expert.

She lined up with the other competitors on the opposite side of the arena, waiting for her next go and watched all her friends fawning over him. She shook her head at their duplicity. He was a total hit with them.

She completed her second run and then a third, thankfully redeeming herself, roping the calf, getting a respectable time and earning her a second place. She jogged over to the group but only had eyes for Dylan.

He fussed her horse, confirming her suspicions that he'd been around horses before. "I didn't realise you were a professional?" he said.

She blushed and said, "No way, but thanks."

Her friends were giggly, but after the initial novelty of him had worn off, they all disappeared, one by one, to pick kids up and cook their husbands' dinners.

Dylan fit right in immediately. During the course of the afternoon, he helped put up and take down cattle pens and played judge's assistant when an extra spotter was needed. Grace was so proud of him that she couldn't speak. Everyone assumed he was her man and she let them. *Why not?* She could pretend just for a day.

At the end of the day, she walked back to the barn, side by side, with him leading her horse, and he leaned down and kissed her cheek. "Well done," he said, simply. "I had no idea you were a cowgirl… It's really cool."

She blushed. "There are a few things you don't know about me."

He cocked his head at that adorable angle she was getting used to. "I guess so."

When they reached the barn, Grace quickly took off Jet's saddle and bridle and replenished her hay and water supply. She smiled to herself when Dylan picked up a brush and began to brush her while she worked.

"You're no beginner… you're too at ease around her?" Grace said, coming over to stand next to him.

"It's easy … she's beautiful," Dylan said, running a hand over her sleek black coat.

Again, he'd sidestepped a question. "You've been around horses, though, I can tell."

"A bit … before I met you … you know, at school." He continued to brush her and Grace remained silent, willing him on. "I was sent to stay with an uncle in Ireland for a few months. He was a horse dealer. I rode a bit then … nothing since though." His eyes flashed over to Grace and back down to Jet's coat.

He feels vulnerable when he tells me something. It seemed preposterous that he could be so confident and overtly sexual and yet painfully introverted when they were alone. And it was those snippets of vulnerability that were drawing her in slowly but surely. She looked at him with wonder. "You never cease to amaze me, Dylan."

A shy grin crept across his face when he looked at her.

"Would you like to try again sometime?" Grace said.

"She's a bit small for me, don't ya think?"

"Very funny. I can borrow a big one for you. We can see how you feel, then we can go out for a ride if you like?"

Dylan bobbed his head. "Yeah, why not."

Grace got out the carrots she'd reserved for Jet's treat at the end of a hard day and shared them with Dylan so he could feed her as well.

"You love this little horse a lot, don't you?" Dylan said, glancing sideways at her.

"She's my partner, you know? We have an understanding. She's sort of misunderstood like me. I just give her the space to be a horse and she appreciates it and tries really hard for me," Grace said, lost in the wonderful bond she felt.

Dylan put his arm around her shoulders and pulled her into his side. "You always take care of people."

Her brow furrowed and she blinked away tears as she looked up into his beautiful blue gaze. It was a strange thing to say. *Was he referring to something she'd forgotten?* A flicker of doubt crossed his face like he'd said the wrong thing. Anxious for him not to clam up, she rambled on, "Sometimes, when you help somebody get better, you end up curing yourself," she said.

He stared into her eyes for a long moment as if boring into her soul, put a hand on her cheek and rubbed his thumb across her cheekbone. "You are one in a million," he whispered. And leant down and gently brushed his lips against hers.

She closed her eyes and absorbed the affection. The contact shot electricity through her body and her heart hammered against her ribs. It was a tender kiss but full of promise. She opened her mouth slightly and stroked his lips with her tongue and longed for him to do the same.

He seemed so restrained; his hand trembled next to her cheek. She licked him again and this time he responded tentatively. He touched her tongue gently with his so softly and cautiously she had to remind herself who he was. He swirled his tongue with hers and his taste swamped her senses, sending a wonderful ache to the juncture of her thighs.

Everything in her screamed to pull him to her hard, so she could devour him hungrily, but something else told her to go slowly, as ludicrous as that seemed. She broke the kiss first and clasped the hand that rested on her cheek "You're shaking," she whispered.

He pulled his hand away slowly and held it out in front of him to watch it closely. It was shaking violently. "I've got to go," he said, turning on his heel.

"Dylan?"

He unbolted the stable door and began to jog away and out of the barn.

"Dylan?" she shouted this time.

Confounded, she ran to the barn door and called again, but he refused to turn and continued to jog down the drive and out to the front car park to his waiting bike. She was left totally confused, with her hands on her hips.

Her heart was still hammering from the kiss and the shock of his sudden departure. *Fuck,* he was such a contradiction. Saying stuff one minute like she was one in a million, then running off like he couldn't escape fast enough.

Hurt and frustration quickly gave way to anger. The guy swooped in, turned her world upside down, and fucked off again after demolishing her defences. And, what's more, he left her gagging for more, never to be the same again.

She kicked a stone in temper. *FUCK!*

CHAPTER 4

*A*nger dissipated into terror after several days and she still hadn't heard from Dylan.

She'd admitted to Janey that they'd kissed but that he'd literally run away afterwards, and she'd come up with the theory that he was a commitment-phobe, which explained why he did the line of work he did. It was feasible, she supposed. But Janey hadn't been there to see the look of sheer horror on his face.

The whole thing had done nothing for her self-confidence. And so she waited for Dylan to call, on tenterhooks – praying that she'd hear from him again.

A week had gone by and she'd heard nothing.

Cursing her own weakness, she caved and texted him: *Are you OK?*

Still nothing.

Several more agonising days passed.

She resolved to try texting him one last time just to make sure: *I'm sorry.*

It wasn't until 3 a.m. the following night that she got her reply: *You didn't do anything wrong.*

She stared at her phone a long time. What she replied now meant everything. She knew so little about him, but what she did know was that he set boundaries without telling her what they were, and when she inadvertently stepped over them, he didn't like it. But if she took the heat off and didn't push him, he relaxed. He was one complicated man.

She picked up her phone. Here goes: *Do you want to ride this Sunday?*

She waited an agonising thirty minutes and then: *What should I wear?*

She breathed a sigh of relief. *Jeans 'n' boots. I'll borrow a Stetson for you. Shall we say 2?*

Straight back: *C U then.*

She cuddled the phone to her chest and closed her eyes. It felt like she had another chance. She couldn't fuck this up. She now realised how much he had come to mean to her already. And if all he could offer was friendship, well then, she would take that for now. She knew that she had to go at his speed or not at all.

It all seemed so ridiculous considering what he did for a living, but he was quickly becoming a drug she had to have more of.

WHEN HE TURNED up at her stables the following Sunday, it was as if nothing had happened. He smiled and kissed her on the cheek as soon as he arrived and, to save any awkwardness, she quickly introduced him to the horse he'd be riding: a beautiful, large chestnut mare called Storm. He loved her on sight.

Grace found him a black Stetson, which fitted him perfectly and looked great. He looked so hot that Grace had to try not to stare at him too much. The cowboy look totally suited him, but then again, everything did.

The owner wanted to see his standard of riding to make sure he'd be safe going out, so Grace adjusted his stirrups and he hopped on. It made her wonder how he kept so fit. *A question for later.*

He told her he had only ever ridden in the traditional English style, but after a few pointers, he was soon steering this way and that with loose reins held in one hand – stopping and moving off like an old pro. When he put the horse into a jog, Grace recognised straight away that he had a natural seat and was deep and steady in the saddle and had lovely light hands on the horse's mouth.

Leaving Dylan to practice, she tacked up Jet and they were soon miles out in the farmers' fields, following the tractor tracks.

The day was sunny, but a cool breeze kept them and the horses from getting too hot. They chatted freely along the way, Grace always mindful of keeping it light and surface. Favourite bands – hers: Pearl Jam, his: various artists she didn't recognise. Films – hers: *It's a Wonderful Life*, his: *The Long Good Friday*. And stuff like that.

Pretty soon Dylan's confidence in his horse had grown so much that they could lope side by side at the edge of the cornfields, until they eventually slowed to a walk and took a path through the cool green of the woods.

They found a clearing, dismounted and let their horses graze while they sat and rested on a log.

"Can I ask you about your work, Dylan?" she asked cautiously.

He looked down at the floor. "What do you want to know?"

She watched him closely, not sure whether she should continue, *but fuck,* there was so much about him that confused her. They'd seen each other just a couple of times, but he threw her off balance constantly – pulling her to him like a magnet and then pushing her away. Her head was in a whirl. "It's just that when I imagine someone who... You know, does that sort of thing for a job..."

Dylan narrowed his eyes as she spoke.

She wavered and took a fortifying breath and pushed on. "I don't imagine him to be shy?"

He visibly relaxed, smiled slightly and leaned forward with his elbows on his knees. "It's not me when I'm working," he said softly, looking ahead of him, far off through the trees.

Grace frowned. "I get it... like you're acting."

He looked sideways at her sharply, his brow furrowed. "More than that... I have to become someone else." And he looked ahead of him again.

It felt as though she had angered him. "I'm sorry, Dylan. I'm just trying to understand."

He fidgeted and was moodily quiet for a few moments.

Grace really tried to phrase her words carefully. "So you have to get into character and that's why you don't speak to anyone?"

When his face turned to her again, it wasn't anger she saw but misery and it cut her to the quick. She felt terrible, but she simply could not continue with him as friends (or whatever they were) until she understood him a little. She held her breath and waited for him to speak.

"That's it, Grace. That's totally it."

Relieved, she reached out a hesitant hand to touch his cheek. He closed his eyes, accepting the contact. She inched closer and held his face and kissed his forehead, then his nose, his mouth, desperately hoping it wasn't the wrong thing to do. She simply could not gauge this man or the rules of this relationship.

When she pulled apart from him, he slowly opened his eyes. "You're such a contradiction," she said.

He smiled ruefully. "I know."

"I'm still trying to work you out."

"I know you are," he repeated, and pulled her into him, cuddled her to his chest and rested his chin on the top of her head. "I can't give you what you need, Grace."

She swallowed hard, not knowing how to reply to that. "What are they called… your films?"

He stiffened and remained quiet for a beat. "Diablo … they always have Diablo in the title. Google that, and something will come up," he said, quietly.

Sadness seemed to be coming off him in waves and she longed to question him further, about his films, his inability to get too close to her, but she was still in his arms and she knew the intimacy of the moment would be lost if she continued. And so she let him just hold her for what seemed a very long time, until eventually, he kissed the top of her head. "Hadn't we better get back before we're missed?"

She reluctantly nodded.

They walked over to their horses, still grazing a little way off, mounted and rode back to the stables in companionable silence. Her eyes returned to him often, he was just so beautiful. A perfect specimen of a man on the outside, but a puzzle underneath; a puzzle that she was determined to piece together.

As soon as she'd got the chance, Grace had phoned Janey and got her on the case to find the Diablo films. She needed a clue, any clue, as to who the real Dylan was. When she disconnected her call, a text message came through from Dylan:

Keep Saturday free. I have a surprise. D

EVEN IF SHE had been booked, her diary would have been cleared for Dylan. She barely knew him and was getting in deep. A fact that weighed heavily on her, making her feel like a hopeless sap.

It felt like a year, but Saturday arrived and he collected her early, informing her they had a little way to travel. Cuddled into the warmth of his body throughout the two-hour journey on his bike, they eventually arrived at the Milton Keynes Bowl.

Realising where she was and seeing all the people already making their way in, she hitched a breath. "We're seeing a band?"

He nodded, came to a stop and took off his crash helmet. Reaching into his jacket pocket, he pulled out the tickets.

"Pearl Jam!" she squealed, and leapt off the bike. "You remembered."

"I listen," he said, quietly.

She looked at his face, slightly blushing; *yes, you do.* She was humbled by his thoughtfulness. *It was a real boyfriend-type thing to do.*

Before she could get soppy, he picked up her hand and walked with her into the stadium to find their places.

Grace floated through the best evening of her life. Singing along to all the songs, Dylan was reserved as always, but when they stood, he held her in front of the shelter of his big body and she snuggled into the heat of him. And he let her. Everything was perfect. Her favourite band she'd waited years to see, and her perfect man to escort her. It felt as though they were a real couple.

She had to keep telling herself they were only friends.

Dylan had made it crystal clear more than once that that was all he wanted. But standing in the circle of his arms with him touching her skin at every opportunity, she couldn't help but read the signals.

When the concert finished, he bought her a programme as a keepsake and they made the long journey home.

He kept the engine running outside her house and she reluctantly gave him the crash helmet back. "Come in," she said, keeping her eyes downcast.

When he didn't answer or move, she chanced a glance at his face and he looked uncertain, as if he were weighing something up. "No pressure," she added, and went to turn away towards the house. When she heard the engine switch off, butterflies tickled her stomach.

Now that he'd agreed, she was barraged with insecurities. *Shit,* she'd half expected a knockback. What would she do with him when she had him? She just entered the house without looking at him, threw her keys down on the table next to the door and busied herself making coffee.

Every now and then, she peeked at him waiting in her small living room. His eyes were roaming about the place, taking in her personal space.

When he caught her watching him, he said, "This place is so…?"

"Girlie?" she finished for him.

"Yeah," he admitted.

The whole cottage was white, shabby-chic with splashes of colour, mainly pink. Crystals hung from the light fittings and lamps, and white furry rugs covered the pale, sanded wood floors.

"It's nice though… very you."

"Are you trying to say I'm frivolous?" she said, bringing in the coffee.

He took a cup. "Not at all, you seem to love beautiful

things," he said, smiling. She looked in his eyes for a hint of a tease and there was none.

Her two sofas were arranged in an L-shape; he sat on one and she on the other. He'd distanced himself again. "What's your place like then… masculine bachelor's pad?"

He nodded and sipped his coffee. "Pretty much."

"Will I ever get to go there?" she said, looking down, knowing it was a cheeky question.

He put his coffee down on the table. "Do you want to?"

"Course I do. I'm nosy like that," she said, trying to make light of it.

She no longer suspected he lived with anyone. She supposed it came from not believing a man as gorgeous as him could possibly be single. But seeing where someone lived was a big deal, like meeting their parents or something.

He laughed and stood up. "I'd better go."

She stood up, put her cup down and walked to stand right in front of him, looking up into his eyes. "Thank you for today. It was the nicest thing anyone's ever done for me."

A look of concern quickly crossed his face and he ran a finger down the side of her cheek. "My pleasure."

She'd have given anything to know what he was thinking in that moment. "Stay…" came out of her mouth before she could stop it. Her eyes were wide and she bit her bottom lip as soon as the word left her mouth.

He exhaled and drew her to him and put his forehead down on hers, his fingers still holding the side of her cheek. "Grace…" He sounded agonised. "It wouldn't be nice with me."

It felt as though her stomach had fallen to the floor, her heart sank so low. She pushed away from him and turned. "Forget I said anything." Her eyes closed while the wave of humiliation washed over her. *Of all the stupid things to say.*

She felt his hand touch her shoulder and she shrugged it

off. "Please, Dylan, it's not your fault. You've told me time and time again and I didn't listen," she said, turning back to face him with her arms firmly folded across her chest, fighting and biting back the hurt. "I'm just being silly," she said, shrugging. "I should know you wouldn't fancy someone like me… Plain Jane Grace."

Dylan's brow furrowed angrily. "That's not it… no… not at all. You're beautiful. If ever I was gonna… Listen… I don't date." He went to close the gap between them. "You deserve… Look, it's nothing to do with you, it's me."

She threw her arms down by her sides in exasperation. "Oh my god! I don't believe you are actually giving me the 'It's not you, it's me,' line." She marched over to the front door and opened it wide while she looked at the floor. "Goodbye, Dylan."

He stood for a moment, not knowing what to say or do, rocking from foot to foot until he strode out the door.

Grace slammed the door after him, leaned her back on it and slid down to the floor. Her body shook with her sobs while she hugged her knees to her chest. She knew she wasn't really entitled to feel so let down by him as he'd broken no promises, but she felt so terribly alone.

Not more than a few moments had gone by when the door knocked loudly behind her.

She ignored it.

"Open the door, Grace," Dylan's voice said from the other side.

She slowly stood, wiping her tears on her hand and opened the door. "What?" she said, flashing her reddened, angry eyes at him.

"Can I come in?" he said, softly.

"I thought you wanted to go?"

"Please, Grace."

She pushed the door open wider and he stepped around her and back into the house.

His body language was pissed off, to say the least. Grace closed the door softly behind her and felt like a little girl about to get told off.

Dylan just quietly watched her. "Did you watch any of the films yet?" he said, seriously.

"I haven't had a chance yet… anyway, it doesn't matter."

He looked away from her and back again in frustration. "When you do, you'll understand."

She nodded and sagged. "I get it… but I don't care."

He shifted his weight impatiently. "For fuck's sake, Grace."

She raised her eyes to his angrily, but what she saw in his wasn't anger but anguish. "You say one thing, though, Dylan, and your body says another," she said, with conviction.

He stepped in closer, so he loomed over her menacingly, pushing her back against the door with his hands on either side of her head. "And what does my body language say now?" he said, with his head on an angle.

Her bravado began to evaporate and she shrank away from him. "You're just trying to scare me," she said, in a small voice. She swallowed, gathering her courage again. "Because *you're* scared." Her eyes narrowed, waiting.

As if she'd stunned him, he stood motionless for a beat. Then he slowly took his hands from the door and stepped closer, flush against her body. He bent his head and brushed her lips gently with his.

Clasping at the kiss like a lifeline, she nipped at his lips, needing more of him – all of him. He knew exactly what she needed and covered her mouth with his forcefully. His tongue probed, circled and twirled with hers, while his strong hands pulled her tight to him, crushing her for a moment.

Then, as if he had come to his senses, he broke away and rested his forehead on hers.

"Stay," she repeated. "Please… Just for a while."

Dylan shifted his feet with his inner turmoil, groaned then lifted her on a growl, as if it went against everything he stood for, but was doing it anyway. She didn't care and clamped her legs around his waist. He found her mouth again while he walked purposely up the narrow staircase and to her bedroom.

CHAPTER 5

*H*er room was as white and frothy as the rest of the house. He put her down gently on the bed and loomed over her. Afraid he would change his mind, Grace patted the bed next to her. "Just for a while," she repeated.

He frowned slightly with indecision, but took his jacket off and placed it over a chair. Then he stretched out next to her and leant up on an elbow.

She smiled up at him and cautiously ran a finger down the side of his cheek.

"You make me feel like a nervous teenager," he said, with a small smile on his lips.

She laughed at the absurd reversal of roles. "I find that hard to believe. There's no pressure... I just want to spend some time with you, that's all."

He stooped down and kissed her lips gently, cupping her jaw with his free hand.

"Talk to me," she whispered.

He grinned next to her mouth. "You get me up into your room and you wanna talk?"

She giggled and then nodded solemnly. "It's important."

He adjusted his position so he was on his stomach, put his arms under the pillow and rested his head, facing her. "What do you want to talk about?"

She had to be careful. Experience with him had taught her one wrong word sent him running to the hills. "Were you born in Ireland?" she said, turning on her stomach to mirror his position.

"No."

"You see?"

"What?"

"You never elaborate… ever."

He laughed, turning on his side again and picked up a lock of her hair and played with it between his fingers. "What do you want to know?"

"Do you have brothers and sisters?"

"Three brothers."

She was mildly surprised but waited and, as usual, nothing further was forthcoming.

"You?" he said, smiling.

"No, it's just me. Where do your mum and dad live?"

"Mum lives 'round here still, I never knew my dad… went back to Ireland when I was small."

She nodded and pushed the hair off his face. She would have liked to probe more into that subject, but decided not to overdo it.

"What about you?"

She rolled her eyes at his evasion and turned over onto her back and looked up at the ceiling. "My mum and dad had me quite late in life. They were retired, went sailing, had an accident and never came back, so it's just me," she said, flashing a glance at him.

Dylan just remained quiet, studying her.

"That's how I got my own house, not because I could afford to buy it or anything," she continued.

Dylan leant across and kissed her cheek. "Why do you do that?"

"What?" She turned onto her side to face him again.

"Put yourself down all the time."

She shrugged. "I don't mean to… I've just never done anything, you know… out of the ordinary."

Those hypnotic eyes of his were studying her again. Feeling under scrutiny, she ran her hand along his arm, following the lines of the swirls and arcs of his tattoos. "Do these go everywhere?" she said, her eyes low with the obvious deflection.

Dylan watched her, expressionless. "Yeah."

"Can I see more of them?" she said, biting her lip.

He smiled slightly as he turned to sit up, "You trying to get my shirt off?" He was already pulling it over his head.

She knew he was sexy, but when he was semi-naked, hair ruffled, with tattoos covering the whole top half of his hairless, tanned body, she blushed from head to foot. Her hand reached out in spite of herself; she simply couldn't help it. "Turn over," she ordered.

He indulged her and lay on his stomach again while she ran a gentle hand over the large eagle's wings that were spread across his shoulder blades.

"What do these mean?" she asked, tracing a finger over the symbols underneath.

"I don't know," he said, turning back over and obscuring them from view.

She was sensing his unease, which meant the question session was going to come to an end soon. Quickly, she touched the five large dots in the centre of his chest, arranged like fingerprints within the outline of a hand. "What are these?"

His eyes were hooded. "I don't know what they mean."

She slowly pulled her hand away from him.

"Do you have any?" he asked.

She was sure he was just swerving again. The idea seemed preposterous. "Me? No."

"None?" he said, smiling, but his face looked sceptical.

She shook her head.

"That's rare… I don't believe you."

She laughed. "Are you trying to get my top off… I thought you were supposed to be shy?"

He dragged her nearer to him by the belt on her jeans. "I never said I was shy; you seem determined to assume that I am." He ran a thumb gently over the skin of her abdomen under her shirt. "You always want to see the good in me, no matter what I say." And he nimbly opened the buttons of the front of her shirt with one hand.

That was well practised. Shit! He was right, she was outmanoeuvred. Her heart was hammering. She was always determined to see him as poor little Dylan, no matter how he warned her. She swallowed hard. "You don't seem bad to me."

He pulled her underneath him and brought his mouth down to hers. "You make me want to be better," he whispered, next to her lips.

"Don't be too good," she whispered back.

He laughed into a kiss and moved his weight to lie fully on top of her, pushing his tongue into her mouth. He pinned her with his weight and his hips rolled and gyrated slowly into hers. His taste and smell overran her and she gave herself over to the sensation of having him so close. Warm and silky smooth skin slid beneath her hands while they meandered over his back and she pulled him to her tighter.

He groaned with approval and kissed and nipped down her neck, moving her already open shirt down over her shoulder, exposing the round of her breast covered by white lace. She writhed against him, unable to keep still while he moved down her body.

So adept, he slipped her shirt down from both shoulders until it reached her elbows, but instead of pulling it completely off, he held it behind her back, trapping her arms and pushing out her chest to his mouth.

Before her brain had chance to catch up to what he'd done, his mouth closed over the peak of her breast, pushed pertly up to it like an offering. She felt completely trapped.

She gasped. *Fuck!* She felt way over her head. This man was a professional and he'd warned her.

Despite her fear, her resolve was buckling; it felt good – so good.

She'd barely caught up with what was happening when he held her shirt behind her with one hand, flicked open her belt and popped her jeans button with the other, and she couldn't do a thing. "Dylan," she gasped again.

He stilled this time, then released her arms and came back up to her eyeline. He rested on his forearms and nipped her lips.

She looked deeply into his eyes, still breathing hard.

"You're so beautiful," he whispered. "But you're not ready for this."

She frowned and her stomach fell away with disappointment, which she was sure he read in her eyes.

"Shh," he said, pushing her hair away from her face. "I won't go yet ... I'll stay till you fall asleep."

It was a caring, lovely thing to say, but she couldn't help the feeling in the pit of her stomach that just made her want to cry. "You will?" she said, trying to bring a smile to her lips.

He rolled off her, taking her with him to rest her head on his smooth chest. She listened to the comforting thud of his heart while he held her and tried not to let a tell-tale tear fall onto his skin and give herself away.

Despite his obvious care for her and not rushing straight off, she racked her brains over the evening's events, at what she had done to turn him on, and what it was that had turned him off. Everything just pointed to her being clumsy and unsophisticated. *That's all it could be.*

"Stop thinking," his rumbling voice ordered.

She took a peek at his face and his eyes were shut. She hoped he would fall asleep and still be there in the morning.

She snuggled back into him and splayed her fingers out over the symbols on his chest. For the first time, she realised there were small ridges under the dots of the handprint tattoo. At the angle she was lying, she could clearly see the raised skin, like scars or burns. *Was the tattoo there to disguise it? Or was it deliberately put in the markings?*

She couldn't ask him, not now and relaxed into him again.

"Sleep," he rumbled again.

Gradually, because of the events of the day and his close proximity and warmth, she did just that. It must have been a while, as she turned over and ran her hand over the bed space he'd occupied and he'd gone.

Her sleepy eyes flickered and she leaned up slightly to look around the room to make sure.

There he was, sitting in the chair in the corner watching her, except he was dressed now, with his jacket and boots on. One leg was crossed over the knee of the other and his elbow rested on the arm of the chair. But his look was dark, *no wait,* really dark. His blue eyes looked black and soulless. He was somehow dark and evil, sitting there studying her, and even though she tried not to, she watched him for what seemed like ages.

He has blue eyes; it must be a dream. You are asleep. And she allowed her eyelids to flutter shut again.

Some time later, she felt the soft brush of his lips next

to hers, "I'm going," he whispered next to her skin. "Don't get up." She stirred, but he put a finger to her lips. "I'll call you."

WHEN SHE AWOKE some time later, it was morning, judging by the sunlight prying through the gap between the curtains. She glanced at the empty armchair in the corner of the room. The unsettling feeling of the dream still clung to her. *Did she dream that?* She shuddered.

Refusing to dwell on it, she threw her legs over the side of the bed and padded out to the hall and down the narrow staircase. He had definitely gone.

Thank god it was Sunday. She was tired, miserable at herself for ruining the first chance of intimacy she'd had with him, and still a little creeped out by the disturbing dream. No, she decided, it was back to bed for her. The whole world could go away for a few more hours before she had to go and see to her horse.

Not that she could stop her mind working: *Were they out of the friend category now? Shit,* she had no idea. Perhaps some warm milk was a good idea. She found she was wandering around aimlessly. *What had she done with her keys?* She knew she must have had them last night to get in with, and she always chucked them on the same small table by the door. But there was nothing there.

Maybe Dylan had picked them up by mistake?

GRACE'S STOMACH flipped when she returned from the stables later that day to find Dylan sitting on her doorstep. All her humiliation from the night before evaporated as soon as she saw him. She beamed a smile when she walked up her tiny garden path. "What brings you here?"

He held up a bunch of keys. "I must have picked them up with mine."

She nodded, pleased, put her spare in her bag and took them from him. "Do you want to come in?"

"Okay… I can't stop long though," he said, standing to follow her inside.

"You have to be somewhere?" fell out of her mouth before she could stop herself. *Shit*, the last thing she wanted was to sound like the Inquisition.

But, true to form, he just nodded.

Secrets. She tried to school her features to hide her rising frustration with him, but failed abysmally.

"Have I upset you?" he said, quietly, pulling her toward him when she would have walked away.

She didn't reply. It seemed better than lying.

"Is it because of last night?" he persisted.

Grace hated to cause a scene or argue with him, but, in that second, everything seemed intolerable – his behaviour, his lack of communication, everything.

"It is… talk to me, Grace," he said, putting her away from him slightly so he could search her face.

Her eyes flashed at him, transmitting all the anger and hurt.

He blanched, mildly amused.

Incensed, she went to push away from him.

"Ah, no you don't," he said, pulling her back. "Talk!" he ordered. "You say I don't open up, but you're just as bad."

Her expression was all kinds of pissed off when she faced him again. "Okay… I don't know where I am with you. You blow hot and cold. You kiss me, then you say we're just friends… then last night?" She threw her hands down by her sides in exasperation, pulled out of his hands and paced the room.

His eyes followed her movements the whole time.

"Do you know how that made me feel?"

He took a deep breath and blinked slowly as if she'd slapped his face. She doubted if anyone had spoken to him like that, ever.

"And not ready… what the fuck does that mean?" she said, incredulous, with hands on her hips.

His eyes went wide and he stood up straighter and frowned, as if he'd ridden the gambit of what she'd said all over again. "It's better if we're just friends."

"Oh, fuck off, Dylan, that's bollocks and you know it."

His eyebrows popped again as if she'd surprised him.

"Listen to yourself," she went on, "everything you say to me is so patronising. I'm a big girl, I've been on my own for six years and I can look after myself."

He stood, riveted to the spot, staring at her for quite a few moments. She couldn't tell if he was stunned or considering what she'd said. She'd tried to rile him up to fight just to get a reaction, but he was too cool for any of that; she should have known.

Just when she would have given up, he stalked towards her, stopping way too close, narrowing his eyes down at her. She did her utmost not to shrink from him. "I'll come for you tonight at 9. Be ready with a bag packed for the night." And he turned and walked towards the door.

She stood, stunned, eyes wide, her mouth opening and closing and nothing coming out.

"Don't say I didn't warn you, Grace." And he was gone.

Shit. She sagged in relief. She hadn't realised she had been holding her breath for god knows how long. *Where was he taking her? And what the fuck should she wear? Shit, Shit, Shit!*

She started pacing manically, thinking of all her options, when her phone rang. She snatched it up. "Thank god it's you, Janey. I have an emergency"

"Shut up, Grace… you have to come to mine tonight!"

"What? I can't."

"No, you have to… I've found one of his films and you need to see it."

Fuck, fuck, fuck! Her mind was turning cartwheels. She knew Janey had her best interests at heart, but tonight could be one of the most important nights of her life and it didn't matter what Janey said; she knew she wouldn't miss this chance with him. So she resolved to just block it out of her conscience, for now. "I can't, Janey. I'll come tomorrow. He's taking me out tonight… I'm staying with him… I think tonight's going to be the night."

"Oh fuck, Grace, please, you need to see this first."

Grace was shaking her head before Janey had even finished speaking. She'd made up her mind and nothing and no one was going to ruin it for her.

CHAPTER 6

Dylan picked her up as promised, a little after nine, and they were soon speeding up the A20 towards London. He had said very little, just made sure she had packed a bag. When she had asked where they were staying, all he'd said was, "mine."

He was very subdued with her. Maybe he didn't like being told straight how he made her feel. Excitement was quickly giving way to nerves. He wasn't exactly angry, but he simmered, and she found herself hoping that nothing happened to make him boil over.

Hugging into the heat of his body, she briefly wondered what it could have been that had got Janey in such a tizzy. Well, she'd see her tomorrow and everything would be clearer then.

The place they were going to was in Brixton. Not a place she had ever been to; not ever having had reason to, it just never came up.

They drove into an underground car park where he parked the bike near a lift entrance to the building above them. Two huge black bouncers stood guard and shook his hand when he neared them with a simple acknowledgement as "D". They entered the lift and Dylan hit the top floor button.

She looked at him sheepishly. It was beginning to dawn on her how little she really knew him. "Aren't you going to talk to me?"

He glanced at her moodily. "Let's see if you still want to talk afterwards."

She frowned. She didn't deserve this cold shoulder. How bad could it be? "Where are we going?" she said, as the lift reached the floor.

"A party."

"Whose?"

The lift doors opened. Loud voices and thumping reggae bass hit her immediately.

"My best friend."

Surprised, she followed him into the party, sticking as close as she could to him. Everything was so far out of her comfort zone that she could hardly breathe. The air was balmy, damp, thick with smoke and musk perfume. The bass vibrated her chest. Scantily clad people were packed tightly together. Every face was black and a hundred eyes appeared to stare at her.

Shit, she should have gone to Janey's. She had to remind herself that he was showing her his world, even if it was solely to put her off. All she had to do was show him she could handle it.

Glancing up at him for reassurance, she could see no sign of discomfort – he was completely at home. Everyone seemed to know him, male and female, and referred to him simply as D. It was there that her impression of shy Dylan began to fall away. Reserved didn't mean shy.

The whole feel of the scene around her reminded her of a slow-motion gangster-rap video. The way the women draped themselves over and moved around the men, whose movements were fluid.

A very handsome man came over to them when they reached the kitchen, "D-man," he said, pulling Dylan to him into a hug. His eyes rested on her from across Dylan's shoulder, then looked at Dylan in surprise. "D... where have you been hiding this one?" Then he picked up her hand dramatically and kissed it.

Dylan turned. "This is Grace... Grace, this is Fenton."

Grace smiled as confidently as she could manage, but the feeling of being way out of her depth was reaching fever pitch.

Then, before she knew what had happened, a tall, lithe woman with green eyes and scraped-back hair pushed rudely between her and Dylan and pulled him with her towards the other room, where the loud music was playing and people were dancing.

Grace was momentarily stunned into inactivity. Never had she felt so rudely sidelined. She didn't know whether to stay, go, or follow them and tap the girl on the shoulder. As she went to turn on her heel, Fenton grabbed her arm.

Nonplussed, she stole a glance in the direction Dylan had gone to see him with the woman stuck to him like glue, draped around his neck, moving against him sensually in time to the music.

"Hey!" Fenton said loudly, to break her stare. "Look at me," he ordered, knowing damn well where her thoughts were going.

"Who is she?" Grace said, her face red with anger, fixing her glare on Fenton.

He handed her a drink. "It's wine... You know what D is?"

Grace gave him her best snarky bored look. "You're just trying to distract me... yes, he's told me."

Fenton looked sceptical, then relented. "Well, Serena is the nearest thing to a girlfriend D's ever had."

Grace felt her face drop along with her heart, straight to the floor, and she closed her eyes.

Fenton touched her arm gently and shook his head. "Slow up, baby, it's not like that. She just takes the edge off, you know?"

"No, I don't know." *For fuck sake, why did everyone talk in riddles?* "I don't know what you mean," she said, through gritted teeth. She needed to get out of there.

"D's two people," Fenton grinned. "I can honestly say he's never brought anyone to something like this, let alone someone like you."

She knew he was just trying to distract her with flattery. "Like me?" she said flatly. *Here comes the patronising old flannel.*

"Graceful by name and graceful by nature, babe."

Bingo!

He laughed, "The Devil's found an angel."

She frowned at the truly weird thing to say, then dismissed it as the ramblings of someone who was drugged up or mad. It wouldn't hurt to press him for information, though, while he was being so talkative, something completely lacking with Dylan.

"Who are all these people… I mean, are they all to do with Dylan's work?"

He smiled slightly.

God, she was getting so sick of the patronising looks.

"Some of them," he said, more kindly.

"Serena?"

He nodded. "He works with her sometimes."

Her heart sank. *Could it get any worse?* She was growing to despise the woman already.

Fenton laughed as if he knew.

"What about you?" she threw at him.

"Me?… I'm his agent… but we're good friends."

"How did you meet?"

"I've known D since he was about eighteen. We met through a martial arts club not far from here."

At least she knew now how he kept so in shape. She flicked a glance to make sure Dylan was still dancing and her teeth clenched at how close they were, literally poured all over each other and moving as one. *Fuck!* They looked great together.

That did it. "I'm going!" she announced.

"Ah no, babe… You can't leave on your own… D!" he shouted.

At least he was taking her seriously now.

Dylan lifted his head from Serena's shoulder and frowned as if the kitchen light hurt his eyes. Fenton motioned with his hand for him to come over.

Grace had had it and rushed out. She wasn't prepared to have the inevitable shouting match with Dylan here. This whole thing had been a bad idea. *What a deluded idiot.*

She reached the lift and was about to press the button when Dylan's hand got it for her. "I warned you," he said, close to her ear.

She snapped her head round to him, done with fucking around. "No, you didn't, Dylan. Because if you'd said: I'm an insensitive prick with a stable of women and don't want to lower my standards with you, I'm pretty sure I would have taken notice." She narrowed her eyes and spoke through her teeth. "Even a silly, naive girl like me would get that hint." And she stamped into the lift.

Fenton's laughter could be heard from behind Dylan. "I like her, D. She's tougher than she looks." And he slapped Dylan on the back and sidestepped him to pick up her hand and kiss it again. "Enchanted, Angel." Then he winked at Dylan and walked back into the party.

Grace scowled at Fenton for calling her that stupid nickname and then at Dylan, who had joined her in the lift. "Where do you think you are going?" he asked, quietly.

"Home!" she spat, not able to look at him.

He stood next to her, shifting his weight from foot to foot as he did when he was agitated or indecisive about something.

After what felt like a lifetime, the lift opened and she stormed out into the underground garage.

She had to jog to try to get away from him. "Let me take you, it's not safe," Dylan said from behind her.

She spun round on him. "Oh, it's not safe? You're not safe! Fucking up there's not safe!" she screamed at him. "Talk fucking straight for the first time in your life," she shouted, pushing him hard in the chest.

They'd reached the bike and he pushed her helmet at her. "Get on, I'll take you back."

She snatched it and put it on, figuring she hadn't a fucking clue where she was anyway.

He started the bike and she got on behind him but made sure she held onto the back of the seat. Snuggle time was well and truly over. And he knew it by the way he shook his head before pulling away.

She was still steaming with anger. New angles and arguments crowded and vied in her head. Okay, they hadn't been seeing each other that long and, yes, they weren't exactly an item, but *bloody hell*, you don't take a girl to a party to humiliate her like that.

It was dark and the streets were wet where it had been raining. Everywhere looked the same, but as unfamiliar as it was, Grace knew that they were going in the wrong direction to take her home.

Briefly, it did cross her mind how vulnerable she was alone with him and with no idea where she was, but she shelved it, thinking that he had never hurt her–well, until tonight. She stifled a sob.

They came to a stop on a concrete square, off the road, between two buildings. They got off and she followed him to an old-looking door off the street. He unlocked it and guided her to a lift. The place seemed derelict and abandoned, like a disused warehouse or something.

The lift took them to the top floor and the doors opened into a small, dimly lit hallway with a door in front of them. He went in front of her and opened it. "Go in," he said, following her and bolting the door behind them.

Inside, it was a different world. It was a huge space with a vaulted ceiling, like one of those bachelor's pads she'd seen in the films, all exposed brick and sparsely furnished. A huge bed dominated the room and a martial arts dummy hung from the ceiling at one end, along with some suspect-looking chains, which she guessed were also to do with training. There were a couple of soft chairs, an impressive music system and a small kitchen. This was his space.

"Bathroom's through there," he said, pointing to the opposite end of the room.

He slowly eased off his jacket and threw it onto a chair, then chucked his keys down onto a coffee table. He looked dog-tired.

"Why did you bring me here?" she said, leaning on a hip with her arms firmly folded across her chest. She wasn't about to have the mind-fuck of an evening pushed under the carpet.

He breathed out a sigh and walked slowly to her and pulled her in close to him by the hips – much the same as she'd seen him do with Serena earlier. It brought her back to her senses and she pushed away from him. He thought he could whitewash over everything by just getting near her.

He stood still, seeming defeated and exhausted. "What do you want, Grace?"

Her brow furrowed in disbelief. "No, Dylan, what do you want, 'cause I'm buggered if I know?"

He exhaled slowly and closed his eyes for a long moment. When he looked at her again, he looked ruined – like he was devastated and had the weight of the world on his shoulders. "I've tried to keep away from you, but I can't..." Then he shifted his weight to his other foot. "Then I thought if we could be just friends, then it'd be okay. But I don't seem to be able to do that." He looked at the floor, shaking his head.

She studied him, agonising for a long moment, absorbing his words. "What was tonight about then?... I don't get it... Deliberate, so I hate you?"

He shrugged, "No, I didn't know she'd be there."

Grace looked around her, trying to make sense of it. "What are you afraid of, Dylan?"

He looked her squarely in the eye. "That I might hurt you... that when you know who I am, you'll hate me." He looked in agony and faced away from her.

She closed the gap between them and touched his face with her hands. "How could you hurt me, Dylan?" she said, looking up into his pained, glazed eyes. "Help me, I'm trying to understand."

He allowed her to pull him close to her mouth and she put her lips to his. He remained impassive, letting her move her mouth over his. Then, as if his resolve snapped, his arms came about her and he moved against her, forcing her lips apart, probing and invading her mouth with his tongue just as she battled him with her own.

She groaned into his mouth and the most sensual kiss of her life. "Please, Dylan," she whispered. She wanted more. She wanted all of him.

There was no coming back from a kiss like that and he

swept her up and carried her over to his bed where he lay her gently on top. He took off his T-shirt and lay down next to her, half covering her with his big body.

He kissed her again, deeper and passionately this time, as if he'd finally realised she wasn't made of glass. He rolled onto her and she was forced to open her legs to relieve his great weight. He nudged at her core in gentle strokes, the heat of her melting for him already.

"I want you, Grace," he whispered, next to her mouth and nipped down the side of her neck, "I shouldn't, but I do." She dissolved into those words.

She gasped and clutched him tightly to her, entwining her fingers into his beautiful bed hair. His hands seemed to be everywhere until they found the hem of her top and pulled it upwards so she could wriggle free of it and he could pull it over her head.

Before she knew what had happened, her bra went loose and disappeared as well. He overwhelmed her so expertly. His mouth, light as a feather, moved across her skin, lighting up everywhere it touched, every nerve ending. Always moving downwards while his nimble fingers flicked open her belt buckle.

Then, when his mouth closed over her nipple, *fuck!* She almost combusted.

Perceptive after the last time, he paused to allow her mind to catch up with what he was doing. She lay still, breathing hard, until she had to touch him again, and her fingers stroked up from his smooth shoulders to intertwine with his hair again. Then he continued, more slowly this time.

Dylan moved across to the other breast, licking, kissing, taking her nipple delicately between his teeth. She moaned and her body arched and writhed beneath him.

He leaned up slightly to watch her. "God, Grace, you're so

beautiful."

Her eyes flickered open for a moment to see the adoration in his eyes. No one had ever looked at her in her life like that. He made her feel beautiful.

He immediately moved back further and put his thumb into the waistband of her jeans and tugged them down to her knees. Then she felt him leave her to tug off her boots, then a second tug to her jeans and they were off.

Dylan was standing now, never taking his eyes from hers. He released his own belt, popped the button and stepped out of his jeans. Not a second of bashfulness when his boxers came off next. Totally hairless and covered in the strange black ink symbols, he crawled back onto the bed. Reverently, he pulled down her silk briefs.

Grace held her breath while his eyes roamed her body, followed by his hand with a feather-light touch. She shivered and exploded into goosebumps.

He lay down next to her again, leaning up on one elbow. "Are you cold?"

She shook her head.

Dylan leant over and took her mouth again, confidently demanding full submission from her. She didn't resist and let him in, so in that moment, he owned her by her mouth alone. The hand that held her jaw began to skim down to brush an already hardened nipple waiting for attention. Then lower, to pull her leg from under her knee so he could slide his fingers through the wetness of her folds, alive with sensitivity. Circling her bud, he spread the wetness and probed with his fingers at her entrance slowly with one finger and then two.

Grace gasped into his mouth. He was driving her wild, way beyond any limits of arousal she'd reached before.

He stilled again and looked into her eyes for reassurance, reading her as always.

"I'm okay," she whispered, nipping at him, taking his lower lip between her teeth.

Dylan rolled onto her with a groan. Her breaths were noisy and ragged next to his cheek. He began to nudge at her rhythmically, finding the heat of her instinctively, gradually penetrating her little by little.

Her heart was hammering. It was actually finally happening.

"I need to be inside you," he whispered in her ear.

"Yes… " She found his mouth and drew his tongue into hers hungrily, finally robbing him of any restraint and he plunged deeply into her.

CHAPTER 7

Grace cried out his name while she clung to him with everything: feet, legs, nails and teeth. He was gloriously large and filled her to bursting and she revelled in the twinge of pain it gave her. He moved gradually, hips undulating slowly, stroking her innermost muscles.

Ruled by her instincts to taste and bite, she moved down his neck while his strokes strengthened and lengthened. Never had she felt so thoroughly taken in her life.

Dylan leaned up on his elbows to look into her eyes. His were bleary with lust and she looked into them deeply, her brow creased in a blissful pain. The kind you never wanted to stop. He kissed her hard again and increased the pace, pulling one of her legs over his arm for deeper penetration.

Their breaths were loud and in time with each other, bodies moving as one while the bed creaked a symphony with the springs squeaking and frame scraping the wooden floor.

Despite the ferocious pace he was building, he continually checked her eyes, she realised, for clues as to whether she was still with him.

Dylan rolled onto his side, keeping her knee over his hip, allowing him to lengthen and slow down his strokes, delectably slow.

Grace wanted to scream with frustration; he teased her so. Then he'd push so forcefully, she'd never felt anything so deeply within her.

Then he rolled onto his back, taking her with him with his strong arms. Always keeping them joined so she straddled his hips and he could gyrate beneath her slowly. Her weight met his hips while he stroked deeply into her womb.

Her muscles clenched around him and he moaned. Her stomach flipped at the sound and she was the cause of it. She'd never felt such intimacy and closeness. She closed her eyes and gave herself over to sensation, while his hands held her hips like a vice and ground her tightly onto him.

Fuck, he was good. It was like having sex for the first time. Nothing previously came close to this, not even on the radar.

Her hands rested on the ridges of his abs and felt them harden as he sat up. He clasped her around her back and sensually kneaded her back with his fingers while he sucked the hard peaks of her breasts and moved gracefully beneath her. He encased every part of her, owned her, devoured her and she loved the feeling of ownership in it.

"How do you want to come?" he whispered, biting her neck, then sucking in rhythm with his hips.

God... She gasped. "I don't know... I've never."

Dylan stilled for a moment as if he'd just understood what she meant. Her heart stopped for fear she'd said the wrong thing.

Then he nodded slightly, "I know what you need."

Her heart fluttered while her mind panicked at what that could be. But she had no time for fear when he lifted her up and she felt herself falling backwards with her head to the foot of the bed. Still joined, Dylan pushed the top half of her so her head hung over the edge and he lifted her hips to his so she was lying down-hill. "Hold my legs," he said.

She clasped her hands around his thighs to stop herself sliding backwards.

With one hand, he pushed a thumb between their bodies, immediately finding her engorged bud and making her jolt. The sensation was mind-blowing. When she could cope, he began to stroke it while he circled his hips and moved inside her. She groaned in indescribable ecstasy.

Then his other hand slowly came across the front of her to her throat, pushing her further over the bed so she had to clasp his legs to stop herself falling and pulled them tighter together. *Clever man.*

"I'm going to take you with me," he said. The whispered words were almost her undoing.

Then he began to close his fingers around her throat, limiting her air supply.

At first, she wondered if he realised how strong his grip was. The blood was going to her head anyway, and with the lack of air, her face felt raging hot, like it would explode. At the point she thought she couldn't breathe, he worked her mercilessly and thrust into her over and over.

Something deep within her started to unfurl. She clenched and rippled and it built to teeter on a huge precipice. "Dylan?" she croaked.

"No… I want this one."

Despite herself, she opened her eyes at these words; they sounded so strange and out of place, and for a moment, he looked like he was a stranger. But a second later, rational thought deserted her as he removed his hand from her throat and moved in and out of her in long, deliberate strokes. The rush of oxygen, mixed with the strength of his thrusts, sent her head spinning, driving her towards the edge. Then, when he grabbed her breast roughly, rubbing his thumb across her nipple, and with his other hand, pinched her intimately between his fingers, every nerve exploded. She screamed his name. Letting go, he clamped both hands onto her hips and pulled her onto him hard while he hammered deeply inside her. Her own arms, holding her up, were now useless. A million lights went on all over her body, shooting outwards to the tips of her fingers and toes. He prolonged the sensations and strung her out for so long she thought she couldn't stand it and would pass out.

Beseeching him with her eyes while her body bowed and arched, he pulled her to his gyrating hips, wringing every last spasm from her body and working her mercilessly through her first orgasm, because that was undoubtedly what it was. She literally came to pieces in his hands.

After what seemed like an age of blessed torture, his hips slowed to small shudders and he pulled her rag doll body up against him and gently lay back so she floated into the pillows with him in a tangled heap.

GRACE'S HEART was still beating like a train and her breath came thick and fast. Tangled together, she felt Dylan's chest rise and fall next to hers, but his eyes remained shut. Her body thrummed with a sense of exhausted contentment such as she had never experienced. She couldn't even move her limbs, nor did she want to.

"You really never came before?" he said, quietly.

"No," she whispered, realising how typically inexperienced that sounded.

"Not even on your own?

Oh my god! Her face blasted redder than it already was from her mind-blowing orgasm. She thanked God for the dim light. She had to remember that sex was as natural as breathing to him. "No," she said, warily.

He pulled her more tightly into him. "Then I'm honoured to have been part of your first."

Wow, part of? It was totally down to him. She smiled to herself.

"What?… I can feel you smiling."

She'd had the best sex of her life. How do you tell a man something like that? "It wasn't bad, was it?"

He chuckled. "No it wasn't."

She lifted her head slightly to look up at him. Had the rules of the game changed now? His eyes were still closed. "You're not afraid now?"

He opened his eyes a tiny fraction so he could look at her. His expression was amused. "You seem to bring out the good in me."

She grinned, thrilled he was now so relaxed with her. He was still a puzzle, but she wasn't about to ruin the moment with questions. She snuggled back into his chest.

"If you wake and I'm not here, I'll just be out for my run, so don't worry," he said.

"Okay, don't you ever give yourself a day off?"

"No… I don't sleep much and I'll only keep you awake."

She heard the amusement in his voice and guessed what he meant. Her stomach flipped. Every time she thought about what they'd just done, her butterflies played basketball.

"Sleep," he ordered.

She smiled and went into a lovely, contented doze.

It was no more than an hour or two later when she felt him leave the bed. The excitement, strange surroundings and not being used to sharing a bed meant she slept lightly. Her eyes cracked open a little and she watched his gloriously naked body, ribbed and corded with muscle, move, as graceful as a cat, towards the bathroom. She almost purred while she stretched and luxuriated in the rumpled bed.

The hiss sounded from the shower and he re-emerged glistening and tempting with a towel around his waist. He dressed in grey sweats and running shoes and slipped quietly out.

Grace allowed herself to doze a bit longer, then roused herself to go to the bathroom to make herself look an effortless natural beauty before he came back. Grabbing one of his clean T-shirts on the way, she piled her hair on top of her head and took a quick shower, sprayed some perfume and put some concealer on the dark circles under her eyes. A little blusher and rose-coloured lip-gloss and she was good to go.

Teeth! She remembered just in time and opened the small vanity cupboard above the sink, looking for toothpaste. All the male products made her smile.

A stab of hatred hit her at the thought she might find something of Serena's, and it prompted her to take a quick root around. Relieved, she grabbed the toothpaste tucked away behind some bottles. *Ah, crap.* She'd knocked one into the sink. Luckily, the glass bottle didn't smash. She turned it in her hand to glance at the label: Zyprexia. She grabbed another: Clorazil. And another: Prolixin.

The names intrigued her. They weren't anything she'd ever heard of before; definitely not painkillers, or any commonly known medicine.

Steroids? Perhaps, but he wasn't beefed up and stacked with muscle like a bodybuilder. He looked like an athlete, fit and trim. No, they looked like properly prescribed medicines for some kind of condition. Her mind boggled.

The door closing echoed in the other room. She felt so guilty, as if she'd been rifling through his stuff. She quickly tried to replace everything as she found it, opened the bathroom door and quietly closed it behind her. Turning without looking, she slammed straight into a chest. A chest that wasn't Dylan's.

She yelped in fright.

Fenton looked momentarily as surprised as she was. "Angel?"

Her eyes were still wide; he'd really made her jump.

Fenton's eyes roamed around the large room, then back to her. They looked bloodshot; he probably hadn't slept yet. "No D?"

"He's gone out for his run," she managed to say breathily. "How did you get in?" The fact that she didn't know this man from Adam was beginning to dawn on her and made her feel uneasy.

He held up a bunch of keys. "I wasn't expecting you here, honey… I come to check on him sometimes."

Why did he need to be checked on? Before she could think more deeply, the door opened and closed behind them.

Dylan walked in looking hot and sweaty, cheeks flushed and hair wet. His expression was closed as he walked slowly over to them. He looked into her face, then at Fenton. "Fent?"

Grace watched Dylan closely and realised he wasn't pleased to see his so-called best friend. Not like he had been at the party.

He dragged his eyes back to her, "Can you go into the bathroom for a minute, babe? I just want to talk to Fenton, okay?"

She felt wary of leaving the two of them alone. Her eyes flicked between them, but she nodded, guessing there wasn't a lot else she could do. The bathroom door clicked shut and she pressed her ear up against it. *Shit,* she couldn't hear a thing. They must have walked away from the door.

Grace left it a moment and, holding her breath and

squinting her eyes, she cracked open the door a fraction. They were speaking in raised whispers.

"What are you doing, D?"

"You don't need to worry, I have it under control."

"You think you can have a normal relationship with her… is that it? … What happens when you flip?"

"I know I can control it… tonight we… I came close, but I managed to bring it back."

"Fucking hell, D… you could kill her. Is that what you want?… It's closest to the surface when you … Fuck, you take enough shit, you shouldn't even be able to get it up."

"I was scared, but it's fine."

"And when you're off your meds?"

There was a pause for a long moment.

"I'm going to quit, Fent."

Another pause.

"Shit, D… How long have I known you?"

A huff. "I know what you're saying."

"Ten years… I've helped you have some kind of life. It will out… it *needs* an outlet. You know this… If you don't do it in the controlled way we do? Then god knows when it will come and how strong it will be.

Silence.

"And you have at least one commitment coming up which you are contracted to do."

"I'll do that one, then I'm out."

A loud sigh. "Look, I'm outta here. Think about it. Think of her, okay?"

Grace heard the front door open.

"Fent?… Don't come here when she's here again."

The door closed.

Fuck. Her mind was reeling, a jumble of words: meds, having control, killing her, for her sake… *what the hell had she just heard?*

Her mind went back to the bottles in the cupboard.

"Grace?"

She jumped out of her skin and held her throat. "Won't be a minute," she said, as upbeat as she could.

She opened the little cupboard quickly and memorised the drug names over and over. She'd Google them as soon as she had a chance. *Janey!* Suddenly, seeing Janey became really important. Perhaps what she had seen would shed some light on all this?

Taking some deep breaths, she adjusted herself in the mirror. Her eyes were dilated with fright. *Fuck,* in one two, out one two, she breathed, then went out the door.

When she came out of the bathroom, Dylan was sitting on the edge of the bed waiting for her. He looked at her questioningly and she hoped she didn't look guilty. Looking at his face, adorably insecure, she reminded herself how she felt about him before she'd found the pills, before Fenton had turned up. He was the same man, for god's sake.

He shifted forward with his elbows on his knees. "Are you okay?"

He looked as if he expected her to have changed her mind. She tried to act bright and breezy. "Yeah, fine. I need to go soon. I have to go and see to Jet."

With a micro-flinch crossing his face, he stood without saying anything further. Half of her wanted to run and throw herself at him and tell him everything was okay, but she needed to get away from him to think straight, to be objective.

He didn't make eye contact, just looked at the floor. "I'll have a quick shower, then take you home."

Her eyes tracked him to the bathroom. "Thanks, I'll get dressed."

He grabbed a towel and went in without a word.

After getting hurriedly dressed, she plonked onto the

edge of the bed with her head in her hands. She could have got all this wrong. What's the saying about eavesdropping?

He appeared out of the bathroom a moment later. "Are you sure you are okay?" he said, whilst sorting out some clothes to put on.

"Yeah, he just gave me a fright, that was all."

Dylan frowned like he was considering whether or not she was telling the truth. "He wouldn't hurt you."

All she could do was give him a slight nod of acceptance. He dressed in no time, grabbed his keys and they left his apartment.

It was light by the time he pulled up outside her cottage and she got off the bike. She went to hand back her helmet. He pulled his off but left the engine running. "You may as well keep it here." But the way he said the words was like a question, like a small test.

She nodded, smiled weakly and kept hold of it.

"No invite to come in today, then?" He wasn't looking at her, in fact, anywhere else but.

Shit, everything seemed to be spiralling in the wrong direction. Why was she feeling so awful? Why was she feeling like the worst bitch in the world?

All she could think of doing was moving in closer to physically touch her body next to his. She touched his cheek and kissed him on the lips. "I just need to process last night. It was a big deal to me, okay?" She said the words softly next to his face. "Also, I didn't want to say anything earlier, but Janey phoned just before I came out last night. She has one of your films and said I should watch it." She studied his face for his reaction. There was no anger there.

All he did was sigh and nod slowly as if he totally understood. "I said you should all along."

"I know." It was true, he hadn't hidden anything from her;

in fact, he had tried his hardest to put her off him, which raised questions of its own.

She took his face between her hands and kissed him chastely on the lips again. "The way I feel about you, Dylan, I can't imagine anything being bad enough to change that."

His smile was one of sad regret or resignation. A pain hit her square in her chest when he replied, "I'll see you," and ended the conversation by putting his helmet back on.

Panic surged through her when he pulled away. *Did he assume that was it?*

As he disappeared, all she could do was rush into the house and dial Janey. She would be worried about her, and it seemed more important than ever that she find out everything about him, and that included his films.

CHAPTER 8

Grace was on her phone to Janey while she fired up her computer. The way Dylan had left would have haunted her if she wasn't so intent on discovering what Dylan's tablets were for.

The phone was ringing while her fingers nimbly tapped away clicking like knitting needles. She typed the first name: *What does Zyprexia treat?*

Her eyes skimmed across the screen and her blood began to run cold.

Janey picked up. "Hello … Grace … is that you?"

Totally absorbed in what she was reading, she forgot to respond verbally and sat there nodding slowly.

"Grace! Are you okay?"

"Yes," she said, finally, still distracted. "Sorry, I was reading something… I have to go… speak to you later."

"Hold it right there, Grace, or I'm coming over."

Grace huffed in irritation. The thought of Janey coming over now, demanding her attention while she needed to read – needed to think of the implications of all this, almost made her snap at her old friend, but she got a grip just in the nick of time. "I'm okay," she said evenly. "Just haven't had much sleep."

"Oh," Janey said, deflated. There was silence for a beat. "I just assumed… You know… How did it go?" She spoke warily, not a hint of the excitement she would normally exhibit when any gossip was in the offing – especially of the sexual variety.

"Good."

"You don't sound full of the joys of spring about it, Grace?"

"Neither do you." Silence again. "Look, I'm just exhausted, Janey, okay?"

"Are you coming over to see the film?"

Grace's heart sank. She had intended to, but she could only deal with one crisis at a time. "Not today, Janey. I need some sleep and to catch up on a ton of stuff."

"Well, okay, but you *are* okay, though?

"Yeah," Grace said. "Honestly."

"Bye then… Fuck, Grace, don't keep me in suspense. Was it good?"

Grace couldn't keep the smile out of her voice. "Yes… The best ever," she said, wistfully.

"Nothing kinky?"

A pang of concern stabbed her in the heart. Janey was obviously thinking of something connected to the content of the film.

"No… He just, you know… knew what he was doing." She tried not to let the annoyance come out in her tone of voice.

Janey audibly relaxed. "Well okay then, but I still think you need to go into it with open eyes, armed with all the facts about him."

"I will… and thanks."

Grace clicked off her phone, took a deep breath, and went straight back to reading the webpage.

Zyprexia belonged to a group of medicines known as antipsychotics used to treat schizophrenia, acute manic episodes, particularly related to bipolar disorder and depression. Clorazil and Prolixin both said basically the same thing and were taken to improve thinking, mood and behaviour.

She sat back in her chair and racked her brains over the time she'd spent with Dylan. Apart from the time he'd run away after the first time he'd kissed her, he was always perfectly behaved. Her only bugbear was his inability to open up about anything to do with himself. Was that it? Was he so quiet because he was harbouring this massive secret?

Her heart ached for him. She had prepared herself for the worst – that he was an unpredictable drug addict and Fenton was his pusher, and scenarios like that, so it was kind of a relief to think that he couldn't help it.

Her mind flashed back to Janey and the film. It wasn't going to go away. She was going to have to watch it sometime, if only to get Janey off her back, but not today. She was going to swot up on everything to do with the illnesses associated with those medicines.

This she did until she had to reread a paragraph several times in order for it to go in. Hot chocolate and bed were the only things left to do. She was useless until she had some sleep. Bed seemed the most inviting place in the world, and then perhaps she could think clearly about what to do next.

IT WAS 7 p.m. when Grace finally got into bed. Unable to absorb any more medical jargon, she fell asleep as soon as her head hit the pillow.

Dreams plagued her. Anxious, stressful and always out of

reach, Dylan was in them all. The most disturbing were the ones where she was running from him. It seemed vitally important that he never caught her, but her arms and legs wouldn't move and his hands would come around her throat to suffocate her.

She awoke bolt upright, panting and dripping with sweat. Everything was pitch black. A glance at her alarm clock told her it was 3.45 a.m.

A car pulled into the parking space next door and its headlights broke through the gap in her curtains, spearing a beam like a searchlight along the ceiling and down to the chair placed in the corner of the room.

Her brain stalled, she stopped breathing and her eyes went so wide with fright they stung. He was sitting there watching her, as he had been the other day. She blinked several times. Dark soulless eyes and the stark lines of his gaunt features stared back at her. It was Dylan, but not Dylan. It didn't make any sense even to her. He just looked and seemed different.

Was she still asleep? It can't be real. Dylan couldn't get in, not unless he'd forced his way in and then she'd have heard something, wouldn't she? She was overwrought; that must be it.

The engine of the car was switched off, along with its lights and the room was thrown into total darkness. Her fear spiked and her breath became so shallow that she was panting. Her heart was almost coming out of her mouth.

Warm breath tickled her skin mere kissing distance from her face, and she let out a small squeal of fright. His presence was all around her in the blackness, making her small hairs stand on end. "Dylan?" came out like a desperate croak. "Is that you?" She was sick with fear; it felt so real.

Cautiously, her hand ventured ahead of her into the blackness but sliced easily through the air. Sagging in relief, she let out a huge breath. Lying on her side she flicked on the lamp. Her blood was still pumping in her ears while her eyes roamed the room to see if she had been dreaming. Nothing was there, and no evidence to suggest otherwise. She strained her ears to see if she could hear anything anywhere else in the house.

Fuck! She flopped back onto the bed. That was the mother of all nightmares.

THE DREAM PLAGUED her all the next day at work – that and Dylan. He hadn't contacted her once since dropping her off yesterday. Did he think she wouldn't want to see him again after seeing the film?

Janey had phoned twice, but not Dylan.

By 3 o'clock in the afternoon, she caved and tried his mobile – no answer. She almost threw her phone in frustration. The creeping, crawling tendrils of paranoia were taking hold: he didn't want her, he'd cast her off and the worst of all, now he'd had sex with her she'd outstayed her welcome. She couldn't concentrate or eat; her nerves were shot to pieces.

She had to text him, but what to write? She decided on keeping it simple so she didn't make a complete prat of herself. So she just put: *I miss you.* There, see what he makes of that.

Grace agonised her way through the rest of the day at work, dealing with endless disgruntled clients that her boss had asked to cancel because he'd rather go out and play golf. Then, when she'd typed the last letter and her last set of minutes, she reluctantly made her way back to her empty house, a little scared since her nightmare.

No messages waited for her on voicemail. No calls during the time she spent at the stables. Staying out as long as she could and feeling exhausted, she forced herself to drive the two miles home through the winding country lanes at around 9 p.m. Still nothing.

She had never felt so alone. She moped and felt sorry for herself. She hadn't really done anything wrong, had she? All she'd said was she wanted some time to think and, of course, the film thing. Why had he suddenly gone cold on her?

Deciding to sleep with a lamp on from now on, she went to bed after warming a can of soup. It was all she could manage with her stomach in knots. Huddled in a ball of misery, she wished she'd invited him in when she'd got home; if only she could turn the clock back.

Flinging herself from one side to the other, she tossed and turned for what felt like hours. Her eyes rested longingly on her phone next to the lamp. *Shit!* It was flashing. A text must have come while she'd dozed off. And yet she swore she hadn't slept a wink.

She bounded up and pounced on it. Opening the text, her heart skipped. It was from Dylan.

Holding her breath, her eyes gobbled up the words: *Did you watch the film?*

She stared straight ahead of her. What did he mean by that, besides the obvious? He knew she would have had time to. Should she lie? Would he know? God, she was such a crap liar.

She typed "No" and sent it.

She stared at her phone, willing it to beep back at her immediately, but it didn't. *Shit.* He was doing her head in. What was she supposed to do now? There was absolutely no chance of sleep, so she padded down her little steep staircase to the kitchen to put the kettle on.

The phone beeped from the kitchen counter.

She grabbed it. *Why not?*

Now, did she say she had bigger fish to fry like playing Miss Marple with his antipsychotic drugs, or did she say the real truth; that quite frankly, she was scared to, because she was having to admit to herself that she was falling for him hook, line and sinker, and she would rather be an ostrich and think of him as simply the wonderful sexy man she knew him, deep down, to be?

Blah, blah, who was she kidding? She would never have the guts to say all that.

Then she thought about all those people he mixed with at the party – particularly Serena. Maybe he liked her because she was different to them? She might not be all street and swagger, but she was strong in her own way.

She snatched up the phone and tapped: *Scared to.*

It was as close to honest as she was going to get without looking like a mad woman and making him run a mile.

She stirred her cup of drinking chocolate.

Her phone beeped again.

Why?

What was he doing to her? Did he want to turn her into a gibbering ball of mush and admit her feelings for him? Did he want to strip her bare and leave her more vulnerable than she was already?

She thought long and hard and just went for it: *Janey thinks it's bad, u think it's bad. I don't want 2 think bad of u.*

Thinking she probably just made a huge mistake, she thumped back up the stairs to bed, turning lights off as she went.

Beep.

There's a lot about me you don't know.

Fuck, you don't say. Her heart played a drum solo. *U don't think I could take it?*

Straight back: *I don't know if anyone could.*

Anyone except Serena, she wanted to scream in capitals. She felt so weary. She hadn't slept properly in days. Was he giving up, saying it was all hopeless, because quite honestly, she wasn't sure she could take that.

Please, Dylan, tell me exactly what u want? She pressed send, hoping he took the plea in the right way. She was beset with paranoia after she'd sent it. Loathing herself for being so uncool and needy.

No reply. She'd fucked it up now, she was sure of it. Maybe a hot bath would wilt her enough for sleep. The tap squeaked as she turned it, and she sloshed the water around with some blue muscle-soak bubble bath.

A hopeless last glance at the phone on top of the loo – nothing.

With the bath full to brimming, she gingerly got in, careful not to slurp it over the sides and give herself the tiresome job of cleaning it up.

She rested her head back over the roll top and sweat beaded her lip and brow when the phone beeped again.

Shit! She lurched forward, sending a tidal wave forward and back and cascading a waterfall all over the floor. Standing up and drying her hands quickly, she looked at the phone. Her heart somersaulted at the simple words: *I want you.*

She swallowed a lump in her throat the size of a small apple, tears of relief streamed down her cheeks and she clutched the phone to her heart. *Silly cow.*

Beep.

Clearing her vision, she read: *If you want me too, you have to accept all of me and that means you have to know everything.*

Her heart skipped. That was all she'd ever wanted. She'd never wanted anyone so much in her life. She replied straight back: *I want u, I wish you were with me now.*

Beep.

I'm outside...

. . .

GRACE FLEW DOWN the stairs in nothing but her bathrobe, flung open the front door, ran with bare feet and threw herself at Dylan halfway up the garden path.

He caught her on impact and waddled with her glued to his body and lips, through the front door and into the little living room where he gently set her down on her feet.

Grace still clung on around his neck and looked up at him with tired eyes wet from crying happy tears. "You came."

Dylan rubbed the pad of his thumb under her eye to take the tears away. "I meant what I said though, Grace. We need to talk."

Grace nodded, let go of her hold on his neck, held his hand and began leading him towards the stairs.

Dylan laughed a little. "Grace. Did you hear what I said?"

She stopped and turned abruptly. "Yes!" Then continued to pull him with her. "We can talk in bed. It's the middle of the night."

Dylan shook his head, half amused, but allowed her to lead him.

They were soon minus their clothes and nestled under the frilly duvet in each other's arms, facing each other.

"Go ahead," she said, all serious.

Dylan laughed and looked away, then back at her again, a little bemused. "So you didn't get me up here on false pretences?"

Grace grinned. "Well, as much as I'd like that, it would be nice to just… you know, cuddle."

Something flashed across his face for a second, then the edges of his mouth twitched.

"What… was that the wrong thing to say?" she said, suddenly alarmed.

His look was one of bewildered amazement. "No, it's just no one has ever been interested in doing that with me before."

My god. It was seldom you'd feel sorry for a man like Dylan, with a problem of women using him for his body, but she found that she did. "Well, I do." And she snuggled in closer.

"Don't you have to be up in a couple of hours?" he said, kissing the top of her head.

She groaned. "Don't remind me." Then she shook her head. "I'm going to throw my first ever sickie." And she looked up at him shrewdly, like a co-conspirator.

His expression took her breath away, like love or adoration or something. His lips were so distracting. She had to remind herself of the importance of what they were doing and drag her eyes back to his, still searching her face in wonder.

She crossed her legs in a definite no to her one-track mind. "Before we start, I have a confession to make, Dylan."

His eyebrows popped in surprise.

"When I was in your bathroom, before Fenton came, I… I found your medicines in the cupboard."

When he frowned, she quickly tacked on, "I wasn't snooping, I promise. I was looking for toothpaste."

He pulled her in close so he could kiss the top of her head, but she got the impression that he was escaping her gaze and giving himself time to think.

"That's why you wanted to leave?"

Grace nodded against his chest. "That, and feeling a little overwhelmed by everything."

"And you know what they are?" he said, pulling back so he could look into her eyes.

"I looked them up as soon as I got home."

Dylan exhaled loudly and rolled over onto his back as if the inevitable conversation he'd been dreading had finally come.

Grace kissed his shoulder. "Talk to me, Dylan. It's okay."

He looked sideways at her and his eyes held a hopeless-ness that said he didn't believe her for a minute. "Is it though?"

She looked at him steadily. "I need to know everything… your words."

CHAPTER 9

*D*ylan nodded once, took a deep breath and dragged her onto his chest so all she could do was listen.

"The summer before I came to school and met you, I went on a school trip with my old school. I was good at science, you know… a real whizkid at it."

Grace was fascinated and moved her head further back to the edge of his shoulder so she could watch his face. The lines of it were stark and his eyes haunted.

"Something bad happened while I was there; I don't know what exactly. They told me afterwards that my mind had blocked it out because it was so horrific. The friend I went with – my best friend –was killed. We were both injured, but he died. I had to have therapy to come to terms with the injustice of that."

"Did you ever find out what happened?"

"Yeah… we went out in a storm, messing about, a power cable got struck by lightning, killed Pete and threw me clear." He inadvertently touched his chest.

Grace gently ran her fingers over the handprint, to the burns in the fingerprints disguised by the tattoo. Then watched his Adam's apple move, as if he had to swallow down his emotion. The worst thing she could do was wimp out around him with pity.

"Everyone thought it was just a case of me getting over the trauma, but I felt different instantly. I've never been the same since." His eyelids lowered.

Grace remained silent, waiting.

His voice wavered and it nearly broke her heart.

"I started getting these blackouts; periods of time I just lost. I'd been aggressive towards my mum… She made light of it, but sent me back to the doctors and said I was having mood swings. They put it down to post-traumatic stress, but it happened a few times with my brothers as well. Then, when it happened with my mum again, instead of having me hospitalised, which is probably what they should have done, they packed me off to my uncle in Ireland."

"The one with the horses."

He nodded. "I know it sounds mad, Grace, but it was as though I was sharing my mind with someone else and there just wasn't enough room, and when I blacked out, *he* took over."

Grace noted that his eyes lowered, filled with hatred, as he referred to the *he*.

"I started to fight to stay conscious during those times so I knew what the hell he was doing."

The word "schizophrenia" floated to Grace's mind from the webpage. The word alone was terrifying.

"I hated it, Grace. He was the total antithesis of me, everything I despised, and all that was disgusting, he loved."

"I was in a mess. Finally, I confided in my uncle, who paid for me to see a doctor privately. That was when I finally got diagnosed. The weird thing was when they said it was schiz-ophrenia; I still thought, no, you're wrong. There is another entity inside me... that was the exact word I thought... enti-ty... it was so much more than hearing voices."

Grace closed her eyes and turned her mouth to kiss his collarbone. "When did Fenton and the film-making come into it?"

Dylan looked up at the ceiling. Grace was amazed to see Dylan's face transform, as if it were a happy memory.

"They had me doped up to the eyeballs, so I couldn't think straight, I couldn't even string a sentence together, let alone cause any trouble, so they let me go home. That was when I started a new school."

"Where you met me... No wonder you were so quiet."

"And failed all my exams... I walked around in a druggie haze, not bothering to open my mouth." Dylan ran a finger down her cheek. "But you never judged me, or questioned me, you just sat down in the chair next to me and made me feel normal... you don't know how grateful I was for that. Everyone just treated me as the quiet kid who was friends with Grace, and left me alone."

God, she had no idea such a thoughtless gesture like that held so much importance to him. She just never gave it a thought. It was humbling. "And Fenton?"

Dylan relaxed back into the pillows again and sighed. "There were still periods when he would break through, no matter how many pills I took. My mum and brothers covered for me all the time, so I didn't get committed."

The reality of the nightmare he'd suffered hit her and she swallowed down her emotion.

"I begged my mother to take me to a priest in the end, I was so convinced I was possessed by a demon."

Grace tutted. She just couldn't believe things like that still went on in the twenty-first century.

"No, I believed it, Grace. That's exactly what it felt like. But after the priest said a few prayers and splashed me with holy water, it became obvious that my demon had become comfortable and had no intention of coming out."

Grace giggled. Dylan smiled down at her. How she loved that he could make light of something so horrendous.

"That's when my older brother took me to the gym with him and started to train with me. I started with regular boxing first of all, then Thai and martial arts. That's how I met Fenton."

"He trained with you?"

"Yeah… He's about ten years older than me and an experienced martial artist. He was already representing several people in the blue film industry."

Yeah, the sleazeball, totally taking advantage of a young, impressionable man and exploiting him.

Dylan read her mind or her scowl. "It wasn't like that, Grace. Fenton saved me."

Pur-lease.

"He started to train with me really hard. I'd grown tall, as tall as I am now, and I trained like a lunatic. It sharpened my thinking and gave me purpose."

Grace softened a bit. Exercise would totally do that.

"Fenton started encouraging me to enter tournaments and became like my coach. He was brilliant when I think back."

"He groomed you, Dylan."

Dylan laughed, flipped her over onto her back and pounced on her. "No he didn't," he said, touching her lip with his finger, telling her off. "I was about twenty and an adult by then."

"Mmm," she hummed, unconvinced. "So you're a good fighter?" Her eyes were lowered, waiting for what he would do next.

Dylan's mind went straight back to the past and he moved off her and onto his back again. "No, not me… it was *him* who fought. *He* always took over and completely annihilated my opponents. That meant *I* became known for being a dirty fighter and putting several people in hospital."

She absorbed the information for a moment. He was basically telling her that he was like some kind of Jekyll and Hyde type character and she wasn't sure how she truly felt about that. Instead, she went for humour. "That's lucky," she whispered. "That it was the other you." And she bit her lip.

Dylan scowled at her, then tried to hold back a smile. "Now you're taking the piss out of me?"

She continued to bite her lip. Schooling her features, she urged him to continue with a regal wave of the hand. "How does that get you into nudey films?"

Dylan threw his head back and laughed loudly, then rolled onto her again, his eyes hooded. "When I imagined telling you, Grace, it scared the life out of me." He grinned and kissed her on the mouth. "I never thought you'd just take the piss."

The truth was – with him here and now, warm and sexy in her bed, it all seemed unreal somehow. It wasn't that she thought he was lying or exaggerating, more that he seemed perfectly well to her. And so what if he took medication? Thousands of people did that every day for all kinds of conditions. His just happened to be for his mood, or personality, or whatever. So instead of getting all serious and down about it all, she did what she always did with him: she made everything seem surface and light. "Sorry… I just have a short attention span." She grinned.

He barked a blast of laughter again. "That I totally love you for," he said softly.

They stilled and their eyes locked for a moment.

"Do you love me?" she whispered.

His look was one of wonder, as if he'd just come to a realisation. Then he closed the distance between them and nodded slightly. "Yeah… I do."

Grace fought tears, reached into his hair and pulled him to her mouth. The touch was electricity transmitted straight to her core that immediately ran wet for him. His arousal pushed into her pelvic bone, longing to be lower.

Gasps and swirling tongues, tasting and stroking each other, with no clothes to inhibit them, Dylan shimmied down so he could nudge at her, ramping her heart rate to dangerous levels.

Dylan's arms pushed underneath her, pulling her tighter to him while his hips rotated, teasing his hardness into her super-slick, sensitive folds, aching to envelope him. "We're supposed to be talking serious stuff," he moaned, grazing his teeth down the column of her neck.

Grace panted in frustration as his large arousal moved away from where she wanted it to be. "Bloody hell, Dylan, we'll have to talk in a minute." And she pushed him over so she could kiss down his hard chest and abs to the throbbing thickness waiting for her mouth.

Dylan's laughter evaporated when her lips circled him and he hissed. She stilled, waiting for his permission to continue. Then fingers stabbed through her hair and moved her where he wanted her mouth. She cupped him underneath and he moaned, while she worked her mouth, slowly building in speed, up and down, flicking her tongue over the broad head.

"Ah, Grace, what are you doing to me?" he whispered.

Her reply was to take him in deeper still.

His muscles became rigid and she sensed him so close, but he pulled her gently away from him and rolled on top of her again, kissing her full and deeply on her mouth. "I want to be in you." And he entered her in one full, hard thrust.

With no preamble, he began a punishing rhythm, causing her to cry out his name. All she could do was bite into his shoulder and score his back with her nails. He was literally pounding her into the bed. Everything in her screamed to pull him closer and deeper within her, teeth and nails only served to drive him on harder and faster.

The punishing pace meant that neither would last for long. "Come with me," Dylan whispered.

"I don't know if I can," she whimpered.

No sooner had the words left her lips than she was flipped over onto her stomach with an arm under her belly, hoisting her bottom up to him like an offering which he plunged straight into, causing her to cry out again.

Dylan placed one arm under her chest, holding her firmly by one breast. He moved down to find her clitoris and circled and milked it until the warmth of buzzing, tingling nerve endings exploded all over her. Her womb clenched and retracted and her sheath gripped onto him like it never wanted to let him go.

Grace felt him ripple inside her and he clamped onto her neck with his teeth and groaned loudly. The erotic moan totally did it and she dissolved into pulse after pulse and let the release wash over her again and again.

Dylan continued to rotate his hips into her for a long while after and continued to suck her neck gently. The feelings of ownership were complete. Trapped underneath him, while he was still inside her and gripped onto her neck, it was instinctual and primaeval and profoundly satisfying on a level she didn't totally understand.

Dylan relaxed down his full weight and stopped moving while he caught his breath. "Are you okay?" he said, eventually.

"I love you," she replied, simply and honestly. There was no point in playing silly games; she loved the bones of him.

GRACE WAS SO TIRED, but determined not to sleep yet. Dylan, on the other hand, seemed to never need sleep. After a quick shower, he disappeared and went downstairs and put together an early breakfast and returned with a tray. It was almost light.

"Come on, eat something," he said, perched on the edge of the bed with it.

Grace realised he was stark naked. "Did you walk around the house like that?" She sat up and rested against the headboard and nibbled a piece of toast.

He shrugged. "I don't have a problem with nudity."

No, she supposed he didn't. There was an uncomfortable silence for a moment. "You didn't finish your story," she said, reaching for a glass of orange juice with lowered eyes.

Dylan was scrutinising her, she guessed to see if he should continue. "You want me to?"

"Everything, remember?"

He walked around the bed and got back in next to her. "Where did I get to?"

"You became a badass fighter."

Dylan composed himself and nodded. "Yeah, I started to be treated as this kind of Terminator character on the circuit and we started to get invited to all these social events and parties. Some were pretty wild, and with that scene came all the women."

"Was that you or *him*?"

Dylan studied her for any humour, then looked as if he was impressed that she'd cottoned on so quickly. Grace didn't understand it all, but it had suddenly become really important that Dylan's alter ego was the guy who did all the bad stuff.

His face suddenly became sad. "I wish I could say to you that it was all him, Grace, but the truth of it was that I was strong enough to break through to consciousness at any time, especially while I was medicated. So if a situation came up that I liked or wanted, I could remain there."

Grace looked at him long and hard. "Like the two of you?" she said flatly.

Dylan nodded, looking her dead in the eye, gauging her reaction.

He was basically saying that, depending on the situation, he could be involved, or not, as the case may be. "So, you mean if *you* liked the woman?" she said, looking down, pulling a corner off her toast and putting it in her mouth.

"Yeah."

"Like Serena?"

She felt him sag next to her.

"Sometimes."

Jealousy raged through her like a rabid animal. God, she wanted to scratch the woman's eyes out.

"Is she yours or *his*?" she said, swallowing hard and dropping her eyes away from him. She knew she was coming across as a petulant child, but fuck it.

"We shared her," he said, softly.

Grace screwed her face up in disgust. "Does she know... about you?... The two of you?" she corrected.

Dylan's face was contrite as he tried to explain it. Her anger was uncalled for, she knew, after all, it was all before she came along, and Dylan was just trying to survive, but she just couldn't help herself.

"I've told no one except you... Fenton knows. Whether people guessed or what, I don't know, but I never told her."

There was a little comfort in that, she supposed. Feeling

totally insecure where that woman was concerned, she was glad she had something she didn't – his confidence. "Do you become aware during the film-making?"

"Yeah, sometimes."

Her eyes snapped up to his. "So it *is* you?"

He sighed, slightly exasperated with her, shaking his head. "No, it's not."

She threw her hands up. "So let me get this straight… You take the tablets – why?"

Dylan frowned. "They keep me calm and in control… *he's* quieter then."

She huffed, totally confused. "Then why, Dylan, do you have to make the films at all, if you take your tablets?" she finished at a loss.

"It was Fenton who first worked it out."

Hoo-bloody-ray for Fenton! But she remained quiet and tight-lipped.

"If I left off the meds, *he* would always come to the surface."

Grace grabbed his hand and looked deeply into his eyes. "Well, that's it then. Surely, you take the meds nonstop and keep him suppressed."

Dylan was already shaking his head before she had finished.

"What?… Why would you come off your meds when you know he takes over?"

Dylan took another deep breath and stroked the hand that held his. "It doesn't work like that, Grace. He's unpredictable and breaks out at any time – he's incredibly strong. Fenton thought up the idea of setting aside certain times where we would allow *him* out, where *he* was in a controlled environment… and that doesn't always guarantee he doesn't wake up at times… Of course, I fight him, but it happens."

Grace stared at him for a long moment, then a horrible

thought struck her and she swallowed hard. "Is he with you when you are with me?" *Please say no.*

"He tries, but I am adamant about it only being me. He doesn't like it, because it's the only time it's happened.'

The thought of Dylan ever having sex with other women killed her, but his saying that thawed her a little. Then she remembered. "That first time we had sex. You said something weird?" She tried to reel off the exact words, but he was ahead of her, already nodding.

"Yeah, I know when you mean. Sex is always dodgy; it is when he's closest to the surface, even when I am on the pills."

After a few moments of letting it all sink in, "So let me get this straight: you take medication to keep him suppressed, but he breaks out... so you leave them off at certain times so you know when?"

All the while Dylan was nodding. "Exactly."

"But why fighting... why blue films, Dylan, I don't get it... can't you do a regular job?"

He put his head at an angle and smiled as if to say, if only it were that easy, then he composed himself again. "After I... we...won our first few fights, it became clear that it was *him* who had the killer instinct, so Fenton had the idea of leaving off the meds leading up to a fight. It meant we had control. We knew exactly when he would break through, and it seemed to be the outlet he needed, allowing me to be myself at other times."

"How do you make sure you come back... I mean, doesn't he want to stay all the time?" she asked.

He nodded. "True... Fenton supervises the tablets for the first forty-eight hours – and he made it very clear to *him* from the start, that he only gets to indulge in this extreme lifestyle if he plays ball – he needs Fenton to get him gigs, you know? Plus, I only cooperate because we do it this way.

He doesn't want a constant fight to do what he wants, any more than I do… It seems to work."

She had to concede that it kind of made sense. "But why the films?"

"Pretty soon, tournaments started to refuse me entry because of my reputation. The partying became more wild; endless women, sex, orgies, sometimes even men… I dunno, it's a blur."

Grace's eyes went wide with shock. She knew he'd been on the fringes, but still, hearing it spelled out… But there was no boasting in his voice; if anything, he sounded as if he regretted it all.

He must have read it on her face. "Everything, remember?" he said, with a weak smile. He closed his eyes and pressed on. "Fenton witnessed most of it, and what with my size and physique, plus my fighting reputation, he set about putting it all to use, and I made my first film."

"How convenient for Fenton," she sniped.

Dylan looped his arm around her, pulled her over and kissed the top of her head. "Still protecting me?" he laughed. "The trouble is, with him being so strong and unpredictable, if I couldn't fight, then I had to have something else."

Dylan watched her face for a few moments. "It gave me an income … I needed a job, Grace. Not a lot doing for a headcase like me," he said, smiling.

Grace was still pulling apart her toast, but eating very little. She was angry, but her heart bled for him. "Is he here now?" she whispered, chills coming out on her skin as she thought it.

"No," Dylan said, affronted. "There is no way I'd let him anywhere near you; he's evil, Grace. I didn't even want him to have access to your phone number in the beginning… You don't understand."

Her writing her number on the beer mat that first night

came back to her. She'd thought it odd at the time, but it all started to fall into place. Grace searched his face; he seemed so emphatic about it, she had to believe him. "So when you said you're getting into character for a film and can't speak to anyone?"

Dylan's eyes became soulful. "Yeah, I come off my meds and let *him* out, *he* does his thing for the film… I go to sleep. Then, after, I try to recalibrate myself and start the tablets again and go back to being me."

"Do you remember anything?"

"Sometimes… I get images or flashbacks like in a dream." He looked away, ashamed. "But most of the time, I don't want to know."

She continued to watch him, not daring to ask the obvious question, dreading to know the answer.

He answered it anyway. "You want to know when it's going to happen again?" he said, sadly. "In two weeks' time, I have to disappear."

"For how long?"

"I come off the meds about a week before filming." He looked at her sharply. "You should go away."

Her eyes went wide with fear. "Why? I don't want to."

"Please, Grace. For me… I'd feel better."

"When will you be back?"

"I insist on all my scenes being shot back to back, then I have to stabilise after… so about three weeks, a month, tops."

Grace put the tray on the floor and snuggled into him and he shimmied down into the bed with her. How on earth would she get through that time without him?

She thought of all those people at the party – Serena, being close to him and her not being able to, made her want to commit murder. "All those people at the party… who do they know, you or him?" she hedged.

"Both… they just call me D. They assume we are the same person. They think I'm *him.*"

Grace stroked the side of his face lovingly. "Do you prefer D to Dylan, is that it… like you can separate yourself from it or something?"

Dylan kissed her lips softly and searched her face, but shook his head slowly. "No, Grace, D is for Diablo, it's Spanish for Devil… I'm known as the Devil, Grace."

CHAPTER 10

Grace phoned in sick at work and eventually fell asleep through sheer exhaustion. Dylan never left her, although he was awake most of the time.

When she awoke sometime in the afternoon, Dylan made her eat again and said he had a few things to do and would return later. She followed him downstairs, but he paused in the doorway. "Ring your friend, Grace. Tell her you'll see the film tonight."

Grace froze and felt alarmed. Why would he want to ruin everything now? "It's okay, I'll search for it on my computer. I can watch it here."

Dylan shook his head. "There's no running away from it. I'll drop you off there; you shouldn't be alone."

Why was he pushing her into it? "I can drive myself there. I won't drink," she said, scowling. *Believe me, I'll want a clear head.*

"I want to make sure you go, Grace."

She stamped her foot. *Shit!* He was getting to know her pretty well.

Then he looked down and shifted his weight from foot to

foot. "Then, if you don't call me to pick you up, I'll know," he finished, looking at her with flat, expressionless eyes, already prepared for rejection.

Grace walked over to him and reached her hands up around his neck. "Do you think I'd dismiss you just like that?" she whispered. Did he think her feelings were that shallow, that easy to get over?

Dylan bent his head and kissed her on the mouth. They'd kissed a hundred times that day and it just didn't get old. "No," he said, quietly. "But that is what you *should* do. I want you to be clear in your mind, what you are dealing with… what you're letting yourself in for."

He put her away from him. "Tonight, Grace."

GRACE HADN'T REALLY HAD enough sleep to cope with the enormity of what she was about to do. She felt spaced-out and headachy, like she had a bad bout of jet lag.

Janey said to come over around eight when the kids were safely in bed. Dylan watched from the bike as she knocked on the door, then nodded once when it opened and rode away. A lump came up in her throat to see him disappear. It felt prophetic.

"Bloody hell, Grace… he brought you here?"

Grace huffed. "You've got him all wrong, Janey." She stepped in over the threshold.

Janey wasted no time and took the disk from a plain DVD cover and put it in the player.

"You've got it on DVD?" Grace said, surprised.

"Dave had to get a friend to burn it onto a disk for us. He has to really be careful what he watches or downloads online, Grace.

"God, Janey, does Dave know?" Grace was mortified. Dave was Janey's husband and a police officer. A long time on the force, he was the last person Grace wanted judging Dylan.

"Yes, Grace. He's really concerned for you… He said the Diablo films are hard to download because they are so bad. There are rumours that they don't always use actors."

Grace didn't argue; it was pointless. "Won't he get in trouble if it's so bad?" she said.

"Yes, probably, if they knew about it, but he called in a favour from a contact of a friend on the force because he wants you to see sense."

Grace sighed. This was becoming more complicated by the minute and going to be harder to sit through than she thought, and not just because of the film content.

Janey opened a bottle of wine and gave Grace a glass.

"I can't believe he brought you here… does he know what we're doing?"

"Yes," Grace said, sighing again. "He made me come… he wants me to know everything as much as you do. I would rather not know, to be honest, Janey. He wants me to know what he's done, before we get too involved." Grace swallowed and looked down at her glass.

"My God, Grace. It's too late, isn't it. You've fallen for him."

Grace nodded with a heavy heart. No point in lying. "I can't help myself, Janey. He came into my life like a bomb going off, and nothing will ever be the same again. It's like I've never been in love before, never had sex." Her eyes glanced cautiously at Jane, then back into her glass.

"Shit… you've got it bad. I feel terrible being the one to have to show you this."

Grace studied her friend while she found the start of the film and switched all the lights off. Janey wasn't enjoying this any more than she was. *Just get the bloody thing over with and then she could go.*

The sound boomed, and Janey had to turn down the dramatic atmospheric music. It reminded her of one of the old Hammer films. But the terror inside wasn't from anything spooky; it was of the film actually affecting her, of it making her feel different or unsure about the man she had come to see as the love of her life.

"Have you watched other blue films, Janey?" She asked because she had absolutely nothing to gauge it on.

"Yeah," Janey said, matter-of-fact. "Most couples have some time, but I can honestly say, nothing like this."

Shit. "What's different about this one?" She couldn't help asking, but recoiled inside, sure she wouldn't want to know the answer.

Janey laughed while she thought about it. "They normally have silly plots like the plumber coming round to fix the boiler and gets it on with a highly sexed housewife within minutes, or a boss asking his secretary in his office to take dictation… You get the picture."

Grace waited.

Janey faced the TV screen again. "This is nothing like that."

Grace curled her legs under her and got comfortable to watch the film. Then everything around her disappeared as she became absorbed into the movie. Sucked into a gothic horror of misfits; all the low life and underbelly of society that no regular person ever sees.

It began in an underground club packed with people more at home in a Marilyn Manson video; each one exposing deathly white skin, wearing a combination of tattoos, bondage, piercings, chains and horror-like contact lenses.

They were working themselves up with hardcore rock music to abandon while evil-looking men mingled in and out, reminding her of vampires searching out a victim.

Directly in front of the camera was the back of a mystery man dressed in black who appeared to be watching his minions at work.

The hairs began to stand up on Grace's neck and arms. Although his hair was slicked back with grease and looked jet-black, she instinctively knew it was Dylan. Maybe it was his stature or the way he held his shoulders, but she'd know him anywhere. The camera didn't show his face.

A group of unwitting friends had entered the club, knowing straight away they had entered the wrong place. Their way was barred and there was no escape. The mystery man nodded.

Grace's hackles began to rise. This had nothing to do with sex so far and all to do with fear. "Can we take a break?" she blurted.

Janey looked sardonically over at her. "No, Grace. Nothing's happened yet."

The hapless friends were soon drugged and woke up in what could only be described as a dungeon. Guess that's why the film was called *Diablo's Dungeon*. And that meant Dylan's.

There were three girls and three boys. One of the girls looked noticeably more pure and virginal than the rest. Probably deliberate.

Grace had no experience with sex on the fringes or anything alternative, but she found herself clutching her throat and remembering Dylan's hands around it the first time they'd had sex. Then she forced herself to watch the world of sadomasochistic torture, which included various devices used to humiliate and cause pain. But still there was no sign of Dylan.

"Can we have a break now?" Grace asked again. It was uncomfortable viewing and she wanted out. The whole thing emanated evil and darkness.

The minions had brought the people into the dungeon to

perform despicable acts of sexual torture, who overacted like they were enjoying it. That was disturbing in itself, but the virginal one had been left on an altar like a sacrifice, dressed in nothing but a sheer white lace robe and panties, revealing her nubile body underneath. She looked so young.

The minions left the others and began circling her, chanting like a satanic ritual. A feeling of dread loomed over Grace and she wished she couldn't guess what was coming, but nothing would make her tear her eyes away now.

The wall to the dungeon slowly opened to reveal billowing clouds of dry ice, dissipating slowly to show a lone figure like an apparition. A tall man stood motionless as the smoke cleared, reminding her of Count Dracula, except this one was naked to the waist.

A tanned, tattooed man, hair gelled so it shone black under the lights, stared down at the floor. There was no denying who he was; she'd know him anywhere. He was slimmer, not an ounce of fat, not that he ever carried much, but he looked like a fighter with every sinew and muscle defined.

He wore a studded belt around his low-slung leathers, and studs caught the light in the seams running snugly down his long, slender legs. His hands clenched and unclenched as if he were waking up. His head slowly raised and he prowled towards the girl. He hadn't said a word, but he held the scene with such presence you couldn't take your eyes off him.

Menacingly, he looked up at the camera. His face was gaunt with harder lines from his weight loss, but it was his eyes that spoke and held her. Deepest brown and soulless, he was the man sitting in her chair, the man from her nightmares.

Grace found she was breathless. In her dreams, she had already met Diablo, and in them, he knew who she was. The terrifying knowledge she'd been putting to the back of her mind was now impossible to ignore; she knew he wanted her. And as he looked into the camera and smiled, pure evil, it was as if it were for her alone.

"I don't know if I can watch any more of this," Grace said, desperately.

"Stay where you are, lady, at least for this scene. Remember, even he thinks you need to see it."

Grace faced the screen again. He wasn't Dylan. He didn't even really look like him. "His eyes are a different colour," she sniped.

"Probably contacts, Grace… to make him look scarier."

Yeah, he did look scary – even Janey thought so. Dylan couldn't do this, she reassured herself over and over as she watched the sordid events unfold. He's acting, the girl was acting, she reminded herself. The girl was made to look pure with her pale skin and neat brown hair in a bob. She was a porn star, for fuck's sake. She was probably ten years older than she looked. But she couldn't deny what the film was meant to portray. It was domination and humiliation for all the sickos out there who dreamt of doing things like this to some poor, helpless young girl.

Grace looked away.

"Watch, Grace."

The girl was awake from her trance now, screaming and fighting. She was dragged from her plinth to face Dylan/Diablo. Then he appeared to hypnotise her into compliance and lay her back down. A minion pulled a rope on a pulley across the ceiling. Then Dylan skilfully set about binding her with the thick rope like some kind of magician. But it wasn't soft showbiz cord, it was rough ship's rope that would chafe and rub the skin. It went around her hands and feet and body over and over, until he yanked it hard and pulled it hand over hand, his arm and back muscles bunching and cording, till she hung way over their heads from the ceiling.

The girl hung there, straining against the ropes, her hair falling into her face so you could see her jaw line and her full, slightly parted lips. Her body hung forward and breasts were exposed where the ropes had parted her dress and criss-crossed her chest. Her leg was pulled high by the knee vertically behind her at an unnatural angle with her other leg left tied low, exposing her panties and parting her legs for the camera. The eroticism in the treatment of the girl was obvious but disturbing, and Grace found she couldn't drag her eyes away.

It was strange because the fact that she was dressed made it all the more unsettling, making it look more like something taken, instead of given freely. Then the last thing to be added was a noose around her pale neck.

Grace unconsciously touched her own.

Diablo had to move her hair to do this, exposing her face. Her eyes were half closed and her lips parted as if in ecstasy. It was done gently, almost reverently.

Grace shuddered, but still she was spellbound by the spectacle so far removed from anything she'd ever seen. Then he took a step back while various other painful things were done to her that forced Grace to cover her eyes and watch through the gap in her fingers. But Diablo hadn't yet physically touched her – not sexually anyway. Maybe that wasn't what he did? She hoped so and she clung to that thought, but everything had been hardcore up to that point and the suspense was building to when he'd let loose on her.

Grace was drawn into the film like a vortex. Nothing else existed. She was disgusted and yet compelled, like some horrific car crash. Diablo did the despicable things, not Dylan, the man she loved. He worked the girl over like a master torturer, until she hung quivering and begging for mercy. The smile of evil was a prelude to what came next.

Grace was overcome with dread, but couldn't tear her eyes away.

When he had her lowered and braced against the plinth, Grace audibly yelped. "That's it… That's enough!" Grace shouted, jumping up in a mixture of anger and distress.

Janey flinched and looked shocked at her reaction, but didn't argue, sensing she'd reached her limit. She rose sheepishly and went towards the DVD player to switch it off.

Following her actions, Grace's eye caught the screen and she gasped. Turning away, she covered her eyes with her hand. "Turn it off, Janey… please!" she shrieked.

"Okay… okay. I will."

"Wait!" Grace yelped. "Forward it to the credits." She just had to know.

Janey did as she was asked and forwarded the rest of the film, switching it back on a minute or so before the end.

Grace hitched a breath at the state of him. Covered completely with the girl's blood, and laughing, he looked so evil; in fact, the whole scene looked demonic.

Appalled and mesmerised, her eyes were glued to him. Smiling and covered in blood, he turned and sauntered away, returning to his crypt. *Fucking hell!*

Janey switched on the lights, and relief flooded her. The bright suburban room acted like a huge weight lifted from her shoulders and heart. The credits moved quickly up the screen and Grace could finally breathe again. Her fists had been clenched so tightly that her nails had pitted her palms.

She still didn't say a word but followed the credits to see if Dylan's name came up. Relieved, she let out a breath when all it said was: 'featuring Diablo' and that was it – one name, that was all he needed.

Grace let her head fall into her hands. What was she meant to do now with what she knew? There was no way she could undo what she'd seen. Pain stabbed her in the chest and gut when she contemplated finishing it with Dylan, but at the same time, whatever way you dressed it up, that *was* Dylan. Schizophrenic or not, it was him.

"Are you okay?" Janey said, with sympathetic eyes.

Grace wasn't sure how long she had been sitting there, staring into space. Her glass was topped up. She was tired and overwrought. "I don't know what to say... what to think," she said, shaking her head in exhaustion.

"I guess you could take comfort in that it isn't real and it's just a film... however sick." Janey smiled weakly. "It's not even real blood."

Grace loved her for that, but whatever way she thought about it, from what she knew of Diablo, it was real enough for him. The film just gave him a legitimate platform to indulge his sick perversions, where he wouldn't get locked up.

"What Dave couldn't understand was why he was covered in maths?"

CHAPTER 11

Grace's hand dropped away from her head like a stone and she frowned at her friend. She sat up straighter. She was right, some were like hieroglyphs, but a lot were numerals and letters set out like equations. She shook her head and the thought away; too much to take in right now.

"Dylan doesn't even know what they are." *Shit.* She blasted red. Janey frowned, but didn't question her, thankfully. The last thing she needed was to spill about the whole schizophrenia deal as well. Janey would blow a gasket.

Janey came and put her arms around her shoulders. "What are you going to do?"

Grace shook her head wearily. "It's as if he's two different people, Janey. The Dylan I love doesn't do things like that."

"You've got to stop making excuses for him, Grace," Janey said, clearly exasperated with her. Then she hugged her to her chest. "I know you love him… I just want you to be safe."

They both looked around sharply as Dave walked in through the door. He smiled at her sympathetically. He was thirty-five, six feet tall, once muscular, now more portly, with a receding hairline. But he was a lovely bloke and a good husband and father. And Grace loved him. He was like the big brother she never had.

"She watched it then?"

They both nodded.

"Well?"

"Well what?" Janey said, getting annoyed with him. Go and have your dinner."

"She gonna sack him off?"

"Go away, Dave, you're not helping."

But he wasn't about to be brushed off and stood with his hands on his hips. "Blokes like him make my job ten times harder... should be locked up with all the other nonces.

"Dave!" Janey shouted.

"She ain't got no one else looking out for her."

Janey narrowed her eyes and told him where to go through thin lips, so he slammed out of the room.

Hearing Dylan described like that just tipped her over the edge. Not the Dylan in the film, but her Dylan. The one who'd been in bed with her all day, caring for her, making her food and making love to her. She couldn't bear it. Tears brimmed in her eyes and ran down her cheeks.

"Oh, Grace." Janey pulled her into her body to comfort her. "Don't cry, we're here... I'll kill Dave when I get him on my own."

Grace sniffed. "If you could see what he's like when he's with me, Janey. He's nothing like that.

"I know... I know," Janey said in soft, soothing tones while stroking her hair like she would one of her kids. "What are you gonna do?" she said, eventually.

Grace shook her head. "He dropped me off so that he would know how I'd taken it. He said if I didn't call him, then he'd know."

Janey's eyebrows popped. "Shit, Grace, I can see why he confuses you so much."

Grace began to sob anew in Janey's arms. She was tired, hadn't slept properly in days and strangely, all she wanted to do was sleep for a year in Dylan's arms, while he told her everything would be okay.

"I overheard him talking; he said he's going to quit," Grace said, extracting herself from Janey's hug.

"Well that's good," Janey said, pushing the hair off her face.

Grace nodded like a small child being told everything would be all right in the morning.

"Maybe you can put this behind you then?" Janey said, smiling.

Janey didn't know the half of it and so Grace burst out crying again. "He's committed to one more film," she sobbed.

"Oh god, Grace." Janey cuddled her again. "When?"

"Two weeks' time… He'll be away a month… Said I should go away."

"Sod him, Grace. Do what *you* want, not what *he* tells you to do."

Grace nodded, sitting back up. She was absolutely drained. "I'm going to ring him."

"You sure that's a good idea?… Why don't you stay here?"

Grace touched her friend's hair. "Thank you, Janey, but I have to work this out and I can't do it here." She walked out to the bathroom and splashed her face with water. She looked hideous. There was a reason to stay right there.

Not trusting herself to speak to him, she sent a text: *Please pick me up now.*

Straight back: *Sure… are you okay?*

No.

Then she went back out and sat with Janey until the phone beeped to tell her he was outside.

Grace got up to leave.

Dave came bounding down the stairs. He'd showered and changed his clothes. "You off?"

"Yeah," she said, sniffing.

"You sure you're okay to drive?" Dave said, no doubt concerned about how much she'd been drinking.

"It's okay, Dave, Dylan's picking her up," Janey explained.

"What?… she's going home with the bloke after that?" Dave said, angrily pointing at the TV. "Are you mad?" he shouted.

"Leave it, Dave. It's up to her." Janey said, pushing him out of the way while she led Grace to the door.

"Fuck this!" Dave pushed past the pair of them and marched out to the road where Dylan waited next to the kerb with his engine running.

Grace ran out after Dave in panic, followed quickly by Janey, who grabbed Dave's arm to slow him down. "Calm down, Dave. Leave it."

The road was well lit by a security light from the house and a street light right above Dylan. He looked an impressive figure, tall, dressed in head-to-foot black leather, blacked-out helmet and astride a big, powerful bike.

Dylan slipped it onto its stand as soon as he heard the first "Oi you!" from Dave as he left the house. He got off, removed his helmet and shook out his hair. Dave only stopped when he was right in front of him, a little shorter and a little wider, too.

Dylan's eyes moved from Dave to find Grace's. "You okay?" he asked, quietly.

Grace just nodded, conscious of diffusing an explosive situation and getting away.

Dylan turned his gaze back to Dave, who was still determined to have a go at him.

"No, she's not okay after watching that shit."

Dylan didn't move a muscle but continued to watch Dave. Grace knew he was coiled and waiting for Dave to make a move, standing still but not relaxed.

Dave moved in chest to chest and pointed into Dylan's face. Janey grabbed firmly onto his arms, ready to yank him back. "Dave, calm down."

He shrugged her off.

"I'm watching you, do you hear me?"

Dylan didn't even blink.

"If I hear you so much as touch a hair on her head… you'll have me to deal with."

Dylan didn't back down or alter the tone of his voice. "You have my word."

Dave tutted and allowed Janey to pull him a step back.

Grace came closer to Dylan and tugged on his arm to break his fixation. Dave was a police officer with fifteen years on the force, but Dylan was a fighter, retired or not. The quiet assurance he'd given to Dave had made her shiver and scared her that he could snap if Dave pushed it too far.

"It's okay, Dave… don't worry." Grace took the spare helmet from Dylan's hand and he finally broke the stand off and remounted the bike. She climbed on behind him. Grace watched Dave put his arm around Janey, who looked really worried. Gripping her arms around Dylan's waist, she watched the pair until they were out of sight.

THE TWO OF them entered Grace's house in silence. Dylan hovered by the door.

"Look, I'm sorry about Dave, okay?"

"Don't be… he was looking out for you," Dylan said, unwilling to meet her eyes.

He was restless and Grace could tell he was unsure of what to say or do.

"Look, I'm gonna go… Let you have some time to yourself." He looked angry with himself.

Grace, who had been composing herself really well up until that point, felt like she was beginning to crumble. Her face screwed up in pain and her voice barely came out a croak. "You're going to leave me here like this?" A sob escaped her. She put her hands to her mouth in a vain attempt to stop any more.

Dylan's eyes widened in bewildered surprise. He clearly didn't know what on earth he should do. "I just thought… you might need…"

His shocked expression was enough to make her burst into tears. He strode over and circled his arms around her and swayed with her gently. "Shh… hey, I won't go anywhere if you don't want me to… Ah fuck, Grace, I'm so sorry."

She felt wretched; she'd gone against her best friend's advice tonight. "I'm all on my own, Dylan… so on my own," she sobbed. And although it had been six long years since she'd lost her parents, she'd never felt so utterly alone as she did at that moment.

Dylan didn't say anything, just kissed the top of her head until her sobs eased to the odd hiccup now and again. "Better now?" he whispered next to her cheek.

"I want to sleep for a year," she sniffed, next to his chest. Every emotion had been wrung out of her over the last few days.

"Come on, I'll put you to bed." He picked her up as if she weighed nothing and carried her up the stairs.

She tried to peel off her clothes, but her arms felt like lead weights and her eyes were half closed, making everything take ages.

"Here, let me help you." Dylan was scrutinising her while he made short work of the tricky buttons on her shirt.

Even in her lethargic state, Grace could tell that he didn't understand her one bit. Maybe he'd been expecting her to rant and rave at him, or be violent, but all she felt was raw, like an open wound and would cry again any minute. "I need the bathroom." She scooted around him to find the privacy to break down. His hands dropped helplessly to his sides.

In her little bathroom, Grace put down the loo seat and sat for a minute. Tiredness swamped her and her brain refused to work, so she sat and stared into space. This was no good, so she flicked on the shower, took off the rest of her clothes and stepped into the bath. Tucked into a ball in the bottom of the tub, the spray battered her head and back. Perhaps if she sat long enough and small enough, everything would wash away.

Grace wasn't sure how long she sat huddled there, but the water was almost cold when Dylan came into the bathroom. He pulled his T-shirt over his head, discarded it and reached in to turn off the spray. "Come on, Grace. You'll freeze." He grabbed a towel from the rail, put it around her and pulled her to her feet. Then he helped her out over the side and put a second towel around her head.

Grace allowed her despairing eyes to look up into his for the first time and saw he was in misery too.

"I'm sorry," he said. "I should never have made you do it..."

While she watched him kicking himself for making her do something that was never going to end well, she felt strangely better. After all, he couldn't help what he'd been in the past; the real dilemma for both of them was where they went from here.

Dylan carried her back to the bedroom and sat on the edge of the bed with her in his lap like a small child.

"I know you want to talk, Dylan, but I can't. I feel numb at the moment... I just need to sleep."

He nodded and pulled back the quilt. "In."

Grace did as she was told and he folded a towel to put under her head to stop her hair from wetting the pillow. It was so ridiculous that all she thought was how her hair would look when it dried like that.

"You always look beautiful."

Did she speak out loud? God, she was losing the plot.

She blinked her heavy eyes. "Sleep with me."

He hesitated with a look that said he didn't know what was going on, then stood, unbuttoned his jeans and stepped out of them. He slid into the bed next to her and pulled her close.

He was so warm, she took a deep breath of him – his own distinctive smell she could never get enough of and sighed. His heat seeped into her and, before long, she knew nothing else.

THE NEXT THING GRACE KNEW, the room was bathed in the soft pink glow of her bedside lamp. It must be nearly morning. She was groggy and still half asleep.

Dylan's face was a few inches from hers and he was asleep. She moved her head back slightly to study him. It was the first time she'd ever seen him like this. He reminded her of the little boy he must have been; he looked so young and pure with every facial muscle relaxed.

Her fingers traced the small laughter lines at the corner of his eye, on his forehead and at the corner of his mouth. His eyes flickered open. "Sorry, I didn't mean to wake you, but you looked so beautiful asleep."

Dylan's smile was small and uncertain. "I feel safe here."

If it had been anyone else, it would have been a weird thing to say, but because it was Dylan, she understood, and it tugged at her heartstrings. "Does he leave you alone here?"

He nodded slightly; he was cautious, baffled by her. He

shifted to face her. "Why don't you hate me?" It was the question he'd obviously needed to ask since he picked her up.

Grace was as curious as he was. "What did you expect me to do?"

He frowned like it was a trick question.

"No, really… I'm interested to know." Did he honestly not know how deep her feelings ran for him? Maybe if he did, he'd never have made her do it.

He rolled onto his back, closed his eyes and pinched the bridge of his nose. He didn't seem to want to say; it was like no one had ever questioned him like this. "I didn't expect you to want me to pick you up."

Grace leaned up on her elbow. "But you didn't take long so you didn't go home."

His hand dropped and his head turned to her and he frowned. The thought hadn't occurred to him, or had she caught him out? "No, I didn't." His frown deepened.

"So you did expect me to call you."

Again, that frown and vacant look; he was apparently examining himself deeply. This was definitely new territory for him. "I guess I hoped."

So he couldn't go too far away just in case. Her heart quickened, but she had to push on. "How did you expect me to feel when I saw the film, Dylan?"

His eyes narrowed on her; he was beginning to understand what she was doing and deciding whether he was okay with it. He came back with both barrels, fearless and self-destructive. "That I was some kind of dangerous pervert."

It was her turn to be surprised. His expression was hard, like he offered no excuses. He was what he was. She nodded but kept her mouth shut. He watched her closely and waited. She was not going to give him the inevitable row. Instead, she changed tack. "Have *you* watched the films you make?"

He rolled onto his back again. Discomfort. "In the beginning, I watched bits. I couldn't stand seeing myself like that."

Was he seeing himself somewhere in it all, or did he see solely Diablo?

"Did you ever wake up and find yourself doing any of the gross acts in the films?"

Dylan put his arm up to his forehead, then turned his face to her. "What are you trying to find out, Grace?"

"It's obvious, isn't it... I need to know how much of that was you?"

Dylan's face clouded over. "You don't believe me..." He said it as a statement and not a question and went to sit up to get out of bed.

She grabbed his arm. "Stop, Dylan ... I can't turn back the clock and pretend I haven't seen it any more than you can change the fact you did it, but you have to acknowledge that I had to watch you not only have sex with another woman, but do it in the most brutal way. You've got another one coming up in two weeks and I don't know what I'm going to do." Her voice quavered and her eyes brimmed with tears.

Dylan softened immediately, pulling her back down with him and holding her to him, half crushing her with his body and kissing her face in small nips. "Stop, please... I'm sorry," he said, wiping her tears with his thumb. "I'm sorry."

"You're breaking my heart, Dylan." She began to cry harder.

He closed his eyes like he was the worst kind of bastard. "I'll quit, okay? I'm not going to do it any more."

Grace sniffed away her tears and pulled back from him slightly to see the sincerity in his eyes. "What about the one you said you had to do?"

Dylan shook his head. "I'll try to get out of it. I'll speak to Fenton tomorrow... You can come with me, then you'll know for sure."

She grabbed onto him like her life depended on it. "Thank you."

He drew back and kissed her on the lips.

"What about Diablo? Will you be able to handle him?" It was so weird speaking about Dylan's alter ego like he was a completely separate person, but that was how he felt to both of them.

Dylan nodded and looked into her eyes, "I'll work something out." His expression held no doubt.

"Like a normal couple," Grace said, gazing into Dylan's beautiful, unblinking sky-blue eyes.

He nodded and closed the distance between their mouths. They passed the next two hours talking, making plans, kissing, stroking, tasting, feeling and loving. Getting to know each other's bodies slowly and thoroughly.

Grace needed to reaffirm how different her Dylan was from the Diablo in the film, and she was positive Dylan wanted that too. He also needed to prove he could hold back the tempest within him.

Grace wanted him to grow in confidence around her because that was the only way he'd ever let go of his past life, so they had a chance of a future together. So when in the heat of passion, though her blood ran cold, she hid her terror. Because as he hovered his weight above her and looked deeply into her eyes, his gaze appeared deepest mahogany.

Was she being irrational? For the briefest moment, she felt she was in the arms of Diablo, and his smile was as evil as it had been on the screen. It was as though he was taunting her to let her know he was there, just beneath the surface. And he wanted her, and knew he would have her soon.

Grace kept her deepest fear to herself.

CHAPTER 12

The next day, Grace put her unsettling feelings back into her mental closet and walked with Dylan into Fenton's apartment. They'd slept late, but it didn't seem like Fenton had been up that long either, dressed in only a T-shirt and tartan PJ bottoms.

He clapped hands with Dylan and pulled him in for a man-hug; just long enough to show affection, not too long to look sappy. "Angel!" Fenton said, with genuine warmth, which surprised her as she expected animosity from him as the girl taking his best buddy and meal ticket. "You still spending time with this dog?" he said, playfully jabbing Dylan in the stomach. Then he bent forward and kissed her on the cheek. "He ain't put you off yet then?"

Grace felt her cheeks go pink and cast a furtive glance at Dylan, who gave her a small smile. That under-the-surface, latent sexuality punched her in the gut every time.

"I still don't know how you managed to pull her, D?"

Dylan's face broke open into a beautiful smile. "I don't know either, got lucky, I guess."

Fenton motioned with his hand for them to follow. "Come in… Cerise is making coffee."

Dylan put his arm around her back for her to go first and they walked through the hall that had been packed on her previous visit until they reached the kitchen. In fact, the place that had reminded her of a drug baron's luxury crib now looked like a tasteful modern family home.

A beautiful black woman greeted them and Fenton introduced her as his wife, Cerise.

Grace barely hid her surprise. She'd got Fenton so pigeon-holed in her mind, determined that he was this womanising druggie bad boy who had lured her impressionable Dylan into the sex industry. Then she was almost floored when two adorable children, a boy and a girl, bounded in from another room and flung themselves at Dylan's legs and hung from them like Spider Monkeys. Dylan was forced to do this comical walk like Frankenstein while the kids giggled and hung on for the ride. Her heart hitched at how good he was with them and how well they knew him, treating him as part of the family. *Was she wrong about Fenton?*

The kids nagged to show Dylan a new PlayStation game. He looked over at Grace. The question was clear on his face: did she mind? *God, how could she?* She smiled indulgently and he grinned, rough-housing with the boy as he went off with the little girl on his back.

Fenton and Cerise must have caught their exchange and looked at each other with widened eyes.

"I'll have to go referee… Dylan cheats," Fenton said, not convincing anyone that it was a chore. "You two get to know each other," he said, with a wave of his hand, and left the two women alone.

Cerise put a cup of coffee in front of her on the counter, got some biscuits from a cupboard and put them on a plate.

"Sit, honey, then you can tell me your secret," she said, with a friendly smile.

Grace climbed onto a high stool at the breakfast island. "What secret?"

"With D. How'd you reel him in, girl? That man is off the market."

Grace's eyes went wide in spite of herself and she sipped her coffee, not sure how to answer that. "We haven't known each other that long ... well, we met at school."

Cerise nodded sagely. "That figures... 'cause you're so not like the normal girls he mixes with."

Whatever mixes with meant... girls he slept with socially, or worked with? Her face must have betrayed her because Cerise quickly explained, "D doesn't do girlfriends, honey."

"Oh, really?" Grace couldn't resist answering.

"No, he usually whisks 'em into his bed and merrily on their way."

The stab of pain Grace felt in the centre of her chest was irrational. She already knew what Cerise was saying, but hearing it spelt out still hurt like a bitch.

"You know, when Fenton told me D had met someone, I couldn't believe it, but I was pleased... You know... He deserves something good."

Grace smiled and accepted the compliment. Then picked up a biscuit and began to nibble on it to hide her embarrassment. The sugar was welcome as she hadn't been eating much lately with all that had been happening.

Then, just as she took a big mouthful, Cerise dropped the clanger: "So, have you met Diablo yet?"

Grace nearly choked. It was so bad that Cerise had to come and pat her on the back and pass her a glass of water. You didn't expect Dylan's second personality to be brought into conversation as if he was a long-lost brother or something.

She shook her head nervously. She wasn't even sure this conversation was appropriate with Dylan only in the next room.

Cerise faced her sardonically. "Look, honey, I know you don't know me, but you need to be careful, okay? Fenton loves that man like a baby brother, but when Diablo comes out to play, he won't let him anywhere near me or the kids."

Grace's pulse was already racing. "Fenton handles him okay, though, doesn't he?"

Cerise conceded a small bob of the head. "Yeah… but even he sometimes has to full-on fight with him to keep him in line." She sat back and let her words sink in.

"Do you know what I used to do for a living before I had kids?"

Grace's mind raced. *Dancer, actress, model, porn star?* "No… I didn't even know Fenton was married until today." Not a lie.

"I was a psychiatric nurse for seven years."

Grace's heart thudded. That was a shock. She felt immediately guilty at the conclusions she'd jumped to, but curiosity tortured her for any info about Dylan and she waited for her to go on.

"They treat him for schizophrenia," she said.

Slightly disappointed, Grace just nodded. "He told me."

"I'm not convinced that's what it is."

"What else could it be?"

Cerise sat back. "Look, girl. People suffering from schizophrenia hear voices and suffer paranoia; they don't have a whole other personality like Jekyll and Hyde. And never once, in all my time working with people with mental illness, did a person's eyes change colour with their mood swings." And she nodded once to emphasise what she'd said.

The words hit Grace in the solar plexus. Cerise had only spoken the words that the tiny voice in the back of her mind had already said, and of course, she'd skirted around it or ignored it, afraid of the alternative. "Why are you telling me this?"

"Because Fenton is worried for you… you're gonna come up against Diablo sometime, if you haven't already." The spectre of Diablo's face last night, so close to her own, made her shudder. The fact that Cerise looked genuinely frightened for her made it worse.

The chaos of kids' voices broke the atmosphere and both women turned their heads as the men came back into the kitchen. The kids were moaning for another game.

"Go and set it up then," Fenton ordered, and the kids ran back into the other room, leaving the four adults together.

Dylan came straight over to where Grace sat. He rested his hands on her shoulders and bent and kissed her cheek while he rubbed his thumb across the nape of her neck.

Such a simple touch, but it ran molten straight through her body, lighting up her butterflies and pooling between her thighs.

Fenton and Cerise swapped looks.

Grace felt Dylan stiffen and he pinched her neck and let go. "What's up with you two?"

They swapped looks again and Fenton spoke up. "We're worried about you, D… well both of you."

"You don't need to be. We're working it out … We're fine."

It was what he left out in that explanation that revealed how much of Dylan's life the two of them knew. She glanced up behind her at Dylan's face and he looked annoyed.

"Does she know you've got a film coming up?"

Dylan shifted his feet.

Fenton sagged, "Ah, no… you're not gonna quit on me?" he said, with a mixture of disappointment and anger.

Dylan let out a deep sigh and looked down with his hands

on his hips, then into Grace's eyes as if drawing strength. She gave him a small, nervous smile.

"I can't do it any more," Dylan said quietly, and smiled back at her as if he'd accomplished something special.

But their moment was short-lived. Fenton pointed an angry finger at Dylan. "I told you, you can't get out of this one. They'll tie you up in court for years and take you to the cleaners."

Dylan shook his head, not willing to be moved. "Can't do it."

Grace picked up his hand and held it with both of hers to show her solidarity.

"You're a fool if you think Diablo can be controlled any other way," Fenton continued.

Hearing Diablo referred to as a separate person was seriously weird, but what caught Grace's eye more was Cerise, who was beginning to look really scared. "Listen to him, D. None of us will be safe then."

Grace's heart was beating a military tattoo. Dylan pinched the bridge of his nose and walked away to think in the larger space of the room.

"Isn't there anything else he can do?" Grace said, grasping at straws.

"Well, he's got to do this film, that's a given," Fenton said, ignoring Dylan's exasperated look and speaking directly to her. "The thing is, Angel…"

God, she hated him calling her that!

"Is that D… Diablo needs extremes."

Dylan looked up at the ceiling as if it was excruciating for him to listen.

"Come on, D… let's be truthful here," Fenton said, with his arms out wide. "The girl deserves the truth."

Dylan blew out a breath and shrugged for him to continue.

"Diablo thrives on extreme sex and extreme violence. Shades in between? Not interested."

Grace frowned. "Any fool can work out that he's just the complete opposite of Dylan, it's obvious," she reasoned, standing up.

Fenton's eyes widened and he nodded over to Dylan in appreciation of her balls, but faced her again. "Is he, though?"

Grace immediately snapped her head around to Dylan. She frowned. What was Fenton driving at?

Dylan's face was deadpan, but he was not taking his eyes from Fenton's.

"What does he mean by that, Dylan?" she asked, watching him closely.

Dylan walked back over to her, but she continued to watch his face as his hand rested on her shoulder. He still hadn't broken eye contact with Fenton. There was obviously so much the pair weren't saying. "He means that it's not always that black and white."

Grace's eyes went from one man to the other; neither broke their stares or elaborated further. You could cut the atmosphere with a knife. Were they going to have one of those fights Cerise spoke of?

"Nothing else you wanna say?" Dylan said, but there was no humour in his voice.

Shit, Grace was beginning to feel a little scared. There were children in the house, for god's sake. "If he does this one, can he get out then?" she found herself saying.

All three pairs of eyes went to Grace as if she'd shouted some profanity. She was looking between them all for some help, then her gaze rested on Dylan, whose look went from amazed to pained and then disappointed. Whether it was at himself or at her, she wasn't sure. "But I thought..." he started.

"It's just one last time," she said, the sorrow dripping from her.

Dylan turned his attention back to Fenton and pointed at him. "The last time."

Fenton nodded once, realising it was the best deal he was going to get.

"Then we can all get our heads together and work out a plan for after that," Cerise said, with a hint of hysteria in her voice, obviously as keen as Grace was to diffuse an awkward and possibly dangerous situation.

Grace nodded manically and smiled at her new ally.

Dylan pulled her to him and kissed the top of her head. She threaded her arms around his waist. "I love you," he whispered into her hair.

She squeezed him hard and relief washed over her. She knew he would have fought Fenton not to have done the film and possibly lost his best friend in the process. Mad though she seemed, this was damage limitation and she was sure now she would need Fenton and Cerise's help in the future, if she could just get through the coming weeks.

After they left Fenton's, Dylan grabbed some things from his place and they went back to Grace's. Dylan never went home. Not that she minded; she was in seventh heaven. She booked a couple of weeks off work and gave herself over totally to Dylan.

They cooked together, rode the horses, watched soppy movies and cuddled on the sofa. Dylan even said he could get used to her tiny white frilly cottage. Grace felt her heart would burst, she was so in love.

But the times she treasured most of all were just after they'd made love for hours and would talk softly about a future together, relaxed and blissfully at home in each other's arms. It was all her dreams come true.

Initially, she'd been terrified of another appearance of Diablo, but it was as if their happiness kept him at bay. Whether Dylan had any control over that, she wasn't sure. He was still an enigma to her. All she knew was that they had a lifetime to work it out.

The day Dylan had to go crept up on them. He'd explained that he needed a few days before he was due to fly to Germany to come off his meds.

They'd made love slowly and passionately and Grace gazed up into his ice-blue eyes while their heart rates returned to normal. He kissed her slowly, stroking her tongue with his. Her hands ran gently over his muscled back and she let out a contented sigh.

"I love you," he said, resting his forehead on hers.

"Come back as quick as you can."

"I will." He rolled off onto his back. "What will you do while I'm away?" he said, not looking at her.

She hadn't planned anything, actually. "I'm going to carry on as normal, just work and stables. Maybe I'll pop over and see Janey one night if I get lonely."

Dylan turned onto his side and searched her face for a few moments.

"What's the matter… what are you worried about?" she asked, touching his lips with her finger.

Grace could tell he was troubled and could guess he didn't trust himself off his meds. "Don't worry. I'll be fine," she said, smiling.

He leant over and kissed her lips and seemed to snap himself out of it. "I've got something for you."

"What?" she said, surprised.

Dylan sat up and leaned over, grabbed his holdall and

pulled it nearer to the bed. When he sat back up, he was holding three small tatty books.

"What are they?" Grace said, sitting up with him. He was running a hand over them as if they were precious.

"You've given me so much, Grace. I wanted to give you something that meant a lot to me. Something of me that I've never shown anyone."

Grace looked from the books to Dylan's face, then back again. She kissed his cheek. "I don't need presents, Dylan."

He nodded, still looking down at the books. "I know." His eyes tracked to hers and looked soulful. "There's a lot you want to ask, and have a right to know, Grace. Stuff I can't talk about." He handed them over to her slowly.

She cautiously took them, deciding it was something he needed to do.

He held onto her hand as she took them from his. "Don't look at them now... while I'm gone, okay?" He looked intently into her eyes as he spoke, so she knew he meant it.

How could she deny him anything? And she nodded with a small smile. "Thank you, Dylan." She recognised he was in virgin territory even though he'd been with hundreds of women. He was laying himself wide open. She clutched them to her heart.

It took only twenty minutes for Dylan to shower, dress and put his few things back in his bag. Grace walked him to her front door and he turned to face her.

"I'll miss you," she said, looking up at him.

His face was so full of regret that it brought a lump to her throat. What he didn't say was blindingly obvious: that he probably wouldn't miss her because Diablo would be at the front of his consciousness.

"I understand," she said, smiling weakly.

Dylan hugged her tight and pulled away as if his emotions

were riding him as hard as hers. He didn't look her way again. She knew he couldn't.

CHAPTER 13

G race didn't even bother to dress the rest of the day. She just curled into a miserable ball on the sofa, blowing her nose and crying over a silly film, which reminded her of Dylan because she'd watched it last with him.

Evening was approaching and the sunlight was going when she finally made herself a hot drink and sat with her feet up to read the books Dylan had left her.

She turned the hardback cover and ran a hand over the first yellowed page...

DYLAN O'SHEA AGED *twelve and a half.*

SHE FLICKED QUICKLY through the pages. *My God.* It was his childhood diary. She wasn't sure why he wanted to share it with her, but it called to every part of her, ravenous for any detail about him. Drawn in immediately, he was explaining in his own words what happened the night his friend died.

Dylan had more or less already told her what happened, but this was a frightening insight into his deepest innermost thoughts and feelings at the time ...

THE MORE *I talk about him, the more mad they think I am. I've got to keep quiet.*

The doctor knows I'm holding a lot back about what happened, so he told me to write this. Said it was just for me and no one had to look at it if I didn't want them to. He said it would help. I'm not sure about that.

DYLAN HADN'T WRITTEN the diary every day; some days there were just doodles, and the smallest entries like what he'd had for tea. Grace flicked through to the next substantial entry of writing.

DYLAN AGED THIRTEEN.

I'm starting to forget what happened. He's taking over so bad. It feels like my memories are getting mixed up with his.

I don't want that.

I hate that. I don't want to become him.

So I'm going to fight to stay apart,

I'm going to write again what happened that night before it goes. He wants me to forget about it. He doesn't want anyone to know where he came from.

GRACE BLEW her nose and dabbed her eyes with her tissue. He seemed to have to write the events of that night over and over every few weeks, as if to formalise it in his mind, as if he was fighting not to forget. It was heartbreaking.

She stopped reading and ran her fingers across a picture he'd drawn, coloured in vivid reds and blues. It showed two men – one had tattoos. There was smoke, fire and lightning everywhere.

She turned the page and read on until she came to a clear description of what he believed he saw. It was the first time he'd given the details of the exact moment when his personality must have split ...

WE WERE in this field not far from the centre, having a right laugh, when we saw flashes of lightning. It looked really cool. We couldn't believe how much there was and no thunder. It was weird; so quiet – just a buzz like electricity.

In front of us, the lightning kept landing on one spot on the ground. It was smoking.

The light was so bright we couldn't stop watching. That was when we saw him, just an outline of white light – the shape of a man.

I looked at Pete to make sure he was seeing what I was seeing, and he looked back at me. We got really scared. We couldn't move. I wanted to run or shout, but we just froze.

The shape was moving closer, slowly, like it was walking. Another lightning strike and the lightning man came towards us.

I looked at my chest. It was burning. The lightning coming from the man was like an arm with fingers and everything. It felt like a spear went right through my heart.

I looked up at the sky. Lightning was all around us like a spider's web of light. It was beautiful.

Then I looked at Pete. He was falling to the ground.

I was falling, but I wasn't alone.

. . .

*F*ROM THAT DAY, *he was with me, inside my skin, looking out from my eyes.*

Then I was awake all the time. He pulled and pushed me around.

They told me Pete was dead, hit by a cable from the pylon. But I know it was the space man. He could be a ghost or a ~~angel~~ Devil, but I think he's a spaceman who came through a time warp and landed here by accident. He stole my body, but I'm still inside.

I can't tell anybody anything; otherwise, they'll think I'm mad, so all I say is I can't remember.

Now it's all mixed up and we are both called Dylan.

I told him he had to pick his own name and he said I had to.

I call him D. He doesn't like it. Tough shit.

*D'*S THOUGHTS *are all bad. He doesn't like people very much. He wants to hurt them all the time. They give us medicine to calm us down and not worry. But I worry about my mum and my brothers because D doesn't even like them when they love us no matter what. He wants to hurt anyone I like, so we fight and he makes me go to sleep.*

*T*ODAY *I* WOKE *up with my hands around my mum's throat. She was trying to scream and nothing came out. Her eyes were wide and bloodshot and her face was red.*

I cried when I saw her like that and let go fast.

She hugged me and told me I couldn't help it. I cried more because I was so relieved she didn't hate me.

I'm scared it will happen again, so I told her about D, about what he thinks and what he does.

She took me back up the doctor's and he gave me different pills. Mum didn't tell him about D, though. She said they'd take me away if she did.

.   .   .

OUTSIDE, it was now quite dark. Grace drew the curtains and took the diaries up to bed with her. She couldn't put them down.

After snuggling down in the bed, she read on...

D FIGHTS *with all my brothers, especially the older ones. He says it proves he's rock solid and I'm a poof.*

Today he knocked my mum across the kitchen, so they're sending us away.

I'M at my Uncle Sean's now, in Ireland. It's beautiful here, but I miss my family. D doesn't give two shits.

There is loads of countryside and horses. They make me feel calm. D's bored though and wants to shag my cousin. Fucking hell, what if he does? I'll get caught for it and then I'll be put in prison or, worse, the looney bin.

I'm going to talk to Sean.

DYLAN'S FEAR transcended the page. It was a palpable thing and Grace felt it deeply. She found herself hating D as much as Dylan did. *Ridiculous.* She shook her head. You could go mad trying to get your head around all this.

TONIGHT I TOLD SEAN EVERYTHING *– well, except the spaceman part. He's made me an appointment with a proper doctor.*

PARANOID SCHIZOPHRENIA, they're calling it. Fucking shit, bollocks, cunt. That's what I'm calling it... not it... him.

.   .   .

G{\small RACE} {\small TURNED} page after empty page. *What happened... why did he stop writing?* He'd stopped writing for weeks. Then he resumed...

T{\small HERE} {\small IS} a big gap in my diary coz I couldn't think. I used to sleep all the time at my uncle's. The good thing was that D slept as well, so he couldn't do anything bad.

Now they are sending us back home. I should be excited, and I want to see my family, I really do, but I don't feel anything any more.

M{\small UM} {\small HAS} {\small SENT} me to a new school away from all the memories of Pete.

I wander around not knowing anyone; I'm not that bothered.

Kids push me around and I look at them, but I can't remember what to say, so I just look at them. They get bored and leave me alone.

I've got used to sitting in all the lessons on my own. I don't write anything. The teachers seem to know I'm a freak and ignore me.

All the desks in the class are arranged in twos. Today, a girl sat next to me. Her name is Grace Fellows. She's really cool and pretty.

Everyone seems to know her and she talks to everyone. She even asked me if I was all right today. I just nodded.

I don't have all the same lessons as her, but she sits with me in Science and Maths. They all say I'm Grace's mate now.

G{\small RACE} {\small READ} page after page and every entry mentioned her: what she wore, how she'd done her hair, and what she'd said to him – even if it was the smallest, most throwaway comment. He'd recorded it all. It began to dawn on her, what had seemed like a trivial acquaintance to her, she could barely remember, had meant a hell of a lot more to him. So much so, it was overwhelming. That was why he wanted her to read them, so she knew how much she really meant to him, and had always meant to him. She was stunned.

Last day of school today. Everyone is going to college or work now.

I know I've failed all my exams. I couldn't think what to write, so I just wrote my name over and over.

I want to say something to Grace before she goes, like thank you, but I haven't got the guts.

I'll probably never see her again to tell her.

I hope I meet her again one day.

By those final words, tears were streaming down her face. It was the last thing he wrote in the diaries apart from some weird-looking diagrams that could have been maps or something. They could have just been doodles except he'd done them with a ruler. She dismissed them from her mind as unimportant.

The thought that haunted her was that she had made such a difference to his life back then and had no idea at the time. He'd just always been the kid in the background to her. If only she had known.

She curled into a ball in the bed and bawled loudly. Her heart ached to hold him in her arms now and apologise and tell him she was so sorry she didn't know. To think of everything he had been through and totally on his own.

Then she sniffed and stopped crying. He was as alone as she was – two lonely souls together. It made sense now that they had found each other.

Grace passed a fitful night sleeping lightly, dreaming vividly, and always about Dylan.

SHE WENT BACK to work and the next couple of days passed agonisingly slowly. How on earth would she last a whole month without him?

Then, around the fourth day after he had gone, an idea pinged into her head: what if she visited him? He had told her that he holed himself up for a few days before filming started to come off his meds.

Briefly, the voice of reason broke through to warn her that he would be unmedicated and had asked her specifically to steer clear of him. Blah blah, but it was still him. Surely he would still be able to see it was her, and would not be too angry.

The image of Diablo couldn't be ignored and it made her shudder. But it was just Dylan's other side, she reminded herself, and to stop being such a bigot. Thousands of people suffer from mental illness in this day and age and manage to function in healthy, happy lives.

That settled it. Grace decided to visit Dylan after she finished work that day.

CHAPTER 14

Instead of taking her usual train home, Grace took the train from Victoria to Brixton. She could think of nothing else since she'd made up her mind after reading Dylan's diaries. She'd had no sleep, little food and no peace of mind. She simply had to meet Diablo and decide for herself what she thought of him. He *was* Dylan, for god's sake.

Then why did she feel so guilty in the pit of her stomach? There was no justification for it; she just did. It was probably because Dylan thought Diablo was a different person that it seemed like she was being disloyal.

Grace stood for quite a few moments outside Dylan's street door. Her heart hammered and she tried to take some deep breaths to calm herself. Passers-by were looking at her as though she was weird. It was beginning to get dark, so she had to do something, either go in or go home before it got any darker.

Not sure if she could get in at all, she tried the handle and the door creaked wide. Was he usually so slack with his security when he was off his meds? This was a rough area, after all. An image of him languishing in a drug-like stupor, letting everything go to rack and ruin, sprang to her mind.

The disturbing thought gave her the courage to get in the lift. It clanked upwards through the floors till it reached the top. Her heart beat harder the higher she got. She paused again at his apartment door with her heart in her mouth.

Perhaps he wasn't even in? She hitched a breath. Perhaps he wasn't alone?

Anger blasted through her when she thought of perfect Serena. That thought alone justified her visit, she told herself. The "schizophrenic" excuse so wouldn't wash here. *It wasn't me shagging her, honest, it was the schizo other half of me. Pur-lease.* But wasn't that exactly what he said about the films? *Bloody hell.*

Grace was shallow breathing as she grasped the door handle and pulled it downwards. Click.

Shit, it was on the latch.

She pushed it slowly open. Her heart thudded in her ears. One foot touched the carpet. Then another step until she peeked her head around the door.

There was silence – no sound at all.

Her eyes started a sweep from one side of the apartment to the other. Just as she was about to assume he'd gone out, the jangle of chains brought her eyes straight to him, hanging in the crucifix position from the apparatus she'd seen the first time she came. He remained suspended from the ceiling as if he had all the time in the world.

Every ridged muscle ripped and corded before her eyes on his naked back. His body looked like the honed piece of machinery it undoubtedly was. The large wingspan of the black inked eagle spread and rippled across the tops of his shoulders. His back was straight and his head was bent slightly forward. She would have thought he was dozing or meditating if she weren't aware of the sheer physical strength needed for such an exercise, not forgetting the pain the chain wound around his hands must cause. *Rock solid*, she remembered.

"Come in, Angel," he said, dropping down to land on his feet like a cat.

She shuddered at him calling her the same pet name as Fenton. *What were they saying?*

The chains jangled as he let them go, his hands pitted and bruised from the links. "What's the matter, Angel, did you imagine the chains biting into you?" He was facing the other way, but his voice sounded really quiet and unlike his own.

She was stunned into silence.

Thankfully, he didn't seem to expect an answer. "I've been expecting you." His head rose slowly as if he were gathering himself, still breathing through his exercise.

Her heart hammered and she had to remind herself to breathe at all.

"Close the door." He turned his head to the side as he spoke, but he still hadn't looked at her.

The door clicked shut.

He looked much leaner; his hair darker and swept back like it had been in the film.

"Who am I talking to?" she asked cautiously, but she already knew. She could tell by the different way he carried himself.

"You shouldn't have come here, Angel," he said, with sadness like the inevitability was unavoidable. Perhaps it was.

"Who are you?" she repeated, needing it spelt out, but he ignored her.

"It's not safe for you here," he said in his gentle voice and turned his head slowly to look at her over his shoulder.

The familiar yet strange face chilled her to the bone. With his evil smile and his amused brown eyes half closed. "You know who I am, Angel. That's why you've come."

Grace recoiled in anger, but as she felt the emotion, his smile broadened. He knew he was right.

He chuckled and faced front again and sank to the floor in a cross-legged position. "Ask your questions."

The fact that he knew her so well was unnerving. She had to keep reminding herself that it *was* Dylan. Under all this, he was a man who had got to know her intimately in the short time they'd been together; of course, he would know her reactions. And yet it still felt as though he was someone else. It was chilling.

Grace inched closer. He seemed calm enough. She stopped a few feet away. "Is Dylan there with you, awake?" It felt really important that *her* Dylan didn't see this visit as a betrayal.

He turned his head to the side again with his mocking smile. "It bothers you if he saw you here?" Then he cocked his head on an angle as if he were considering the notion for a long moment. "Are you planning on being bad then, Angel?" his quiet voice purred.

Grace frowned, *God no... yes... ah fuck.* She'd come to see Dylan.

Still, he sat unmoving, danger coming off him in waves, terrifying her, yet his blatant sexuality and complete composure intrigued her.

Her heart stopped when his legs unfurled and he stood effortlessly and fluidly as a predator, turned to face her. He smiled and looked her straight in the eyes, insolently, confidently, shouting 'fuck you' from every pore. She was trembling.

Diablo was naked from the waist up as he'd been in the film, wearing nothing but baggy black sweatpants. His feet were bare. The weight he'd lost was drastic; in just a couple of days, his cheeks were hollow, giving his face a more sinister, haunted look. His eyes were dark-brown and appeared shadowed and deeper set. His hair looked oiled and shone darker in the light. The corners of his lips twitched with amusement. "What do you want, Grace?"

The use of her real name threw her. She frowned and stuttered, "I wanted to… meet you."

His smile broadened as if it was as he expected.

"… To see if you were different," she continued. The words sounded ridiculous as she stood in front of her own boyfriend, that she'd been in bed with no more than four days ago. But everything about him now seemed so different: the way he stood, his facial expressions, voice.

"Dylan is asleep," he said, answering the question she'd asked and given up on. His smile evaporated as if he were looking inward and not at her at all.

She nodded slightly, a little relieved.

He took a slow step closer, and then another. Her eyes widened in fear and he paused. "You want me to touch you, Angel." Said as a statement of fact.

She was shaking her head. He continued past her. "That is why you are here," he breathed, next to her cheek. Tempting. Enthralling.

Her heart thumped, her eyes closed and she didn't move a muscle. What a stupid idea to come here and face Hannibal Lecter with muscles because she sure as hell felt like dinner. And to prove her point, he licked the side of her face in one long drag. She gulped, finding her breath was stabbing the air in shallow pants. *She mustn't faint, she mustn't faint.*

"You want to know if fucking me is better than fucking Dylan," he purred next to her ear and kissed down her neck.

Grace swallowed and shook her head. She had to remind herself it *was* Dylan over and over.

"You want to be bad, Grace."

She was shaking her head emphatically. "No… no. You're

wrong." But her heart was racing and every nerve ending was awake and pulsing southward to the juncture of her thighs.

His hand immediately cupped her there as if he read her body instinctively. She groaned, unable to help herself.

"You want to give yourself to Diablo," he said, massaging her through her jeans.

His voice was lulling – hypnotising. *My god!* What was she doing? She found herself wanting him. He was Dylan. His body was Dylan's; she knew it so well. But she had to snap herself out of it. Dylan wouldn't see it that way. *For fuck's sake*, he didn't even smell the same.

Like a bolt from the blue, and for the first time, she entertained the thought that Dylan could possibly be right – as mad as it sounded. What if Diablo was a separate person entirely?

Seeming to sense her wavering, he increased the strength in his fingers, pushing the seam of her jeans into her most sensitive place. She gasped. Coaxing and whispering, he licked across her lips. "Give yourself to me, Grace... you'll never know for sure if you don't."

"I thought part of your character was to take," she said, panting.

He laughed, a different sound to Dylan's. "Not with you, Grace. You must come to me voluntarily."

Her brow furrowed. She wanted to ask why, but he was nipping at her lips with his and slowly pulling the shirt from her waistband. *Oh my god.* Her pulse was through the roof.

"He won't help you against me."

Fuck, had she spoken out loud? Or was she such an open book?

His hand had slipped under her shirt and was next to her skin now, his thumb passing delicately across the lace covering her nipple. She whimpered pathetically. "Give yourself to me, Grace, and I will make you feel so good."

His lips were close to hers and she could feel his hot breath. His hips were moving against hers and she could feel the hard bulge of his erection barely contained by his sweatpants – the familiar hardness. *My god, she was so totally confused.*

The top of her jeans suddenly felt loose and she hadn't even felt him undo the button. "You hurt people," she groaned next to his mouth, which he opened and covered hers.

"Only in a good way," he whispered, and pushed his tongue deeply into her mouth. "I promise." Plundering her deliciously, sinfully, taking her in a single kiss that eroded everything.

Grace's knees gave way at the strength of it, no longer possessing any coordination; he swept her up and carried her helplessly to the bed.

"Tell me what you want, Grace?" he said, between blistering kisses that ignited every nerve.

"I want… I want."

He placed her down gently on the bed and covered her with his weight. "Do you want Diablo inside you in every way?"

Her shirt was ripped open in one tug, buttons pinging in every direction, followed swiftly by the bra she had picked especially. The man had her naked in under five seconds. She only had time to gasp and his mouth captured that. He took everything.

His kiss built in force and ferocity, pushing her hard so she thought she would orgasm from a kiss alone. He bit her wherever his mouth travelled and sucked the blood through her skin, leaving marks.

Grace cried out when he treated her breasts in the same rough way. She was so close to the edge.

He stopped what he was doing suddenly. "No!" he ordered. "You come only when I say."

She was left panting and almost crying with need.

"Tell me what you want?"

He was all over her, everywhere, punishing her body relentlessly. Bruising her skin with his hands and mouth wherever they made contact. She no longer recognised the noises coming from her own mouth. "I want you."

"You want me to, what?" he said, flipping her and biting her behind hard, leaving deep teeth marks.

"Ah, fuck."

"Yes… say it." His mouth was moving down the back of her thigh.

"Fuck… I want you to fuck me."

No further words were needed. His arm reached beneath her and he hoisted her behind, high, and he plunged into her on a single thrust and pounded into her.

Grace was rammed forward on every thrust so that everything she tried to get a hold of was knocked to the floor. The clock, the table lamp, all went over until she was forced to hold the edge of the small table next to the bed. She shouted with every thrust.

He responded by pulling her head back by the hair painfully and pounding into her unmercifully. Then he left her suddenly and she was yanked back by the feet and onto her back and he was on top of her again. Legs pushed up to her ears, he plunged into her again, except this time, he had leverage and it was deep, so deep.

"Open!" he ordered. As her eyes had been tightly closed. "Look into my eyes." He was thrusting in hard jabs, as if spearing her through. His eyes were half closed, dark and cruel, dancing with enjoyment and drunk on the power he had over her. Relishing the position to batter her small body.

Her breath hitched and her heart stopped when he reached between them and touched her engorged clitoris and worked it in circles. The look in his eyes told her, like nothing else, that he knew her body well and he'd learnt it from Dylan. He made her feel like she'd sold her soul to the Devil.

When he watched her begin to tumble over the edge, he laughed and laughed. "Yes, Angel, come for Diablo... come for me."

Everything exploded, coiled, clenched and pulsated in the biggest climax of her life. The more she tried to hold back, the stronger and higher it built, making it mind-blowing when she finally had to let go and accept it.

When she finally came to her senses, what she had let happen sickened her, because despite trying to convince herself otherwise, she felt so guilty, as if Dylan was right; that Diablo was a separate being living inside his body. That was the reason Diablo knew everything about her, because he was with Dylan continually. Like he had tricked her and lured her to be unfaithful to Dylan because he knew it was the worst thing she could possibly do. As ridiculous as it all seemed even to her, it was how she felt.

Smug didn't come close to the look of self-satisfaction on his face. He was still moving on top of her and not finished by a long shot.

"I need to go," she said, flatly.

His face hardened. "We've a way to go yet, Grace. I've waited a long time to deflower my Angel."

His words sent a chill right down to the bone, not helped by her head now being completely back on line and not clouded by misguided lust. Dylan's words, *They call me the Devil*, echoed in her head. The reality of the situation she found herself in now started to hit her hard. Because now he felt he had the right to do whatever he wanted with her; she only hoped she could survive the night, and Dylan remained oblivious to her betrayal.

The thought terrified her.

Diablo seemed to read her mind and moved his lips down level with her ear. "You wanted me to fuck you, Grace. Remember?" he whispered. "No going back."

Her heart sank so low she swore it bounced off the floor. His eyes, dancing with mischief, looked into hers, frozen in fear. "Does he know?" came out barely a rasp.

He seemed to grow harder with the thought, as if having that over her was another source of power and he renewed his thrusts, with which he spoke in time. "It'll… be… our… secret, Grace."

She recoiled into her misery.

Diablo laughed and adjusted himself for deeper penetration.

Tears began to stream from the corners of her eyes because she knew without doubt that if Dylan knew what she had done, whether he and Diablo were the same person or not, it would destroy him. That, or he would kill her himself. It was the sole reason it had been so important to Diablo that she go to him willingly, so her betrayal was utter and complete.

CHAPTER 15

wo hours later, Diablo was finally sated. He pushed off her and told her to go. His appetite had been insatiable. He said he was leaving and needed to shower. So, in effect, she'd been used, abused and booted out.

Grace was exhausted. He'd used her hard. Made her do things no polite girl should do, and her body was battered, bruised and in shock. She couldn't stop shaking.

Maybe it was partly because she had eaten so little? But deep down, she knew it was from the shock of what he'd put her through. She didn't even have the energy to go home, afraid of collapsing in the street and then having to explain herself to ambulance men or, worse still, the police.

Grace opted to go to Cerise and Fenton's place. Luckily, she remembered roughly where it was and somehow managed to get a taxi to take her there. Her legs would never have made the ten-minute walk.

She didn't have a clue what the time was when she buzzed the entry phone to their apartment. They might still be asleep. She sagged in relief when Cerise told her to come up.

Somehow, Grace made it to the front door, but when it was opened, she stumbled and almost fell over.

"Oh my god … Fenton, come quick."

"What, Cerise?" Fenton's voice came from somewhere in the flat.

"It's Grace. She's hurt."

Grace wasn't sure if she passed out for a moment, but the next thing she knew, she was being lifted from the floor. The pain from her bruises made her wince.

Fenton placed her gently down on the edge of the sofa in the living room. Luckily, there were no children around, so she guessed they were either still asleep or already gone to school. She'd lost all sense of time. He looked intently into her eyes. "What happened, Grace? We need to get you to a hospital."

"No," she groaned in misery and began to cry.

Fenton looked uncomfortably across to Cerise, then back again. "What happened, Angel?" he said, more gently.

"Don't call me that," she shrieked. Then was calmed with soothing hands and apologies. All she could do was look hopelessly into his eyes, as she could tell he already knew. "I went to see Dylan." Tears rolled down her cheeks and Fenton sagged, slumped down onto his haunches and closed his eyes. It was as though he'd heard someone had died.

"Why the fuck did you do that?" Fenton said, with real anger in his voice.

"Fenton?" Cerise scolded. "You can see she's in a state."

He stood up sharply and pushed away from her in disgust. "Well… for fuck's sake… it wasn't like she wasn't warned."

A sob escaped her. "Don't tell him… don't tell Dylan," she pleaded.

Cerise squeezed her hand. "Don't worry, babe. We won't

say a word. Will we, Fenton?" she said, casting a warning eye at Fenton.

"Fuck!" he shouted. He bent down and looked Grace in the eye, just a few inches away. "Do you have any clue what you've fucking done?" He kissed his teeth and pushed away from her again.

Grace was now openly sobbing.

Fenton looked back at her and pointed. "We won't say a word, but you better hope Diablo really likes you, because if he don't, he'll take great pleasure in opening Dylan's eyes... literally."

FENTON KEPT Dylan in Germany as long as he could to give Grace's bruises the necessary time to disappear, but the day came when Cerise got the call that they were on their way home.

It had been an agonisingly slow month. Well, three weeks, five days, and six hours to be exact.

Grace had phoned in sick for work and moped around with Cerise at her apartment. She hadn't gone home. She somehow felt closer to Dylan there. The bruises had subsided, but the worry of what Dylan had been doing at any given moment (and who with), and whether he knew what she'd done, was eating her alive.

As the receiver hit the cradle, Grace pounced. "Is he coming back?"

Cerise nodded, but her expression was guarded, not giving anything away.

"Tell me what's going on, Cerise?" Grace pleaded.

"Nothing... It's just the same as always. They'll be back tonight." Cerise looked her dead in the eye. "You mustn't see him yet, Grace."

"Why... he's back on his meds, isn't he?"

Cerise conceded with a nod. Yes, but Fenton said he's only been on them for the last forty-eight hours. You need to give it another couple of days before it's safe."

"Did he say anything, Cerise... Was Dylan okay... Does he remember anything?" Grace's heart hammered in her chest and her stomach churned when she contemplated the consequences of Dylan knowing. Her life would be over whether he killed her himself or not.

"No, nothing. I very much doubt it, Grace. I'm sure we'd know about it if he did." Cerise finished sardonically.

That Cerise alluded to her stupidity was water off a duck's back. It was no more than Grace had thought herself. If only she could turn back the clock.

The rest of the evening passed slowly. Grace constantly glanced at the clock and bit her nails down to the quick. Cerise seemed equally on edge.

The phone rang and they both looked at it and held their breath.

Cerise swallowed and picked it up.

Grace watched eagerly, knowing it was Fenton. "Are they home?" Grace interrupted. As soon as Fenton stepped foot back in the apartment, she would at least know if Dylan knew anything.

Cerise clicked off the phone. "They're back," she said flatly.

Grace stared at her for a minute. *Where the bloody hell was Fenton then, when she needed to speak to him?* "Can't I even speak to Dylan on the phone... surely that won't hurt?"

"No, it's not that," Cerise said, looking very uncomfortable.

"For God's sake, Cerise. Don't keep me in the dark?"

Cerise put her hands up in surrender. "Fenton's not sure when he'll be home because they've gone out."

Grace blinked. "What do you mean, gone out?… Gone out where?"

Cerise sighed and appeared to deflate slightly. "To a club."

Grace frowned, trying to compute what was being said to her. "Let me get this straight. I am at my wits' end with worry, and Fenton and Dylan are out on a boys' night?"

She had to sit down for a second, running thought after thought through her mind at rapid speed. "I thought he was dangerous?" she said, throwing her hands up.

Cerise's face was sympathetic. "He functions okay, and he's got Fenton with him, but you have to understand, Grace, this is what Fenton meant about there not being black and white where D's concerned."

"So it was Dylan's idea?"

Cerise just nodded. "I think so… Fenton won't let him near us tonight."

Grace seethed. After everything she'd been through and Dylan showed no sign of needing to get back to her. *Shit, Serena. He was seeing her first.*

She jumped up, frightening the life out of Cerise. "You'd better take me to wherever they are, Cerise, otherwise, I swear to god, I'll trawl every nightspot within a five-mile radius until I find them."

Cerise stared at her for a moment and quickly came to a decision. "Let me just get someone to sit with the kids."

It was around midnight when Cerise led the way into the small private club not too far from where they lived. To think he was this close and hadn't tried to see her. Her blood boiled anew. But wasn't this Dylan's lifestyle, party after party, fast bikes and faster women?

Flimflams was all glass, chrome and soft green lighting. Not majorly busy as it was only a Thursday night. Grace scanned the room. He wasn't hard to find; taller than everyone else. The party of three stood at the edge of the room in a cosy little huddle – Fenton, Dylan and the bitch.

With her heart beating like a freight train, she absorbed the scene; Dylan's face at ease and smiling, his hair tousled and falling over his forehead and into his pale-blue eyes. Yes, blue, Dylan, not Diablo, was in this club and chatting to *that* woman.

He hadn't rushed home and thought to ring her after not speaking to her for a month. No, he couldn't wait to get home and see *her*.

"Easy, girl," Cerise said from next to her. "You don't know anything yet."

All Grace could do was look at Cerise with contempt. The time for excuses had passed and she stormed in the direction of the group. Cerise quickly followed.

Grace didn't slow down until she was right in front of Dylan.

Fenton appeared to jump out of his skin and then put his head in his hands. Grace flashed a glance at Serena and willed her to say one word. Thankfully, the girl thought better of it, raised an eyebrow to Dylan and walked off the way they'd come. That only left Dylan facing her; he looked mildly surprised. There was not even a flinch of guilt at being caught red-handed. And, more importantly, no anger directed at her for any knowledge he may have of her meeting with Diablo.

"Grace?" was all that escaped him.

"Dylan?" she threw right back at him. He couldn't miss the animosity in her tone.

Dylan was smiling, mildly confused. "What are you doing here?" Then he looked at Cerise, standing sheepishly next to her, for an explanation.

Fenton looked downright agitated.

"She's been staying with me while you were away," Cerise explained.

Dylan just smiled with a small nod, then looked back to Grace, not fully understanding her hostility.

"What are *you* doing here?" Grace flung at him. "With her?" she finished nodding her head in the direction Serena had gone.

Dylan flashed his beautiful smile then and was about to speak, but Grace didn't give him time. Her fuse had blown and she shoved him in the chest.

Dylan had to take a step back with the force to right himself. His eyes widened, but his expression was still one of amused bewilderment.

She screamed at him, "Why are you laughing?" Fenton began to push and herd her towards the exit.

Grace began to struggle with him until Dylan decided the joke was over, got between them and marched her to the exit by the elbow. He was now deadly serious, not wanting a scene.

"Let me go!" Grace shouted. "Fuck off, you bastard!" But her protests fell on deaf ears.

Within seconds of being outside, Dylan bent and lifted her off the ground and threw her into the back of a cab while she flailed, kicked and screamed.

Fenton held Dylan back, not sure what he was going to do. Grace scrambled along the back seat to get back out the other door, but was halted by Cerise, who waggled her finger in her face through the glass, and mouthed for her to stay put. Cerise's expression alone sucked the venom out of her when she realised that Dylan and Fenton were now nose-to-nose, arguing.

Grace's hand went to her throat when Fenton pointed a finger at Dylan's face. "You can't take her with you yet, D."

Dylan leant into Fenton's full weight menacingly. A small

circle of onlookers waited with bated breath. No one knew whether it was going to go off between them and neither of them looked like they were backing down. But Dylan made no reply.

Grace was terrified that Diablo was there somewhere underneath the surface and watched his blue eyes intently. The knowledge was no comfort; it just underscored the unpredictability of either of them.

Eventually, Dylan broke the standoff and went to the other side of the cab, but never took his eyes from Fenton's. He opened the door to the backseat where she sat. "Don't ever cross the line with me, Fent," he said over the car roof. Then he got in and slammed the car door.

Dylan gave his address to the cab driver like an order and they drove home without him looking at her once.

THEY GOT out of the cab and rode up in the lift in silence. Dylan unlocked the door, pushed it open and gestured for her to go first.

Almost overcome with the memory of the last time she'd been there, she stood awkwardly in the centre of the room with her heart beating like a train, terrified *his* memory would be jogged.

Dylan sighed and threw his keys down on the table. "Do you want anything?" he asked quietly, his anger replaced by fatigue.

Grace shook her head, only daring a furtive glance at him every now and then.

"Relax," Dylan said. "I'm not going to hurt you."

Her eyes flashed to his and she felt her cheeks burn red. Guilt. *Did he know?* Her heart thudded while he walked towards her in his easy, fluid gait.

He stopped right in front of her and just stared into her

eyes for what felt like the longest moments of her life. She didn't know what scared her more; the appearance of Diablo any minute or Dylan confronting her with what she'd done.

She swallowed hard.

"What was that all about?" he said eventually.

Was he joking? She narrowed her eyes. "Have you any idea what it's been like for me this last month?"

"No," he said simply, "but I can imagine."

"And you didn't think to at least call me when you got back?" She went to turn away from him, but he held her still by her arm.

"I haven't been away enjoying myself, Grace."

"You certainly seemed to be tonight," she sniped and went to struggle out of his grip.

He let her go. Confusion flickered across his face, which only seemed to enrage her even more. He sagged, clearly exhausted, and leant his weight on his hip. "I'm sorry you had a month of worry. I only woke two days ago. It wasn't the same for me," he finished, with a small smile of regret.

Shit! She looked up at the ceiling. He made her feel terrible. How could he miss her when he was unconscious? *But still…* "Why were you with Serena?" she said, resuming her anger.

Dylan smiled and took a step closer. "Please, Grace, I didn't know she'd be there." His hand came up to touch her cheek.

She continued to scowl at him. "That's not an answer."

"I normally give it four days before I go out of these four walls, but this time I needed to. It's hard to explain, but he kept me locked down tight this time."

Grace concentrated on not going red again. If Dylan felt caged, then Diablo did too when the shoe was on the other foot. Little wonder he needed an outlet. A feeling of hopelessness was beginning to overwhelm her when Dylan bent his head and brushed her lips with his. "Are you safe to be around now?" she asked with her lips still against his and her eyes closed, savouring the closeness to him.

Dylan pulled back slightly to look her in the eyes. "Honestly… I don't know. This is new territory for me. But right now… I feel fine."

"And Serena… how do you feel about her?" She couldn't help herself and watched his face closely for the slightest twitch.

He frowned slightly. "She's just a friend."

"Do you still sleep with her?" she persisted, hating how weak and needy she was sounding.

"*I* won't sleep with her," he said, but she couldn't help but notice the emphasis on the 'I'. Of course, he couldn't speak for Diablo.

They stared at each other in silence for a few moments until she was forced to look away. "I'm sorry, I didn't mean to cause an argument between you and Fenton."

Sensing her softening, he pulled her to him by the waist. "Don't worry, we've had worse. I'll speak to him tomorrow."

She wound her arms around him and pushed her face into his shoulder and breathed in deeply. It felt so like home, so right. "Can I stay with you tonight?" she said, gazing up at him.

Dylan pulled her into him tighter and ground his hips into hers. He was already getting hard.

But buzzing through her brain were a million questions like: how many women had he had sex with over the last month, what did he do to them or, worse still, they do to him, *arghhh!* It was torture. But it wasn't him, was it? She tried to tell herself over and over. *God*, a girl could go crazy.

He pulled her chin up so she was forced to look at him. "Stop worrying, Grace. It's done… It's over now," and he began to nip at her lips to coax her to kiss him.

"Maybe I should go?" she whispered half-heartedly, trying to pull apart.

"I won't let you go now."

The words were her undoing and she succumbed to a blistering kiss. Because the words didn't just mean right now in this apartment, they meant ever, and they both knew it.

CHAPTER 16

*D*ylan made short work of undressing her and she was lifted and placed carefully on the bed. Placing his weight gently on top of her, she gazed lovingly up into his impossibly blue eyes. She touched his cheek with her shaking hand. "Stay with me, Dylan."

Turning his head and kissing it, he knew what she was saying. She needed reassurance that he wouldn't change on her. "You're mine, Grace… only mine."

His skilful mouth worked its way down her body, seeking and longing for his touch.

He swept away any fear she may have had that he didn't feel the same way for her, or that he wasn't totally in control. He made love to her utterly and completely with the passion and care of a lover and the skill and stamina of a professional.

No one else could ever come close to this. She was lost to sensation. Even when he roughly slammed her into the shower wall, flipping her around and plunging into her from behind, she gave herself over to it, enjoying every thrust and proof of his unrestrained need for her.

And when at last his own release overcame him, she fell asleep in his arms, blissfully exhausted, aching and bruised. Revelling in the feeling that tickled her stomach when she remembered how she got that way.

DAWN APPROACHED and she groaned when she felt Dylan try to extricate himself from the tangle of their limbs to leave the bed.

"Shh," he said, stroking back the hair from her face. "Sleep. I'm just going for my run."

She murmured some gibberish and turned over and went back to sleep.

The buzzing of the mobile phone on the bedside table brought her back to consciousness. Briefly, she ignored it until the thought pierced through her foggy brain that it was Dylan's phone.

Looking around to make sure she was alone, she leant up and tilted the screen to face her.

Serena calling, it said.

Immediately, she snapped awake with her heart pounding. *The cheek of the woman. Who the hell did she think she was?*

Anger made her come to a quick decision before it rang off and she put the phone to her ear. "What?" she answered bluntly.

There was a brief pause at the other end as if the caller was taken by surprise.

"Pass the phone to D," Serena said, equally blunt.

"I can't, he's not here."

Again, a pause, probably while she assessed whether Grace was telling the truth. "Tell him I called."

"Yeah… I'll tell him," Grace said, letting the sarcasm drip from her voice. She held all the cards and Serena knew it.

Then she totally surprised her. "We need to talk."

"What would I possibly want to speak to you for?"

"You don't know what you're dealing with."

"Don't I?" Grace was sure that if they'd been face-to-face, they would have been nose-to-nose at that point. Never had anyone riled up so much hatred in her.

"Meet me at the coffee shop on the corner of Dylan's road at one." Then Serena was gone.

Grace was left looking at the phone with her heart still hammering. But when she tried to relax and put the call from her mind, she found it impossible. Because, infuriating as it was, she knew that she would have to meet her.

It wasn't hard to get away. Dylan wanted to go and see Fenton. Grace offered to go food shopping to give them some space and Dylan had happily gone on his way.

She paused at the busy coffee shop door, gathering herself. She took a deep breath, whispered, 'here goes' and yanked the door open.

Serena was sitting at a small table for two in the corner and gave her a small nod of recognition. Grace detoured to the counter first to buy a coffee and then carried it over to join her.

"I didn't think you'd come," Serena sneered.

Grace sat and sprinkled sugar into her drink from a small packet. "Neither did I?" In fact, she still wasn't sure why she was there. She stirred her cup. "What's this all about?"

Serena smirked. "You think you've got it all sussed, don't you?... You haven't gotta clue."

Grace sipped her drink and blew over the surface. "So what is this?" she said, holding out her hand. "You got me here, so enlighten me... " she added, raising her eyebrows.

"You'll never be enough for D."

Grace narrowed her eyes. "And you are?... It felt pretty

okay from where I was lying last night?" The snipe was out before she had time to check herself. This woman brought out the fishwife in her.

Serena visibly flinched. She loved him. It was more than sex to her, of course it was.

"You know what he does?" she threw back.

Grace had been waiting for her to bring out the porn card and rolled her eyes like she was bored with the whole subject. "Of course. We are completely open with each other."

"So you know he has certain… appetites?"

Grace stared at Serena, taking in the look of spite and gritting her teeth while she concentrated on not rising to it. "That was in the past."

Serena smiled as if she had delighted her. "You're a fool if you think a man like that can ever change… My god, you're deluded."

Grace felt her temper riding her, but kept a lid on it, just. "You misunderstand me," she said through tight lips, "what I meant was, it is in the past with you." *Yes, you bitch.*

Serena blinked at the blow. Grace was sure she wasn't expecting her to bite back, but she was buggered if she wanted to talk about her sex life with this trollop. She nodded once and, satisfied, she began to stand. "If you don't mind… I thought you had something to say that I didn't know."

Serena grabbed her forearm. "Then why did D ring me last night? Believe me, when D calls, he doesn't want to talk about the weather."

Grace was momentarily stunned. "You're lying," she managed eventually.

"No, I'm not, you don't know his dark side," Serena said and let go of her arm and sat back in her chair.

"Oh, don't I?" She was furious about what she'd learnt.

She needed time to think about it on her own, but she wasn't about to give this bitch the satisfaction of letting her know she'd got to her. "You know what they say about the quiet ones." And she went to turn away.

But just as she was about to go, she paused, "Dylan and me are a couple. Get used to it." And she strode towards the door.

"Until he comes to me. He always does," Serena sang from behind her.

Grace closed her eyes but continued walking.

Her phone beeped. She was a bag of nerves when she reached the street outside and took a peek with shaking hands.

It was Dylan.

Where are you? It simply said.

Grace took some deep breaths and turned off the phone. She needed to think. She needed to be on her own for a while.

GRACE WASN'T sure how long she had wandered the streets, but it was starting to get dark. She found herself back where she started outside Dylan's flat and had to make up her mind what to do.

Everything had gone round in her head over and over and she was no nearer to knowing the answer now than she was when she'd met with Serena. Deep down, she knew she wasn't lying and Dylan did probably ring her, but the question of which Dylan it was, and did it really matter going forward, made her head feel like it was in a blender. Because even if it was Diablo; which should make it slightly better, it meant that it would come up again, and that she would have to put up with him going to Serena over and over, especially now Dylan was giving up working and Diablo could break free at any time.

Shit! She looked up at the dreary building in the half-light and thought of Dylan waiting for her up there. What should she do? She was cold and hungry and tired of walking. Should she go to Fenton's? *No.* If she did that, she would have to give Dylan some sort of explanation and it would all come out.

With a deep sigh, she opened the street door. Perhaps she could say she'd got carried away at the shops? She looked down at her empty hands; that wouldn't work.

The doors to the lift opened and she'd run out of time. Her heart was hammering in her chest. She'd just have to wing it.

The lift doors closed behind her and she stood in front of Dylan's apartment door. Her knuckles tapped gently and it snicked open. It had been held on the latch. Weird. Ice began to creep through her veins at the reminder of the night she'd spent with Diablo.

Her breaths were coming in shallow puffs as she crept around the door and into the room. Everything about her was on high alert. The lights were on, but after a quick scan of the large room, it looked as if there was no one home. Perhaps Dylan had nipped out to look for her and left it open in case she came back?

Grace allowed herself to relax a little. She was exhausted and strung out. She simply was not being rational. With her head hung low, she allowed her bag to drop onto the large bed and walked to the bathroom to switch on the shower.

Turning the dial to hot, she began to pull out her shirt and undo the buttons while she wandered back into the main room to leave her clothes there, not wanting them to get wet.

But she didn't get that far.

Grabbed from behind, she was slammed against the wall.

Her cheekbone screamed in pain at the impact. A hot mouth came next to her ear. "Where have you been all afternoon, bitch?"

Dylan's voice sounded lower, gravelly, husky – Diablo.

"Answer me!" he shouted, making her jump when he slammed her into the wall again to demand she speak.

"Stop… you're hurting me," she whimpered.

His body caged her in entirely. His nose was resting on her cheek. "I'll ask you one more time. Where. Have. You. Been?"

"In town," she managed to squeeze out.

"Where in town?" He bit her cheek and held it.

Her eyes were squeezed shut. "All over… just walking."

Diablo yanked her head back by the hair, painfully, at an impossible angle. She thought he would break her neck. "Who did you meet?"

"No one."

He laughed and ground his hips into her backside as if the lie delighted him. "The truth, Angel, you don't want me to wake Dylan to watch, do you?"

Grace felt paralysed with fear. There was no doubt that Diablo would and could carry out his threat. Dylan would hate himself for putting her in danger; god knows what he would do.

Diablo laughed again, knowing he had the upper hand. He reached in front of her and began to unbuckle her belt and pull it from the loops of her jeans.

"Please don't," she whimpered, closing her eyes. Her breaths were so shallow, she began to pant with fear.

Her belt was pulled free and he popped the button next. "Okay… please stop. I met Serena earlier… in a coffee shop."

"Now we're getting somewhere," he said, kissing down her neck. "The truth at last. I saw you there."

Her brain stalled. Had he been following her the whole time … watching and waiting to pounce?

While her brain worked, Diablo's hands got busy and yanked down her jeans, using his large body to pin her to the wall so she couldn't escape. "Was it you who phoned Serena last night? she asked, desperate to halt his progress.

It worked as he did pause for a moment. "It matters to you which one of us it was?"

She didn't answer. Was it a test? Was he curious because he saw it making no difference? Or did he intend to use the answer against her?

Her jeans were now around her ankles and he trod on them and shook her so she was forced to step out of them. Then he kicked her legs apart and positioned himself at her core.

"Wait!" she shouted. "Tell me first, I need to know."

A cruel chuckle next to her ear and he slowly sank himself inside her.

Grace gave up on getting an answer as he began a pounding rhythm while he held her rigidly by the waist. He lowered his head next to her ear, "I called her, Angel. But he only needs a nudge… you see he loves fucking her as much as I love fucking you," He sank his teeth into her shoulder and bit her hard and thrust into her relentlessly.

Overwhelmed and dazed, she sagged beneath him, her legs completely giving way. He quickly caught her, picked up the belt and walked with her and threw her onto the bed. He gave her little time to clamber away; he grabbed her wrists and tied her to the bars of the headboard.

Gasping for breath, she stilled and opened her eyes when he paused. He was kneeling up, watching her with his cruel brown eyes and demonic smile. He cocked his head on an angle as if a new thought just occurred to him. "I've decided you're mine, Angel." And he laughed as if the thought astounded him. "You know that?"

Grace began to kick and flail with her legs to keep him away from her, but he laughed heartily. "Don't... please... Dylan will know when he comes back."

Diablo continued to laugh as if she delighted him. He covered her with his large body. "Shh, Angel. Relax. You'll get used to it." And he entered her again, slowly, reverently, as if he wanted to take her over. Kissing her on the mouth, on the neck and shoulders, building his pace. "Yeah, Angel. I am taking you... I am taking over. You belong to me now."

*D*iablo was insatiable, but eventually flopped down on top of Grace, squashing her flat, face down on the bed. Kissing her shoulder blade abruptly, he got up and sat on the edge of the bed. Then studied her as if he were waiting for a reaction.

Sensing his scrutiny, she cracked open her eyes with effort as every part of her ached and longed for sleep. But she found she could not take her eyes off him, as tired as she was; not just because she didn't know what he would do next, but because she just couldn't believe that the savage man staring back at her could be Dylan.

He gave her a slight nod. Was that some kind of thank-you – appreciation for the fight now gone out of her? Or was it a, 'take that, you bitch?' She couldn't be sure.

He smiled, stood up and walked lazily to the bathroom. The shower came on with a hiss.

Grace forced herself to move and wriggled her wrists, still bound to the headboard. Her arms had pins and needles and she needed to get some blood through.

She jumped when Diablo's arm came in front of her face and loosened the buckle so she could pull her arms free. She hadn't even heard him coming.

She rubbed her wrists back to life and raised her eyes to his. "What now?" she asked.

He said nothing but reached into a small drawer and became preoccupied with what looked like a pillbox with compartments with the days of the week on it – Dylan's medicine. "What are you doing?" she asked, sitting up. "That's Dylan's medicine."

Diablo grinned. "Replenishing his supply."

Her heart stopped. He was putting new pills in the compartments, but she'd put money on them not being the right ones. "What are you putting in there?" she asked, trying to keep the anxiety out of her voice.

"Harmless. Don't worry. But I can't have him locking me down tight now, can I, Angel? How else would I see you?"

"I'll tell him."

The smile dropped from his face and then returned just as quickly. "Will you tell him about our night of passion?"

All she could do was stare blankly at him. He was black-mailing her. What the hell was she going to do? "He'll see my bruises," she said in triumph, her nose in the air.

"He will, won't he… whatever will you do?" He reached out his hand to touch her reddened wrist, making her flinch at first. But he just rubbed a thumb across the raw skin. "I reckon you have till morning till the bruising comes out… then it's up to you."

She was flabbergasted. He won either way and he knew it. He stood and pushed his legs into some jeans, slipped his shirt over his head and pulled on some trainers.

"Where are you going?' she said, desperately.

He grinned again. "Out… I can't be here when Dylan

comes back. You have a reprieve. It's up to you what you do with it." He went to the door and slipped out, leaving her alone.

Her brain raced. Fucking hell. She was losing her mind. He was going to go out as one half of Dylan and come back as the other. Diablo even thought they were two different people. Who was she kidding? So did she.

The question was: what should she do now? She could go to Janey's? *No.* She would have to tell them the whole story and that meant Dave would go ballistic.

Fenton's? *No.* Diablo may be heading there. She could phone him, but she'd have to be quick.

Hurriedly, she rummaged in her bag and found her phone. Flicking through the address list, she clicked on Fenton's entry. The phone rang twice and he picked up. *Thank god.*

"Grace?" the deep voice said.

"Fenton, please listen. I'm not sure how long I have. Diablo's back and he was waiting for me …"

"Slow down, Angel. Say it again slowly."

Grace was exasperated with him but tried to calm herself to speak more clearly and relayed the afternoon's events right from when she'd met Serena, till when Diablo jumped her in Dylan's flat – minus the gory details, but he got her drift.

"So you think he's tampering with Dylan's medication?"

"I'm sure he is."

The line went quiet for a beat. "Fuck me… I dunno what the best thing to do is?"

"I'm going to be smothered in bruises by the morning, Fenton. Dylan's going to go mad."

There was silence on the line.

"Fenton?"

"Sorry, Angel, I was just thinking."

Then Grace heard a muffled conversation as Fenton held the receiver to his chest and spoke to Cerise. Then he came back on the line, "Right… this is what you're gonna do. I'm gonna call you a cab and you will get straight in it. Leave Dylan to me. Cerise will already be in the cab with the kids. It's not safe for any of you here any more."

PART II
DIABLO

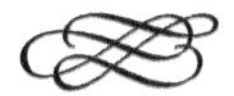

CHAPTER 18

Grace did exactly what Fenton told her to do. The cab pulled up twenty minutes later and she got in with Cerise and the kids, already in the back seat.

"Where are we going?" she said, as soon as the car moved off.

"Shh!" Cerise said, widening her eyes. "Station."

The cab driver looked in the rear-view mirror and nodded.

Grace's heart began to thump. Everything was getting really serious. Cerise obviously didn't even want the cab driver to know where they were going. Did she think Dylan would go to those lengths? They weren't supposed to be running away from him, just giving her time to heal, weren't they?

Grace studied Cerise's face while she stared out the window, then realised she wasn't getting any more information and relaxed back into her own seat.

They were soon out of the cab and onto a train to Victoria, then a tube to Paddington Station, where they got on yet another train to Oxford.

When they were settled into their seats for the hour-and-a-half journey, Grace felt justified in finally getting some answers from Cerise. "You going to tell me where we are going yet?" She was exhausted, but her nerves were on edge.

There was silence in the carriage. All they could hear was the clackety-clack as the train rocked and moved through the darkness.

"We're going to stay with a friend of mine."

Grace rolled her head on the headrest to look over at Cerise. "Who?"

"Someone I went to college with. Someone who might be able to help."

Grace smiled weakly, not convinced. What could anybody possibly do? Dylan had seen enough health professionals; in the end, it was Fenton who had helped him get by the most. "I don't understand why you had to go to all this trouble, Cerise?" She looked guiltily at the kids, one curled up on Cerise's lap, the other leaning on her arm. "Poor little mites." What had started off as a bit of an adventure for them had now worn them out.

Cerise checked that both the kids were asleep and whispered, "You don't understand, Grace. D's capable of anything when he's out, especially when he's pissed off."

Grace swallowed. She got what she was saying, but "It won't be Diablo, though, Cerise. He said it will be Dylan when he comes back."

Cerise nodded but looked slightly impatient with her. "Yes, that might be true, Grace, but he's now unmedicated, and when he finds you gone, D could easily return, and Dylan may not be able to get out if Diablo doesn't want him to." Cerise glanced out of the opposite window and blinked rapidly as if to get rid of her emotion. "He'll go straight for Fenton." She shook her head and tears returned to her eyes.

"Oh, Cerise." Grace felt terrible. To think she had brought all this trouble on them all.

"Fenton will cop the lot. D will know that he helped us get away... he'll go mad."

Grace looked up at the ceiling of the train. Everything had got so way out of control. She looked back at Cerise abruptly. "He wouldn't hurt him though, Cerise... I mean, he loves him, doesn't he?"

"I don't know, Grace, D's capable of everything."

At last, they arrived by yet another taxi at the old-fashioned apartment on the campus of Oxford University. A geeky-looking, tall, blonde, slim older man welcomed them warmly, and Cerise introduced him as Anton.

They quickly settled the kids down together in a spare bed already prepared for them. Anton made them hot chocolate and Grace curled up in an armchair next to a real fire. She barely touched her drink before she fell asleep.

Anton found a soft blanket and covered her where she lay with her head on the arm of the chair. He left her to sleep while he and Cerise sat talking well into the night, and she explained everything she knew about Dylan – from Fenton's meeting him until the events of that night.

After a hasty kiss goodbye, Fenton ran back upstairs and got himself ready for the inevitable trouble to come. He wasn't sure what mood Dylan would be in when he eventually rocked up, but he knew him of old. His Mr Nice side could be as handy as his evil one, and whatever personality he was met with, the fact that it had been Fenton who had spirited his woman away would piss him off, no matter what.

He quickly phoned two mutual friends. They were

brothers who had trained in martial arts with both him and D, and who also worked his door for him at parties; his tightest friends after D. He could hold his own in a fight with D, but this was different, and he wasn't taking any chances.

When he put down the receiver, he went to the fridge and made up some orange juice (D's soft drink of choice) and crushed several of Cerise's sleeping pills into it. He gave it a shake and put it back in the fridge. He then set about hiding any sharp objects, knives, his samurai swords and nunchucks, which hung on his walls, just in case D decided they were a useful prop to kill him with.

Lastly, he removed any evidence of Cerise and the kids' hasty departure, and then flopped down on his sofa. He cracked open a beer and drank deeply. It was going to be a long night.

Beep!

He stared at his phone for a second, then leant forward and tilted the screen towards him.

D.

He quickly skimmed the text.

Is Grace with you?

Fenton sat back into his sofa, but his brain was on high alert. He quickly tapped back: *No. Why? Is everything okay?* He decided hedging his bets was the best policy at this stage, plus he wanted to make sure which one he was dealing with. Diablo was a crafty bastard.

Beep!

Not sure. She went out lunchtime and she's still not back. Getting worried now.

Fenton stared at the screen, not sure what to reply next, when a second text came through.

Fent? I blacked out today.

Fenton quickly came to a decision; sure it was Dylan he was dealing with.

· · ·

*C*OME *HERE*, *D. I'll help you look for her. Where are you now?*
Mine.
Okay, C U in ten.

FENTON SIGHED DEEPLY. He knew he had around ten minutes to decide how he was going to play this. Either way, it wasn't going to be good.

WHEN DYLAN WALKED in and their eyes met, Fenton felt like he was being assessed. Diablo or Dylan, he had a way about him of making a person feel uneasy when he wanted to. A ticking bomb; thank fuck his eyes were blue for the time being.

"Juice?" he asked as flippantly as he could, already opening the fridge and peering inside.

Dylan's face was closed and not up for joking; he pointed to the can Fenton had left on the coffee table. "Nah, beer."

Fenton paused for a millisecond, then grabbed a cold one and passed it to him. "So you blacked out?" he said, keeping up the light chit-chat.

Dylan sighed and nodded. "I came to on my bike and it was dark… the last thing I remember, I was coming over to you just before lunchtime today."

"And you haven't seen Grace since?" Fenton eyed Dylan cautiously.

He just shook his head and looked heartsick.

Fenton took some deep swigs of his beer, watching Dylan the whole time.

The entry buzzer sounded.

Dylan looked at the door and back to Fenton expectantly.

"Don't get your hopes up. It's probably just Dean and Herbs."

Dylan deflated and nodded.

Fenton walked out to the hallway and buzzed them up.

Dylan paced.

The black brothers walked in and nodded a greeting to Fenton and then Dylan. Their presence meant that Fenton could now cut to the chase. "Have you been taking your medication properly, D?"

Dylan's eyes flickered across furtively to the two guys.

Fenton was grateful that they were chatting between themselves, tactfully taking the heat from Dylan. They knew the score, though; not everything, but that Dylan had severe and unpredictable mood swings and needed handling with care.

"Yes," Dylan said eventually. "Every day like clockwork." He was frowning like he couldn't understand the line of questioning. "Can we get going, Fent. I mean… we ought to start looking."

Fenton raised a placating hand. "Could he have done something like swap your pills?'

Dylan frowned and then shifted his feet uncomfortably. "Well, I suppose he could have…" He was becoming impatient.

Fenton wasted no more time. "Here." He reached into a kitchen cupboard where the family medicines and first-aid stuff were kept. He took out a bottle and threw it over to Dylan, who caught it easily. "Take these. I keep an emergency supply just in case."

Dylan looked confused, but was becoming exasperated with the lack of action. "Just in case of what… shouldn't we get going?"

When he said the words and fixed him in the eye, Fenton

knew he feared the worst. There was no point beating around the bush any longer. "There's no point."

Dylan narrowed his eyes.

"I know where she is."

"I don't get—"

"Cerise phoned after I spoke to you. She's with Grace… She's safe," Fenton said, holding his hands up in front of him to steady Dylan.

Dylan was shaking his head and frowning. "Why?" But the look of building concern and fear on his face told Fenton more than anything else that he was dreading what he would say.

Fenton paused for a beat.

"What did I do?" Dylan persisted, beginning to shout.

The brothers tuned in and took a step closer.

Fuck it… "Serena called to meet her."

Dylan was dumbfounded. "What the—?"

"You… I mean, D, followed her."

The colour visibly drained from Dylan's face, then his jaw clenched. "What did he do?" he said, low with menace.

Fenton took a brief glance at Dean and Herbs, who were standing by, ready to jump in at any moment.

Dylan didn't miss the exchange and it angered him even more. "Tell me!" he demanded.

"You scared her…" Fenton saw no point in adding details and hoped he wouldn't need to.

Dylan looked at everyone's face in disgust at the non-answer. Come on, Fent, what did I do?" he said, more controlled this time.

Fenton took a deep, fortifying breath. "From what I can gather, you roughed her up a bit."

Dylan blinked slowly, as if he'd been hit in the gut, then looked up through tired eyes straight at Fenton. "Where is she now?" He sounded ruined.

"I can't tell you, D… it's not safe."

Dylan turned away abruptly and pinched the bridge of his nose. Then he used the same hand to rub his closed eyes and run his fingers back through his overlong hair, pushing it back away from his face.

When he turned around again slowly, Fenton's heart sank and began to thump. Gone was the look of total devastation in Dylan's eyes, replaced by the hard, cruel darkness of Diablo. He pointed a mocking finger at Fenton. "You tell me where the fuck she's gone, Fenton, before we fall out." His tone was soft and taunting; Diablo rarely shouted. His intense violence usually did the talking for him.

He grinned at the other two men, who were already bracing themselves, ready for him to kick off. "You thought to bring back-up, Fent? Impressed."

"Now that's not it at all, D," Fenton said, edging back slowly towards the fridge. "She's out with Cerise, that's all… Beer?" he said, eyebrows up in question.

Diablo wasn't having any of it and narrowed his eyes at him. "Juice," he said, flatly.

Fenton really concentrated on not appearing too eager by his choice and just busied himself pouring the drink, making sure he gave it a good shake first.

"Save the bullshit for Dylan, it's me you're talking to. Now. Where. Is. She?" he said in his most reasonable voice. But Fenton wasn't fooled at all by his easy-going tone; he knew of old the threat beneath. *Just drink the fucking drink!*

He worked really fucking hard not to glance at the drink and give himself away. He tried a different tack. "You were really rough with her, D."

Bingo!

Diablo grinned and took a large gulp of the orange juice. Then he shrugged.

"It was all Cerise could think of to stop Dylan from seeing her."

Diablo's look was calculating. Then he downed the rest of the drink and nodded as if satisfied with the explanation. "Good… Okay, when Dylan comes back, let him phone her. That should keep him from kicking up too much of a fuss."

Fenton nodded. The two brothers visibly stood down. Diablo sauntered towards the door as if to go. Fenton made eye contact with the brothers as if they'd just pulled it off and went to follow Diablo out.

Then, faster than anyone could track, Diablo turned suddenly and violently smacked Fenton against the wall by the throat, using a pinch hold that he knew well.

The two brothers took a step forward in sudden consternation. Diablo halted them with his spare hand and spoke quietly: "Hold on, boys… I don't want to crush my best friend's windpipe… don't make me do that."

Fenton remained motionless. He'd seen this manoeuvre many times and knew D had no compunction to use it to its full force.

Everyone froze in a stalemate.

"Just a little reminder, Fent… You ever fuck with me again, I will kill you… and that pretty wife of yours." Then his face cracked into a huge grin right in Fenton's face. "Eventually."

Fenton went to struggle, but Diablo increased the pressure in his grip and there was no escape.

They all felt so helpless, as if in the power of the school-yard bully. Then, as if by miracle, Diablo released his pressure slightly, then shook his head and staggered. No one wasted a second and Fenton pushed hard on Diablo's chest as the brothers bounded forward and grabbed D's arms and pulled them behind his back.

He began to fight back wildly, his strength still formidable, but he was clumsy and uncoordinated.

"Take him over to the sofa," Fenton shouted as they all struggled to avoid his kicks. It was like trying to contain a wild animal. A breakfast barstool and the glass top on the coffee table were casualties and got smashed on the way. With enormous effort, they managed to push him down flat onto the sofa until the fighting lessened.

Diablo's head rolled on his shoulders and his eyes flickered white until he eventually lay still.

"Wait!" Fenton ordered. There was no way he would release him until he was absolutely sure he wasn't faking unconsciousness. He would kill them for sure.

Eventually, Fenton let him go and straightened up. The brothers followed him and sighed with relief.

"Hang around a while, boys, can you, just in case?" Fenton said, still breathing hard.

They both nodded. They all knew what an unpredictable fucker D was.

Fenton picked up his phone and dialled Cerise. Thankfully, Grace had already fallen asleep, so he could talk freely. "I'm going to allow him to phone you in the morning. Tell Grace she can speak to him, but on no account must she tell him where she is."

Cerise agreed with the wisdom of that and hung up.

Fenton then set about clearing the place up. The brothers helped, gave it an hour, and then left, after shaking Fenton's hand and wishing him luck.

Fenton flopped into a chair opposite the sofa, exhausted but not willing to sleep. No, he wouldn't allow himself that luxury until he was sure it was Dylan who woke up.

When Grace finally woke the next morning, she was achy and stiff and felt like she'd gone a few rounds with a heavyweight boxer. Cerise brought her a steaming cuppa and she stretched and took it gratefully. "Any news?"

Cerise sat down in the chair opposite her. "Yeah. Dylan spent the night with Fenton. He'll ring you soon."

Grace's eyes went wide. "Really ... Does he know?"

Cerise nodded, "Not the details, though. Fenton just told him he scared you."

Grace breathed a sigh of relief. It was a good-enough excuse; one she could spin out as long as she needed. She glanced down at her wrists. They were now a nice shade of purple; along with other places she was sure, matched. *Would Dylan buy it, though? Possibly.* She'd have to box clever.

"Anton's agreed to see Dylan; that is, if *he* agrees. He hasn't been that trusting of health professionals in the past," Cerise continued.

"And he is a proper shrink?" Grace said, feeling the first glimmer of hope in a long while.

Cerise laughed at the label. "Not exactly. Let's just say he is on the experimental side of psychiatry. It's a science for him – a passion, but that I think could be our selling point."

Grace watched Cerise's positive confidence with the whole thing and wasn't convinced. "I'm scared, Cerise... that if Dylan finds out what he's done,..." Tears welled and she covered her face with her hands.

Cerise rushed over and perched on the arm of the chair and pulled her to her. "Shh ... I know ... you love him."

"He'll leave me for my own good." And she turned her face into Cerise and sobbed. "He might even do something stupid to get rid of Diablo."

"Hey, don't."

But Grace could tell by her tone that Cerise was thinking the same thing and was just as worried. *Shit.* It looked as though they were the blind leading the blind here.

Cerise kissed her head and whispered into her hair, "Look, we all love Dylan, okay? And Anton is brilliant. If anyone can help him, he can. We'll get to the bottom of it."

When her sobs were just shudders every now and then, she pushed apart from Cerise and looked up into her face. "What can he do... honestly, I mean."

Cerise bobbed her head. "Well... he wants to see whether he agrees with the diagnosis for a start."

Grace frowned. Weirdly, Dylan's diary and the drawing of the two men in the lightning came to mind. "You mean he may not be schizophrenic at all?"

Cerise's smile was wan and not too enthusiastic on that score. "Anton has dealt with some pretty complex characters. He thinks Dylan will be an interesting study." She finished with her eyebrows up.

Her phone rang and halted Grace's train of thought.

Cerise and Grace looked at each other.

"You gonna pick it up?" Cerise said.

Grace reached out a shaky hand, glanced at the screen, slowly put it to her ear and swallowed. "Hello," came out breathily.

Silence.

"Dylan … is that you?"

"Yeah," came back eventually. Just one word and he sounded devastated.

Grace fought with every instinct inside her not to tell him to stay where he was and she would come right to him. "Are you okay?" she said instead.

"Argh," he said, clearly in pain, "I should be asking you."

"Listen to me. I'm fine, I promise. We just thought… Cerise and I, that you needed some time for your medicine to work. That's all, it's no big deal."

Silence.

"Okay, Dylan? Talk to me."

There was a long silence and Grace's heart was thumping. She had no idea how much he actually knew about what he'd done, but she suspected he was just going on gut instinct and what he knew of Diablo's character.

"I don't think it's safe for you to be around me any more, Grace. Fuck, it's never been safe," he said, with exhausted resignation.

"Don't say that… Please, Dylan, just give it a few days. It'll be fine. I promise."

"No, something is off… something is changing. I can feel it … he's getting stronger. It's getting harder, Grace… for me to stay."

For a second, panic clutched at her because he wasn't talking about staying around her as a partner; he was talking about staying at the surface – staying the conscious one in his body, and the thought terrified her. She blinked away her tears and swallowed hard. "Listen to me, Dylan. I love you, and you love me, right?"

"You know I do, it's… I can't …"

"If you love me, you'll do anything, okay? Anything to fight this." Her mind raced. He was giving up. Giving in to that animal he shared a body with, and there was no bloody way she would ever let that happen, not in a million years. She had to think fast. "Now you listen to me, you idiot," she said through gritted teeth, "you fucking owe me. Do you think he won't try to find me when he's out?" *Shit*, she didn't want him to think Diablo had some sort of sick connection to her. "Just to piss you off," she added. "I need you to keep me safe."

Bloody hell, the gaping great silence told her more than anything else that she had still given away a major fucking clue as to how much she had interacted with Diablo. But hey, what the hell, now it was out.

"What do you suggest?" Dylan said eventually. He sounded at a loss, but thankfully, didn't pull her up on what she'd said.

"Cerise has a friend here, a professor in psychiatry or something. Cerise says he may be able to help us."

"Us?" Cynicism dripped from his voice.

"Yes, you lummox, of course us."

He laughed genuinely then. "What's a lummox?"

"I don't know," she said, laughing as well, "but you definitely are one," and she was reminded how she always managed to dispel his discomfort or stress by being light-hearted.

"Okay," he said, relenting in his lovely, easy-going way. The Dylan way she knew and loved.

Grace nodded silently at Cerise, who had been listening and watching intently. She beckoned for Grace to hand her the phone.

"Bye, babe, I have to go. Cerise wants to talk to you. I'll see you really soon, okay?"

"Okay," he repeated, heartbreakingly quietly.

She passed the phone reluctantly to Cerise, who, after a hasty hello, asked for Fenton. Between the two of them, they planned how they would meet in a few days. Hopefully, enough time would have elapsed for Fenton to get some real drugs into Dylan and her bruises to fade. God knows what she would say to Dylan if they hadn't.

GRACE WAITED in the anteroom just off the study in one of the old-fashioned buildings at the university.

There was a knock on the door.

"Come in," she said, in a squeaky voice a little too high with nerves.

The door opened and her heart leapt when Dylan shyly entered. She stood up immediately and ran at him. He let out a blast of air on impact as she slammed into his chest and his arms enveloped her.

"I've missed you so much," she croaked, clinging tightly to him with her face against his shirt, breathing him in.

"Me too," he whispered into her hair.

They clung for a few moments until he eventually pushed her away from him to look into her face.

"I'm okay," she said, blinking away tears.

He searched her eyes until he was satisfied and pulled her to him again. "I dunno what good this will do?"

She extricated her arms to look up again; "We have to try, though, right?"

He exhaled loudly and nodded.

Another door opened to the left of them and Anton poked his head into the room. "Would you like to come into my study now, Dylan?"

Dylan looked briefly uncertain and Grace nodded her encouragement. He bent and kissed her chastely on the lips and walked past Anton and into the study. Anton smiled at her kindly. "I won't be long, and then you can have him back."

She smiled weakly and nodded. He went back inside the room and closed the door.

Grace watched the old mantelpiece clock. It ticked loudly but the hands didn't seem to move. Absently, she shuffled Dylan's old diaries perched on her lap. Ten, fifteen, thirty, fifty minutes passed agonizingly slowly. The clock dinged on the hour and finally, after an hour and a quarter, the door opened and Dylan walked out, none the worse for wear. Anton accompanied him, smiled and warmly shook his hand.

"Did everything go okay?" she said anxiously, standing up.

Dylan nodded and gave her his gorgeous, unsure smile.

"Everything went fine," Anton said. "I've just got to spend a little time putting my thoughts down. Dylan has been very open and honest. Cerise has also been helpful with any relevant things she knows about Dylan. So shall we meet again in say … a couple of hours?"

Grace had almost forgotten. "I brought these…" And she held them up to Dylan, asking for his silent permission.

"My diaries?" Dylan said, a little surprised.

"I know you said you've never shown anyone but me, but I thought they would be helpful… do you mind if Anton sees them, Dylan?"

He looked into her eyes for a few moments as if deciding and then nodded. "If you think it will help?" Then he faced Anton. "I was just a kid."

Grace squeezed his hand in reassurance. He didn't need to explain himself to anyone.

Anton held out his hands and Grace passed over the precious diaries. "Any information is important, I assure you," Anton said, smiled again and disappeared back into his sanctum.

GRACE AND DYLAN sat opposite each other in one of the campus canteens. Both had a steaming mug of tea. Neither of them was saying much.

"I'm sorry, Grace," Dylan said, breaking the silence first.

"Sorry for what?" she said, stirring her cup, frightened to look at him.

"For scaring you so much you felt like you had to run away." He looked up at the ceiling like the answer could be up there somewhere. "Fuck, I knew it would happen… I'm so fucking stupid."

"Stop, Dylan. Stop it now!" Grace snapped.

Dylan's eyes flashed to hers, surprised by her outburst.

"It wasn't you, it was him."

He looked away, exasperated. "I just got out from seeing a shrink, Grace."

"Don't you believe in Diablo any more, Dylan?" she said desperately. It seemed more important than ever that *he* believed he was a separate person, especially now.

He seemed to lose patience with her. "It's getting kind of hard, ya know, Grace?"

Both their tempers had fired up and their eyes locked for a few moments. Dylan looked away first. "I'm sorry, it's just…"

"Just what?"

"We have to face it that I'm just nuts, Grace." His sad face belied the smile on his lips and her heart broke for him.

"You are not nuts, do you hear me? You are the strongest person I know to put up with this for so long. And we are here to find out how we can beat it… that's all. So we can have a normal life. Okay?" she said, red in the face, furious with him.

He'd watched her with his brow furrowed throughout the whole tirade, raising and lowering his eyebrows until he relaxed and the corners of his mouth turned slowly upwards. He reached forward, picked up her hands and brought them to his mouth and kissed them.

Suddenly conscious of the ring of green and yellow bruising around each wrist of which he still seemed oblivious, she pulled back her hands and sipped her tea nervously.

Dylan watched her, puzzled, and picked up his own tea. "Are you staying near here?"

Grace nodded into her drink. The last thing Cerise had said to her was on no account should she tell Dylan where she was staying. "Where is Fenton?" she asked, changing the subject.

A flicker of a frown crossed his face, but it went as quickly as it came. "With Cerise, I guess." He was still watching her intently. "Are you okay, Grace?"

Shit. "Yes, of course I am," she said, a little offhand. "Why?"

He paused, still watching her closely. "Is there anyone home?"

When her eyes darted to his, he was waiting for her answer, his head to the side. "No. I don't think so... why?"

He smiled his shy smile, picked up her hand and rubbed his thumb absently over it. "We have a little while to kill?" His eyes were bright, devilish and boring their meaning into hers.

When her cheeks seared red and her pulse raced, she had to get a grip on herself and remember the reason she'd been explicitly told not to reveal where she was staying or to go anywhere alone with him. But his head went to the side again, as if he were curious at her response. How could she ever resist his quiet confidence, that gentleness that also held such power? The man just oozed sex appeal. *But fuck, her bruising. He would see. They had gone down a lot, but...* Then again, if she refused him, would he be even more suspicious? *Who was she kidding?* The heart was definitely treacherous – well, hers was, anyway. But honestly, when she looked at him now, she couldn't see a shred of the brutal, heartless person he became. The separateness of their characters seemed so clear to her at that moment.

Then, as if he read her turmoil, "Are you refusing me, Grace?" His look was goading, with a sly smile on his lips as if he didn't expect her to deny him for a minute. *Hell! What could she do?* "Have you taken your tablets?" she found herself saying to buy some time to think – her voice cracked and broken with the strain.

He put his hand up to his left pectoral dramatically. "I swear."

Despite knowing it was unwise, she simply couldn't help but smile at his playfulness; after all, he could have taken it the wrong way. "Would you have told me if you hadn't?"

He frowned but was still mildly amused. "Actually, yes, I would... I think."

Satisfied, she took a deep breath and came to a quick decision: "Come on then. We're wasting time." And her chair scraped the floor as she stood up.

Dylan laughed easily and followed her.

WHEN THE TWO of them walked into Anton's apartment, Grace called out, "Anyone at home?" There was no reply. She wasn't sure if she was relieved or more apprehensive. Her conscience was still pricking her. But when she turned and saw Dylan's gaze riveted on nothing else but her, she picked up his hand and led him to the spare room that she now occupied. Cerise and the kids now used rooms down the hall belonging to another lecturer who was away for a few weeks.

Grace closed the door to the bedroom just in case, and Dylan waited patiently while she procrastinated and faffed with putting things away in drawers and cupboards.

"Come here," he said, having waited long enough.

Grace stopped what she was doing and walked slowly up to him. She stopped a little way off and dragged her eyes slowly up to his. Her heart felt like it was in her mouth, it was beating so wildly.

Her eyes rested on his, so impossibly angelic and blue. She frowned at the irony. His hand was on hers and drew her towards him, while his mouth slowly closed the distance to hers. She was breathing hard, thinking he would kiss her. "You're scared of me, Grace," he whispered incredibly quietly next to her lips.

Scared he would change personalities and even more scared he would change his mind, her eyes flashed to his, wide open and blue – still blue. *Fuck.* As long as she kept an eye on them, she decided. "I love you… not him," she said, by way of explanation. Her hands wended their way up his neck and into his hair, floppy and wayward with neglect. *God, he felt so good.*

After a terrifying pause, he seemed to understand. And when she parted her mouth, he penetrated her lips immediately with his tongue, tentative and seeking.

Eyes still locked on his, she felt herself lifted and carried as if she weighed nothing over to the bed and placed down gently. Dylan released her and stood back watching her while he unbuttoned his shirt. His muscles bunched and flexed underneath his many tattoos as he placed his shirt over a nearby chair. Then repeated it with his jeans. It was so graceful, it was hypnotic.

Aroused just watching him, her temperature rose further

when he bent forward and gently slipped the boots from her feet, then her socks. He crawled up her body like a panther and popped the button on her jeans. "Lift!" he ordered quietly.

Digging her heels into the bed, she arched up her pelvis, and with a flick of the wrist, he yanked them down from her hips, then whisked them off her feet. Everything was well practised and smooth and nothing was fumbled.

Dylan slid up her body again, straddled her hips and nimbly undid each button on her shirt. Neither spoke, nor did they break eye contact. She was spellbound.

He pulled her up to sitting and slowly slid the shirt from her shoulders and down her arms. Soft, gentle and efficient, he kissed the top of her shoulder when it was completely removed. Then he gently laid her back down and began a gentle line of kisses, beginning with her mouth, down her neck to her collarbone. Her breathing became shallow, and heat pooled between her legs, ready for his touch.

As he neared her wrist, she closed her eyes for a second and breathed deeply, partly wanting to lose herself in the mind-blowing sensation of his worshipping her in this way, but terrified of him coming up against the multicoloured bruising now inches from his gaze. Her body was undulating beneath him and taking on a mind of its own. She couldn't stop this now if she wanted to. It felt too good, too right.

Dylan began kissing along her forearm. Her breaths were now so shallow that she was barely breathing as he neared her wrists.

She held her breath.

His kissing stopped.

She didn't move a muscle and neither did he.

CHAPTER 20

The clock ticked impossibly loudly, but time stood still. They remained frozen, her heartbeat pounding in her ears. Surely he could feel it against him? But his eyes were riveted to her bruising. Then his finger slowly traced its circumference around her wrist, while he held her hand – his mind working the whole time. The spectacle was mesmerising and the wait was torture.

Just when she thought she would die with dread and he must surely say something, he bent his head slowly and put his mouth to the green and yellow skin and planted the gentlest of kisses all around where he had previously run his finger, ending with a kiss to her palm. It was seductively compelling to watch, and at the same time heartbreaking. She swallowed hard.

Breathing at last, when he sat back up, she braced herself for the inevitable questioning, but it never came. Instead, he stooped the other way and repeated the same thing with the other arm. Stopping and examining the bruising, checking it was the same, his mind seemingly calculating the maths of how she would have got them.

Think, think, think, what could she say to him? Anything but the truth: that his alter ego had tied her to the bed with her own belt and fucked her senseless.

When he sat back up, he was still frowning and lost in thought. His eyes roamed over her body, making her self-conscious. Thankfully, there were only a few thumbprint-sized bruises on her torso left by him being heavy-handed; the worst ones were on her wrist and across her shoulder blades.

"Turn over," he said quietly, but it still made her jump. He didn't look at her face and she was thankful, so she did as he asked.

His calloused hands smoothed across her back as if he wanted to feel any texture to the bruising. But the teeth marks were barely recognisable oval blobs now. He bent his head and kissed them gently. Her heart plummeted. He knew what they were and was kissing them better. It was a reverent act, but felt strange, like a penance. She would have preferred it if he'd just got angry and questioned her about them, instead of this grim, almost ceremonial, overwhelming regret. The pain was coming off him in waves and crashing into her. It was unbearable.

Tears were now soaking the pillow around her face. They were not tears of self-pity, but of what this would do to him – was doing to him, and their relationship together, and whether they could survive it. A sob escaped her before she could stop it.

The bed dipped next to her with the transfer of his weight, and he lay next to her and pulled her to him. He planted kisses all over her head and face in succession in an attempt to take the pain away. But all it did was open the floodgates and the grief poured out of her loudly and without restraint. She sobbed into his chest and all the while he stroked her hair and rocked her, running a hand over the sensitive skin on her back.

When at last the sobs died down, he continued to stroke her over and over in a hypnotic path. It was soothing and lulling and she guessed it was the only thing he could do. He couldn't say he was sorry and would never do it again, because he knew damn well that it was an empty promise he had no idea whether he could keep.

His mouth came down next to her cheek so she could feel his hot breath next to it, hot and hard. Moving hers, she kissed his cheek, feeling it moist with tears, she had no idea whose – probably from them both. She continued to kiss across their tears until she found his mouth, moving slowly, in small circles, over and over, coaxing and asking.

Reluctant at first, Dylan responded gradually, growing in strength and ferocity until they clung together with all their strength, hungrily nipping and biting. Lips, cheeks, neck, everywhere their lips or tongue touched. Plunging and tasting, hoping to find solace, needing to come home, anything to cure this bone-deep pain.

Emotion gave way to lust and they were soon panting and groaning, moving down each other's bodies, sucking and biting on their journey, beyond any likelihood of going back.

Grace rolled onto her back, pulling Dylan with her, scoring his back with her nails and making him gasp. She pushed the waistband of his boxers down until he took over and they were gone; hers quickly followed.

She moaned when his weight forced her legs apart and he suspended his body above her and they looked into each other's eyes for the first time. His eyes looked red and sore, but before she could move her hand to touch his face lovingly, the head of his erection barely nudged her before he sank it home in one long, brutal thrust, making her cry out his name.

There was no time before he established a relentless rhythm. She opened her legs wider to accommodate him, wanting as much of him inside her as she could. It was hard, fierce and almost brutal. It was as though he were marking her totally as his. And with every thrust she began to cry out, not with pain but to welcome it, to welcome him, all of him, even in this animal and savage way – she needed it.

He pistonned into her over and over, hammering himself into her as if to pound away the badness, to take over, pushing himself deeply within her, where only he should be.

"Only you," she panted next to his ear.

And he turned his face to look at her, still grinding into her hard, and for a few seconds, he looked intensely into her eyes. Then he covered her mouth and moaned when their tongues battled and swirled. The build was shockingly swift and their crescendo swamped them over and over. Dylan was all over her when her release vibrated through her, from the tips of her toes to the depths of her soul, and they gradually slowed until they panted in a heap with her arms and legs still pulling him to her, refusing to let him go.

"Dylan!... Dylan!"

Grace's mind came back online and she groggily tried to sit up. It took some moments to realise that she had fallen asleep with Dylan and it was Fenton's voice and angry face glaring round the door at them. He was furious and his eyes looked daggers at her.

Shit, well and truly busted. She shrank back down in the bed.

When she had withered, he turned his attention back to Dylan, who was blinking awake. "Get up … Anton's here. He wants to talk to you."

"Okay… I'm getting up," Dylan said with effort, sitting up and swinging his legs over the side of the bed.

Fenton just kissed his teeth loudly, turned and closed the door behind him.

Dylan bent down, gathered his clothes and began putting them on. Grace lay on her side, running the tips of her fingers over his smooth back.

"He's angry with us," Dylan said, looking over his shoulder at her.

She nodded, feeling a bit guilty. "I wasn't supposed to bring you here."

Dylan paused dressing for a moment, then nodded. It wasn't that hard to work out why. "You'd better get dressed as well. You should probably hear what he has to say."

FIVE MINUTES later and the pair of them stood in Anton's living room; a little ruffled, but there.

"Take a seat." Anton indicated the empty space on the sofa. Fenton and Cerise each sat in an armchair. Anton remained standing centre stage. "Would you prefer the privacy of my study, Dylan?"

Dylan shook his head, "No, I've no secrets from my friends."

Anton nodded, satisfied and took his notes out of a worn cardboard folder. "Okay… on the surface it would appear Dylan presents classic schizophrenic traits: breakdown in the relation between thought, emotion and behaviour, leading to impaired perception of what's real – a withdrawal from reality… But what was most fascinating was his entries in these diaries as a young boy." And he leant forward and passed them back to Dylan, who took them from him awkwardly, as if their mere touch exposed him as crazy.

Grace butted in. "So you don't think it's schizophrenia?" she said, hopefully.

Anton held his hands up and nodded slightly to get her to hold her horses for a second. "It is more likely, from my experience, the entries in the diaries, and indeed the information Cerise was able to give me, that Dissociative Identity Disorder, or DID, would be a more accurate diagnosis."

Everyone stared at him blankly.

"This is where the subject believes that one or more identities exist within themselves. The identities can talk to the person and the person can answer back. And the most significant point to note is that very often the identities are formed to help the subject cope with difficult parts of their life, like a trauma or a tragic event."

Grace looked at Dylan and squeezed his hand in moral support. He looked back at her, answering the unspoken recognition of the facts.

"The identity may show a very different set of values from the subject's core personality." Anton continued, "They lose track of time and can't account for blocks of time during the day. This usually occurs when the identity takes control of the subject and engages in activities or behaviours the subject would not otherwise engage in."

Everything was sounding really damning and Grace and Dylan exchanged looks again. He seemed to be accepting of everything being said. Even Fenton seemed to be agreeing as if everything were making perfect sense and if only they had learnt this years ago.

"It seems all these other cases have loads of personalities; how come Dylan only has one?" Grace demanded, feeling indignant that everyone was taking this prognosis without even challenging it.

Anton smiled at her kindly as if he knew exactly what she was trying to do. "This is only a preliminary diagnosis,

Grace. I would want to have several consultations to make a definite conclusion, but one answer is that his psyche has only needed one so far in which to cope; there is no guarantee that he wouldn't fragment further should the need arise."

She tutted. "But this personality doesn't come out to get him through a job interview or to cope with social situations. He hates people. He hurts them and enjoys it!" Grace shouted with her fists clenched.

Everyone was staring at her in astonishment. Grace reined it in quickly. The last thing she wanted to do was hurt Dylan in front of everyone.

"Chaotic behaviour very often presents itself during periods of intoxication, but again I would need to spend some time with Dylan to get to the bottom of his personality's motivations."

Grace felt exasperated with the non-answer to something she felt was so key to what Dylan had to deal with.

"What's your viewpoint on the change to Dylan's eye colour, Anton?" Cerise said.

Thank you, Cerise. "That's right. I've seen it first hand," Grace agreed, nodding her head.

Dylan was watching each of them in turn, partly in bewilderment, partly in wonder at their defence of him.

Anton took a moment to consider the question. "That, I agree, has puzzled me. To my knowledge, there has never been a case study published where that has happened before. But it has been documented the lengths and cleverness of the mind to perpetuate the separate identity, like one wearing glasses and one not, for instance."

"So you are saying he probably pops in contact lenses?" Fenton said, looking at Dylan, eyebrows up, obviously sceptical.

Dylan shook his head. "I've never found anything like that when I come round."

Fenton agreed. "Yeah, I'm with him in a lot of hotel rooms when he films and when he used to fight, and I never came across anything like that."

Anton looked confused.

"The other one does those things," Dylan explained quietly.

Grace wanted to scream that Dylan was being put through the ringer like this.

"Intriguing… Intriguing," was all Anton could offer to that.

"What about all the maths signs then?"

All eyes shot to Grace.

"Well, how can he not know what they mean if he put them on himself… whichever half did it?"

They all continued to gape at her. She shrugged unapologetically, waiting for her answer.

Anton looked at Fenton for confirmation and he bobbed his head. "He does."

"And he has no recollection of getting them done or why they are there," Grace continued.

Anton pulled some faces while he thought about it. "Interesting. Do you think I could take a look, Dylan?"

Dylan looked left at Grace, then right towards Fenton and stood up. He untucked his T-shirt and pulled it forward over his head, dragging his hair forward and obscuring his face. He ran his fingers back through it and shuffled his feet awkwardly.

"Fascinating," Anton said, walking in an arc around him. "Turn please."

Dylan did as he asked while Anton's eyes wandered over the large eagle on the top of his back, then lower over the sets of brackets and numbers strewn across the rest.

"Do they continue below the waist?" Anton asked.

Dylan looked over his shoulder at him and nodded. "All the way down my legs."

"Do you have any idea what they mean?" Grace asked Anton.

Anton shook his head. "And you have no idea, Dylan?"

"No… I just kept on waking up with more and more of them as soon as I turned eighteen."

"I wonder what the significance of the eagle and the handprint is?" Anton mused while he continued to circle him. "This kind of maths is way beyond me. Do you mind if I ask the opinion of a colleague? He's a physicist."

Dylan shrugged. "Can't hurt, I suppose."

Anton walked over to his landline on the sideboard, picked up the receiver and dialled. "Simon? Do you have a minute?…"

CHAPTER 21

Ten minutes later and Dylan was standing in his Calvins. Thankfully, his experience in the adult film industry meant he wasn't too bothered about standing with next to nothing on. But the subject they were discussing, as if he were a lab specimen, did make him all kinds of uncomfortable.

Professor Simon Kincaid was standing, rubbing his chin next to Anton, both looking over Dylan's strapping physique with eyes only for the numbers.

"Amazing," was all he kept saying.

"Would you like a pencil and paper?" Anton offered.

Grace, Fenton and Cerise were all watching and waiting for Simon to reveal to them the answer to the mystery.

"Do you mind if I photograph them? There could be something I miss."

Dylan motioned with his hand for him to go ahead, so Simon took out his smartphone and began taking pictures of Dylan from all angles.

When he'd finished, all eyes were on him expectantly. Dylan had started to pull on his jeans.

"Can you shed any light, Professor?" Fenton asked.

"Well, it's pretty high-brow stuff and really quite amazing from what I can see… It appears to encompass Chaos and String Theory … incredibly advanced stuff." He was looking closely at Dylan. "And you have no recollection of it?"

"No," Dylan said. "I was good at science at school, but left at sixteen with no qualifications."

"Look, I'll take these pictures and print them out and study them more closely if it's okay with you?"

Dylan nodded with a wan smile that said what choice did he have?

"So you think you know what it means?" Fenton said, getting up and showing the professor to the door.

"Some. It's incredibly advanced. There are some fascinating ideas that I'd love to spend some time over and take a closer look at." He stood and turned back in the doorway. "I'll work on it straightaway and try and get back to you tomorrow, okay?"

"Thanks," Dylan said. "We're on a bit of a time constraint, you know?"

When the professor had gone and Anton followed shortly afterwards, Grace couldn't help hugging into Dylan and asking, "What time constraint, Dylan?"

"I can't trust myself around you, Grace. We can't go on like this."

He looked down into her eyes with such sadness; she swallowed a lump in her throat. "You can't leave me now. We have to do this together," she said vehemently.

He kissed her tenderly. "I'll try to, babe, but the first sign of anything, and I'll have to go."

Staring up at him, she knew it was pointless to argue. All she knew was she couldn't bear to be apart from him.

.   .   .

DYLAN MOVED TOWARDS THE DOOR. "I'll book into a hotel nearby. I think there's a Travel Lodge just up the road."

"You may as well stay here now," Grace said in dismay, much to Fenton's clear annoyance and he pinned her with a tight expression. "What?" she said. "We spent all afternoon together, I don't get what difference it makes?"

Fenton exchanged glances with Cerise and bit his tongue.

Dylan put up a hand. "It's okay… I'll go. I understand."

"Fenton. Make him stay."

Despite clearly being torn, Fenton relented. "No, man, stay." He stood up and walked over to Dylan, hovering by the door, and pulled him into a tight embrace.

Grace sagged in relief.

"I'll be just down the hall," Fenton said quietly and pulled apart, motioning sideways with his head for Cerise to leave with him, but not before he fixed Grace with a meaningful stare. Something along the lines of, 'on your own head be it', passed between them.

They all said quiet goodbyes and Grace and Dylan were left alone.

Dylan wasn't stupid and totally got the awkwardness over where he would stay. He stood with his head hung low on his shoulders, with his hands on his hips. There was nothing Grace or anyone else could do to take away his feelings of wretchedness; the realisation that he wasn't safe for any of them to be around. Instead, she got up and ran into him and wound her arms tightly around his back, laying her cheek against his chest. She was rewarded when she felt his arms slowly come around her and his lips rest on the top of her head.

"I'm not safe to be around… not really." He sounded completely defeated.

"Shh!" She wouldn't hear of him giving up. It just wasn't an option.

"You heard the man, I'm a fucking fruit loop, Grace."

"He didn't exactly say that, Dylan. Let's see what the physics guy comes back with." She pulled away from the warmth of Dylan's chest to look up into his face, taut with worry. "And anyway, if you *are* a fruit loop, then you're my fruit loop," she said with a grin creeping over her face.

Dylan shook his head and pulled her back to him, almost squeezing the life out of her.

DYLAN LEFT SOON after to go and get some food for them. They ate and went to bed early. Both of them were emotionally drained and subdued. They sensed they'd reached a crossroads where there was no going back. Things had to be faced now head-on.

A cuddle in bed, intended to help them go off to sleep, soon escalated into feverish lovemaking. It was the kind that was hard and urgent; all about the passion and the longing each felt for the other.

Dylan never took his eyes from hers. He seemed to know how important it was to ground her with the confirmation of their colour. There were times, she knew, when he fought to keep control. And she wasn't totally sure whether it was an internal battle with Diablo for supremacy or just an animal urge not to be too rough and bury himself deeply to claim her.

When Dylan brought them skilfully to orgasm quite some time later, he moved slowly, undulating his hips while he leaned on his elbows, trying to relieve her of his weight. He pushed back her damp hair from her flushed face with his fingers, then closed the distance between their mouths and kissed her languidly and thoroughly. Her hands glided over his back, covered in a film of sweat.

They gazed into each other's eyes for quite some time

until he took her by surprise; "Did he hurt you... badly?" His eyes blinked slowly in pain as he said the last word.

She knew the question had to come, but remained silent and continued to look into his hypnotic blue gaze. There was no point in lying; he'd seen the bruises. She was surprised he hadn't said anything before. "More terrorised, really."

He nodded slightly as if it were what he expected, but he knew she was holding back.

"He tied me up with my belt."

His eyes were searching hers while she waited, breathing as evenly as she could. She knew he was gauging her. She sensed his tension.

"That was the bruising you saw." She stated the obvious. Somehow, she knew if she could focus his thoughts on that, then perhaps his imagination wouldn't run away too much.

He nodded almost imperceptibly and swallowed. Her own heart began to thump. A muscle ticked in his jaw. He was reining in his anger.

"There wasn't anything I could do." She knew he was joining the dots. He knew Diablo well enough that he would have gone the whole way with her, to spite him if nothing else.

He took a deep breath, closed his eyes to get a grip, got off her slowly and sat on the edge of the bed.

Grace scrambled up after him and laid gentle hands on his bare back. "Please, Dylan... I'm sorry."

"You did nothing to be sorry for," he said, low and deliberate. But he didn't look at her. Instead, he stood and began pulling on his worn jeans.

Tears now brimmed in Grace's eyes and she struggled not to fling herself at him and wail miserably. She felt so guilty. "Where are you going?"

"I need to get out for a while." He walked to the door, pulling his T-shirt on over his head as he went.

Grace was left empty, stunned and scared.

GRACE PASSED the rest of the night fitfully and Dylan didn't come back. At 8.30 a.m. her mobile phone rang. She snatched it up. "Hello?" came out more like a yelp.

"Grace, is that you?"

It took a minute for Grace to get her head around the female voice. "Janey?" She was the last person Grace expected on the end of the phone.

"Yes, of course, it's me, Grace. Are you okay?" We've been worried sick about you. We haven't seen or heard from you in weeks."

Grace sighed and slid back down into the cocooning warmth of the bed covers. "I'm fine," she said on an exhale, "I thought you were someone else, that's all."

"Grace, we've been by your house several times and everyone's been ringing you. Where have you been?"

Right there and then the huge weight of everything became intolerable, and the concern of her dearest friends only served to crack open the floodgates. A sob escaped her.

"Grace… Grace? Come on, you can tell me. You're worrying me now. Did he do something?"

She pulled herself together. Janey was her best friend in the world. She had to trust someone, otherwise she'd go mad. So she began to relay all the events since she'd last seen her on the night her husband Dave had lost it with Dylan outside their house. She included a brief explanation of Dylan's mental disorder – glossed over, and didn't go into graphic details about the sex she'd had with Diablo and her stupidity in going to him when she shouldn't have.

But Janey knew her well; possibly better than any other living soul and she got the point. To her credit, she listened to the bitter end, without interrupting, right up till the events of the night before and Dylan's exit. "Well, if you ask me, he did the right thing," Janey said when she'd finished speaking.

"It doesn't feel like it, Janey. He could be anywhere. What if he doesn't come back?"

"I know, babe, but it shows he loves you. He doesn't want to put you in danger."

Grace knew she was right, but still… life just didn't bear thinking about without him. She doubted it ever would again.

"So what are you gonna do?" Janey said, getting practical.

"Pray he comes back before the professor does, so we can get some answers."

"Well, okay then, babe."

Grace could tell Janey didn't hold out much hope.

"You know where we are, and make sure you give me the address of where you are… just in case… And if you need us, call!" Janey said sternly.

Grace half laughed and half cried, grateful for her friend being there. It warmed her like nothing else. Except maybe… speak of the Devil. Her heart hitched and she sat bolt upright as the door opened. "I will…" she trailed off.

Dylan walked in and glanced at her.

Was he just showing her his eyes? "Gotta go, Janey." She just about caught "Call me" in the distance as she pulled the phone away from her ear and clicked it off absently. Her heart revved dangerously.

Dylan stood a few feet from the bed with noticeable distance and silence between them.

"Where have you been?" she ventured eventually, trying to keep the hint of accusation out of her voice. She didn't want to come across as whiny.

"Hotel up the road," he said quietly, with a bob of his head sideways to indicate the direction.

There followed a gaping great silence after that. Grace

could honestly not think of a single thing to say, except, "I'm glad you came back."

"Just to see the physics bloke," he said, flashing his eyes at her with meaning.

Fuck, then he would be off. Grace swallowed and prayed the guy had something helpful to say, because she sure as hell didn't know how she would stop him from going. And this was when he believed she was faultless with Diablo. What would he do if he ever found out that she'd gone to him willingly?

GRACE PASSED several awkward hours with Dylan, quiet and subdued, until Anton returned with Simon, the physics expert. Fenton and Cerise joined them. Everyone was eager to find out what he had to say.

Grace sadly watched as Dylan sat as far away from her as possible and didn't look over at her once. She swallowed down a lump in her throat and turned her attention to Simon, who stood with his back to the fireplace, the central point of the room.

"Apologies for keeping you waiting," he said cheerfully. "But I wanted to get a second opinion from a colleague who has made String Theory his absolute expertise." He put his hands up in front of him. "I didn't divulge the source of the information."

"Did he come up with anything?" Fenton said, steering him back to the point.

Simon looked amazed and then frowned as if Fenton really didn't get it and should of. "Come up with anything? If this proves correct, it could be the breakthrough of the century."

Grace looked around and everyone else did the same.

"Perhaps you could explain it as simply as you can for us lesser mortals," Anton joked.

Simon laughed. "Of course," He began to open his brief-case, pulled out a clipboard and on it he quickly drew some long, wavy lines and circles like doughnuts here and there. Then he held it up, smiling.

Everyone still stared at him blankly.

"String Theory," he said, grinning widely, looking at everyone in turn. "The first theory ever to be the answer to everything." He allowed a pause for effect. "And if what Dylan has on his body is correct... no longer a theory." Another pause.

Grace looked around to make sure everyone else was following because she sure as hell wasn't.

"You're gonna have to spell it out a bit, Doc," Fenton said, shaking his head.

"Okay," Simon said, perching on the arm of an armchair. "String Theory explains everything from the very large, i.e. the universe and beyond, and the very small – smaller than atomic particles."

"Absolutely everything is made up of strings that move and vibrate. Even our universe is encompassed in a membrane or Brane as we call them, and instead of going off in all directions into infinity, it is actually a very large string, and could be one of many strings," and he pointed to his crude diagram. "And some forming circles. But in order for this theory to work, it can no longer function in just four dimensions but would require a minimum of ten. So in fact there could be infinite Branes, containing an infinite number of universes. Some could support life like our own or contain nothing at all. The possibilities are endless. The mind simply boggles," he said wistfully.

"Sorry, Doctor, but can you tell us what all those universes have to do with what Dylan has on his body?"

Cerise asked, pointing to the diagram Simon was holding like the World Cup next to his face.

Simon relaxed a little and smiled ruefully. "Well, I have no idea why Dylan should have pure maths decorating his entire body, but what I do know is this: that just like the strings vibrating in the smallest of particles, the membranes existing in other dimensions and containing other universes do the same on a massive scale. In other words, they collide to varying degrees… possibly solving the mystery of the sudden extinction of the dinosaurs, but almost definitely the cause of the Big Bang starting all life as we know it."

"You see another dimension could be mere millimetres from our noses," he said with delight, looking round at everyone. "Don't you see?… There must be instances when they pass so close that if you know where to go, and have enough electromagnetic energy, you could actually move across, or jump between them."

It was at that point that Grace got the significance of what he was saying and suddenly looked across at Dylan. He must have got the point at exactly the same time as he looked back at her. A moment of total understanding passed between them. The diaries. The spaceman. It fit, it so fucking fit.

Dylan faced Simon again. "So the numbers… they're telling the story of how someone came here from another dimension?"

"No," Simon said, adamantly. "It is telling us how to go from this world to another. It not only says it's possible, but the group of numbers I didn't recognise at first, tells us where."

A deathly silence fell over the room.

"They were coordinates… we know exactly when and where it will happen," Simon said, laughing in his excitement.

Grace and Dylan looked at each other again in shock. This could be it. This could be the answer to all their prayers. Could it actually be true?

"Come, come now, Simon," Anton said, rising from his chair to try and calm everyone down and get sensible. "I'm not sure all this is beneficial to Dylan. It is my opinion that he suffers from Dissociative Identity Disorder, and filling him with false hope would not be beneficial to his therapy and gaining a normal life. Typically, this kind of disorder presents itself as a coping mechanism after an extreme trauma such as losing a close friend, as was the case for Dylan when he was a boy."

Grace had heard enough and scrambled to her feet. "No, Anton. Don't you get it? Didn't you read the diaries?"

"Yes, of course..." Anton tried to sound sympathetic, but his tone said only frustration.

But Grace cut across him. "What if what Simon said actually happened? What if someone passed between the worlds when Dylan was a boy, and that person has been living inside him ever since? What if all this... everything that Dylan has been through, has been in order for that person to get back?" It all sounded fantastic; too fantastic for anyone to get their head around and actually believe, but nothing had been real or ordinary in the whole time she'd known Dylan.

She looked over at him, watching her like he adored her in that moment. Hell, he didn't even believe it. "Dylan, think about it," she said, running over and dropping to her knees in front of him, then picking up his hands. "Remember how you felt as a kid. Remember how convinced you were then... that he was a separate person to you?" She was vaguely aware of Anton's exasperation behind her.

Grace watched as Dylan tried to remember – tried to think of the time when everything wasn't so jumbled up.

He smiled and then frowned, as if he were warring with his own logic.

"Please, Dylan… for us… try?"

He didn't seem convinced, but gave her a small rueful smile. "On one condition," he said, facing Simon again, his face dark and implacable. "No one must know about this… No fuss."

Simon nodded emphatically. "You have my word."

"When does it say… when will it happen again?"

"In two weeks," Simon said in wonder. "Just two weeks."

Whether or not Dylan truly believed it or was just humouring her, Grace didn't care. The fact that he was willing to fight for them was enough. To think they could have missed it, a chance at normality gone for ever. "Where?" she said as the thought suddenly occurred to her.

"Aberdeen in Scotland."

A few phone calls later and Anton had rented a house not far from the coordinates, about an hour into the countryside from Aberdeen. The university there had a good Physics Department too, Simon informed them. Dylan had stipulated his terms privately, to which Simon had agreed. Simon would have done anything to be in on the discovery of the century and quickly cleared his diary, determined to accompany them. The truth was, they couldn't do it without him.

Fenton and Cerise had argued. Fenton didn't want Cerise anywhere near Dylan these days. Least of all when it was a certainty that Diablo would surface. But she stood her ground, making the case that Grace shouldn't be the only woman there. Grace suspected that she was as concerned for Fenton as he was for her. Arrangements were quickly made for the kids. They would be away for two weeks, so it was agreed they would go to her sister's house in West London.

Relief flooded Grace when Dylan gravitated to her and put his arm about her shoulders as if the night before never happened. It was as though the new revelation made everything seem different – That there was now hope. Well, she was totally into that and snuggled into the heat of his body. However he reasoned it, she knew that whatever the outcome, she was in it for keeps with him.

When all the bickering died down, arrangements were finalised, and Fenton came back from dropping the kids off, they boarded a plane from London Gatwick to Aberdeen. From there, they piled into a rented large seven-seater, four-wheeled drive. It would take them to the holiday cottage Anton had rented them near the village of Braemar, just over an hour's drive from the airport.

It was starting to get dark during the journey. The atmosphere was charged, partly with excitement and antici-pation, but for Grace, it was apprehension. After all, no one really knew whether any of this would work, and the conse-quences of that didn't even bear thinking about. She looked at the serious faces intent on the road ahead of them. This was important, one way or another, to every single one of them. That kind of pressure didn't lend itself to chatter. So instead she stared out onto the greying countryside; its rugged beauty soothing her jagged nerves.

Pitch dark now, the car whined as it climbed the windy lanes till it eventually reached the large grey-stoned cottage. It had to be big, she reasoned, there were six of them. Situ-ated quite a way outside the envelope of the village, it looked bleak and imposing and not at all cosy.

It was getting quite late when they finally pulled onto a worn, rutted driveway next to the cottage that went the length of the right-hand side of the house. They finally came to a halt in front of a line of unkempt bushes and a rickety shed towards the back. The garden was surrounded partially by a low wall, a wire fence and bushes dotted sparsely here and there. A little stone path led from the road up to the small green front door. A feeling of foreboding shadowed her heart again. The windows seemed soulless and black despite the newly painted white sashes.

Trying to shake her sensation of unease off, she went to grab her holdall from the boot, but Dylan took it from her. She trudged along the little path behind him.

Anton opened the door with a key left under a stone in a flowerpot, went in and switched on the light. They all trooped in after him. It smelt musty in the way all holiday homes did when they've been shut up for a long time. It was sparsely furnished but adequate. The gloomy lights did nothing to cheer the place up. It was clean, though.

"There are four bedrooms," Anton was saying, while he led the way up the narrow staircase that divided the house into two from the middle.

A pang of fear stabbed the centre of her chest. *Four bedrooms, would Dylan sleep with her? Or would he bunk in with one of the other single men?* Her nerves were in shreds. She wasn't sure if she could take that kind of rejection right now.

Anton allocated the bedrooms as they all reached the top landing. There was another smaller staircase leading up into the loft. "You two can take that room. It's the biggest and most private," he said, averting his gaze with embarrassment.

Grace stood in a daze, rooted to the spot and hugging her handbag to her chest.

"Do you want me to sleep somewhere else?" Dylan's quiet voice came from behind her.

Coming out of her daydream, she turned. "Do you want to?"

"No." His voice was steady; his gaze was as brooding and intense as ever.

After staring at him for a long moment and without saying anything further, she turned and walked slowly up the little staircase and felt him following behind her.

The room was large, covering most of the area of the

house. There was a double bed against the centre of the opposite wall, a small wardrobe and dressing table and a door to the right leading to a small shower room.

Grace perched on the edge of the bed, still clutching her bag to her. Dylan dropped their stuff down onto the floor and never took his eyes off her. He was concerned, she could tell. He walked slowly over to her and stopped; stooped down and prised her fingers from her bag and let it drop on the floor next to the bed. He pulled her up to standing, placed his hands on either side of her face and tilted her head so she had to look up at him. His eyes – his beautiful blue eyes, the colour of duck eggs – scrutinised her. "What's changed?" she said, not helping the hint of scorn in her voice.

He paused before answering, as if registering the 'ouch', then nodded a little as if accepting he deserved it. "Nothing."

It felt like a slap. Hurt made her persevere. "You didn't want to spend last night with me, what's different tonight, apart from a lack of beds?" she finished spitefully.

He frowned without biting and ran his thumb gently along her cheekbone, which made her feel the worst kind of person. Nothing was his fault; she was just lashing out.

"I'm sorry," he said eventually. "I was angry… I was scared I'd hurt you again."

Shit. He lived in turmoil all the time. She was getting just the smallest glimpse of the internal battle he faced every day, and she was punishing him on top of all that.

Yesterday, he believed *he* hurt her, albeit unwittingly. Today, everything was different. There could be a chance, however fantastic it sounded, that it wasn't him at all. That all the shit and bad things he'd put up with since he was a boy were not down to him. It must be a huge weight off him.

A tear rolled down her cheek. His eyes followed it and he caught it on his thumb.

"We have to believe this is true, Dylan," she said on a sob.

He got what she meant immediately and nodded slowly. They both needed it to be true. His mouth closed the distance between them and he kissed her softly. She melted into him and pushed her tongue into his mouth while her need seared through her.

Suddenly, he stopped and staggered back. He shook his head and reeled again as if he were drunk.

"What?… What is it, Dylan?" she said, grabbing his forearms to stop him from stepping further backwards into the bed.

His hands went up to his face. He groaned.

"Dylan!" she shouted in panic, trying to pull his hands away from his face.

He shook his head again and turned away from her. She ran around him, not letting him escape.

His eyes flashed open. She hitched a breath. Cruel, narrowed, brown eyes glared back at her.

His eyelids closed slowly and he shook his head again and his legs gave way.

She screamed. All she could do was watch, not knowing whether to run and find one of the others or help him back onto his feet. Refusing to bow to her fear, she bent down and went to gently touch his arm.

"Get away!" Dylan shouted, and his eyes opened and flashed with blue.

She jumped back in shock, while he stood slowly holding his head.

"My pills," he croaked, and pointed a shaky hand towards his holdall.

She rushed over, dropped to her knees and pulled back the zipper. She rummaged, not having a clue where they might be amongst the jumble of clothes.

"Side pocket," he rasped, grabbing his head again.

She fumbled with clumsy fingers inside the separate

pocket and took out two thin strips and a brown bottle. "Which ones?' she cried, turning her head to him.

"The little ones… in the strip."

She ejected the tiny pill from the foil and almost dropped it in her haste, but caught it again. She quickly passed it to him, then rushed into the small bathroom, ran the basin tap and came back with a small glass of water.

Dylan had already swallowed the tablet, but drank the water anyway. Then he sat on the bed as if his legs were still unsteady. He appeared to be trying to get his breathing back to normal.

Grace watched him intently, not moving a muscle. It seemed to be passing. "Are you okay?" she asked cautiously, inching closer to him.

He nodded. "I nearly lost it, Grace. He's so strong… stronger than ever." He shook his head in misery. "I don't know how much longer…" he said, trailing off.

She took the final step closer, no longer scared of him, and pulled his head into her chest. Her arms rested on his shoulders and her cheek on his head.

He remained there for what felt like ages, letting her run her fingers through his hair. Heat radiated through his skin as if he'd been running. It never occurred to her how this constant battle must take its toll on him physically.

Eventually, she took a step away from him and picked up his hand. "Come on… let's take a shower. It will cool you down and relax you."

He paused for a second, then stood and allowed her to lead him like a small child. When they reached the bathroom, he stood placidly while she popped the button on his jeans and pushed them down. She efficiently undressed him, then shucked her own clothes in seconds.

She turned the shower dial and felt the spray until she

was sure that the shower was warm and not too hot. Then she pulled him into the cubicle with her.

They stood facing each other and she grabbed the shower gel, squeezed the blue liquid and rubbed it between her hands. Now full of suds, they travelled all over the smooth skin of his torso, following the lines of his tattoos and ridges of muscle. When his eyes closed and he gave himself over to the pleasure of being touched, she lathered her hands again and began a slow worship of his entire body.

When she went to grab the soap again, his hand stopped her. "Let me."

She paused and drew back her hand.

"Turn," he said, quietly.

She did as she was told and felt his rough hands, now slippery with soap, massage away all the stress of the last few days. Soon his hands found their way around her rib cage where he cupped her breasts and pulled her in close to him. She felt his erection hard like iron against her backside. She rested her head back against him. "Dylan," she whispered.

Before she had time to relax, her head was jolted and she was shoved violently against the cold tiled wall. Shocked into compliance, his foot kicked her legs apart.

Her cheek was stinging next to the tiles after the impact when his mouth found hers, smothering her yelp as his fingers found her wetness between her legs, and he pushed himself deeply inside her.

Her eyelids fluttered open to find his eyes narrowed with pleasure and the colour of azure blue. Her confusion must have registered as he bit her neck hard to bring her mind back to him.

She desperately wanted to stop him or slow him down, to let her catch up with what was actually happening, but there was no time. He flipped her around to face him and then knocked the air out of her as he smacked her against the wall again.

One of her legs were lifted over his arm and his other sought the heat of her and dragged his fingers through her wetness. She gasped and he groaned, then he bent his knees, placed himself and resumed pumping as hard and fast as he was before. Then he slowed to long strokes, hitting her so deeply she was forced to pant in time with them. Briefly, the others in the house popped into her mind. Then, as if he read her lack of concentration, he bit into her shoulder and lifted her other leg, taking her full weight and pushing her legs around him to clamp around his back.

Her fear was dissipating. It was Dylan, but not Dylan. But it felt so good. She was building, and he knew it, and he wedged her into the corner to put his full weight into her and slowed but remained so hard, so good so … "Dylan!" she screamed.

Her orgasm exploded all over her and he pushed himself deep and held her gyrating in small circles, creating total friction on her engorged bud. She continued to mewl, gone to all reason.

Dylan gradually slowed and she felt his breath hard on her face as he sagged onto her, pinning her so she still couldn't move. Her hands meandered over his back and into his hair, but she was troubled. What had just happened? Was he losing himself so he didn't know who he was any more?

Then she was roughly turned again and felt a sharp sting as he smacked her right buttock. The sound reverberated around the tiled room. But instead of being horrified, after the initial shock, she found warmth flooding between her legs.

"Yeah," he whispered, feeling her there with his fingers.

Shit, she'd thought he'd finished – clearly not.

He pulled her away from the wall and pushed her head

down so she had to touch her toes and entered her swiftly again. No longer satisfied with the depth or friction, he clasped her hands behind her back and twisted them slowly, creating leverage by pushing her chest out and himself deeper still.

Oh, my god! she muttered. Dylan had never been this deep, this rough, this totally dominating.

When her sheath muscles began to spasm again, he groaned. "Fuck, yeah!" He released her arms and braced them on the handholds on the wall while he hammered into her. The orgasm that hit her then swept over her totally.

His arms linked in front of her abdomen, he pulled her onto his lap and held her tightly, wringing every last sensation from her. And just when she thought she would pass out from the strength of it, he bent forward and massaged her swollen bud with his finger, and bit her shoulder blade so hard he must have drawn blood.

At that point, her legs gave way, her brain shorted out, and he caught her.

When Grace came to, she was wrapped in towels in the bed, enveloped in Dylan's arms while he slept soundly. The bedside lamp was still on, bathing the room in a soft glow. She freed her hand from the swaddling and reached for her phone and tilted it so she could see the time: 1.30 a.m.

Lifting Dylan's heavy arm, she wriggled free and discarded the towel over the side of the bed, got back in and faced him. He was at peace. Breathing softly, his chest gently rising and falling. There was no sign of the dangerous character that lurked within him.

Grace ran through the evening's events over and over, and passed a disturbed night with barely any sleep. At least she thought she had, but when she awoke and it was light, Dylan's side of the bed was empty.

Fear clutched her heart for a second, but then she remembered he probably woke early and went for his run.

She sat up. Her head spun for a moment, probably because she'd had so little sleep. Swinging her legs over the edge of the bed, she padded to the bathroom and pulled the light cord. After using the loo quickly, she turned to the mirror over the basin to see how deathly she looked.

Shit! She put her fingertips to her cheek. There, right on the bone, was an oval-shaped bruise about two inches long, varying from shades of blue to deep purple in the middle. *Fuck! fuck! fuck!* She racked her brains. Mind-blowing sex though it was, it worried her. His eyes had been blue the whole time, but the way he'd moved with her – hard and unyielding, he felt more like Diablo than Dylan. That, she couldn't shake off. And that wasn't the only worry: what would this do to him if he saw her bruises? He'd send her away for sure, for her own safety. She shook her head. There was no way she would let him do that. Twisting her body, she tried to get a look at her right shoulder blade. There it was. A perfect set of teethmarks in scarlet with blue bruising coming out all around it. At least she could cover it with her clothes.

Right, cover it! She dressed as fast as she could, then raked around in her bag and found her make-up. Then she set about covering the bruising on her face. *Thank god for concealer.* And despite the tendrils of unease creeping through her, she resolved to sweep the whole episode under the carpet – at least for the time being. She simply wouldn't allow him to push her away.

When she'd finished, she scrutinised herself in the mirror to make sure it was covered from all angles. If you really got up close, you could just make it out, but a light dusting of blusher and it was good to go. She crammed her make-up bag into her handbag. Regular touch-ups would be needed today.

The door opened and Dylan walked back in. She'd been right; he'd been running. He was hot and sweaty and his eyes regarded her intensely, as if he were giving her the once-over. She forced a smile so he didn't think anything was up, but couldn't help wondering if he knew he'd been too rough with her. She couldn't think about that now.

"We'd better hurry and have breakfast, Simon wants to leave soon," he said.

Simon was driving them into Aberdeen to the university to confer with his friend in the Physics Department. There, they would decide what was to be done. It was a big day.

Dylan took less than ten minutes to shower and dress. Meanwhile, Grace gathered the things she wanted to take with them, like a pen and notepad and, of course, Dylan's diaries, which she thought were crucial to what they were trying to do.

"Everything they need is on me," Dylan said, with a small smile, referring to his many tattoos.

She stilled to take him all in. *God, he was gorgeous*. As troubled as she was, she just couldn't help herself. "Come on," she said, smiling back. There was absolutely no hint of the turbulence in him from the night before, so she put it to the back of her mind.

When they got downstairs, everyone else was ready to go. They ate a hurried breakfast of toast and tea and piled into the four-wheel drive and set off to Aberdeen.

An hour and a half later and they were seated in a small room in the Physics Department of Aberdeen University, amongst the many books and diagrams on the walls. Nicholas Cornell, PhD had excitedly welcomed them and explained that he was a lifelong friend of Simon's and was thrilled to be included in what they were trying to do.

"Simon emailed me some photocopies of the symbols on your body, Dylan. And a small part of your diary and, quite honestly, it is astounding," he said mildly, shaking his head in disbelief.

"Can you solve it, Doctor? Can you do something for us?" Fenton asked.

Grace looked at Fenton briefly, and for a second, it hit her how he loved Dylan. This was as important to him as it was to her.

Her eyes went back to Nicholas, who was getting up from

behind his desk and walking over to his whiteboard on the left wall of the room.

"The complex mathematics on Dylan's body does not need solving. It is complete," he said, scribbling some letters and numbers, then underlining it in a flourish as if he were teaching some students. "The Theory of Everything in its entirety!" He looked around at everyone's blank faces with an incredulous grin. "Something some of the greatest minds in the world have dreamt of. The only thing we need to do now is rendezvous at a particular place in space and time... and wait."

Dylan, who had been silent throughout, spoke for the first time. "Can you get him out of me?" he said, sounding impatient.

Grace looked at Dylan. Of course, it was what mattered to him. She focused back on Nicholas, who had begun to speak again.

"According to this..." And he underlined his equation on the whiteboard again. "We have slightly less than two weeks. I have conferred with Simon and we have an idea from the sketchy blueprints that were in the diaries. We can build it, but not alone."

"Blueprints?" Grace said, confused.

"The diagrams," Dylan said quietly, as if it was only just making sense to him.

Grace remembered the weird drawings at the back of the diaries.

"The thing is, we need to publish this to get the funding we need ... blow it open wide," Simon was saying.

"No way!" Dylan said. "You gave me your word."

"And I have kept it, not a soul knows I'm here, but this is huge," Simon tried to reason. "You have no idea."

"Wait!" Fenton said, putting up his hand to Dylan for a minute. "Build what?"

Nicholas faced the board again and began to draw squiggly lines. "Imagine this Brane is where our universe inhabits, and this one, a neighbouring one. And they are constantly oscillating. At the point Dylan speaks of in his diaries, this one came within a hair's-breadth of us, and a living being was pushed through by the enormous electromagnetic energy created," he said, looking around to make sure everyone was with him so far.

"So you think it will be as easy as that?" Dylan said angrily. "That he'll just walk out? He's fought tooth and nail to stay here all these years."

Grace reached over and touched Dylan's arm. He looked at her, but his mind was still preoccupied.

"Dylan, let's just hear what he has to say, okay?" she said softly.

The physicists looked at each other, then at Anton, who had just been a spectator up until that point. Everything depended on Dylan being on board with all of this before they started the presumably expensive process.

"Why would Diablo leave instructions to do this if he didn't want to go?" Anton said quietly.

Grace studied his face. Although Anton appeared to be backing them up, she could tell he was still using reasoning from a purely psychiatric point of view.

"Maybe he couldn't survive in this world without you," Simon added. "Perhaps inhabiting you has purely been a case of survival?"

"Indeed, in his dimension, they may not even inhabit fleshly bodies," Nicholas said.

"Like spirits?" Grace said.

"Maybe. Who's to know if our nearest neighbours aren't the spirit realm or the heavens that we have long sought to contact?"

It was all too fantastic, and Grace shook her head to clear

it. She turned to Dylan and picked up his hand, knowing his anger came from it all seeming so unrealistic and far-fetched. "What do we have to lose?" she said to him quietly.

He took a deep breath and nodded, not convinced. "Guess so."

There was nowhere left for them to go after this and he knew it. She squeezed his hand.

Simon coughed as if what he was about to say was uncomfortable for him. "There is just one thing."

Everyone looked at him and waited.

Grace's pulse increased.

"We can create an electromagnetic field at the exact spot with the help of our engineering department, that's no problem ..."

"But?" said Fenton.

Simon looked guiltily at Nicholas for backup.

Nicholas continued for him. "We are still unsure how exactly the entity will leave you or, indeed, if we will have enough power. There was a thunderstorm on the night he came. There is no guarantee we will have the same conditions."

"So you are saying it might not work?" Fenton said, starting to sound angry.

Grace glanced at Dylan, who was looking decidedly hostile. "He means he can't tell which one of us will get kicked out."

THERE WAS a moment's delay and then consternation erupted with everyone talking at the same time. Simon held out his arms to try to hush everyone.

"Is that right?" Fenton said.

Nicholas nodded guiltily and then everyone was talking again.

"Let him speak!" Simon shouted. "You all have to understand that this is virgin territory for us. We've never attempted anything like this before."

"What can we do?" Fenton said, bewildered.

"We've talked about it at great length, and we've conferred with Anton concerning Dylan's personality traits, and we feel the safest guarantee for this to work is for Diablo to be the one conscious throughout."

"Don't forget Diablo is an interloper. Dylan is the host and bound to the very fabric of his DNA. If we have enough power to extract anyone, we are pretty certain it will be the entity," Nicholas added.

Everyone was talking and arguing. Grace saw Dylan clench his fists so his knuckles became white. He got up and stormed from the room. Grace stood, unsure whether to follow. "Can you build it in time?" she said to Simon and Nicholas.

They both nodded.

"I've talked to the engineers, who are working on a blueprint as we speak. They say we can have it in place and tested by the 16th."

She nodded and went to walk to the door.

"There is one more thing," Nicholas said.

She stopped and turned, not sure she wanted to hear any more bad news.

"Even if the entity leaves Dylan's body, we have no way of knowing what damage the process will do to Dylan."

"What, physically?" Grace said.

He nodded. "Or how much of the Dylan you know will be left behind."

"So this could kill him?" Fenton said.

Simon shook his head. "To be honest with you, we just don't know."

"We'll give you and Dylan till tomorrow morning to

decide, before we start work. You need to be completely clear on the risks involved."

Grace looked around at all the eyes on her, hers brimming with tears. She swallowed and left the room.

"Wait up," Grace said, out of breath from running.

Dylan was striding purposefully ahead to who knew where, completely oblivious to her trying to catch up with him.

She yanked back on his arm. "Where are you going?" She held it tight and dug her heels in to force him to spin around to face her.

He didn't answer. His face was a tight mask, but his blue eyes radiated the anger that bubbled under the surface.

"Please, Dylan, don't run. We need to talk about this."

He went to turn and pull out of her grip.

"Stop!" she shouted. "What are you afraid of?"

When he turned back, his eyelids were low with a contempt that shocked her for a second. "If you don't want to do it, we can carry on as we are... I don't want to lose you," she said more quietly. She was fighting every instinct in her not to selfishly fall to pieces.

Dylan's face went from amazement to confusion, then finally disgust. "That's not an option," he said flatly.

"What then?" She still held his arm as if he would run away, not fully understanding his animosity towards her.

"Look at your fucking cheek, Grace."

She hitched a breath and snatched her hand up to her face, where she had covered the bruising earlier. *Shit.* She'd forgotten to check it was still hidden. Desperate for things not to spiral out of control, she put her hands up to touch his face. "It could be all over soon, Dylan, don't you want to believe that?"

He shook his head slowly. "You don't get it, do you?"

"Get what?" His defeatist mood was every bit as scary as Diablo appearing.

"That I don't know what's me and what's him any more." And he went to pull away and continue walking.

She held onto his arm. "It was you last night, Dylan, wasn't it… your eyes were blue?"

He paused as if trying to remember. His brow furrowed and he shook his head. "Yes… no… FUCK! he shouted, and he pulled out of her grip.

Grace jumped at his outburst, then stood hurt and dejected, her hands flopped down to her sides. "So that's it, you're giving up?"

He turned back and regarded her closely, then sagged wearily as if beaten. "The lines are so blurred now, Grace, and have been for a long time. Even if they get something out of me, how will we know what will be left?"

PRETTY SOON, everyone met at the car. They piled in, but the mood was sombre, and they spoke little on the way back to the cottage. Dylan brooded and Grace watched him closely, terri-fied if he decided to go through with it and terrified if he did not.

A meal was rustled up quickly when they got back, but no one really had an appetite. The atmosphere was awkward. Everyone was in their own place of turmoil, but no one wanted to voice it for fear of upsetting Dylan.

Grace was grateful when it got so unbearable that Dylan excused himself and said he wanted a lie down, and she could follow him up.

Neither spoke while they shed their clothes and got into the bed, exhausted. They both lay facing each other. Dylan reached out a hand and traced his finger over the bruise on her cheekbone, now clearly visible.

"We need to come to a decision," she whispered, needing the skin contact but hating that the bruise was going to affect how he thought.

His face turned dark as if he'd read her mind. "I'm not afraid of death, Grace. Fuck knows, I've prayed for it often enough... but I won't leave him behind... with you." He closed his eyes as if the mere thought brought him chills. Then he opened them again and pinned her with his intense blue stare to emphasise his point.

Grace went to protest, but Dylan put his finger to her lips to hush her. "You don't get to make this decision for me," he said, a slow smile creeping across his face.

She sagged in defeat. He was right, of course. "What will you do then?" She dreaded his answer either way.

He nodded. "As long as Simon and everyone else involved never breathes a word about my connection with the experiment, I'm gonna do it... I always imagined I'd have to top myself one day, anyway."

She went to open her mouth to rail against what he was saying, but he stopped her. "But..." he continued, "no matter what Simon and Nicholas say tomorrow about how it's going to be okay, I'm gonna insist on two things." His gaze was penetrating and he paused to make sure he had her full attention.

She swallowed hard, preparing herself. "What?" Her heart began to hammer in her chest. "Please, Dylan... bloody hell, just tell me."

"I don't want you anywhere near when it happens."

"What?" she said in dismay, and she tried to sit up, but he held her shoulder down so she was forced to hear him out. "How can you say that after everything we..." she trailed off and tears welled in her eyes and began to stream down her cheeks. "I have to be there," she sobbed.

He shook his head. "No you don't." His face was implacable. There was no negotiating this one.

Then she remembered the second condition: "What was the other thing?"

He pulled her in close to his body, but recognising it as a distraction, she struggled out of his arms to look into his eyes, so impossibly and beautifully blue. "You're scaring me now, Dylan."

He hesitated as if he were memorising her face. "I won't let him stay, Grace."

She stared blankly at him, trying to get a thread on what he meant. Then horror struck her and she began to shake her head. "No… no you can't."

"Shh," Dylan soothed and tried to gather her into his arms, but she refused to be placated.

"They are scientists, Dylan, they won't agree to murder," and she clung to that thought.

Dylan pushed a lock of hair out of her angry face and smiled with regret. "No," he agreed, "but Fenton will."

CHAPTER 24

The next few days were spent in a constant whirl of toing and froing from the university. While Dylan was poked, prodded and measured, his medicine was administered by injection, so there was no chance that Diablo could tamper with it or affect Dylan taking it. His heart rate and breathing were monitored, so everything was prepared and the machine calibrated specifically for him. The 16th of the month loomed like Doomsday.

Grace supported Dylan in every way she could, shamelessly trying to make herself indispensable, so he wouldn't send her away, even trying to use Cerise and Fenton as allies, but Dylan would have none of it and neither would Fenton. He would take no chances with Cerise and she was to be exiled as well.

With only a few days to go, Grace captured Fenton on his own when Dylan was out for his morning run. Used to waking up early to train with Dylan, he was busy making fresh coffee. He looked over his shoulder as he sensed her walk into the kitchen. "Coffee?"

"Please," she answered, and took a seat at the large pine table in the centre of the room.

Fenton brought over two cups and sat opposite her at the table. They sipped their drinks in silence for a few moments. Fenton, she knew, was not given to being overly talkative at the best of times, let alone when someone they both loved could quite possibly be committing suicide in a few days.

Grace studied Fenton as he blew over the top of his coffee, not sure how she was going to broach the subject, and looked back over the short time she'd known him. How she'd grown from assuming he was a no-good villain to seeing him as a trusted friend who could be relied on.

"What's on your mind, Angel?" he said, with a mischievous smile.

"Why do you call me that?" she said with a frown. It had bugged her the whole time she'd known him.

He chuckled. "It bothers you?"

"Only that he... You know, Diablo... calls me that. I just wondered what it is you see in me that he seems to, too?" She swallowed and looked down at her nails while he scrutinised her.

He exhaled. "The thing is— Grace," he corrected. "The minute I clapped eyes on you, I knew what Dylan saw in you."

Her eyes snapped up to his. "Dylan or Diablo?"

"Both... it makes no difference."

Now she was confused.

"You see, Dylan *thinks* he's evil and Diablo is evil. That doesn't make for a lot of difference with the people they're attracted to."

Grace waited for him to elaborate.

"You are so far out of their circle. You look squeaky clean, you live a good, wholesome life."

"Boring," she added.

Fenton was shaking his head. "No, darling... You are everything Dylan would love to be a part of, and everything Diablo would love to corrupt. Even the way you look – fresh and peachy." He shook his head, laughing. "Yep, the minute I saw you."

Grace was speechless for quite a few moments. It did make frightening sense. She wasn't entirely sure she liked that Dylan saw her like that. It irked her that it had more to do with a reaction to his life and what it stood for, and less to do with him finding her hot and sexy.

When an image of Dylan rolling around with Serena slammed into her head, she pushed the subject from her mind with a huff.

"But that wasn't what you came in here to talk to me about, was it. Spit it out, girl," Fenton said, raising his eyebrows with amusement dancing in his eyes.

"I can't believe he's making me go?" she said, avoiding looking at him in the eyes.

"Ah, come on, Angel. Give him a break. What can he do, huh?"

Grace felt foolish knowing that Fenton was right. But it was infuriating at the same time. She tried to swallow down her emotion that seemed to live so near the surface these days, failed miserably, and her eyes filled with tears. She wiped them away irritably with her fingers. "I may lose him and he wants to send me away?"

Fenton appeared to soften slightly and reached for her hand. "But this ain't about you, darling, is it... He needs his head in the game, and he can't if you're there."

She glared at Fenton sulkily, knowing he was right and she was being selfish.

Fenton let his words sink in for a moment and watched her closely. "Why don't you go stay with one of your friends?"

She held his eyes, looking kindly at her and nodded. "I'll probably go to Janey's."

He squeezed her hand. "Good." Then he appeared to consider something.

"What?"

"Oh, it's nothing... I was just thinking, you could pay a visit to his mum if you wanted. I'm sure Dylan wouldn't mind. Might make you feel better... You know, be closer to him?"

Grace looked deeply into Fenton's eyes. *Was he palming her off?* He looked sincere. It was a good idea if she had to leave.

Then she saw a flicker of uncertainty flash across his face. Was she to deliver the heartbreaking news? Like one of those TV shows where someone's long-lost son was never coming home. *He knows.* "Has he asked you yet?" she blurted. Finally, the real reason for the conversation. Her blood ran cold with the realisation that Dylan had already made his bargain with him.

Fenton only paused in surprise for a beat at the abruptness of the question, but recovered his composure quickly and nodded slowly.

Shit, he has asked him. She knew there was only so much Fenton would tell her before he clammed up. "Do Nicholas and Simon know what you two have planned?"

He shook his head slowly, "Nope."

She just couldn't help herself; "And when it comes down to it, you think you can do it?" she asked angrily.

Fenton looked around him with impatience, as if she didn't get something basic. He fixed her dead in the eye and she knew it would be the last he'd say on the subject. "Yes... I will do it. I will do it for Dylan. Because if it comes to it, Angel, it won't be Dylan, it will be Diablo, severely pissed off, who is a cold-hearted, psychotic bastard, who will enjoy terrorising us all when he can no longer be suppressed… For fuck's sake, think about it. He didn't get his name by accident." And with that, he stood up, scraping his chair. He walked to the sink, rinsed his cup under the tap and walked past her and out of the room.

Grace was left stunned.

It was the evening of the 11th. Tomorrow, Dylan was to come off his medication, allowing Diablo to come to the fore. Grace was to leave to go to Janey's. Cerise would accompany her and split up when they reached London to go and spend some time with the kids.

Tonight, Fenton had booked a table for everyone else in town, giving them the house to themselves. Grace was grateful to Fenton for the alone time.

Dylan showered upstairs while Grace cooked them an intimate dinner for two – pasta and salad. She was no Delia in the kitchen and she sure as hell didn't want to waste any of their precious time cooking.

Dylan walked into the kitchen in a dark grey, worn T-shirt and beaten-up jeans, hair still shining with damp and smelling great. She shook her head as she tossed some vinaigrette into the salad and put it in the centre of the table.

He stood, watching her intently with a smile playing on his lips.

"Eat!" she said, curtly. "What's so funny?"

He pulled out his chair and sat down now, openly grinning. "Nothing."

"Come on… no secrets, remember?"

He laughed. A wonderful sound, she realised he made so little.

"Okay, I was thinking, how did someone like me manage to land such a domestic goddess?"

"Hey!" Grace said in mock anger, stuffing a tortellini in her mouth. "No need for sarcasm."

He raised his eyebrows, still smiling. "I wasn't being sarcastic, actually."

She was sobered momentarily, still, studying his face for evidence of a joke and found none. She frowned. Perhaps he was telling the truth. Cookery would have been the least important skill in the women he knew. And, as usual, a pain stabbed her heart. Serena.

He was oblivious and began eating steadily. She poured them some wine. "Are you scared?" she asked.

"Of food poisoning?… Nah." He grinned.

She laughed and threw her napkin at him and he dodged it, laughing as well. He sobered quickly and thought about the question. "Only of him not going," he said, and placed some salad onto his plate.

Grace had suddenly lost her appetite and began to push her food around. She knew the scientists had no guarantee who would go, but surely after all the trouble Diablo had taken, with the tattoos and everything. "Surely he wants to go… Isn't that what all this has been about?"

Dylan bobbed his head in acknowledgement. "But what if it ends up a fight for survival?" he said, fixing her with that intense stare of his.

Shit, she hadn't thought of it like that. If Diablo thought one of them would be killed, then it would be as though one was holding the other's head underwater. There could only be one winner. "Like a fight to the death," she muttered to herself.

Dylan had stopped eating and was staring at her. "Yes," he said, quietly. "But more than that. Everything… all our lives, has been a competition to him, one he must always win, and to hell with who he hurts on the way. As long as he beats me… is all that matters."

Oh my god, the time she'd gone to his apartment and spent that night with Diablo came crashing into her mind. How stupid could she have been? She now understood why Diablo had revelled in her coming to him voluntarily. It had been game, set and match to him. Her heart sank. Thank god Dylan had no idea and mostly slept through Diablo's episodes.

"This time… with Diablo… will you sleep?"

Dylan shook his head. "Not if I can help it. I need to know what he's up to… He's been really quiet," he said, smiling ruefully. "Never thought I'd say that."

He ate another mouthful, then placed his knife and fork on his plate. "I'll have a fight though… if he wants me asleep."

Grace let out a ragged breath. *God,* the sheer horror of what Dylan must face over the next few days, and her not being around, was just overwhelming. She mustn't let it ruin their last night. She stood, grabbed the bottle from the table and reached for Dylan's hand.

He looked at her, took it tentatively, stood and allowed her to lead him up the stairs. "Make sure he sleeps now," she said over her shoulder.

Dylan was looking straight at her through heavy-lidded eyes. "He will… like a fucking log."

Her heart skipped a beat.

They didn't quite reach the bedroom when Dylan halted her, braced her hands on the doorframe, loosened her jeans and pushed them to her knees. Tilting her upper body slightly forward, he pushed into her in a single thrust. Thinking their lovemaking would be hard and urgent, she was surprised when she felt herself pulled backwards with his arms wrapped tightly around her waist to almost a sitting position on his lap and almost combusted at the closeness. She sighed into him and melted. It felt so right, so loving.

She began to move in undulating circles.

"Ah fuck, Grace," he whispered at her ear.

Instead of building his pace, she almost yelped in disappointment when he released his grip and cool air rushed between them. Instead of pushing her on in his usual, dominant way, he gently straightened, then put her away from him and withdrew. It was torture and she whimpered in frustration.

"Shh," he said. "Patience… it'll be worth it." He led her into the bedroom and pulled her with him onto the bed. "I want us to take our time tonight."

Trusting him sexually, as she always did, she lay down and faced him on the bed. His eyes looked back at her, deep blue and earnest. He was right – as always. Tonight wasn't about lust and fucking, although that was so much a part of Dylan, it was more solemn than that, kind of sacred – a reverence to each other. Although she daren't imagine, it could be their last time.

Grace closed the distance between them on the pillow and kissed him slowly, slanting her mouth over his and pushing in her tongue deeply. It was dominant and possessive and totally unlike her. She rolled onto him, pushing him over onto his back, taking his arms up to either side of his face by the wrists and pinning him there.

She pulled out of the kiss and they both paused. Clear blue eyes, like a lagoon she could lose herself in, stared adoringly back. They held a hint of longing, or was it lust and something else? Was it surprise – amazement?

She realised she was in a position of dominance; a place she rarely occupied – if ever, especially with Dylan. Then, she completely understood the meaning in his eyes. This was the thing that Diablo could never stand. And the one thing that Dylan alone could give her. A smile crept across her face and his answering smile told her he knew she understood.

She ran her thumb along his lower lip and he parted his mouth slightly and his tongue came out to delicately lick her finger, inviting her to do delicious things to him. "I love you, Dylan," she whispered.

A moment of meaning passed between them and Dylan looked above him at the bars of the headboard and reached up and put his hands through and held them fast. He looked back at her through lust-heavy eyes. "Then you know what you have to do."

She nodded. No further explanation was necessary. She moved towards him and kissed him hard on the mouth, biting his tongue and lips. His arms strained against the headboard and the muscles corded in his neck and shoulders.

The effect her treatment of him was having excited her like nothing else. To have such a powerful man at her mercy just totally turned her on and she grazed her teeth sharply down his neck, nipping and biting as she went. Everything was about marking and owning. It was what he needed and she was happy to give it to him. His back arched beneath her, lifting her off the bed and reminding her of his strength, given freely as a gift.

Her tongue journeyed down his body, swirling and licking, absorbing the taste of him. Travelling the smooth path from his navel, she skated around the straining length of him to the weights beneath, hairless and sensitive. She licked them and allowed her tongue to move along the long, silky smooth skin of his shaft that twitched and strained for her mouth to totally engulf it. The bars creaked and complained above her in Dylan's grip.

Spurred on by her absolute power, she clasped the length of him in her hand, gripped him hard and lifted him to her mouth, then licked a lingering circle around the large head. His loud curse was gratifying.

Moving it across the closed cushion of her lips, she teased him until she allowed it to push between her lips, parting them a little at a time, driving him wild, flicking her tongue and stroking him beneath, gripping his girth, moving it with her mouth in a slow, relentless rhythm.

"Fuck, Grace," escaped him on a breath.

There was no giving up her power now and she covered her teeth with her lips so she could glide the length of him to the back of her throat and not hinder her progress. Then she withdrew completely to begin the whole blissful process again. Over and over she worked him until Dylan's hips undulated and he writhed beneath her, lost to sensation.

The bars creaked so loudly she thought he would snap them. "Fuck, Grace, you better fuck me, I can't hold out much longer," Dylan said, between breaths.

He was leaning his head forward, watching what she was doing, and his gaze was searing and tortured, the veins protruding from his forehead and neck. The absolute need in him was the most beautiful sight she'd ever seen, but he would break the bed any minute. His resolve would snap and he'd throw her over and fuck her senseless.

She toyed with letting him do just that – it was so tempting. But she remembered the purpose of what she was doing. "Sit up against the headboard," she ordered. "Put your hands back through." Her voice was husky and unrecognisable.

He did as she asked, but his expression was quizzical while he waited for her next move. His eyes followed her while she stood, put a leg on either side of him and squatted down. Gripping him, she placed him at her core and lowered herself onto him little by little.

He exhaled loudly and the bars complained.

Her excellent leg muscles from riding allowed her the perfect control. Lowering, rising and holding her weight, forcing him to move his hips to meet her. Her breasts grazed his chest and his cheek was tantalizingly close.

He clenched his jaw and grit out the words, "You've got me now, so you better fuck me."

The words snapped something within her and she gave way to her inner animal. She bit his cheek and slammed down hard and used all the strength in her legs to build pace and ferocity until she was riding him mercilessly.

They moaned together. The bed squeaked. And just when she thought her legs would begin to fail her, she felt Dylan's arms come around her and grip her backside. There, he helped take some of her weight so she could keep up her punishing speed.

When Dylan bent his knees, tipping her into his body, her engorged bud got added friction and she felt herself coiling deeply within her. "Dylan," she cried.

Dylan groaned into her shoulder and bit her hard. "Fuck me hard, babe."

His words were her undoing, and while she tried to increase her pace, she was sent hurtling over the edge and her release whiplashed through her nervous system.

Dylan instantly welcomed it and ground her into his gyrating hips. He bit her neck, sucking her blood through the skin, taking everything from her. "Ah, fuck," he breathed.

"Dylan!" she screamed as she peaked, and her spasms pulsed deeply inside her. As if the energy were sucked out of her, she flopped down onto him and he caught her easily. Her leg muscles were shot to pieces and she was completely wrung out.

He didn't allow her to rest, but continued to grind his hips into her, his length still a rod of iron, drawing the last sensations from her, radiating through her from the tingle on her lips and heating her to the tips of her toes.

Holy mother! It was the orgasm of her life, and she'd had a few whoppers with this man. *Fuck!*

She relaxed against him, still breathing hard. His chest rose and fell beneath her while he still held her in his heavy arms. Neither of them moved nor spoke for what felt like ages.

Eventually, Dylan shuffled them down into the bed, too shattered to even go to the bathroom. There was no discussion about what had happened between them. Nothing was needed. They just fell into an exhausted sleep, Grace lying flat on top of him. His warmth permeated and settled her, while his heart beat a solid and reliable rhythm next to her ear. They lay, content and replete, and slept in each other's arms.

GRACE STOOD WAITING with her bag packed next to the front door in the living room. Dylan held her close to his chest; she couldn't bear to let him go. They seemed to have reached a new closeness; a new understanding of each other and the timing of it was heartbreaking.

With her head next to his heart, her eyes rested on Fenton kissing Cerise a tender farewell. Guilt pricked her for an instant when she remembered that Cerise would be fearful for Fenton's well-being too – for what he may have to do to Dylan, and what Diablo might do to him. She closed her eyes momentarily. It was as though their men were going off to war. This situation was so fucked up for so many people.

Dylan seemed to sense her emotion and squeezed her tighter. She opened her eyes again and Cerise and Fenton were whispering words of affection to each other. It was easy to tell. She and Dylan had said theirs silently and privately an hour ago, intimately meaningful and heart-rending. There were no words left to say. She'd done with pleading. All that was left was 'I love you' and both knew it without a shadow of doubt.

"Ready?" Anton said, walking briskly into the room from the kitchen.

She nodded and pulled reluctantly apart from the warmth of Dylan's body.

Cerise kissed Fenton for a final time. "Be careful," she ordered over her shoulder as she walked towards Grace and the door.

Dylan drew her attention back to him, gently taking her by her chin. "Four days… that's all, okay?" he said.

She nodded; it felt like she was in a dream and would wake up any minute.

He kissed her gently and hugged her tightly one last time.

"Do something for me, Dylan," she said, looking up at him.

He searched her eyes and nodded slightly.

"Win." Then she pulled out of his arms and walked straight out of the door, not daring to look at him again. But she felt his eyes on her all the way to the car and when it pulled away.

Anton had offered to drive Cerise and Grace to the airport, allowing the others to get on with the busy schedule that Grace didn't even want to think about. He tried to make light conversation, but Cerise looked out of her window from the front passenger seat and Grace looked out of hers from the back. Neither woman felt much like talking. Both were lost in their own separate worlds of worry.

Grace tuned back in to Anton asking Cerise a question, "What?" she said absent-mindedly. Then she shook her head to whatever the question was and looked back out of the window. She realised that Cerise was worried sick. The risks for Dylan were obvious, but for Fenton, he was the first line of defence and the only one who stood any chance of handling Diablo. Grace wasn't sure why it made her feel guilty, but it did.

She caught Anton spying on her in the rear-view mirror and something in his expression niggled at her. "Why are you here, Anton?"

He frowned, not understanding the question.

Cerise actually snapped out of her daydream and paid attention. Looking at Anton, then at Grace as if she'd temporarily taken leave of her senses.

"I'm not sure I follow?" Anton said. "I had the free time…"

"Not the bloody lift… here at all… in Scotland?"

"Grace?" Cerise said, shocked.

Grace threw Cerise an exasperated look. "I was just wondering why Anton would be going along with all of this when he obviously doesn't believe a word of it?" she explained.

Anton sighed deeply, blinked and shook his head while he continued to drive. "It's not that I don't believe it." He huffed in frustration.

"What is it then... enlighten me?"

"Grace?" Cerise said, again. Anton was *her* friend after all.

"I'm sorry, Cerise, but Dylan and Fenton are risking their lives here and Anton doesn't believe any of it is real, I can tell."

"It doesn't matter whether it's real or not," Anton said, holding her eyes via the rear-view mirror.

Grace rolled her eyes. "What's that supposed to mean?"

Even Cerise looked at him with a frown for clarification.

"It means even if none of this is real, and is just some elaborate fabrication to perpetuate Dylan's delusion, the fact that he wants to sort it out can only be a good thing."

Grace just stared at him blankly, trying to process what he just said.

"If he sees it through to the end, it might just be the last he sees of Diablo... closure, so to speak." He looked across at Cerise, clearly hoping she was with him.

Grace's eyes went from Anton to Cerise. The whole thing was enough to send you mad. Cerise looked out of the windshield, proving she was trying to make sense of it too.

Grace tutted. "No. I'm not willing to accept that. What about all the maths, String Theory stuff ... the blueprints, coordinates ... how could Dylan possibly know all that?"

Even Cerise had to nod to that. No regular bloke with little or no education could solve that level of highbrow theory.

Anton's face spoke reams. He didn't want to get into the whys and wherefores of his opinion. "Look, whichever way you look at it, Diablo is dangerous. Whether you choose to believe he is a separate person or a fundamental part of Dylan's personality disorder…"

"For fuck's sake, Anton. In four days time, Dylan's going to be standing on a machine – which was designed from his fucking tattoos, with god knows how many volts of electricity going through him at a particular spot, dictated again from his tattoos, to send Diablo back to his own fucking dimension!" she ended up shrieking. And the more it sounded ridiculous, the louder she got. *Fucking hell!*

Anton was red in the face, trying to suppress his own temper.

Cerise put her head in her hands, as if she couldn't take much more.

"I must admit that question did trouble me, but Dylan was a bright child prior to his trauma. Perhaps his second personality was so deeply embedded that he was able to study maths and physics to an incredibly advanced level and nobody knew about it. Then it was stored away somewhere in his psyche, only surfacing in the form of his tattoos?"

Grace looked at Cerise in exasperation for back-up.

She looked weary. "It is possible, I suppose," she said with a slight shrug. "What was that film… *A Beautiful Mind?*"

"Yes!" Anton said, like a hallelujah. "Based on a real-life schizophrenic with a brilliant mathematical mind."

"Oh, come on, I don't believe you two," Grace said angrily. She felt like she was fighting for their lives here. "Dylan … solving the theory of the universe, or whatever they bloody well call it?" And crazy as it seemed, Grace thought of the eagle spread across Dylan's back and the handprint on his chest. They were Dylan's tattoos; normal, human and heartwarmingly corny. Her voice cracked. "Dylan loves me... *he wouldn't ever want to hurt me.*"

Anton looked at her for a few moments in the mirror as if deciding whether to say something.

"Well, say it... You may as well," she sniped.

"Did it ever occur to you that one of the things he may see in you is your isolation?" And he left the comment floating in the air.

Grace was stunned, then fumed. *How dare he?* She wanted to cry and rail against what he said, but was he just echoing a tiny little voice way back in the recesses of her mind? Afraid of crying, she just raised her eyebrows in question for Cerise to answer.

Her eyes quickly avoided hers. "All I know is that Fenton's got one hell of a fight on his hands, either way," Cerise said, shifting huffily in her seat to look out of the window again. The conversation was over as far as she was concerned.

Shit! Grace was left to her own thoughts again. *No!... no, she wouldn't even entertain the idea that Dylan had singled her out because she was alone and vulnerable.* It went against everything she knew about him.

Anton had put his attention back to the road as they had reached the airport. There was no point in arguing the toss with Cerise, because as far as she was concerned, it was right; Fenton was in danger, whatever. But just supposing Anton was right, and Dylan was mentally ill, that meant his disorder could come back at any time. Any upset or trauma could trigger it. *No, that just wasn't an option.* She flatly refused to accept it.

"What about Simon and Nicholas... what do they have to say about it?"

Anton continued to look where he was going and pulled into a space at the drop-off point. He turned the engine off and twisted to face her in his seat. "They have their science and I have mine."

Grace stared at him for a long moment. They had agreed to disagree. Then a moment of clarity came to her. He simply couldn't accept it because the implications of it blew his mind. That was enough for her. She wasn't about to over-think it. It was his problem. "Guess you'll know on the 16th?" Grace said flippantly as she opened the car door.

Cerise was already ahead of her and out of the car.

"Maybe," she heard him say, apparently not convinced.

CHAPTER 26

*G*race stood like a waif on Janey's doorstep.

The door opened. "Grace!" Janey yanked her in close for a hug. "Dave… Dave! Grace is here," she called, pulling her inside.

Grace allowed herself to be pulled in and steered. She felt numb and in a bit of a daze when Janey plonked her down on the worn leather chair and fussed and made them all tea. Then Janey and Dave sat opposite her on the sofa and looked at her expectantly.

Shit! Where did she begin? Figuring she should just go for it and not try to give her friends a load of bull, she took a deep breath and launched in. She explained everything that was going on in her absence in Scotland and why she and Cerise had to leave.

When she finished, Janey and Dave sat in stunned silence. Then Dave pulled a confused face and looked at Janey, who frowned back at him. They didn't believe a word of it and she couldn't blame them. *Hell*, she hardly believed it herself.

"Look, I know how it sounds… The important thing is that I need to be here, okay?" Anton's words, that it made no difference to the outcome whether it was the truth or not, echoed. She grit her teeth and huffed.

Dave and Janey nodded enthusiastically, relieved they didn't have to pretend they were convinced. "Stay as long as you like," Janey said, kindly.

"It's just for a few days… till the 16th…" Her voice trailed off. She really had no clue as to what would happen after that. The day was so final.

Janey interrupted her maudlin thoughts. "Great! We can do loads of stuff while you're here; catch up with the girls, maybe go for a spa day even?"

Grace smiled at her, trying to look enthusiastic, but it was half-hearted. "That'll be nice… I'm going to go and visit Dylan's mum while I'm here, though… let her know what's going on."

She caught the exchange of looks between the couple again. "For Christ's sake, Janey, his mum needs to know what's going on… besides, Cerise will come with me." She couldn't tell whether Janey and Dave were worried about her going there in case his mum was as mad as he was, or they didn't want everyone thinking she was mad. It didn't matter. "I'm going, whatever you say, so save your breath."

They nodded, resigned to the fact that they would be there for her no matter what, and she was grateful. Dave stood, motioned for her to follow, and carried her holdall for her to one of the kids' rooms she was to commandeer for the duration.

GRACE SPENT the longest three days of her life trying to look enthusiastic while Janey took her to lunch, beauty treatments and shopping. But she simply couldn't throw herself into it. Her mind was on only one person.

Tempting though it was, it had been agreed that she must

have no contact with Dylan, either by phone, email or text, for fear that Diablo would answer and the project compromised in some way.

She had reluctantly agreed. The night she disobeyed and spent with Diablo was enough to teach her a lesson, that and a warning from Anton: that she could ruin everything they were trying to achieve.

Cerise had been in touch, though. No one had banned her. Fenton had told her everything was going according to plan. The machine was completely finished and they were carrying out trials and tests with it.

Dylan was sleeping more and more, allowing Diablo to surface. He was careful not to let on too much about that, not wanting to worry them. All he said was that he was now being kept in a locked room at the university. Grace hated that.

Fenton had given Cerise Dylan's mum's address in the small village of Horton Kirby in Kent, just fifteen minutes away. He also said they couldn't go there until the 15th, as she wouldn't be there until then. Both Grace and Cerise suspected Fenton was lying about that, hoping to drag it out and not make them tempted to return before the 16th.

At last, the day came. Cerise bibbed outside Janey's, signalling it was time to go. Grace kissed Janey and ran out to the car. She hurriedly plugged in her seatbelt and they were away.

"What shall we say when we get there?" Grace said, seriously worried now that it was imminent. How on earth would they broach the subject?

"I dunno," Cerise said at a loss. "But Fenton has phoned ahead… she's expecting us."

Grace breathed a ragged breath and tried to get a grip on her feelings of dread.

· · ·

WHEN DYLAN'S mum opened the door, Grace was struck by how tired she looked. She looked worn out by an obviously hard life. Her greying hair was long and pulled back into a loose ponytail and her skin was lined with no trace of makeup. She was neatly dressed with a plain beige sweater over navy slacks, which hung loosely on her thin frame.

She seemed pleased to see them and ushered them into the surprisingly large kitchen at the back of the small terrace. She put the kettle on straightaway and asked them to sit at the rectangular table in the middle of the room.

The room smelled of toast and was clean and tidy. The decor was dated, Grace thought, as her eyes roamed the room. She must live alone now.

"Dylan's friend said you were popping in," she said brightly, putting what looked like her best bone china out on the table and a plate of biscuits.

"That was my husband, Fenton," Cerise explained.

"Really?… He's your husband? Such a lovely man… Been such a good friend to my boy." The woman positively beamed.

Cerise smiled and inclined her head, accepting the compliment. "Fenton will be so pleased you think so." She sat forward and took a biscuit. "This is Grace, Mrs O'Shea."

"Call me Helen. Pleased to meet you, Grace."

"Grace is Dylan's girlfriend," Cerise continued. "She wanted to come and meet you."

Helen's eyes went wide with surprise and she sat on the edge of her chair as if she'd received a shock and her legs threatened to give way. Her hand went to her mouth and a noise like a small sob escaped her.

For an awful second, Grace thought she was upset.

"Oh my dear god, Grace. I am so pleased to meet you," Helen gushed. "I'd just given up all hope, you see?… I'm so pleased." She appeared to laugh, then sob at the same time.

Then she stood up and grabbed a box of tissues from the counter. Ripping out a tissue, she dabbed her eyes. "Forgive me," she said, shaking her head.

Relief flooded Grace. She hadn't known what to expect, but she'd never anticipated such an overwhelmingly happy reception.

Helen managed to calm herself down enough to speak normally. "Tell me... how long?" She laughed aloud.

Grace told her a scaled-down version of how she had met Dylan at school and how they'd bumped into each other again a few months ago and started seeing each other.

Helen listened avidly, eating up every word. "I haven't seen Dylan in such a long time... I know he can't help it."

Grace could tell by the way she averted her eyes that she was used to making excuses for Dylan, and she made up her mind there and then to make him visit her more often.

"It's his work... it takes him away a lot."

Grace couldn't help wondering if she knew what Dylan had been doing for a living since leaving school. It was probably a watered-down version if she did.

"He works with my husband," Cerise said, filling an empty silence.

"Yes, of course," Helen said, smiling at her. "Takes him away a lot, too, I bet?"

"Yes, it does..."

Helen turned her attention back to Grace and her face became serious. "He's been okay... well, I mean?" Her eyes bore into her as if she was trying to communicate something. Like she wasn't sure what Grace knew about Dylan's problems.

Grace held her gaze steadily. "That's the main reason I'm here," she said.

Fear flickered in Helen's eyes. "What's happened... is he in trouble?"

"No… no, it's nothing like that… It's just that we have been seeking professional help…" Grace said, looking at Cerise to chime in at that point.

"Yes, a close friend of mine is a psychiatrist," Cerise said.

Helen visibly shrank in her chair, waiting for the worst.

Grace decided to change tack. "Did you ever see any of the tattoos Dylan has?"

Helen looked between them quickly. "Well, he got them after he left home, but I've seen the ones that his shirt doesn't always cover." She frowned, starting to look a little bewildered. "But I don't get what that has to do with…" Her voice trailed off.

Grace wasn't sure whether she could take the information they were meant to deliver.

"So you must know about Dylan's health problems," Helen said as a statement with a sigh.

"We both do," Grace said. "Cerise has known for a long time."

"Fenton has always helped Dylan," Cerise explained.

Helen nodded. "I know, and I am eternally grateful for it." She looked back at Grace. "But I thought… I never thought Dylan could hold down a relationship?"

Grace smiled. "We have had our ups and downs."

Helen smiled back.

A rare thing, Grace was sure.

"I'm so pleased," Helen said, holding her hand to her heart. Then her face fell. "Fenton said on the phone that Dylan had sent you here," she said, looking between them.

"He wanted me to meet you, but he also wanted me to explain what's going on," Grace said.

Helen put her hands in her lap and waited. "What is going on?" she asked eventually.

"Dylan is trying to make himself better," Cerise said.

Helen's face remained blank, then she shifted impatiently

in her seat. "Please don't beat around the bush. Tell me what's going on?" She was looking directly at Grace for the answer.

"He is in Aberdeen, at the university there. They have built a machine made from the plans written on Dylan's body that can extract…" She paused, not quite sure how to continue. It was sounding more absurd by the minute.

"Diablo," Helen finished simply for her. "The evil one."

"Yes," Grace answered lamely. She wasn't sure why she was so surprised that this woman – Dylan's mother – should take all this in her stride. After all, she had been putting up with all this a darn sight longer than she had.

But Helen just nodded as if it were an everyday occurrence. "Do they think it will work?"

"The scientists seem confident," Grace said.

"When?"

"Tomorrow, in the very early hours."

Helen was quiet, as if she was processing the information, then rose and filled the kettle again.

"There are risks," Cerise said.

Grace nodded her agreement. As unpleasant as it was, it was the whole reason for their visit.

Helen flicked the switch on the kettle and turned to face them, leaning on the counter. "That it won't work and the bad one stays?"

"Yes," Grace said.

"Give it to me straight, please… I need to know."

Grace nodded and swallowed, "And there is a chance that neither of them will make it."

Helen exhaled noisily. "Thank you." Then she turned round and continued to make the tea.

Grace looked at Cerise, confused, not knowing what she should say next.

Cerise shrugged.

"I'm sorry," Grace said when Helen placed their cups in front of them.

"Sorry for what… being honest? It's the thing I need most where Dylan is concerned. People have been covering for him his whole life." She sat and smiled genuinely. "I am glad he met you." Helen put her head at an angle and studied her. "At least he had a little bit of happiness." Then she reached for her cup and blew over the surface. "How will they know?"

"Know what?" Grace said, frowning.

"Which one will go?" Helen said, raising her eyebrows as if it were an obvious question.

Grace sighed. That was the 64,000-dollar question. "That's why Dylan sent me away. He has to let Diablo surface. It's supposed to be easier, apparently… I asked the same thing. They said the one connected to his DNA would be the least likely to be extracted."

Helen frowned as if she didn't understand.

Grace didn't blame her. It was all above her head.

"So it is the squatter that will be ejected?"

The expression on Helen's face was beginning to worry her. Grace stared at her for a beat, deciding to phrase her words carefully. "Yes," she answered eventually. "They are expecting Diablo to go."

"The evil one with brown eyes," Helen confirmed.

Grace couldn't tell if she was annoyed with them, or afraid, or just making sure of the facts.

Then Helen stood suddenly and left the room. The two women were left gawping at each other, not sure what to make of it.

"What the fuck?" Cerise mouthed.

Quite a few minutes passed until they began to think that maybe they should go and see if she was all right. Then, at last, she returned carrying two large volumes in her arms and placed them on the table in front of Grace with a thud.

Grace looked up at her, unsure what she was meant to look at.

"Family albums," Helen said flatly. "You need to see them."

Grace frowned, then looked back at the books and slowly opened one. The plastic crackled with age as she leafed through page after page. There was nothing remarkable that she could see at a glance. They were regular family-type photos, which she was sure every household had. There were loads of Dylan with his brothers, going up in height and age. Dylan was instantly recognisable even as a small boy; skinny, lanky and with a mess of dark brown hair.

As she flicked through, she tried to find any of Dylan from the age she would have known him at school and began to notice there were none. She opened the second album, and while his brothers' photos were obviously getting older, he was appearing less and less.

She felt a pang in her heart and smiled apologetically at Helen. Of course, there wouldn't be any of Dylan from then on. It was after that day and he probably wouldn't have wanted any taken. She closed the book and went to hand it back to Helen.

"You didn't notice," Helen said, slightly irritated.

"I did… There were none taken of him when he was older," Grace said, sadly. "Probably because he wouldn't let you."

Helen continued to look frustrated with her. "You love Dylan?"

"Of course I do?" Grace had no idea where she was going with this.

"Beautiful, good, blue-eyed Dylan?" Helen persisted.

"Yes." Fear started to creep through her veins and her heart began to pump.

Helen slapped the book down in front of her again and opened it impatiently to a particular page. "Look at the pictures closely, Grace. There's a great one of Dylan when he was about eighteen months old… there!" she said, smacking the page.

Grace jumped with the smack but looked down at the page.

Then her heart stopped. It was there as clear as day: What Helen was driving at.

The toddler – Dylan, was staring straight at the camera, smiling broadly, showing two little front teeth, with the biggest doe-like brown eyes she had ever seen.

The world seemed to stop and zone in on that point on the page and her hand flew to her mouth.

"What is it?" Cerise said, suddenly.

"Oh my god," Grace said.

"Grace, you're scaring me," Cerise said, rising from her chair to look over Grace's shoulder.

Helen hammered home her point. "That is my son," she said, her words clipped. "Trouble from the minute he could walk."

Cerise pulled the album nearer for a closer look.

Grace pinched the bridge of her nose.

Cerise's eyes went wide when she made the connection. "This means… This means…" she said in panic.

"Dylan is walking into a trap… We must get up there?" Grace finished for her, already rising from her chair.

"I'll ring Fenton," Cerise said, rummaging in her bag for her mobile phone. She put it to her ear and listened. "Shit. It's gone straight to voicemail."

Grace was already walking out of the kitchen towards the front door. "Try him again in the car…" Then she stopped and turned to face Helen. "I'm sorry. Helen, we need to go."

Helen looked so tiny then. Her heart went out to her. The

moment she knew would come one day for her son was coming and she felt responsible for it. She must be in misery.

"After that night… when he came… you knew it wasn't him… your son, I mean?" Grace just had to ask.

Helen nodded slowly, blinked, and tears tracked down her tired face. "When he came out of hospital and he hugged me and looked up at me, all lost with those beautiful blue eyes, I thought god had answered all my prayers and sent me an angel.

"I didn't care less if they called it schitzo-whatsit personality disorder, or whatever they damn well thought it was. He was a good boy some of the time, and that was a whole lot more than before, and I loved him for it," Helen said, sniffing and dabbing her nose on her tissue and standing up straighter.

"But if we go back… if we stop it…" Then Grace was struck with horror. "We could be killing your son?" She couldn't believe she was actually saying the words to Dylan's mother – *no, not his mother. Agh!* It was all sending her crazy. But it was true. Diablo was her flesh and blood.

Helen looked at her sadly. "If it wasn't for that angel, my boy would be dead by now or serving life in prison." Helen went to turn away and paused. "Just tell me when it's done."

Grace was immobilised with shock. She looked at Cerise, whose eyes were sympathetic. "We need to get going," she said quietly.

Shit! If they didn't get there in time? "God, Cerise… if we don't warn them, it won't be Diablo who's leaving." The pair rushed for the door. "I'll keep you posted," Grace said before she disappeared.

Helen nodded. "Go save your angel."

They ran to the car.

"I don't get it?" Cerise said. "If Diablo is conscious, won't he be in danger too?"

That was true – according to what the scientists believed. But Grace had an awful feeling in the pit of her stomach that Diablo knew exactly what he was doing. She kept thinking over and over; this had been Diablo's plan all along. It all made sense now. Everyone assumed he'd planned to get home to his dimension, but it wasn't that at all. He'd used the whole thing to evict Dylan – her Dylan, and to hell with whether it killed him or not.

CHAPTER 27

Cerise drove as fast as she dared. They had to go back to Janey's to pick up her ID and credit card, wasting valuable time. Janey had pleaded with her to hang on for Dave to go back with her, but there just wasn't time. Cerise even had to arrange cover for the kids over the phone.

They tried Fenton's number over and over, as well as everyone else's and had no luck. They arrived at Gatwick airport and still hadn't got hold of anyone. That was worrying in itself.

Grace stood at the booking desk perspiring; stress was eating her alive at the speed – or the lack of it. The booking agent was taking ages trying to find them available seats. "You've just missed one," she said, in a mock apologetic tone. "They've boarded and closed the doors now," her monotone voice droned on.

Grace rolled her eyes and tapped her foot. "When's the next one?" she snapped. It was so hard trying to keep the impatience out of her voice to get the most out of the woman. She reined it in a bit. "It's really important that I get to Aberdeen as soon as possible."

The woman stared at her, then blinked and sighed as if she were doing her a huge favour and clicked on the keyboard again. "There is one to Edinburgh boarding in about ten minutes…"

Grace's heart sank. That was no good. It would mean a long car or train journey as well the other end. She shook her head. "Can you see when the next one is to Aberdeen?"

The woman tutted and pulled faces while she tapped. "The next one is not till 8 o'clock."

"There must be something sooner than that… can't you try the other airlines?"

The woman was losing patience with her. "I have, madam. They've had bad weather up there and what's not been cancelled is full. I can book two seats on the 8 o'clock… It's up to you?" she said with her eyebrows up and no warmth in her face whatsoever.

Grace had to come to a speedy decision before they lost those seats. "Yes, can I book those, please?" She called Cerise over, who still had her phone to her ear. Grace's hopes rose for a second, but Cerise shook her head as she neared. The bad weather must be affecting the phones.

They gave all their details to the ticket agent, then went and sat down in the busy departure lounge. They were in no mood for shopping. Their minds were four hundred miles away.

THEY MUST HAVE TRIED twenty times or more to reach them during their long wait.

"Why won't they answer?" Grace said frantically. *Surely bad weather wouldn't stop the phone signal for that long?* Maybe it could if it was to do with what was about to happen up there. Her fear almost consumed her for a moment, not only because everything was getting frighteningly real, but also because something terrible had already happened. It was eating her alive.

"I don't know," Cerise said, biting her nails. "Maybe they have no signal because they are up at the site and in the middle of nowhere?"

"Yeah… could be." But running through her mind were racing thoughts, like the night when it had all happened before there had been an electric storm. That it was the build-up to the momentous event in time and space. Over and over, her terror kept building; *what if something had already happened... What had Diablo done?*

At last they boarded the plane and found their seats. There they sat for another agonising twenty minutes while they waited for a slot to take off. Both their nerves were now shot to pieces by the time they taxied to the runway. They reluctantly switched off their mobile phones.

"An hour and a half, that's all, and we'll be there," Grace said, thinking aloud.

"Yeah, but at least another hour the other side. That means we won't even get to the cottage before 11 o'clock," Cerise said, worn out with worry.

"Bloody hell," Grace muttered. "Then if they're up at the site… can you remember the way… it'll be pitch dark by then?"

"I think so."

But Cerise didn't sound that convincing. *Shit.* She grabbed them a couple of vodkas from the trolley as it passed and Grace was glad of it. Then they sat quietly and tried to rest as best they could.

Sleep was impossible for Grace. Her mind was a jumble of the photos she'd seen, Helen's sad face and Dylan's beautiful angelic blue eyes. No wonder Helen thought him an angel. That word troubled her. My god, the thought of who he could be just blew her mind, whether he was an alien, angel or whatever. The thought of losing him was real and painful and she felt it stab into her heart like a pickaxe when she contemplated it.

She must cling to what she knows and not get bogged down in thinking too much. Her Dylan was real and good and she loved him and that was enough.

After the longest hour and a half, their plane finally landed and they rushed through Customs. They hired a car in record time and were soon speeding through the car park.

"Where to first?" Cerise said.

"The university… Dylan might still be there."

The wheels squealed up the ramp and out onto the road.

THEY PARKED PRECARIOUSLY and rushed into the older building that housed the Physics Department. It seemed deserted. They headed in the direction of Nicholas's office. There was a caretaker in the corridor buffing the floors.

"Excuse me… Excuse me?" Grace shouted over the machine.

The man noticed he wasn't alone and switched it off.

"Nicholas Cornell – have you seen him tonight, please?… It's really important."

The man looked quite old and stood up straighter, with his hands holding his lower back as if to ease it. "Yes… They were leaving as I got here." He looked at his watch. "There were a few of them… The ones who've been working with him. They all left at the same time."

"Was there a black man with them?" Cerise said.

"With another big white guy," Grace said.

"With tattoos," Cerise added.

"Yeah," the man nodded. "He came and took the other guy

from the room – the one helping them with their experiment," he said, pointing down the corridor.

"Thanks!" both women said and ran in the direction he pointed. They stopped suddenly at the very last room on the right. The door was open to what was more like a storeroom. An unmade cot was against one wall and a cup and a plate were on a small table. There were bars on the small frosted window, but apart from that, the room was bare.

"Come on," Cerise said, snapping Grace to action. "We're too late. We need to catch up with them." They rushed back to their car and out of the city.

GRACE TRIED Fenton's number again while Cerise drove. "It's ringing," she shouted, her eyes wide, adrenaline pumping.

"He... llo," crackled from the other end.

"Fenton?"

"Is... Gra... ce?"

"Have you got him?" Cerise shouted, struggling to keep her eyes on the road.

Grace nodded vigorously. "Yes, Fenton, it's me. Now listen carefully, it's important." The phone connection continued to hiss, crackle and break up intermittently. "We've just come from Dylan's mum's. Diablo is her son... Did you hear me, Fenton? Diablo. Is. Her. Son!" The connection was terrible and getting worse.

"What?... di.... Sa... Beep! Beep! The phone went dead.

"Fenton... Fenton!" Grace shouted as if being louder could somehow be heard. She let her arm fall away from her ear. "He broke up, he's gone," she said to Cerise.

"Did he hear you?"

"I don't know. He was trying to say something. The reception was terrible." Grace hoped he heard. But in all honesty, she couldn't be sure he knew it was even her.

They rode in silence the whole rest of the way, trying everyone's number over and over until they had to save battery power.

"Where to first?" Cerise said as they neared the cottage.

"We may as well rule the house out first before we set off into the middle of nowhere," Grace said, while her eyes scanned the night.

FENTON THOUGHT Diablo had been uncharacteristically well-behaved since he'd started to surface. He usually climbed the walls in frustration unless he could take the edge off, which normally meant hard-core sex or sparring with a worthy opponent who didn't mind bleeding. No, he'd been way too quiet, meaning Fenton had watched him closely. Trust was a commodity you used sparingly where Diablo was concerned.

He was sure the scientists had no concept of the bloke's capabilities. Sure, he'd told them, but they lived in a different world where animals like Diablo didn't exist. Still, if the guy wanted to go home, then he guessed it made sense that he went along with everything.

With his nerves on a knife-edge, he was glad when at last the night came. The plan was that the others would go on ahead to the site with the engineers and run any last-minute tests, and he would go back and release Diablo from the room, bring him to the cottage and wait for the 'all-clear' to bring him up.

Fenton had gone to the room where Diablo had been kept at the university, according to plan. He cuffed him and led him out to the car when the coast was clear. He would have preferred him cuffed behind his back, but it made sitting in the front seat, where he could see him, difficult. There was no way he wanted Diablo behind him. He just smirked and went along like a lamb.

Nothing much was said during the journey back to the cottage, which did nothing for Fenton's nerves. He felt his belt and made sure his radio receiver was switched on, as mobile phone reception was non-existent at the site and patchy everywhere it seemed because of the storms. He didn't like the idea of being out in the middle of nowhere and out of contact, alone with Diablo. Even after all these years, he could never relax with him.

He glanced sideways. Diablo looked ominously smug – no, more than that; charged and waiting to go. He simply wasn't acting like someone who didn't know whether he would survive the night or be ripped from the body he'd inhabited for years. That was, unless he knew something the rest of them didn't. After all, it was his mumbo jumbo they'd used. Maybe he knew a lot more than Dylan about what it all meant?

Diablo turned his head and grinned at him as if he'd been reading his mind. "Keep your eyes on the road, Bro." And he laughed and faced front again.

It made Fenton shiver. Something was going on.

They swung into the lane leading up to the cottage and came to a stop on the square of grass reserved for parking. Fenton switched off the engine. He fumbled in his jacket pocket for his phone and switched it back on. The signal was shit, only one bar. He slipped it into the inside breast pocket of his jacket and got out of the car.

Diablo was already out. Fenton gestured towards the house, "We'll wait here. They'll call us when they're ready."

"Didn't think mobile phones worked up there," Diablo said with a smirk."

Fenton paused for a fraction of a second. Would he know that, being held at the university? How much access did he have to information only Dylan would know? He decided to get inside quickly and went to walk towards the house when he felt the phone vibrate in his pocket. He stopped dead and took it out, tapped it, and put it to his ear. "Hello… Grace?" *Shit.* It sounded like Grace, but the reception was terrible. "He's what?"

The words were sketchy, but he was sure he heard right: "Diablo is her son." He tried to get her to repeat it, but the line soon went dead. His mind whirred on the meaning and implication of what he just heard.

He'd been so deep in thought that he hadn't seen that Diablo had moved from where he thought he was standing. He was out of his peripheral vision for only a second.

Fenton went to turn when a hefty blow to his back sent him hurtling forward. A split second was all he had to tuck and roll back onto his feet again. *Fuck!* The pain in his lower back seared through him.

Diablo stepped out from the shadows. "What she say, Fent?"

"Nothin'." Fenton readied himself for the inevitable onslaught. He knew Diablo. He enjoyed slowly weakening his opponents until he could pick them off easily. It was now his turn. Everything made sense now; why Diablo had been so quiet. He wanted Dylan out and everything had been going according to his plan.

Again, he appeared to read his mind. "You know, don't you?" Diablo said, grinning. "I should have known you'd get it, you old dog."

"Know what?" Fenton said, trying to play dumb to buy some time. Diablo was edging slowly closer. Fenton knew only one of them was going to walk away from this tonight, and he hoped to god it was him.

"We've been friends a long time, Fent." Diablo began to circle him.

Fenton made sure he followed his movements with his whole body, ready for whatever he would do next. "So?"

"We've come a long way together, that's all. Be a shame to throw it all away?" He stepped clear of the shadow of the car and Fenton got a clear glimpse of the length of iron bar he carried in his cuffed hands.

Fenton pointed to it. "Expecting trouble, mate?"

Diablo laughed. "That depends." Then he made a lunge and slashed the air with the iron bar with a whoosh.

Fenton jumped back with it, only just missing him. "On what?"

Diablo put his head at an angle. "Whether you're gonna try and stop me."

Fenton's eyes flicked left to a shovel leaning up against the house, but Diablo followed his line of vision and they both jumped at the same time. Fenton got there a fraction of a second quicker, snatched the handle and spun away just as Diablo's iron bar smashed the wall where the shovel had been.

Diablo laughed like he was really enjoying himself. "It's a long time since we had a good spar, Fent?" Then he swiped the bar at Fenton over and over. Whipping it through the air, so Fenton had to jump back again and again. Each time, he was getting the swipe closer, only missing him by millimetres.

Fenton knew this was just a game. Diablo had no intention of leaving him alive. It was dog-eat-dog tonight and the best man would win – or the dirtiest fighter. Fenton swung the shovel in an arc, bringing it down over Diablo's head, but he held the bar high and blocked it. Then countered with a kick hard to Fenton's side, straight to his ribs, and then quick as lightning to the side of his head.

The air left his lungs to be replaced by searing pain and Fenton was forced to stagger and drop the shovel.

Diablo wasted no more time and swung the bar at the side of Fenton's head. All Fenton had time to do was to block with a raised arm. Diablo let out a war cry and belted him twice. The pain vibrated and felt like knives, like his bone had splintered with the force of it. He twisted his body to protect the arm, but in doing so, he left himself unguarded for a second and Diablo kicked him in the face. He followed it swiftly with a round kick to the side of his knee that collapsed it on impact and it was all over. As he neared the ground, a last crack to the back of his head brought him total darkness.

DIABLO STOOD over Fenton's slumped body, patted his breast pocket for a key and undid the cuffs at his wrists. Then he looked down at his oldest friend devoid of emotion. Of course, he had acquaintances, but Fenton and him had longevity. Even when he saw the blood on his face and the back of his head, it had little effect on him. In fact, he was mulling over the best way to make sure he was dead was to crush his skull with one last blow. He shrugged slightly; he was probably dead already anyway.

He raised the bar and was about to bring it down with all his considerable force when he heard a crackle coming from Fenton's Jacket. He frowned, then crouched and moved his jacket a little to find the small radio receiver. He grinned, removed it, pressed the button and put it to his ear.

Nicholas's voice was clear and authoritative. "Fenton... Come in, Fenton? We're ready for you."

Trying to keep the smile out of his voice, Diablo pressed the transmit button. "On our way." He kept his answer to a minimum, hoping Nicholas wouldn't discern it wasn't Fenton's voice, then he attached the radio to his own belt and raised the bar again. *Where was I?*

Diablo focused the whole of his body's strength when he heard something. He let the bar down slowly while he listened intently. He turned his head slowly in the direction the noise was coming from. It was a car whining up the steep climb of the hill to the cottage.

He stood still for a moment, then came to a decision when he saw a rickety old wooden shed. He bent down and picked up Fenton's legs and dragged him to the ramshackle building. He opened the door, barely on its hinges, and pulled the body inside. Then he closed the door and wedged it shut with the shovel Fenton had used as a weapon.

Car headlights swung towards the cottage and lit up the garden. Diablo crept into the night.

CHAPTER 28

"The car's here!" Grace said, filled with sudden hope. She grabbed the handle, ready to jump out.

"Wait!" Cerise pulled in next to the four-wheeled drive and switched the engine off. She looked worried, as if she were weighing something up.

Grace sat in silence and watched her anxiously, wondering what the problem was.

"Do you think they're inside… the house is in darkness."

Grace followed her gaze in the direction of the house on her left and saw what she meant. Then she shook her head and pulled the handle. "Come on… we'd better check anyway to make sure."

Cerise got out and joined Grace on her side of the car and together they walked to the front of the cottage. Rain had started to spatter and thunder rolled in the distance.

Shit! Another storm was building – as if they weren't on edge enough.

Grace knocked on the door.

No answer.

"Try the latch," Cerise said.

Filled with dread, Grace put her thumb on the black painted metal latch and pushed it downwards. It clanked and the door creaked open, revealing the blackness of the living room. Her heart beat faster, she was sure she could feel it in her mouth.

Cerise lost patience and tutted, pushed past her and felt the wall next to her. With the click, relief flooded them when the light came on. Neither woman realised they'd been holding their breath or how oppressive the darkness was until it was lifted with the light.

"Come on," Cerise said.

"There's no one in," Grace said, trying to hang back.

"For fuck's sake... I'm going to use the loo while I'm here. You can stay here if you want?"

Grace looked at the pissing rain and heard the loud clap of thunder behind her. "Shit, don't go without me."

"Jeez." Cerise walked into the cottage with Grace stuck to her like a shadow.

Grace had never liked it from the moment she'd seen it. Now it just gave her the heebie-jeebies.

Cerise was poking her head in each of the rooms as she passed, thankfully leaving every light on as they went, just to make sure no one was home sleeping.

When they'd got to the landing and checked each of the three bedrooms, they paused. "Right... be two ticks," Cerise said.

Grace just stood, rooted to the spot. "Hurry up, then." She looked all around her anxiously. What she was scared of, exactly, she wasn't sure, or willing to rationalise. All she knew was, she had this overwhelming feeling of foreboding that she just couldn't shake off and she'd had it since they'd pulled up outside.

Her eyes halted on the little staircase still in darkness, which led up to the loft – hers and Dylan's room. She imagined all his stuff still there. She looked back at the bathroom door. Cerise was singing. Grace wasn't sure if it was to reassure her or not. *It wouldn't hurt to have a look?* She dithered, indecisive whether to take the staircase.

Cerise flushing the loo snapped her into action. She switched on the light and climbed the small flight of stairs. The bedroom looked just the same as when she'd left it. Probably because Dylan had been staying at the university. A memory of Diablo flashed into her head. She shuddered.

One of Dylan's faded, worn T-shirts hung over the back of a chair. She walked over, picked it up and put it to her nose. *God,* it totally smelt of him. She breathed it in deeply. A pain so strong clutched at her heart and a sob escaped her.

For a fraction of a second, she thought of her life without him and dismissed it instantly as too painful to even contemplate.

A loud clap of thunder and a flash, then the world around her was thrown into darkness.

Fuck! Fuck! Fuck!

Her heart stopped and she stopped breathing while her ears strained. All she could hear was her heart in her ears. *Just the storm, just the storm... Why hadn't Cerise called out?*

She turned slowly to face the direction she'd just come from. Everywhere was pitch black.

Lightning flashed, then another loud clap of thunder.

The storm must have knocked out the light, that's all.

Her eyes were gradually getting used to the darkness. "Cerise?" she said quietly, not sure why she didn't shout it to the rafters.

There was no answer.

Terror had robbed her of saliva, making her mouth and throat sandpaper dry. Something wasn't right. She must go and see if Cerise was okay. She would have called out as soon as the lights went out. Perhaps she'd hit her head or passed out or something?

While she took tiny pigeon steps towards where she thought the staircase began, she tried to convince herself of a dozen scenarios that could explain why Cerise was so quiet. Like, nipping back out to the car, for instance.

Her hands touched the walls on either side of the staircase and she allowed them to slide as she took each stair carefully until she reached the first-floor landing below. Her steps eventually led her to the bathroom door. She tried the handle.

The door creaked open. "Cerise?" she whispered.

It was deathly quiet.

Stock still, Grace waited on the threshold of the room, too scared to go in.

The longer she stood there, the more terrified she became. The hackles on her neck began to rise. Someone was standing behind her; she was convinced of it. *Don't be silly. Tricks... mind's playing tricks,* she told herself. But the feeling of a presence behind her was unbearably real. Someone was there. She knew it with every fibre of her being.

Warm breaths were blowing like a caress on her neck.

She whimpered and swallowed hard. Then she closed her eyes and told herself to get a grip. It was just the storm and this house. Everything was sending her imagination haywire. *Come on, girl, we can do this.* And she took deep breaths and counted to three. Then she turned around sharply, punching out with her arm. It cut through thin air and she sagged in relief. Paranoia was a terrible thing. She almost laughed.

Her breathing began to get back to normal. She must get to the cupboard under the stairs. It must be a fuse. If she could just get in there, she knew there was a torch and perhaps she could even get the lights going again.

Where the bloody hell was Cerise, though? She might even be outside on her phone. That thought brightened her and she began to edge towards the main staircase.

Then something clanked on the floor in one of the bedrooms, stopping her dead. Her head snapped round to the direction of the noise. "Cerise… is that you?" She hoped and prayed. When no answer came, she knew it couldn't be her. And yet the noise was real enough. Terror began to creep over her again, making her movements stiff and jerky. *Get down to the fusebox,* she told herself.

Her hand reached the banister and she used it to help her move down the stairs more quickly. It was all she could do not to run in absolute panic when another flash of lightning swamped the house in pale-blue light and went again as quickly as it came, robbing her of the little use she had in her eyes.

Finally, she reached the small triangular cupboard and opened the door. The torch normally hung on a hook just inside the door. *Shit!* It wasn't there.

The feeling of not being alone returned with a vengeance. Slowly, she straightened up and began to turn her body. Lightning flashed and revealed the outline of a huge man. Then the blackness engulfed him again.

Grace hitched a breath and froze. "Dylan? she whispered, but it was wishful thinking.

Standing in front of her in the darkness, she heard his low chuckle. "Guess again, Angel."

The whole of her insides plummeted to the floor. "Diablo." Her mind raced. "Where is Cerise?" she managed, but the words barely came out a croak.

"Taking a nap… just you and me."

Grace began to take tiny steps sideways, ready to run, but his arm came out to bar her way. "Where are you going, sweet thing?" His hot breath was at her ear now. She was sweating with fear. His answer was to lick the side of her face in one long drag.

Reason left her for an instant and all she could think of doing was getting out of there. She ducked under his arm and ran towards the front door, shrieking Cerise's name as she went. Sobbing, she flung the door open and ran out into the pouring rain.

If she'd been capable of more rational thought, she would have known he could have easily caught up with her if he'd wanted to, but she was some way off from the house before she realised she wasn't being followed and allowed herself to slow down. *Fuck, where was he?*

Her throat was sore from pulling in great lungfuls of air from her sudden exertion and she frantically looked all around her for a place to go. Did she head into the countryside, having no clue whether she was going in the right direction to find the others? Should she go back down the lane in the direction of the village, or stay put in the hope someone would come back?

There was no way she was going back inside that house. The lightning lit up the sky and the rain continued to lash down on her. There was still no sign of Diablo, but she had to get some shelter.

A shed was set a little apart from the house. That would do. She crouched low next to the wall that formed part of the perimeter of the garden, and crept along it until she came to the gap that allowed the cars in off the lane.

She was soaked through and shivering. Her heart was hammering and she felt sick with fear. Checking the coast was clear, she made a dash for the shed, making sure she stayed low. Up close, it was more like a shack. She tugged on the door, but it refused to move. She almost screamed in frustration. A shovel was wedged at an angle up against it. She kicked it out of the way and wrenched open the door. It smelled musty, but she hurried inside out of the weather. It took all her strength to drag the door shut again.

All around her was pitch-black except for the slits and gaps between the planks that allowed the smallest of light in, but it was better than nothing. She moved deeper inside with small steps until her shin bumped into something soft.

A sack? She crouched down and felt warm, soft cloth.

A bolt of lightning made her jump, but briefly lit up the space enough for her to see for a second. The scream escaped her before she could stop it. She clamped her hands across her mouth to stop any more noise and prayed Diablo hadn't heard it.

"Oh, Fenton," she whispered. "What's he done to you?" She touched his face gently and found it wet. The lightning lit the sky again and she saw it wasn't rainwater but blood. "Oh no, Fenton," she sobbed. *Where was Cerise... was she in here too?*

Grace began to shuffle around on the floor to feel if there was anyone else in there. Tools began to fall and clanked heavily on the floor, making her stop and hold her breath to listen. Her heart was beating like a freight train and her eyes were wide and glued to the door.

A whimper escaped her when she saw the dark shadow loom up slowly, clearly seen through the cracks. With her hands held to her mouth, she watched as the door slowly and noisily opened.

Diablo stood like a grand entrance to one of his films. She could see it now: *Diablo's Revenge!* His hair was plastered to his head in the rain and she could clearly see his cruel and piercing look and the maniacal smile like a painful grimace.

"Angel," he said, like a doting parent. "Out you come... It's time to go."

She looked tearfully down at Fenton, then back at Diablo. He preempted her question. "It's too late for him."

Apathetic in her misery, she stood slowly, seeing nothing else she could do for Fenton or herself. She walked towards Diablo as if he were the Devil. There was nothing left to do but comply.

Diablo steered her by the elbow back to the four-wheel drive and pushed her into the passenger seat. "Don't move." He stalked around the front of the car and got in the driver's seat

"Where are we going?

Diablo started the engine and turned his gaze on her. "We're going to the party, Angel." He laughed and the car pulled off the garden. "It's been a long fucking time coming."

The car bumped over some ruts and joined a dirt track that led up into the hills. Somewhere in the countryside where the coordinates had pointed to the exact spot where two dimensions would touch and the person who came all those years ago would go back. Grace began to cry silently. *Dylan, her Dylan.* Tears streamed down her face, and Diablo was oblivious.

The car trundled along the bumpy track for what felt like ages.

"Why did you have to kill him?" Grace asked. "He was your friend." She had to hold onto the door and the dashboard so she wouldn't bounce out of her seat.

Diablo's face remained blank and unreadable. "He's D's friend, not mine."

"Dylan's," Grace corrected angrily.

Diablo sneered. "No, Angel, I'm Dylan, and you know it." He smiled broadly. "And soon I will get rid of the fucker who stole my life."

Grace stared at him in horror like the madman he was. He was concentrating on driving while the track twisted this way and that. "You've always known... this was going to happen... Tonight, I mean?"

He didn't answer, just turned his head and grinned at her.

"How though… if *he's* the alien?"

He nodded as if it was a fair question and it didn't matter that she knew now. "Because I'm strong." And he pointed at his own temple. "I wouldn't just fucking lay down and take it."

"Take what?" she said, cautiously.

The car slowed to a stop and he switched the engine off and killed the lights. He turned his body to face her in his seat. "After a while, when we were trapped, things started to get a little mixed up." He laughed. "I enjoyed fucking with him… always so fucking straight. Then I started to see the lines between us blurring." Diablo's eyes seemed to take on a far-off look as he spoke. "I realised I had access to him, especially when he was asleep." He shook his head as if it amazed him even now. "And there it all was… the answer… how to get back. And as I started to learn, he started to forget." Diablo's face hardened. "Then you came along."

Grace frowned. She was confused.

"Now he had a reason to live… to stay. He started to get fucking stronger. A real pain in the fucking arse."

Her tears were streaming now. "He'll fight you to stay."

Diablo smiled. "Ya think? We'll see."

"I'll just tell them all up there what you did," she blurted, angrily.

He let out one huff of derisive laughter. "You could, but you won't."

"Oh yeah… and why not?"

"For the same reason D went along with it - Because tonight is a once-only opportunity for it all to end." He studied her face for a moment so intensely that she wasn't sure if he was going to kiss her. "One way or another," he finished eventually. Then he seemed to snap himself out of it and gave her no more time for questions. "Now get out the fucking car."

As usual, he managed to unnerve her and she could do nothing more than obey, so she got out. He walked around the car while he put handcuffs on himself and grinned arrogantly. She yelped when he yanked her to him, but it was just to slip a key in her pocket. Then he nudged her to walk on. The rain had stopped, but thunder still rumbled in the distance. The moon was out now, though, lighting the path that continued, too narrow for a car.

CHAPTER 29

*A*s soon as they walked into the lit area that looked like a scaled-down version of *Close Encounters,* Diablo held out his wrists for Grace to undo the handcuffs. His eyes held hers in arrogant amusement, almost daring her to blow the whistle. She closed her eyes with contempt and fumbled with the key. The cuffs clicked open just as Simon hurried over to them. "You're cutting it fine," he said, pointing to his watch. "Just ten minutes." Then he took a double-take, "What are you doing here?" Then he looked between them. "Where's Fenton?"

Diablo gestured to Grace to answer, grinning, which really pissed her off. He knew as well as she did that it was tonight or never and she wouldn't say anything, no matter how much she wanted to, for fear the moment would be gone forever. "We couldn't get hold of anyone... There was an emergency with one of the kids," she said moodily. "They apologised, they had to rush off."

Diablo smiled back at Simon as if to say "see", but she could tell Simon was troubled by it. But just like her, he was tied to speeding things along. He simply held out his arm to point them in the direction of the machine that would hopefully produce enough electromagnetic energy to split Diablo and Dylan in two.

They were about to move off when Diablo held Simon by the top of the arm and spoke in hushed tones. Grace could only watch as Simon nodded and took a flat packet out of his breast pocket and passed it to Diablo. It was done like a payoff in a drug deal. "Good," Diablo said and slipped it into the back pocket of his fatigues. "Let's get on with it." And he led her with him by the elbow.

She cast a furtive glance at Simon, but he was already concerned about something one of the engineers was showing him. Diablo made her jump when he put his mouth to her ear as if he'd second-guessed her. "You try and fuck this up for me and I'll hurt your friends." All the while, he was walking casually and no one else could hear what he was saying. Just before he stepped onto the platform, he pecked her on the cheek, "And that ain't nothin' compared to what I'll do to you." He winked and pointed to the spot where he wanted her to stand in front of him, where he could see her only a few feet away.

She blasted red with fear and impotent rage. "What did you say to Simon?" she said angrily.

Diablo grinned and leaned back into the apparatus.

Hopelessness washed over her. What could she do? He was so confident, he was up to something. She tried to make her breaths long and even. *Please win, Dylan... please win.*

Simon was now back behind the bank of computer-like machines, conferring with Nicholas. Anton was with them. They all looked over at her, as though her name had been mentioned. Nervously, she checked whether Diablo was watching, but his eyes were fixed in front and unaware. *Was he tormenting Dylan?*

Biting down her fury, she sidestepped a little to see if she could silently get a message across to the others. Cerise could be lying injured somewhere. Whilst she couldn't stop it, she somehow had to warn them what Diablo had done and what he was capable of. His perfect behaviour had lured them all into a false sense of security. They had no idea if he walked away from this, they were all in danger.

"Stay where I can see you," he said, quietly.

With a face like thunder, she shuffled a step back and reluctantly accepted that she had to wait to make her move.

The contraption Diablo was standing on was like a giant upside-down saucer about eight feet across. It covered the exact spot of the coordinates that were etched on his body. A computer was on a table behind it and sensors like stage lighting were arranged all around the outside of the saucer. A tall pipe was behind, stretching high into the air, reminding her of a netball post without the loop, supposedly to act as a lightning rod. A handrail with shackles was on either side of him, she guessed to help him keep his grip. The whole thing looked improvised rather than the space-age device it was, but she guessed they'd only had a few days to make it and very little money.

When she glanced back over at the others at the control panel, Anton was missing. Her heart skipped and she tried not to give anything away. She hoped to god they had sent him back down to the cottage. It was too late for poor Fenton, but maybe they would find Cerise and realise just how dangerous Diablo was.

Nicholas bent forward and spoke into a microphone, "Six minutes to go."

Simon walked over and began to wire and shackle Diablo up to the machine. "You should stay well back, Grace."

"I'll see that she does, Doc. I want to say a proper good-bye... just us," he said, staring straight into her eyes – daring her to move a muscle.

For a split second, she contemplated running, but it was fleeting. He had her and he knew it.

Simon nodded reluctantly and continued with a few safety dos and don'ts, to which Diablo nodded every so often. A pad was stuck on each of his temples, wrists and the front and back of his chest and then a cable connected them to the console behind and to the pole.

Grace looked up at the sky. The clouds hadn't gone away. If anything, they were building again and lightning flashed and thunder rumbled. The storm must be connected to what was about to happen. It all felt like proof that Dylan – her Dylan – wasn't crazy.

"Five minutes to go."

Simon walked back to the control panel. Grace felt terribly alone away from the others, a little like being the only one on a stage. She could just about make out the shapes of the technicians beavering away behind the wall of lights. The generator began to get louder, as if it was being turned up.

"Four minutes to go."

Her eyes went back to Diablo. He was watching her, eyes mischievous. He looked confident; then again, he never looked any different. He was arrogant and cocky, as opposed to Dylan, who was quiet and modest.

"Three minutes to go."

Shit! Panic began to rise in her; it was nearly time. Should she get away, knowing he couldn't get off the platform? Would he ruin his only chance to get to her? No, as much as she hated it, she had to see this through. She hoped to god that Dylan was strong enough to beat this bastard and that she was enough of an incentive for him to fight.

"Two minutes to go."

A loud clap of thunder sounded almost directly overhead and made her jump out of her skin. She recovered her composure and watched Diablo. His eyes were watching the heavens too. Maybe he wasn't as confident as he made out?

She knew without doubt that Dylan would never leave her, not if there was any possible way he could stay.

"One minute to go… please take the brace position, Diablo."

Lightning began to flash all around the area, as if it was attracted to that spot and was being pulled there. It was landing near her feet and scorching the grass with a sizzle. She started to fidget.

"Stay the fuck where you are!" Diablo said, through gritted teeth.

Grace froze. Before she could say a word, the lightning began to strike the pole. Diablo's whole body shook violently, and his eyes disappeared up into his head.

DYLAN WOKE IN SEARING PAIN. Every nerve ending, every sinew, muscle and bone was alive and on fire. He found he was screaming but he wasn't alone as Diablo screamed with him. He felt what Dylan felt. This was their last moment together and they were both awake for it.

Dylan had hardly been conscious over the last four days, but had struggled to the surface periodically just to make sure everything was moving towards the goal. It had surprised him how cooperative Diablo had been with the whole process. It made him ultra suspicious of his angle. Despite what everyone else thought, Dylan knew that Diablo wasn't keen to leave his body and go back home, and he was sure he didn't know that it would be the interloper who would leave. Something wasn't adding up. He told himself over and over, all he had to do was get through the pain and hold on.

He looked up at the contraption above them and saw the

lightning with several forks hitting it continually and now flowing straight through the cables to them. Very little else was visible through the extreme pain – just a white light. His brain was extremely active, though. Amongst the agony came memories of when he was a boy. Everything was so clear and yet snapshots pulsed in quick succession. A tunnel of white light surrounded him, just like that night, and the pain – so much pain.

Before long, Dylan became so engrossed in memories, the lines of which had long ago been blurred. Everything was becoming confused. The heat felt white-hot as if it flowed through his veins. Then it became like a magnet, pulling and sucking him backwards into the furnace of brilliant white light. *Was this death – was this the white light that people who died came back and spoke of?*

He began to drift, his mind became filled with images of an unfamiliar landscape, but before he could rationalise anything, maniacal laughter broke through the haze. The voice sounded like his own for a moment until he remembered where he was and what must be happening.

Diablo. He must be resisting. *Why was* he *floating? Surely it should be Diablo struggling to think straight right now?* But instead, Diablo was pushing him; not to the back of his mind, but out from the confines of his body.

Dylan tried to break through the fuzz in his brain. This was the moment they'd waited almost twenty years for, when at last they would be pulled apart. And it suddenly began to dawn on him that it was he – Dylan – that was leaving. *No, not Dylan ...*

The crazed laughter rang out again.

Feelings of being adrift intensified. He struggled to see through his eyes, to know what was going on, but Diablo blocked his access. It felt as though he was being held underwater, suffocating and unable to breathe. Panic erupted and he fought with everything to reach the air, the last piece of light.

"Very well… take your last look, spaceman." Diablo laughed and retreated.

It was the old argument they'd had over and over as children: Who was Dylan and who was D? It angered him to be having it again now, but he overlooked it and snatched prominence to see through his eyes.

There she was – Grace. Facing him just a few feet away with a fearful expression on her face.

"Dylan!" she shouted, recognising him for a second.

"Stay back, baby," he tried to communicate, but he wasn't sure if she heard over the din of what was happening all around them. It looked like a firework shower of white sparks and the noise was deafening. All he could do was watch the tears track down her face.

"That's enough… you said your farewells!" Diablo pushed in and threw him to the background again.

"What the fuck?" Dylan said. *No more. This was over now.* It was Diablo who was going.

"You don't get it, do you… Can't you feel it? It's *you* who's being pulled away. *You* are the trespasser, D," Diablo said, not bothering to hide the thrill in his voice.

Dylan struggled, refusing to believe it. He'd heard it all before and held on, despite the sucking sensation pulling him like a vacuum. "No!" He held on tighter, straining every fibre of his being. Not allowing any chinks in his resolve, or to doubt himself and to wonder why it seemed Diablo was right and he could feel himself being pulled away.

An image of Grace came to him. Clear and beautiful as the day he had first seen her. He was all she had. The only thing she had asked before she went was for him to win. She didn't deserve to spend her life alone. He'd kill Diablo himself before he left her to him. "No!" he repeated. "You're evil... she was never for you."

Diablo laughed out loud, a full and hearty sound that showed not one ounce of fear or doubt. "But she loves being with me ... needs it even."

Dylan sneered, not even dignifying the ridiculous comment with a response.

"You don't believe me?" Diablo said, highly amused. "That she could actually want what I can give her." He whispered conspiratorially. "You know she likes it rough."

Dylan finally lost his cool and used all his psychic energy to push back at Diablo with all his might, and for a few moments, they fought. "You never got a chance to get near her like that... I saw to it."

Diablo's psychic self avoided the blows while he laughed, enjoying the fight. Eventually, they both began to tire. "I'll show you."

"Fuck off, I don't want to know your fantasies." And the pair tumbled and rolled inside their skin, all the while the lightning encased them for what felt like hours.

Diablo caught Dylan and held him still so he could speak. "Let's look through my eyes at the same time... I'll prove to you I'm not lying."

Dylan tried to resist, but he was weakening fast and needed the last of his strength not to be ripped away. And so he allowed himself to come to the fore.

"Angel," Diablo said, seductively, but loud enough for Grace's eyes to widen in recognition and then shrink again when she realised who was speaking. "I'm just sharing with Dylan our special night ... the one where you came to me knowing Dylan was asleep. How you fucked me willingly and wanted it. Angel, tell him how you wanted it."

Dylan was cognizant and viewing through the eyes of his body long enough to see her blanch and recoil. He witnessed the disappointment, the heartbreak and, lastly, the resignation at being found out.

The air left him as if he'd been winded. He was stunned. And for a second, it felt like his spirit was suspended in nothingness.

Instead of offering any compassion, Diablo hammered home his advantage and revealed his memories to him, that he was now too weak to resist. Picture after sordid picture. "You see … you aren't even human. That's why she came to me. She wants what only a red-blooded human male can give her."

Dylan didn't look at her face again. But in Diablo, he saw pleasure in victory. The masterstroke delivered at just the right moment. Everything seemed to grow quieter and move further and further away. He became more distant until the white light began to call him once more. Memories came to him of a strange land. A place so welcoming that it could soothe all grief, take away all pain, until everything about this world diminished and what threatened to rip his heart from his chest was gone for ever.

When Diablo started to violently shake, Grace's first instinct was to go to him, but arms quickly grabbed her from behind.

"No, stop!" Simon shouted over the noise. "The electricity will kill you."

"It's killing him!" she shrieked over her shoulder and struggled.

Simon held her fast. "We have to see it through, Grace."

She sagged back against him, but Simon continued to hold her arms. All she could do was watch the grizzly sight that reminded her of a person possessed from a horror film. The whites were showing in his eyes and foam frothed from his mouth. Surely no one could survive this onslaught.

His eyes flickered from brown to blue and then back up into his head again. At last, they seemed to stabilise blue for a moment. "Dylan!" she screamed.

He focused on her and seemed to fight to stay conscious. "Stay back, baby… be careful."

She struggled again. "Dylan!" she sobbed.

"Listen to him," Simon said, next to her ear.

She was openly bawling like a baby now. All the pain he must be feeling and he still thought of her safety.

Then, as suddenly as he appeared, Dylan was gone.

Grace shrieked for him to come back, but the blue eyes had disappeared up into his head again and flickered brown intermittently. It was as if a huge battle was going on inside the body, even though she knew he was being subjected to electromagnetic energy flowing directly into him. It reminded her of someone she'd once seen having a fit, except Dylan was standing, and not convulsing on the floor.

Even Simon eyed the ground around them nervously for fear the lightning would come too close and they would be struck. It was like standing too close to a firework display. The air was charged with static and smelled like burnt sulphur.

The sparks continued to rain down on them and Dylan was thrown this way and that. The only thing holding him upright now was the restraints attached to the framework. His juddering eventually began to slow and his eyes squeezed shut.

Grace watched him, willing him to wake up, praying that he would survive this.

They slowly opened. "Angel."

Her blood ran cold.

The look on his face, oblivious to the pain, filled her with absolute terror. She dreaded what he would do next in order to win the struggle. Her body shrank into Simon behind her. A smile crept across Diablo's face.

She felt numb as she watched his lips move. All she caught was the final words steeling from his mouth in a taunt. " Angel… Tell him how you wanted it."

Time seemed to zoom in on her. Above her, lightning built and poured down to earth in long ribbons of light. The static electricity produced by the machine was now rattling the equipment violently. Pieces began to fall apart and drop off.

A glimpse of blue in his eyes filled her with hope for a second, but appeared to fade, as if a dimmer switch was being slowly turned down. "Dylan!" she screamed, and a bolt of lightning shot from his chest, barely missing her. She and Simon jumped instinctively to the left and turned as it appeared to hit an invisible wall and spread outwards into a starburst of light and then disappeared.

Immediately, the lightning around them began to subside. The labouring machine began to slow down and become quieter until it sounded like a car engine ticking over. Only a few intermittent last bursts of energy hit the floor sporadically until it eventually became as silent as a tomb.

No one moved.

Dylan's body sagged and hung limp from the harness. His skin was blackened and charred, especially at the points the pads were stuck to him.

As soon as it was safe, the men all rushed to him, unbuckled his wrists and restraints and caught him as soon as he was freed. But it was a shell. Grace knew that Dylan had gone. With nothing left, she sank to the ground and cried silently, so utterly heartbroken that she didn't even ask if Diablo had survived. What did it matter, the love of her life had gone and, what's more, her parting gift to him was her complete and utter betrayal with the worst person possible.

CHAPTER 30

*P*oor Dylan hadn't seen it coming. He was the visitor and was at a disadvantage. Diablo had always known and hidden the vital piece of information from him. He could even have perpetuated his belief in being the genuine human. Then he bided his time and waited. She foolishly loaded the gun for him that he fired at the very last minute, when Dylan was already exhausted from fighting. With nothing left, he'd simply let go of life, this world, and of her.

She closed her eyes. *I'm so very sorry, Dylan. There is no excuse.* She thought like a prayer.

Her eyes flickered when gentle arms began to pull her up from the floor. She allowed it but continued to cry. "He's gone," was all she could say, over and over.

One of the technicians led her to the Land Rovers. Dylan's body was stretchered to another. Her eyes strayed to him and she briefly wondered if Diablo had gone as well. As if to answer her question, his head rolled and he groaned. Still too stunned to think deeply about the implications, she meekly watched him being loaded into the back door of the vehicle.

Grief consumed her on the ride back to the cottage. The ruts and bumps in the road were the only things that cut through her misery when she bumped her shoulder hard on the door. She couldn't get beyond the repeating thought that he had really gone. Then the whole world tumbled in on her and she cried silently. Tears and snot were running freely down her face and she made no attempt to remove them.

A hand nudged her, and a handkerchief was offered. She absently registered it was Simon. Weird, what you thought of when you were in misery; old-fashioned, was what came to mind – that he still carried a handkerchief.

"He's not dead, you know… just unconscious," Simon said kindly.

She raised her hopeless eyes to his.

He still didn't get it and nodded to confirm what he'd just said and smiled.

She shook her head. "Dylan's gone… didn't you see him go?"

"Back through the rift?" he bobbed his head in acknowledgement. "Something went, we need to analyse our data, but you don't know it was Dylan?" he said, smiling.

Not bothering to argue, she shrugged listlessly. It no longer mattered whether their experiment was a success. "He's not there any more," was all she said.

Simon was putting her behaviour down to shock, she could tell. The patronising pat he gave her hand said everything. "We're taking him straight to hospital as soon as we get back to the house."

She roused for a second. "Fenton!" she said, suddenly remembering.

Simon nodded. "We wondered that too… sent Anton back to find him."

"You don't understand," Grace said. "Diablo killed him … he's dead. You don't know what he's like." She began to get agitated.

Simon continued to "Shhh" and pat her hand, while they pulled into the parking space at the cottage, next to their little hire car left there earlier.

Anton was waiting anxiously for them outside. The first car carrying Diablo pulled in with theirs closely behind it. The technicians and the two medics Simon had hired and sworn to secrecy swarmed around Diablo and carried him inside. His head rolled and an arm moved.

Anton hurried over to them. "It worked?"

Simon nodded while they walked towards the house. "The rift was spectacular and someone definitely left."

Grace scowled. "The wrong one."

Anton tried to pull Simon away to say something to him privately, but Grace was having none of it. She was coming out of her stupor, and shit was about to get very real around here if someone didn't start listening to her. "Don't you dare shut me out, Anton. Did you find Fenton and Cerise?"

Anton frowned. "Cerise is inside… that's what I wanted to tell you. I found her gagged and bound and stuffed into a wardrobe upstairs. She's inside," he said, nodding at the house.

Grace was already jogging in that direction.

"I've called an ambulance… Managed to get a signal at last… They're on their way," Anton shouted after her.

"You need to call the police," she shouted over her shoulder.

No one was taking any notice. Anton probably thought Diablo needed the softly, softly approach and not sending to prison where he belonged. She huffed and hurried inside to see Cerise for herself.

Diablo had been placed on one of the two sofas and

Cerise sat on the other. He still seemed out of action, so Grace went straight to Cerise, who looked shaken and had a swollen, reddened cheek. She ran to her and the two women hugged. Tears of relief flowed for both of them.

Grace put her away from her and held her face, looking at the injury.

"He caught me as soon as I came out of the bathroom. I didn't even have a chance to call out to you." She rubbed her cheek and winced. "Next thing I knew, it was pitch black and I heard Anton calling. He heard me and let me out." She looked around her, worried. "Have you seen Fenton yet?"

Grace just couldn't bring herself to tell her about Fenton – not yet. "Just a minute, babe, I'll ask." She stood up and pulled Simon and Anton with her into the kitchen. "Fenton is in the shed," she said, really quietly, as soon as they were out of earshot. "He killed him." She stabbed the air with her finger in the direction they'd just come from.

The two men looked at her as if she'd lost her mind.

"Did you hear me?… He's in the fucking shed," she said in a shouted whisper, through gritted teeth.

FENTON DIDN'T HAVE a clue where he was. There wasn't a part of him that wasn't screaming out in pain. *Diablo!* Realising that only one of them was coming out of tonight, the slippery bastard had got in there first.

He struggled to get his bearings. It was pitch black, but the smell of earth and mouldy fruit told him he must be in a shed. It took all his effort to just get his arm underneath him to lean up. He groaned with the pain and flopped back down. Shit, cracked ribs and, judging by the headache from hell, a possible fractured skull. He was beat up bad. *The fucker!* He should have been ready for him.

The girls! He relaxed when he remembered that Dylan had

had the sense to send them away before all this happened. *Thank god.*

But where the fuck was he? Whatever happened, Fenton had to be ready to carry out his promise to Dylan. He had to man up and get the fuck up off this floor. He rolled onto his side in an attempt to get on all fours, but ended up flat on his face in the dirt. The pain was so great it threatened to drag him under again. He fought the nausea and breathed through it. *Fuck!* His knee was fucked. Diablo had smashed it, knowing just where to kick to collapse his leg.

With one more gigantic effort, Fenton pushed up on his forearms. Sweat poured from his face with the pain and exertion. His heart was working like a train. Slowly, inch by inch, he pulled himself forward towards the door, grateful for the years of training that gave him the upper body strength. The agony in his ribs and damaged forearm forced him to rest every few moments and take shallow breaths and concentrate on not being sick.

When he finally reached the door, he punched it several times to open it a little at a time. The bastard thing had dropped on its hinges and scraped on the ground. Hand over hand, he crawled, dragging his injured leg behind him and using the other to get more traction and help his tiring arms.

Determined, and eyes closed with concentration, he managed to get half his body outside the shed, until two shiny black boots came clearly into his eye line.

Ah, fuck! His weight collapsed down into the damp earth and he waited for the killer blow. Then darkness enveloped him again.

"JANEY... OVER HERE!"

"What is it, Dave?... There's definitely no one in."

"Some bloke... looks hurt pretty bad." Dave bent down

and felt his neck for a pulse, then put his phone to his ear. There was no signal. *Shit!* There was no way he could call an ambulance. It was this fucking storm. The lightning was all over the sky in the distance, but no thunder. *Weird.*

"Maybe they're not staying here any more?" Janey said. "It's pretty out in the wilds."

Dave clicked off his phone and nodded. Then he looked left and right while he made up his mind. To tell the truth, he didn't know what to do. He looked at the black guy lying at his feet. "This bloke ain't gonna last much longer, his pulse is really weak. We'd better get him to hospital. I'll have a think on the way."

Between the two of them, they managed to heft him into the back seat of their hire car and pulled slowly away. Dave wasn't a great talker and he didn't want to scare Janey, but he didn't just want to get this guy medical attention; he wanted to get Janey the hell out of there, and he knew she wouldn't bloody go anywhere if she thought Grace was still in danger.

He'd never liked that bloody great fucker Grace was seeing right from the off. He shook his head. And her tearing back up here after the bloody Loony Tunes explanation she'd given them about what was going on. It didn't take much for Dave to decide he was coming up here after her when Janey had relayed it to him when he'd finished his shift. And of course Janey was having none of it when he said he was going on his own.

He drove as fast as he dared down the single-track, windy lane towards the village. It seemed to go on forever. They were almost at the point where it widened out as it came towards civilisation, when the flashing lights of an ambulance approached them. *What luck.* Maybe someone called it from back there? He slowed down, stopped in the road and turned to the back seat to check on the injured man. He was in a bad way.

The ambulance blasted its siren briefly to tell them to get out of the way, so Dave got out and jogged around the car to the driver's side.

Something told him not to announce he was a police officer at this stage. He didn't want to get tied up with paperwork until he was sure that Grace was safe. "Got an injured man in the back of my car... he's hurt pretty bad, I was taking him to hospital."

"We're on a 999," the driver said, looking at his colleague in the passenger seat. "Where has he come from?" the driver said, nodding towards Dave's car.

"A cottage, all on its own, a few miles up the lane on the hill."

The two ambulance men nodded at each other. "That sounds like our call."

"Great," Dave said, relieved when the ambulance men got out of the vehicle and headed over to his car. "Someone must have already called you," Dave added. But it didn't sit well with him. The house had been completely empty.

GRACE LED the way out of the back door to the rickety old shed at the side of the garden and near the parked cars. "Does anyone have a torch?"

"Yes. I have one on my phone," Anton said, getting his out of his jacket pocket.

She paused at the door. It was half open. She tried to remember if Diablo had closed it when he had taken her from there earlier. It scuffed the grass as she pulled it open.

"Let me," Anton said, pushing past and shining his torch. It flashed around, first in the centre of the floor, then around the edges and up the walls. Apart from sacks, fruit boxes and rusty tools, the shed was empty.

"But I don't get it?" Grace said in dismay. She had to walk

in and look all around herself before she could believe it was empty. "But he was here... I swear."

They paused before they went back inside the house at the back door. "You've been under a lot of strain," Anton said, touching her gently on the arm.

"I know what I fucking saw, Anton!" Grace snapped.

"Come, come now," Simon said, trying to defuse the situation. "Nerves are a bit frazzled. It could be as simple as he wasn't dead and simply got up and walked out of there." He looked at them both for a reply but met with stony faces. "Cerise *was* just tied up?"

"Well, where is he now?" Grace huffed and supposed he had to be right. Not that she didn't want him to be, it was just she was so sure. She was beginning to doubt everything. That had to be it, didn't it? Diablo couldn't have moved him. He'd been with her the whole time. She nodded, eventually, grateful for Simon's voice of reason. And *Anton could go fuck himself!* "Let's go back inside," she said, huffily, pushing between them. Cerise had been left with Diablo. "The pair of you don't know what you're dealing with."

While the medics saw to Diablo, Nicholas noticed that Cerise was shivering and sitting all alone like a frightened little girl. The cottage wasn't the warmest of places, especially with no one home and no fire lit, but this was undoubtedly the manifestation of shock.

He'd draped his jacket around her shoulders and bent slightly into her eye line. "Would you like me to make you a nice hot sugary tea, dear?

Her eyes strayed to the sofa before she answered. He followed her line of vision.

Diablo lay awake but looked dazed – bleary-eyed. He was quiet, as if he'd just woken from sleep and was coming to.

Cerise dragged her eyes from Diablo and put her attention back on Nicholas. "No, thank you, but do you have a mobile phone that works? I'm getting really worried about Fenton."

"I can do better than that, shall we try him on his two-way radio … probably more reliable out here?" he finished with a chuckle, trying to make light of the situation. He pulled the radio from its case on his belt and pressed the button. "Fenton… Fenton… come in, Fenton?"

All eyes went to the sofa, where the beep, crackle and hiss could be clearly heard.

Diablo was awake enough to smile when he knew he'd been busted and studied every little nuance on Cerise's face while she put two and two together.

It took Nicholas a moment longer to fall in. Only when Cerise flew at him in a blind rage and he only just caught her in time, did he realise the implication of Diablo having Fenton's phone. *Surely not?*

For a few moments, Cerise fought with him. "Let me go…" she said over and over. She screamed with frustration, but her voice, already hoarse from calling out earlier, was a crackled whisper.

"Come with me," Nicholas said, deciding that to remove her from the situation was the best policy, and coaxed her towards the front door. He glanced back over his shoulder at Diablo and was slightly unnerved by how totally relaxed he was just lying there. It was as if the spat just never happened, his feathers not even ruffled.

Together, they walked to the end of the little garden path where there was a small, square rotary washing line. His arm was about her shoulders, holding his jacket around her. It was a cold night and they could see their breath. "He'll turn up, don't you worry," he said in an attempt to comfort her.

"He knows where Fenton is," she spat.

Nicholas had to agree; the evidence was damning. "Doesn't mean he's done him any harm," he said, keeping up his jolly tone as best he could.

She sighed and nodded reluctantly. "Do you mind if I just sit in the car for a while?"

"Sure… that's a good idea. We can put the engine on and give you a blast of heat." He led her to her hire car, which was now blocked in by the Land Rovers. He opened the door. "Here," and held it for her.

Cerise got in, started the engine and let it tick over.

"I'll be back in a minute. I'll see about that tea."

She smiled up at him wanly and he pushed the door shut with a click. He paused briefly, seeing the backs of others walking from the shed towards the back door. It puzzled him. He'd just sort Cerise out first, and he walked briskly back around the front of the house to check on the patient on his way.

He was almost there when he heard a smash of crockery, then wood. He peered through the sashed window to the living room with a clear view, as the curtains hadn't been drawn. The sight in front of him was grotesque and yet compelling. He stood transfixed. It was like some poor-taste film with the sound turned down low. Something in him said to turn and run, but his legs refused to move.

The loud crash was the collapse of the coffee table. One of the technicians was lying across its flattened remains on the floor, his arms and legs all wrong and twisted like a rag doll; his eyes were open and staring up at the ceiling.

Diablo was up on his feet, holding the other technician in some sort of chokehold from behind. His arms were so muscled, the man's face was going red and his eyes began to bulge. Diablo did not so much as grimace with the effort or even break into a sweat. His other arm moved across the man's forehead and then suddenly wrenched his arms in opposite directions. The crack was audible, even from where Nicholas was standing. Then he discarded the body onto the sofa.

The two medics had stood back, eyes wide like saucers and immobilised with fear. When they saw Diablo slowly turn his gaze to them, their hands came up in front of them as if to ward him off, and they edged backwards, trying to talk him down. He stalked towards them and went to grab their throats. They clawed at his wrists with both hands, but he simply stepped back and slammed their bodies into each other. The impact seemed to take their breath, stunning them, and they crumpled to the floor.

Seizing the weakness, Diablo picked up one of them by the hair. His braying was halted when he was hit with a shattering punch to the Adam's apple. The noise was replaced by a horrible choking and gasping for breath through a crushed windpipe. He was silenced completely with a crushing blow to the temple. The poor man went instantly limp, his open eyes glazed and no longer seeing. The last man – a medic, now knew he wasn't going to be left alive and dove for a poker next to the fireplace. Diablo grinned and nodded as if he appreciated the man's gumption. But it was a pathetic, futile attempt as Diablo merely snatched it and yanked the man into range. He punched and wriggled maniacally, trying to get out of Diablo's grip, but he missed and appeared to have limbs of jelly. Briefly, Diablo seemed amused, but his face soon turned back to business. He pulled him forward, bending him over towards him and held him in a headlock. Nicholas thought he was going to choke the life out of him – and that was barbaric enough, but instead he grabbed the back of the man's belt, hauled him into the air vertically, upside down, and threw himself backwards so he landed on the poor man's head. Their combined weight crashed through his head and neck, onto the flagged stoned floor around the fireplace. The rug did little to absorb any of the devastating impact. When Diablo flipped the man back over to face him, a trickle of blood ran from his nostrils and his eyes were blank and staring.

Nicholas was chilled by the efficiency of the killings. It reminded him of a butcher carrying out his everyday work. Not a flinch or the batting of an eyelid. None of them stood a chance against such an effective killing machine.

The room was now silent. Diablo was watching the man on the floor intently.

Was it to make sure there were no further retaliations? Nicholas didn't think so. There was something in the rapt fascination that reminded him of a bully being cruel to a harmless creature he'd once seen at school. It chilled him to the bone.

Then a wave of nausea hit him so strong that it threatened to overwhelm him, and he had to grab his mouth. Leaving his hands there, he watched Diablo tentatively put the tips of his fingers into the blood oozing from the man's nose and mouth, and while he stared the dying man straight in the eyes, he put his fingers to his tongue.

Nicholas retched loudly.

Diablo turned his head to the window sharply.

Nicholas prayed that looking into the dark night from the lit room meant he couldn't see who it was. His eyes appeared to be scanning. Perhaps there was a slim chance. Every instinct in him told him to run, but he fought it and stood still. Diablo would see if anything moved quickly.

The front of Diablo's shirt was covered in dirt and soot, he had smears across his forehead and cheek and a daub of blood at the corner of his mouth. He looked like some kind of demonic savage.

Diablo slowly unfolded his large physique until he stood straight and a slow smile spread across his face.

Heaven help me... The shark's eyes pierced through the glass and right into him while he stalked towards the door.

NOTHING COULD PREPARE them for the sight that greeted them when they stepped back into the living room. Grace surveyed the room, utterly stunned. The twisted bodies of the technicians and medics lay at awkward angles. The smashed furniture and glass were shattered and jagged on the rumpled rug. In the mess, she couldn't believe how little blood there was, and yet they were all undoubtedly dead.

"Cerise?" she shouted suddenly in terror, turning around frantically.

"She's not here," Simon said. "Neither is Nicholas."

Grace was dazed. Why had he done this? Was it because he thought they'd found Fenton? Her eyes rested on Anton. He looked in shock. Simon was no better; none of them could believe their eyes.

"This is our fault," Anton said, low and deliberate.

Grace and Simon both looked at him in bewilderment.

"Pandering to his delusions. I should have put a stop to it." He shook his head and began to pace. "It was against my better judgment."

Simon looked exasperated with him and was just about to speak when they were plunged into darkness.

For a moment, they were completely silent, waiting for their eyes to adjust.

"It's him," Grace whispered, terrified.

The three gravitated together in a huddle, feeling vulnerable and exposed. Grace looked around frantically. "Quick, let's get in the cupboard under the stairs." She began to edge nearer, making sure she had both men's hands and didn't trip over any of the debris or limbs on the floor.

Simon tried to hang back. "Wouldn't it be better to make a run for the car?" he said, sounding as terrified as her. "It makes no sense to stay put."

Grace expected Anton to help her convince him, but he was deathly quiet. She couldn't tell if he was traumatised or weighing up his options. There was no help there. "For fuck's sake, Simon. You wanna get yourself killed?" she whispered, angrily. "That's just what he wants you to do... You don't get it, do you?"

"We could talk to him… Anton could talk to him…" he blabbered.

"I don't think he's in the mood for talking, Simon… now come on." Grace pulled him with her and quietly opened the small cupboard door, not really understanding how she was managing to keep it all together. "Anton, switch your torch on now."

They all squashed in, closed the door and Anton did as she asked.

"This is ridiculous," Simon said.

Anton spoke for the first time in ages: "There's a hatch in the floor, it leads down into the cellar. All these old places have them."

Grace felt relieved. At least she wasn't the only one thinking properly.

Simon knelt, felt around and yanked it open. They all paused when they saw the inky blackness of the hole descending into nothing.

"Go on… We can close it after us. Lock ourselves in and wait it out till morning," Grace said.

No one offered any more argument, and they all followed Anton down the narrow stairway. When they reached the bottom, they realised that the cellar was surprisingly large. There were a few old sticks of furniture, some shelves and some boxes of old clutter.

"How did you know it was here?" Grace said, surveying the room.

"I found it when we got here," Anton explained. "The fridge was too small for all of us. It's a good place to keep bottles cold."

Grace nodded and began to rummage. "Look for some candles, matches or lamps… anything like that." She was totally taking charge, and the two men were letting her.

Anton began to help her, but Simon stood rooted to the

spot as if traumatised. They eventually found some old white candles, a couple of saucers and some big Cook's matches – a real find; the kind you could strike on anything.

Simon still hadn't moved; in fact, he was shaking violently. "Perhaps they weren't dead?... We should have called an ambulance... the police... anything." He was speaking too rapidly and growing in volume until Grace strode over to him quickly and shook him by the shoulders. She looked intently into his eyes. "They *are* dead, Simon. You know it, and I know it. Diablo killed them. He's completely out of control now that Dylan..." And she faltered for a second, then took a breath and continued, "has gone... We've just got to wait it out here, okay?"

She held his eyes until he nodded. Then she spoke more softly, "It'll be alright."

Anton huffed and plonked down into an old wicker chair. "I don't know why the hell I went along with all this?" he said, running his fingers through his hair and pushing it back from his face. "My god, I'm partly responsible for the deaths of all those people upstairs."

Grace came over to him and dropped down onto her haunches in front of him, so he was forced to look at her. "You couldn't have known this would happen, Anton."

"We... I... assumed he would work through this and come out the other side... The truth is, none of us fucking knew, okay. Instead of curing him, he's gone over to a completely psychotic state. I was never happy about the strength and concoction of the drugs he was taking." He was shaking his head, angry at himself.

It felt like a slap in the face to Grace, who was trying to hold it all together. She simply couldn't believe that the thing running around up there killing and terrorising people was some facet of Dylan; she just wouldn't have it. Dylan was a good man and he'd gone. She swallowed hard, blinked away the tears that had welled up in her eyes and coughed while she stood up. "None of us could have foreseen this," she said, with a cracked and broken voice.

It all seemed so ludicrous now when she thought about it. "We all assumed Dylan would win." She almost laughed with bitterness. The memory of Diablo's last revelation to Dylan flashed into her mind. She closed her eyes, but it wouldn't go away. It would never go away. "If anything, I am responsible," she said, walking to the furthest corner away from them. "And if we get out of this alive, I'll never forgive myself."

They were quiet after that and waited in the cellar for what felt like hours, all silently blaming themselves for the part they played in everything turning to shit.

Fenton was consumed and plagued by disturbing dreams. The kind you had when you took a bad trip. It was so real he even felt as if he were bathed in a warm, bright light. It was soothing, as he'd been cold and shivering for so long that the warmth was welcome. Maybe this was death's door.

Fent... Fenton... Fenton! echoed all around him.

He felt so groggy and sluggish, but the voices continued. He tried to turn his aching head towards one of them, but it weighed as much as a medicine ball. He could barely single it out; it reverberated so much.

Fenton... on... on... on! went the echo. He was delirious. *Shit!*

"D... is that you?" *Shit!* His eyes were so heavy he couldn't open them. It sounded like his old friend, *thank fuck!* "D, I'm smashed up pretty bad." His heart ached with relief; with Dylan here, he wouldn't need to rouse himself to get Diablo. "Thank god, man... thank god." Tears came to his eyes when he thought they could all get out of this alive. "The fucker took me by surprise, D. I wasn't ready," he tried to explain.

You're good, they'll patch you up. Then you must get back there. There isn't much time. If you want to save them, you've gotta find the strength, Fent. I'll try to hang on for you as long as I can. But I'm weak, Fent. I'm fading fast.

Nothing was making any sense. Why did he need to get back there?

The girls, Fent... they came back... they came back. And the voice faded away. "D... D," he called, over and over.

Fenton tried to clear his head. Was Dylan there or had he just dreamt it? Dylan's voice sounded so distant and weird that he couldn't tell – probably the latter. So if Dylan wasn't back, then it meant Diablo had won. And if the girls had disobeyed and come back, then Diablo wouldn't be satisfied until everyone who had witnessed tonight had died.

The blurry phone call swirled around in his head. They'd tried to warn him about something. He couldn't put his finger on what it was. The more he thought about it and the strange dream, the more worried he became, and the more he knew he had to get back there and fulfil his promise to Dylan.

CHAPTER 32

It seemed to Grace like they'd waited hours when, in fact, it had only been some minutes. They were all quiet, ears straining for the slightest noise in the house above them.

"Fucking Hell, I could do with a drink!" Anton said.

His sudden outburst made Grace jump. He wasn't in the habit of swearing either. She sighed loudly and got up out of her chair.

"Where are you going?" Simon said, a little too quickly and higher-pitched than normal.

She put up a hand to put him at relative ease. "I'm just taking a look around… see if there's anything to drink down here. It is a cellar. Did we have anything left?" she said, looking at Anton hopefully.

Anton shook his head, but got up quickly and joined her in the search. "Come on, Simon… it'll help us pass the time.

Simon reluctantly got up. "Be quiet," he hissed when they pulled open the complaining wooden drawers that hadn't been opened in a very long time.

Grace began searching the cupboards of an old oak

dresser. She stood up, beaming and holding up a dusty black bulbous bottle.

"What is it?" Anton said, coming over to take a closer look.

She shrugged and blew on the label. "Not sure, it's in French. Cog… nac!"

"Cognac?" Anton took it, pulled the cork and sniffed it. "Let's find something to drink from."

Simon, now seeming to forget his fear, helped Grace look for some kind of receptacle. It didn't take long for him to find some old, white, enamel camping cups.

Anton smiled. "A veritable find." Then he used the hem of his shirt to give each cup a bit of a clean and slurped a good measure of the amber liquid in each cup. "To staying alive," he said, raising his and drinking it down in one gulp.

Grace watched him barely flinch; he was obviously a seasoned drinker. She looked at Simon, who tapped his cup to hers and downed his. "Oh well." And she followed their lead. She almost choked when the liquid burnt her chest and hit her stomach with a blast of warmth, and pulled a face throughout.

"Good?" Anton said.

When she'd regained her composure, she nodded and held out her cup for a refill.

THEY'D DISCOVERED another two bottles stashed away in the dresser and settled down with their drinks, prepared to wait out the night. "A bottle each!" Anton laughed mirthlessly. "Enough to tranq the nerves though.'

"Enough to tranq an elephant," Simon added.

The cellar was L-shaped and was probably the layout of the original house, which dated back to the seventeenth century. They chose the corner out of immediate sight of the stairs and placed some old tins on the steps to alert them should they accidentally fall asleep.

A folded put-you-up bed was opened out and offered to Grace. After weak protests, she gratefully accepted. The alcohol, the aftermath of adrenaline, not forgetting suppressed grief, brought with them an overwhelming melancholy and hopeless tiredness such as she'd never experienced before. She turned onto her side and curled into a ball.

The two men brought their chairs in closer so they sat facing her, with a crate acting as a small table in the middle on which they put a candle and their cups.

"What went wrong?" Simon said. "I don't understand it. As far as I could see, the experiment was a resounding success."

Anton didn't answer, but snorted, looking mildly annoyed and knocked back his drink.

"But we clearly saw the rift… we saw him leave," Simon said to Anton, then to Grace, when he got no response.

Grace absorbed the painful blow, nodded and sat up to stop herself from falling asleep. "Yes, we did." She was looking at Anton as she spoke. It was obvious why he was so quiet. He thought Dylan had simply gone mad and gone on a rampage and totally gone over to his dark side. "But it was the wrong one." She spoke softly, still looking at Anton.

"I don't understand," Simon persisted, oblivious to the undertone in the conversation between her and Anton. "We followed everything to the letter… we were so sure."

"Dylan… my Dylan," she said, her voice cracking, "was the visitor, as it turned out." She struggled to compose herself. "We went to his mother's house, you see… she told us."

"Oh, for fuck's sake!" Anton said, stamping his foot and slamming down his cup so the drink slurped over the sides. For a second, there was a scramble as everything rattled and the candle was knocked over. Simon righted it quickly before it went out and plunged them into darkness.

"Anton!" they both said in shouted whispers. "He'll hear you."

"Well…" Anton said with contempt. He held his hands wide. "This… all this is ridiculous… Tonight… the whole thing… hiding down here," he finished, shaking his head.

"Have you forgotten the massacre upstairs?" Grace almost spat in disbelief. "Pardon me, but you've never met Diablo before – not properly anyway. He must have fooled all of you this week." She shook her head. "Not Fenton, though… that's why …" She fought back the tears and put her hands to her mouth before she said too much.

The anger drained from Anton's face and he watched her guiltily. "I'm sorry, it's just…" He got up and walked to the dresser and uncorked another bottle. "I've been a psychiatrist for fifteen years; I'm a man of science." His gaze fell on Simon apologetically. "I'm sorry, but I let my vanity get the better of me. I thought I could cure him… it marred my judgment." He took a swig and grimaced.

Simon narrowed his eyes. "You're wrong, Anton." He turned to Grace and gave her a reassuring smile. "I'm sorry, my dear." Then he turned back to Anton and his face hardened. "The theoretical maths over that man's body was the work of genius; way beyond human understanding."

Anton tutted.

"Shut up, the pair of you," Grace said, sick of listening to them. "Just shut the fuck up!"

Both men stared at her, aghast. The outburst, the swearing, the tears rolling down her cheeks sobered them into silence.

"What difference does it make now, eh?" she said, listlessly. "Dylan's gone, the rift's gone, and we are left with a raving lunatic who, rest assured, will kill us given half the chance."

Simon swallowed. "You don't know that."

Grace rolled her eyes at his inability to see the situation for what it was. "Get real, Simon." Then she remembered and paused, squinting her eyes with distrust. "What were you and him talking about, just before he went onto the machine… up at the site?"

Simon looked uncomfortable and went to get up and walk away, but Anton held his arm. "No, answer her." He wanted to know as much as she did.

Simon held his hands up in front of him. "Okay, it was nothing… really. He just asked for a few concessions, that's all."

"What do you mean, concessions?"

Anton was frowning and waiting too.

Simon took a deep breath and seemed reluctant to speak, which only made Grace feel more uneasy. "Just spit it out, Simon."

"He just asked me to hold some things for him, that's all… It sounded reasonable, not knowing the outcome or anything."

"What things?" Grace and Anton said together.

Simon took another deep breath. "Phone, flight tickets, passport, credit card and money."

Grace was stunned for a minute, trying to work it out. "You made the arrangement with Diablo and not Dylan," she said as a statement of fact. "When was this?"

He paused, not understanding. "Back in Oxford, and yes… I suppose it was."

Grace was reeling – the thought that Diablo was present when they were at Oxford made her shiver.

"And that was it… nothing else you think we should know?" Anton said.

"No… except he asked to make a phone call from my phone earlier today."

Anton and Grace looked at each other. "Who to?" they said at the same time.

Simon shook his head slowly. "I have no idea, he made it privately."

Grace looked around the room while she thought about who that could have been. "And Dylan… he didn't ask for anything?"

"Not since we've been here… At Oxford… only secrecy … I wasn't to tell anyone what I was working on, or where I was going when we came up here. And, of course, not to publish our experiment."

"And did you?"

"Of course, not a word," Simon said, a little affronted.

"What did Diablo offer you?" Anton said shrewdly.

Simon fidgeted with discomfort again and looked everywhere but at Grace. "He just said if I held the stuff for him and gave it back to him tonight, if he came out of it alive and could get right away, then I could do what I wanted with the information," Simon finished, trying to look justified in his actions.

Grace frowned, looked at Anton and then back at Simon and touched her temple with her finger. "For such a brainy guy, you are incredibly dense. Think… He's getting rid of witnesses. He's now got the means to get away. He won't want any of this published in science journals… He wants to wipe out the last seventeen years like they never happened!" she finished in disgust.

Anton sighed and nodded, then looked at Simon. "She's right." Then a thought occurred to him. "But I called an ambulance… where is it?"

Grace shook her head. Something had delayed it. It clearly should have been there by now. "Well, if it is still coming, we need to create one hell of a diversion when it gets here, otherwise they'll be joining the head count upstairs."

They all jumped as a bang sounded from upstairs. Like something falling onto the wooden floorboards. Grace's heart pounded and they looked at each other, wide-eyed, not daring to breathe.

"Should we blow out the candle?" Simon whispered.

Anton put his finger to his lips.

Grace was too petrified for speech; her breaths were shallow, the warm glow of the brandy gone completely.

"Someone's up there," Anton whispered.

They all watched the ceiling, as if it could reveal the answer to them.

Grace yelped when a gust of wind appeared from nowhere, howling around the room, pulling the candle flame with it until it snuffed it out. Grace whimpered and huddled into a ball to make herself as small as possible.

"It's okay," Anton's voice said. Then a crackle and a hiss and a match was struck. He righted the candle and lit it again.

For a moment, Grace frantically scanned the room, battling to get her eyes to focus from the sudden darkness to the light. Her heart was jumping and palpitating all over the place. There was no one there. "Where did the wind come from?" she said, in a tiny voice.

"Must be a draft," Simon said, making a sudden grab for his cup and gulping down its contents.

Grace frowned at him. "There are no windows."

"There must be an airbrick somewhere," Anton said, but his eyes searched the room, clearly as unsure of his explanation as she was. "These old places are drafty."

Simon nodded, grateful for the voice of reason to latch onto.

"Best thing we can do is get some rest." Anton stood and walked over to her, draping his coat over her. "Simon and I will take it in turns to keep a look-out, okay?"

She nodded, placated like a small child after a nightmare and relaxed into the mattress. Surprised after the scare, how sleepy she felt. It was probably the grief, exhaustion and the alcohol. A concoction that made her eyelids heavy and she nodded off as soon as her head rested on the bed.

It couldn't have been more than an hour or two when she woke up with a start. It took her a few minutes to remember where she was. Glancing at the two men, she was relieved to see them slumped over, asleep, sitting up. Even though they were useless as bodyguards, she was glad they were there.

Then the weight of her loss punched her in the chest when she was reminded that Dylan had gone, and she would never see him again. Her eyes closed and a sob escaped her. She was shivering with the cold.

When she eventually drifted back to sleep, she dreamt. It was as though warmth circled her back, down her legs and then around her waist. It was strong, like an electric blanket, and felt glorious in the bleak coldness of the room. It felt like body heat, like the only thing that could truly warm her when she felt this cold: Dylan. The memory of him was as clear as day. The way she fitted perfectly into his lap when they lay together. Even his warm breath as his lips gently brushed the crook of her shoulder.

She awoke and groaned. A need for him wrenched her insides apart. "Dylan," she sobbed. Hopelessness enveloped her when she remembered the last thing he had learnt about her before he disappeared. He must have hated her. "I'm so sorry, Dylan." She was crying with her face pushed into the bed for fear someone would hear her. She said it like a prayer, in the hope that he would know from wherever he was. "I thought he was you… another part of you."

The warmth continued to surround her. It moved and swirled over her like a comforting hand, rubbing and stroking her better, smoothing and caressing all her worries away. She tried to contain her sobs, but they were unrelenting, as if a dam had burst. Not wanting to wake the others, she turned into the warmth. "I'm sorry, Dylan… I'm so sorry. Please forgive me…"

The warmth was all around her now and she continued to be comforted by it. It roamed over her back, kneading and caressing her till her sobs subsided to intermittent hiccups. It felt good, homely, familiar, even the smell; everything reminded her of Dylan. It was as though her nose was next to his skin just as she'd slept so many times before.

Aware she must still be dreaming, sleep clutched at her again, and she felt herself drifting towards it, lulling and pulling her under. Kisses brushed her cheeks, her eyelids and her lips until she completely succumbed to total oblivion.

DIABLO CHUCKLED when his eyes found the scientist, Nicholas, staring at him through the window in macabre curiosity. Human nature never ceased to amuse him; the way a man would assume a stance of horror and outrage and yet could not tear his eyes away from the object of it. He never suffered such an affliction.

When Diablo moved towards the door, he heard the footfalls stumbling away from the house. Nicholas had rediscovered his motor skills. He flung open the front door and walked outside with purposeful strides. Nicholas fell over about twenty yards away, hurriedly picked himself up and glanced at him in terror.

Diablo would have made a beeline for him and put the

man out of his misery if he hadn't witnessed his eye line flick to the parked cars at the side of the house. His first thought was that he would make a run for one to escape. But he became aware that an engine was already running. He narrowed his eyes on the line of cars to pinpoint which one it was and who could be driving. Nicholas took his chance and scurried away down the lane towards the village.

He'll keep! It was miles of winding, narrow lane before even the next house and very few out here were occupied all year round. He checked the phone Simon had given him. Still no signal. He put it back in his back pocket. No, someone else had piqued his curiosity much more, and he prowled towards the running engine.

It was the car the girls had turned up in earlier, now blocked in by the Land Rovers they used to go up to the site. It made no sense.

Cerise! He grinned. With Fenton and the Alien now out of the way, he was free to have some fun with her. It had been something he'd promised himself he would do for as long as he'd known her. Life was suddenly full of opportunity.

CHAPTER 33

*D*iablo silently came up to the passenger side door and she turned her head to see who it was, jumped and gasped. He reached out for the handle, but she had already locked it. "Open the door, Cerise," he said, calmly.

She shook her head dementedly, like nothing on earth would make her do it.

We'll see.

She cowered away from the door.

Diablo arched a brow. *Foolish woman.* She should know there was nothing she could do to save herself from him. She was his to do with what he wanted now. "Don't you want me to tell you where Fenton is?" he said, in his most reasonable voice.

"Tell me!" she shouted up at him, her eyes flashing in anger.

He turned his head to the side and cupped his ear with his open hand. "Pardon? You'll have to wind down the window." A smile played on his lips.

"Tell me!" she demanded.

Diablo shrugged, turned and walked slowly away, but his full attention was on the car behind him. The delay, he assumed, was her risk assessing the situation.

The clunk of the car's central locking system made him pause, but he didn't turn or rush her. He just stood and waited. The passenger door opened and he felt her get out of the car.

"Tell me where he is?" Her voice wavered with a delicious hint of fear and hatred.

He grinned and pointed towards the house. Cerise glanced in that direction. He enjoyed watching the rainbow of emotions cross her face. He could read her like a book. She didn't trust him, but the thought that Fenton could be just a few feet away was too much.

"We had a fight," he explained, "I knocked him out... he came back about ten minutes ago. I came to tell you." *Plausible... just.*

Again, uncertainty crossed her face. She wasn't stupid for a woman. She knew Fenton well. Fenton would never be inside having a cup of tea; he'd be out here looking for her until he found her and could rest easy. Still, she would have to make sure, just in case.

Cerise's eyes darted, trying to find a way past him where she'd be out of reach. This made him laugh at the girl's bottle. He stepped back and flattened himself against the house wall. "Go and check... I won't stop you, I promise," he said, smiling.

Too hard to resist, she took a halting step, and then another.

He held out a hand in dramatic gallantry for her to go first. She suddenly made a run for it and shot past him towards the door.

He followed at a leisurely stroll behind her, counting, *one, two, three...* and waited for the scream. *Aannnd there it was.*

Well, a yelp really. Maybe it was overkill, and he chuckled at his own pun.

She turned and ran unseeing straight into his chest. He caught her up and threw her over his shoulder like a sack of potatoes. She found her voice again and punched, kicked and screamed.

"Shut the fuck up, bitch!" She was a tough bird; he'd already smacked her one tonight, but he couldn't afford her warning the others. He had plans and he wanted them all where he put them.

He put her down roughly, held her by the throat and squeezed, but spoke calmly. "If you don't shut up, I'll hurt you."

She went to struggle and shout for help despite his reasonable warning, so he wasted no time and backhanded her sharply. She crumpled in a heap on the floor. He huffed, rolled his eyes in annoyance and threw her back over his shoulder. Then he strode back inside the house, stepping over bodies as he went as if they were no more than rolled-up carpets. He hadn't forgotten the science bloke – Nicholas. He took his phone out of his back pocket, smiled at the appearance of a signal and hit call. "Where are you?"

NICHOLAS HAD LOST count of how many times he'd fallen over and scrambled back onto his feet in his haste to get away. His hands, knees and elbows were bloody and his clothes were muddy and torn. The air rasped painfully in and out of his lungs and his sore, dry throat. He wasn't sure how much longer he could keep going along the winding, single-track lane. Part of him wanted to get off it for fear that Diablo was following behind and would soon catch up with him, but another knew that to deviate from the road could mean no hope of meeting a car or, worse still, he could die of exposure out on the hillside and no one would find him for days, maybe even weeks.

He slowed down to a walk, stopped and bent, putting his hands on his knees to breathe. *Shit, he'd left Cerise like a sitting duck.* Guilt hit him. He felt like a coward and tried to justify his actions. *The others were still there somewhere; surely they would find her?*

A noise woke him up. The thought that Diablo could be just behind him and snap him in two with his bear hands made him jog on wearily down the road. His legs were shaking so badly with the effort that he could hardly lift them from the ground and kept tripping.

A flash of light on the hill ahead of him pulled him up sharp. Was that the whine of an engine? He strained his ears. Yes, he was sure of it. It must have been headlights. Hope surged through him; he'd given up all hope of meeting anyone since he hadn't seen a single house yet.

The engine sound was getting louder. Nicholas stood in the centre of the road, held up his hands and waved so the car would see him as soon as its headlights reached him. Thankfully, it was impossible to get up too much speed up here.

The car came around the next bend and immediately slowed. Nicholas held his nerve, refusing to move aside for fear the car might try to go around him. It worked, the car came to a halt right in front of him. When he was sure it wouldn't drive off, he ran around to the driver's side.

A young black woman looked up at him without winding down the window. He couldn't blame her; he must look like some escapee from an asylum, and she was a woman on her own.

"Please," he begged. "I need help. A lift into town... I can pay you." He rummaged hurriedly in his pockets and pulled out some crumpled notes. "Look, there's at least fifty quid here if you take me into town."

She opened the window a tiny bit. "Where have you come from?" she asked, eying the state of his clothes.

"A cottage up there," he said, pointing back up the lane he'd just travelled. "Not sure how far, I've been walking for a while."

She paused for a moment. "Get in."

He hurried around the car to the passenger side. He heard the clunk of the central locking and he got in the car. The welcome blast of heat and to sit at last was a relief to his aching back and legs. But even in his exhausted state, he had to marvel at her kindness, taking in a complete stranger, looking like he'd been mauled by something, on a dark road in the middle of nowhere. "Thank you, you have no idea how grateful I am."

She pulled slowly away.

"Er, sorry, you need to go that way. That's the way to the village," he said, a little alarmed.

She gave him a small smile. "I can't turn around here – too narrow."

He nodded hesitantly. She was right, of course. It still made him nervous though, going back in the direction he came. He studied her profile, frowned, then looked ahead through the windscreen. Something about her was off, and he couldn't put his finger on it; probably his overwrought mind playing tricks on him. "Forgive my rudeness, my name's Nicholas."

"I'm Serena," she said, not taking her eyes from the road.

WHEN FENTON AWOKE, it was to the serious-looking faces of a pretty blonde woman and a slightly overweight balding man, whose closely shaved head and serious bearing immediately reminded him of Old Bill. In fact, the more his eyes came into focus, the more sure he became of what he was.

Fenton sat up sharply, then regretted it, clutching his head.

"Easy there, mate," the cop said. "You've had quite a pasting."

Fenton ignored him and threw his legs over the side of the bed, then squinted at the bloke with the pain thumping in his cranium. "What do you know about it?"

The two in front of him looked at each other in surprise, then the bloke spoke. "We found you trying to crawl your way out of an old shed... We brought you here – well, the ambulance we intercepted did."

Fenton looked around him. He was in a curtained-off hospital bed; the smell alone would have given it away. "Where am I?" he said.

"In hospital."

"Yes," he said in frustration, "but which one?"

"Aberdeen."

"Pass me my clothes," he ordered and pointed at the pile on a chair next to the bed.

"I don't think that's a good idea," the bloke said.

Fenton glared at him. "Look, I know you mean well, and thanks for getting me here, but you don't understand. The bloke who did this..." Fenton pointed to his own face. "He's free, and he'll be going after my wife and my friend's girlfriend, and he don't play nice, as you can see."

He flicked his hand at them, "Now get me my clothes. I need to check the house, then head straight to London. That's where he'll head for." He tried to shuffle off the edge of the bed.

The two looked at each other again in silent conversation.

Fenton swayed with the pain and became exasperated. "Fuck!... Who are you anyway?" He tentatively put some weight on his toes. The bloke and the girl steadied him with an arm on each side of him.

"I'm Dave and this is Janey."

Fenton nodded, his attention still on trying to dress.

"We're close friends with a girl called Grace."

Fenton paused without making eye contact and listened.

"She came hurtling up here with her friend on some mission of mercy to help some nutter she's been seeing. As soon as I got in from work, Janey told me and we headed up here to try to stop her from getting into any kind of trouble. The bloke's no good."

Fenton glared at him, but bit his tongue. The bloke obviously knew nothing about the situation, or very little. "You mean they're up here?"

Fenton was now standing up, but wobbly. The scrambled phone calls came back to him now. They'd been trying to warn him. They must have been on their way. *Shit!* He began to dress.

"Yes, we were looking for them at the house when we found you."

"Fuck!" Fenton said, pulling the temporary cast off his leg and swearing in pain as he pushed his legs into his jeans before he fell over or passed out. "You didn't find any sign?"

Dave shook his head and smiled weakly.

Fenton used every expletive when he pulled his bloodied T-shirt back over his stitched head. "We need to hurry."

Dave helped support him as they exited the ward. "This bloke… the one who did this to you …"

Fenton lurched along the corridor, limping badly and clutching his ribs; he knew what question was coming.

"Was it her boyfriend?"

Fenton took a deep, weary breath and looked at Dave sideways. " Yes… no… it's complicated."

They reached the car and it saved Fenton from elaborating further while they all got in and Dave drove. "What I don't get is what made them high-tail it up here… I bloody told them to stay put," Fenton said.

Dave was driving fast and efficiently out of the car park like the pro he was. *Definitely Old Bill.* But the bloke looked uncomfortable, like he didn't want to impart what he had to say. Fenton was watching him intently and waiting for an answer.

"She… Grace, I mean, told us this story…" Dave shook his head as if he still didn't believe a word of it.

Fenton could guess what it was. Dave looked over at him, uncertain whether he should continue. Fenton nodded for him to go on.

"They'd gone over to see his mum, or something."

"They?"

"Grace and her friend."

"She'd told them… now let me get this straight… that her son was the other one?" Dave finished with his eyebrows up and an expression like, "What the fuck?'

Fenton knew it was today that they were meant to go there. Then his fuzzy head went back to the bad phone call. Cerise or Grace, he couldn't remember which, had tried to warn him, but the phone signal had been too bad and reception had broken up. His head reeled with the information. That was why Diablo had turned on him. He knew that he knew. It was all starting to make sense now: they all thought Diablo had gone along with everything as quietly as a lamb because he wanted to go home, but they had it all wrong; it was because he was confident in the knowledge that he would be getting rid of Dylan. *Shit,* Dylan had said over and over that Diablo wouldn't want to leave the body, and no one listened. He knew he would have a fight on his hands.

A pang pierced his heart for a second, and he was forced to look the other way out the window. He loved that guy and he was gone to fuck knows where. The thought choked him up for a minute.

"What does it all mean?" Janey said from the back seat.

Fenton had forgotten she was there. He looked at her, then at Dave. "You Old Bill?"

Dave's eyes widened in surprise at the abrupt question.

"What can I say, it's a gift," Fenton said, deadpan.

"I don't get what that's got to do with anything?"

"D'you have a weapon?" Fenton asked flatly.

Dave paused before he answered, checked Janey first in the rear-view mirror, then looked back at Fenton and nodded.

Fenton's eyes went to Dave's chest, where he silently tapped with his hand, indicating his concealed holster. *Thank fuck the guy was packing.* "Good… we're gonna need it."

"Why, what are we gonna do?" Janey said anxiously from the back seat.

"You two – nothing. There's something I have to do." Emotion welled up in him again, forcing him to look out the window and swallow it back down. "You two can wait back at the hotel." He gritted his teeth and straightened in his chair. "I'll call you when it's done."

Despite having to drive, Dave eyed Fenton for a long time as if he was weighing things up, then he shook his head. "I'm going to have to call this in," and he began to take his mobile phone out of his pocket.

Fenton put out his hand to stop him. "Not yet."

Dave tutted, shaking his head. "I can't let you go off with a gun – *my* gun, besides, you need the back-up if this bloke's dangerous."

Fenton knew he was right. Here he was, already looking like the living dead, thanks to Diablo. "Look, you can call 'em, just give me a head start – an hour, that's all?" He stared intently at Dave.

"I say we should call it in now, if this bloke's as dangerous as you say?"

"No, this is something I need to do," Fenton said, hoping to appeal to the guy's sense of honour or vengeance, or whatever the hell it took for him to give him his gun so he could get the hell up there and finish it.

"I'll come with you," Dave tried.

Fenton shook his head adamantly, "You can't."

"I can't give you my weapon and, besides, look at the state of your leg, how can you drive?"

Fenton glanced at the gear stick. "It's an automatic... I'll get by. Look, you don't understand, right..." Fenton's patience snapped. "This bloke, he won't stop. He'll carry on till he gets us all one by one; believe me, I know him. Starting with them up at that house. Then he'll hunt us down... He'll find us, and he'll enjoy doing it." He continued to stare at Dave long after he'd finished speaking to let his words sink in.

Dave looked back at him, uncertain and not happy at all with it. "Okay... an hour. That's all you've got.

CHAPTER 34

*D*iablo threw the limp weight of Cerise onto the sofa, went to the cupboard under the stairs and flipped the trip switch. All the lights came back on. As he turned to move back out of the cupboard, a loud clank of metal on wood made him pause for a second. He listened hard and looked over his shoulder at Cerise – she hadn't moved. He crouched, putting his head at an angle, listening for the smallest of sounds. Fidgeting to adjust his stance, he accidentally knocked a broom over in front of him, hitting the wall opposite in the small space. When he reached to pick up the broom, something metal clanked by his feet. He ran his hand around on the floor. "What have we here?"

There, on the floor, camouflaged into the pattern of square carpet tiles, was a large oblong hatch. It took him no time at all to find the metal ring embedded in it, hook his finger and pull. He raised it very carefully, no more than a couple of inches and listened. A slow smile spread across his face when he heard hushed voices. *The fuckers were all holed up down there... like sitting ducks.* He knew this had to be the only way in or out as he'd already cased the whole outside

"

perimeter and found nothing. He silently closed the hatch. There was no better holding tank. He chuckled.

A groan behind him made him turn his attention back to Cerise. The bitch was waking up. There was no way he was going to let his little lure escape. He crept back out until he loomed over her.

WHEN CERISE AWOKE, she was strapped to a high-backed wooden chair in the middle of the room that had been filled with dead bodies before. Looking about her, she couldn't help but wonder if she'd actually seen them. The debris from the smashed coffee table and general disarray of the room meant she probably had.

Her eyes halted sharply at Diablo, sitting casually opposite, studying her. She struggled against her bonds behind the chair, furious that he had this power over her. "Agghhh!" she shouted in frustration.

Diablo's rapt expression never altered with her futile struggles. His scrutiny made her feel uncomfortable and she waited for the violence that she knew was inevitable. "Where's Fenton?" she said, warily.

All he did was raise his eyebrows philosophically. "Honestly?… I don't know."

It threw her because he looked genuinely surprised. *How the hell could she trust what he said anyway?* "And the others?" she said, looking around the room as if she would see the answer somewhere. "The dead people?"

Diablo's lips twitched into the smallest of smiles. "I tidied up."

A small part of her had to admit she was a little relieved that she wasn't going mad, but that soon gave way to disgust and horror. He really was a monster, just as Fenton had always warned her. *What was to become of them all?* More to the point: where was Fenton? She decided to try a different tack. "Did you and Fenton fight?"

He nodded slowly and knowingly. "We always fight."

"Was he hurt?"

Diablo grinned as if he had to hand it to him. "Not as much as I thought, apparently."

Diablo appeared to be waiting for something. She was tied to a chair and all he was doing was watching her. But at least she knew Fenton was alive somewhere; all she had to do was keep herself alive long enough to find him. Then, throwing her off balance again, he casually got up and walked out of the front door.

Left completely stunned, all she could do was strain her ears and wait.

Fucking hell! What was he up to now? Her heart thumped while she frantically scanned the room for something to help her. Disappointed, she began to try to shuffle her chair to the edge of the room, away from where Diablo thought she was. Then perhaps she could see if there was something she could snag her bonds with and get free. She pulled and huffed. They were so tight, she shouted in frustration. She started to rock to and fro in a rhythm, using her own momentum to carry her further forward and back. But in her rush, she misjudged it. The world began to tilt and she went over; her shoulder hit the floor painfully when the weight of the rest of her body smashed it into the rug.

Cerise groaned and spat something out of her mouth. *That hurt.* "Help!" she began to shout. "Someone help me, please!" she said a bit louder. Then she listened for a reply or the return of Diablo.

Her cries were met with silence.

What was he waiting for?

.   .   .

"WHAT'S THAT? Grace whispered.

"What?" Anton said, suddenly alert. "I didn't hear anything?"

"Listen!" she said, standing up and walking towards the bottom of the stairs.

"Be careful!" Simon said.

"There!" she said, jabbing a finger. Then motioned for the men to come closer. "Someone's calling for help." She looked into the men's faces, listening intently. She hitched a breath. "It's Cerise!"

"Are you sure? What should we do?" Simon said anxiously.

"Bloody help her, of course," Anton said, going to push between them.

"Wait!" Grace grabbed his arm. "What if Diablo is waiting?"

"We can't just ignore her?"

Grace bit her lip and racked her brains. "I know, but we need to think about this. I think we should wait a bit to make sure it's safe before we go rushing up there."

"What about if just one of us goes up and reports back?" Simon said.

"I'll go." Anton nodded. "We'll have to be careful he doesn't see where I come from."

"Wait... take something with you," Simon said, looking around for something to use as a weapon. He picked up a candlestick to feel its weight, thought better of it and put it back down.

Grace went into the drawers of the dresser and quickly found a large rusty knife. "Take this." She turned it around, put it in his hand and pointed to his waistband. "But don't let him see it." It was questionable whether a weapon was a good idea at all.

He nodded, tucked it behind his belt and looked every bit

the geeky doctor in psychology that he was. *Oh god!* Diablo was a trained killing machine and could snap him in two as soon as look at him.

Despite her misgivings, and after waiting what felt like a lifetime, she nodded and Anton climbed the stairs with her and Simon following closely behind. He began to slowly open the hatch.

None of them knew what to expect and she was sure they all held their breath.

"The lights are on," Anton whispered over his shoulder.

"Shh!" Grace said. "Please be careful, Anton. Let us know as soon as it's safe."

Anton nodded and disappeared through the hatch. Simon and Grace took its weight and closed it softly behind him. All they could do was wait with bated breath for his return.

Eventually, they crept back down the stairs, just in case. Grace didn't want to assume the worst, but it was highly likely that Anton would be caught.

CERISE HAD GIVEN up all hope of seeing any of the others alive by the time she saw Anton's head peer round the doorway of the cupboard under the stairs. She burst into tears.

Anton ran to her immediately to undo her ties. "Where is he?"

"I don't know... he's been gone a while now. He could be anywhere."

Anton helped her to her feet and she rubbed the angry skin around her wrists, trying to get some blood back into them. "It's not safe. Where are the others?"

"In the cellar,' Anton said, quietly next to her ear. Then he nervously looked all around.

Cerise didn't immediately rush to them. She had an

uneasy feeling that Diablo knew where they were. The question was: why was he leaving them to it?

"Wait!" she said when Anton turned to walk back to the cupboard. "What if he knows you're all down there?" Her brain raced. *Fuck!* All together and trapped, they were vulnerable. "Maybe it'd be better if they came up?"

Anton looked in her eyes while he came to the same conclusion as her. He crept to the window and peered outside, careful not to be seen. "They can't stay down there for ever."

He walked back over to her, mulling over their options. "It'll soon be light. If we can just get to one of the cars, maybe we can get away?"

The question of where Diablo had disappeared to played on her mind, but Anton was right. They needed to be proactive. The aftershock of the adrenaline was kicking in and she was beginning to shake all over. "Let's do it," she said, standing up and shaking out her limbs. "We need to be quick."

"I'll keep look out. You call the others," Anton said, resuming his position by the window.

"Is Fenton?" she asked, eyes wide with hope.

Anton shook his head with regret. "None of us has seen him all evening."

She let out a long, ragged breath, nodded, and went to the cupboard under the stairs.

Lifting the hatch, she called softly, "Come up!"

Pretty soon, Grace and Simon came up out of the hole in the floor and hugged her. She was so relieved to see them all alive. "Where's Nicholas?"

"We don't know… we hoped you could tell us?" Grace said.

There was an uncomfortable silence where they all

thought the worst. "Come on, we're gonna get out of here," Anton said, taking the lead.

NICHOLAS BEGAN to get nervous when they passed a perfect place to turn around and they went sailing past. He pointed. "We could have backed into there!" The dirt track came and went until he craned his neck behind him to see it.

"Ah, there'll be another one," Serena said. But her face remained stony, fixed on the road ahead of her.

His unease intensified.

Quite a few minutes had passed since she'd picked him up and she was still continuing the wrong way. Her speed seemed a bit fast too for someone who was just looking for somewhere to turn. At this rate he'd end up back where he started. *Shit!* If only he had his jacket, but he'd lent it to Cerise. It had his two-way radio in the pocket and he could have reached someone. He cursed bitterly.

Nicholas studied Serena's cool profile. She was beautiful. Where could she be going at this time of night, all the way out here? She seemed totally at ease with a complete stranger next to her. There were no other houses that he'd seen. Perhaps he'd missed one set back from the road? It would have been easy to do, in the panic he was in.

"So what brings you all the way out here?" he said, trying to break the silence and his paranoia.

"Visiting a friend," she said, without looking at him.

His foot was tapping with nerves and impatience. It was no good. He simply couldn't just sit there and make polite conversation. It wasn't paranoia. His alarm bells were ringing all over the place. "Look, I'm sorry, but is there no way you could reverse and turn round and go the other way?"

She glanced at him briefly. "Don't worry, we won't be long. There's a house up here."

His chest began to feel tight. Something wasn't right about this whole situation. He'd felt it ever since he'd got in the car. "You don't understand. There's a madman up there. Look at the state of me, for god's sake!"

She looked him up and down quickly without batting an eyelid. "Someone attack you?"

He huffed in exasperation. "Not exactly."

She smirked as if to say, 'I thought so.'

"I did this trying to get away… He's killed people. At least four that I could see." His throat felt like it was closing up while he spoke, as if saying it out loud made it seem more real. "Do you have some water or something?" he croaked.

Serena pulled a small bottle from the door space and handed it to him. "Look, chill out. We'll be at my friend's place in a minute." And she gave him the first smile he'd seen, although it didn't reach her eyes.

It was in that precise moment that he knew for sure. He wasn't sure how, but he knew she was taking him right back to *him.*

His eyes flicked down to the door handle. Were they going slow enough for him to jump?

"I wouldn't," she said, reading his mind. "Central locking."

"I'm a prisoner," his voice quavered.

"No, you can leave the car any time you want."

But before Nicholas had time to say, 'stop the car', she reached down onto the door space and took out a heavy dark object and put it in her lap.

It took him a moment to focus and believe his own eyes. In fact, he hoped this whole evening was nothing but a terrible nightmare, and the gun that nestled between her thighs a figment of his imagination.

·　·　·

"Be careful!" Cerise said. "I don't know where he went; he could be just watching."

After a brief hesitation and looking at each other, unsure what to do next, they crept out one at a time; their eyes scanning the area to make sure the coast was clear.

"Maybe he's gone," Simon whispered. "And got rid of the bodies."

Grace didn't answer. She doubted that very much.

They reached the line of Land Rovers and went to the one at the back that wasn't blocked in. "Does anyone have the keys?" Anton said as he tried the handle to the passenger side. He leapt back and Cerise screamed when the top half of a body flopped sideways onto the ground. It lay at an unnatural angle with its feet still in the footwell.

Anton took a few breaths to compose himself, then he bent down, eased the body out of the car and pulled it a few feet away to lie on the grass.

Grace put a comforting arm around Cerise, who was wiping tears away on her fingers. "There's another one in the driver's seat," she said, pointing through the car at the body sitting motionless, facing front like a mannequin.

Anton nodded and motioned for Simon to help him, and together they carried the other one to lie side by side with the first.

"There were four," Simon said.

"How could someone do something like this?" Cerise sobbed.

Grace hugged her into her body.

"A sick bastard," Anton said.

The comment surprised Grace. Anton was always the professional. But this wasn't some crazy act. It seemed very calculated to her. Not just to scare the life out of them – which it did, but more to slow them down, making any kind of quick getaway impossible.

The fact that she seemed to know how his mind worked bothered her. *He wasn't Dylan for fuck's sake!* She shook her head and the thought away.

"There's only one in this one," Anton called from a little way off, and opened the door of the next car.

Grace walked over to join him. She wouldn't mind betting that the other one was in the car in front of that. The car in the very front was just too boxed in to bother with. *Clever.*

When all four bodies were laid out side by side on the grass, they all began talking at once. Someone was saying to leave the cars and start walking. Someone else was saying they should hunt the house for the keys. Anton was ordering Simon to try to hotwire the car.

"I wouldn't know where to start."

Cerise was still crying.

"Shhh! Shut up, the fucking lot of you!" Grace said as quietly and forcefully as she could. "Listen!"

They all stopped and stared at her. She frowned and concentrated on what she thought she heard. "There!"

"I can hear it… maybe it's the ambulance!" Anton said, wide-eyed. "Come on."

Grace ran to catch up with him, pulling Cerise along with her, who appeared to be going through some kind of meltdown. She eased up guiltily. Maybe they would all take their turn with one of those.

Headlights flashed around the bend and shone into their faces, but it didn't take long to realise the vehicle was too small for an ambulance. Grace went and stood and hoped with the others that the car would contain their saviour. They all stood in a line across the lane while the car came to a standstill a few feet away from them. Grace closed her eyes momentarily in the glare of the headlights and said a quick prayer.

The driver's side door opened and a woman got out of the car. Grace's heart began to sink even before the woman's face came into focus. She indicated for the passenger to join her.

"Nicholas!" Simon said and rushed over to him. "My god man, are you okay?" He looked over at the driver, whose face was still unclear.

"Go stand with the others," she said, holding out her arm.

Grace gasped when she saw that she was holding a gun.

Simon hurriedly helped Nicholas, who appeared to be roughed up pretty badly, over to the rest of them.

The woman stepped closer.

Grace's heart stopped. "Serena," she whispered.

CHAPTER 35

Fenton dropped Dave and Janey off at a hotel, and before Dave had given Fenton his hire car, he'd slipped him his gun without Janey seeing. It wasn't without a warning: "If this all goes pear-shaped, you'll leave me no choice. I'll say you jumped me."

Fenton nodded. "Fair enough… I gotta get going."

Dave had watched him drive out of sight, but Fenton's mind was already on his grim task, and getting there as soon as possible. Even though the car was an automatic, the pain in his leg throbbed and threatened to overcome him with nausea. Just the fear of what Diablo was capable of sent his heart rate racing. His head spun again. *Shit!* He'd taken quite a beating and only hoped he could stay conscious for what he had to do.

He opened the window and spat, breathed in some of the bracing air and sped out of town and into the countryside. It was at least an hour back to the cottage and there were no guarantees that D was still there.

D, Dylan, Diablo; what the fuck did he call him now?

Who would be there to meet him? He knew who he'd rather it was. Did he buy the whole possession thing, really? He shook his head. He'd lived with Diablo as long as he'd lived with Dylan and he'd noticed all the little things that crossed over at times. Like when Diablo had taken offence for him when someone had been disrespectful because of his race, or when Dylan was a little too extreme with the ladies. Neither character always fitted their mould.

The thing he had to remember now was not to get soft and sappy. Diablo had left him for dead. There was no sentiment in that, and no sign of Dylan. He had gone. Whether it was to the other side or to the recesses of his mind to be suppressed forever, he had no way of telling. Now his job was to race to the rendezvous he'd promised Dylan, who'd known this day would come. The time and place never specified, only the promise to end the guy's suffering and the people forced to endure it with him – that meant him, Cerise and Grace. Fenton had an appointment with death.

"I swear." Dylan had made him say. He said it aloud again, right there in the car. His heart raced. What if he was too late? It just didn't bear thinking about.

The wheels screeched around a sharp bend in the country lane.

"You know her?" Nicholas said, nonplussed.

"What are you doing, Serena?" Cerise said, ignoring Nicholas. She'd stopped crying abruptly, as if the absurdity of the situation had now become plain ridiculous.

"Move back to the house," Serena said, waving the gun in the direction they'd just come from.

Grace couldn't believe it when they all slowly turned and did as she said. "What the fuck's she doing here?" Grace said under her breath while she walked with Nicholas.

"She picked me up on the road… I didn't know who she was… Who is she?"

"Shut it, you two," Serena said, shoving Nicholas in the back with the gun.

They were silent after that and trooped back into the trashed living room. Serena looked around at the mess. "What happened here?"

"D happened here," Cerise said, her eyelids low with contempt.

Serena smirked.

"He killed four people," Anton said, outraged.

Serena rolled her eyes. "He fight with Fenton again?"

Cerise flew at her and Anton and Grace grabbed her just in time. Serena held the point of the gun to the middle of her forehead and grit her teeth.

"It's true," Grace said quietly, not wanting to make her angry or do anything rash. "They're out by the cars."

Serena flicked her eyes briefly at her. "Yeah, yeah, and I suppose I follow you out there so one of you can jump me?" She kissed her teeth with a long, drawn-out hiss. "Don't insult me. Where is he?" She switched the gun to point at Grace instead.

Grace and everyone else didn't dare breathe.

"We don't know," Simon said quickly. "We've been hiding in the cellar. He had Cerise tied up."

Serena stepped back from Grace and looked at Cerise as if to say, "Naughty, naughty". Grace squeezed her arm so she didn't bite.

"Sit down!" Serena ordered. "Together!"

They all squashed up on the three-seater settee. Grace's mind began to race. When had Serena managed to speak to him? Surely it must have been before tonight because no one's phone was working up here. Her heart pounded. Did that mean Dylan had been aware of it? Was it him who'd asked her here? Jealousy raged through her for a second and all she wanted was to tear Serena's eyes out of their sockets. It quickly evaporated with the opening of the door.

Diablo stalked in, looking dirty and sweating like he'd been running or working hard. Maybe he'd been burying the bodies? Grace shrank back when his eyes quickly scanned the room and found her. With an evil smile, he pulled Serena to him and kissed her purely for her benefit. *Bastard.*

He affected her. Even though she knew it wasn't Dylan, something physical shifted within her whenever he was in close proximity to her. Science, she told herself. It was no more than a physical chemical reaction that couldn't be switched off just because the previous owner had moved out of the banging-hot body in front of her. Guilt quickly followed when she thought of the people he'd killed tonight.

His eyes reluctantly left her when Serena spoke to him.

"Where you been, baby?" she said, fawning sickeningly all over him.

Grace saw that his hands were filthy with earth.

Diablo seemed to read her mind and smiled. "Just checking out the area," he said, pecking Serena on the lips but still watching Grace's reaction. Then he put her away from him as if he were suddenly bored. Of course, he was incapable of any real feeling.

He sauntered over to her until he towered above her. Then beckoned her with a finger to stand up.

Grace hesitated, then looked left to Cerise, then right to Simon, who shrugged nervously. She looked back at Diablo. "What do you want?"

His face remained impassive. "You're coming with me." Serena came up behind him and went to protest, but he put up a hand to silence her immediately. He blinked slowly in annoyance at the interruption, then looked menacingly at the others. "The rest of you, back in the cellar."

The men grumbled, which he silenced with a look. "No heroes, please." He said it quietly, as if he expected nothing else, then rested his eyes back on Grace.

"What about me?" Serena whined.

Ignoring her and clearly sick of waiting, he yanked Grace to her feet so quickly she gasped. He had her tightly by the top of the arm and pushed her into an empty armchair.

"Cellar... Now!" He glared at the others. They scurried as one unit, any idea of mutiny quickly vanishing as they disappeared one by one down the little staircase and back into the darkness.

He turned to Serena, who now looked a little worried about how things were turning. What the hell did she expect when he gave her a gun to bring along. *Fool!*

"You're gonna guard the trapdoor," he said, and he frog-marched her over to the cupboard under the stairs. He slammed it down, then loomed over Serena to intimidate her – one of his favourite tactics. His hands went around the gun. "If a head comes up out of that cellar, you shoot it off."

They stared at each other for a few moments. For the first time, Grace saw a definite flicker of internal crisis cross Serena's face. But she must have weighed up her chances and swallowed the thoughts down, because she nodded eventually and he let go of the gun. She went to turn and walk over to a seat.

"No!" he barked and pulled her back to the cupboard. "Here!" he said, pushing her in and closing the door.

"D!" Serena shrieked. "It's dark!"

He huffed and marched over to the front door, opened it and disappeared for a few moments.

Grace and Serena only had an instant to lock eyes before he returned. But it was long enough for Grace to know that Serena knew she was in trouble, and Diablo was further off the Richter Scale of madness than she had even given him credit for.

"So you can see," he said, passing Serena a heavy-looking torch and bundling her into the cupboard.

Grace thought she heard her try to say something else, but he closed the door on her. Then he dragged a sideboard over and blocked her in.

He turned to Grace and grinned. "It's you and me time now, Angel."

Grace couldn't take her eyes off him and her heart hammered. His hair had fallen forward in rats' tails around his face and glistened in the light, just how Dylan wore it. Smudges of dirt on his tanned face didn't detract from his chiselled beauty. Only the eyes – those piercing mahogany eyes gave a sinister, harder slant to his features.

She battled the feelings he invoked. Fuck, for all intents and purposes, he was Dylan. The magnificent toned physique, the hair, the stubbled jaw and infinitely kissable lips. But the lines of his face were hard and his dead eyes sobered her.

He enjoyed her studying him, like he wanted her to draw comparisons. There was no modesty in him; he knew what he was to women. Before she knew it, he was getting closer, her eyes were glued to his and she swallowed hard. She jumped when he ran his finger down the side of her face. Diablo simply didn't do gentle.

"You're still not sure, are you?" he said, with his head on a slight angle as if she puzzled him.

She frowned, confused. "Sure about what?"

He laughed on a single breath and yanked her flush to his body, so tightly she could feel him bulging in his fatigues. Despite her body's reaction to him, she tried to pull away, but he held her fast.

He bent down and, after biting her cheek, he put his lips

next to her ear. "You hope he's still in here somewhere, don't you?" He nipped her earlobe.

Her eyes were wide with fear and her breathing heavy.

"Even though I know you saw him leave, you want him and me to be one," he whispered, taunting, grinding his hips into her.

She struggled. *No... Yes.* "Oh fuck off!" she shrieked. He was twisting her, manipulating, changing what it was she really felt. The only real reason she wanted Dylan to be there was so she hadn't lost him for ever. Not because of some masochistic streak she enjoyed exploring, *didn't she?*

Diablo was laughing like he enjoyed her discomfort and confusion. It only proved his point. His laughter died down and he began to bite down her neck, hard. She closed her eyes and it sickened her while he made the excruciatingly painful but erotic journey down her body. *My god, was he right?*

His knee pressed between hers and prised her legs apart so his thigh could make perfect friction.

A door slammed behind him and stopped him in his tracks. He turned his head slowly, with narrowed eyes.

The chance came and she wasn't going to wait to find out what it was. Her leg came up sharply and connected with his balls.

Diablo gulped, groaned and crumpled in one move. It was like felling a tree. Grace ducked under his arm as he fell and ran for the door. She wondered what the horrible shrieking was until she realized it was coming out of her. She just ran blindly in terror. Panic threatened to paralyse her when she reached the perimeter of the cottage. *Where the hell did she go from here?*

First, she ran one way, stopped, then ran another. Eventually she got as far as the lane to the village, convinced he must have got back on his feet by now.

Then she heard a shrill and blood-curdling scream. *Cerise!* She skidded to a halt.

Another scream, then men's shouts of protest. *The others!*

The bastard hadn't even bothered to run after her, just gone and got someone to hurt so she could hear.

For a second, she debated what to do. Did she run down the lane and get help? Surely that was the only route out of there. Then she looked back at the house. He had her and he knew it.

"Angel?"

Slap!

There was a man's shout of objection – Simon.

She squinted to see if she could see anything down the lane; any signs of life, a car, a light – anything.

"D!" It was Serena's voice. "No! Calm down."

There was another loud slap. *God, it must have been hard for her to hear it all the way out here.*

"Angel!" Diablo called again without laughing. All signs of humour had gone.

"Stop!" she shouted.

"Come back here!" Diablo ordered.

With no other option, she looked at the sky for help. "Alright... don't hurt anyone. I'm coming."

THE FRONT DOOR was still open wide. She paused on the threshold; it had all gone deathly quiet. Then she took a deep breath and stepped in.

Simon was dabbing a split lip with a handkerchief. Diablo had Cerise by the hair, so her head was pulled back uncomfortably. The men were flat against the wall, not daring to move, and Serena was rubbing a cheek that looked angry and red. There was no smirk on her face now. "Well, you have us all, Diablo. What do you plan on doing?" Grace said, cautiously. The last thing she wanted to do was anger him further, especially while he had Cerise like that.

The bastard pretended to think about it, dramatically looking up at the ceiling as if he hadn't decided yet. As if holding a beaten woman by the hair was natural to him – but she guessed it probably was.

He sighed deeply with regret. "I thought of taking you with me, but…" He shrugged instead of finishing.

Serena scowled, still holding her red cheek.

Diablo grinned. "Plenty to go around, babe." Then he looked back at Grace, still grinning, to gauge her reaction.

Instead of biting, Grace remained quiet. Serena's hands had tightened around the gun. *My god!* She couldn't believe she still had it. After everything, the woman was still going along with him, and he was so arrogant that he allowed her to keep it. Fools, the pair of them. He'd noticed it too and didn't so much as flinch.

All Serena did was kiss her teeth loudly and rested on a hip. "That wasn't what I signed up for."

He laughed with a derisive snort and put his free arm out wide. "You can't stay away from this, babe," indicating his body with his hand.

"Fuck you, D!"

As this little spat continued, Grace made eye contact with Anton, who got her drift. He nudged the other two men and looked at the doorway, signalling them to inch towards it. Grace stayed put to give the men a chance. Diablo took very little notice of things, she realised. Unless it particularly interested him, he deemed it pointless.

Cerise's eyes were locked on hers, and Grace widened them so she could get what was happening. Fear flickered across her face – after all, she was the one he had.

"You ain't that great," Diablo was saying. Intimating that he didn't score Serena in the sack that highly.

"How dare you… Like you had any complaints?"

Grace saw Serena's finger grip through the trigger loop of the gun as she got angrier and angrier. *Shit!* She would have enjoyed this a week or so ago, but if they carried on and she shot him, a) she could hit Cerise, and b) it suddenly struck her; did she want that? She was confused; it made no sense to think that way. But Dylan did inhabit that body. *But he had gone.*

"You're not as good as you think you are…" he was saying slowly, deliberately and maliciously.

"And she is?" Serena screamed, waving the gun wildly, pointing it at Grace, forgetting she had it.

Everyone seemed to see it and shouted, "No!" at the same time.

At last, Diablo saw the threat, not that he showed an ounce of fear. "Give me the gun, Serena." It wasn't a request, but an order.

She looked at it as if she only just remembered it was there, and frowned in confusion. Then immediately brightened when she realised she held the power and pointed it back at him.

Big Mistake. They all held their breaths. They were doing the maths. If she shot Diablo, then they could rush her. Diablo was a whole other prospect entirely, and no one was willing to take him on.

"Answer my fucking question," Serena shouted.

His answer was to throw Cerise onto the sofa by the hair so he could face Serena squarely. Grace had to hand it to him; she thought he would use Cerise as a human shield. She guessed he didn't need one. *Oh shit!* She'd better at least maim him; he was looking pissed off and she'd never seen him anything but calm, and that was terrifying enough.

"She doesn't bore me," he said slowly, goading her.

Serena baulked and pulled a face. "What's that supposed

to mean… Her?" She flicked the gun towards Grace again, making them all duck. "Miss Goody-Two-Shoes," she sneered.

He shrugged, "You're predictable." Then a grin crept over his face. "A little on the vanilla side."

Then everything happened in a flash.

CHAPTER 36

Serena's eyes widened in shock, at what exactly, Grace couldn't tell. It all happened so fast. Diablo dropped so low and so quickly that for a second, Grace thought Serena had shot him. But instead, he'd kicked out and completely snapped Serena's leg at the knee. It sounded like kindling cracking.

Serena went to the floor.

The gun went off.

Cerise ran to the men, who were all in a huddle on the floor. It seemed they hadn't made it out. All Grace could do was watch the scene play out in grisly slow motion like a bad dream.

Before she knew it, Diablo was back on his feet, had the gun from Serena's hand in one second and at her forehead in the next. A loud blast to her forehead, and the back of her head splayed out in red matter on the floor behind her.

Grace remained frozen to the spot. She thought bullets left neat holes, but her eyes became glued to the melon-like mess that fell from the furniture and the wall in globules.

Diablo wasted no time and strode over to the men who

were not where he'd left them and roughly pulled them apart. Nicholas was gasping and clutching at his chest.

Diablo swore under his breath.

Grace couldn't take her eyes off the blood; Nicholas's blood, and there was so much of it. It ran through his fingers in streaming rivulets. His face was ashen and his thin lips blue. Grace knew instinctively that he had been fatally wounded. He'd been hit in the heart.

"Get up!" Diablo ordered the others. He pointed to the sofa. "Get over there." He was so calm and menacing that they meekly got up and did as they were told.

"We need to call someone," Cerise said quietly, as she walked past him.

"It's too late," he said, simply. Nicholas, not even quite gone, was already written off. But that was Diablo all over, wasn't it. Easy come, easy go.

Grace watched in misery as Nicholas began to pant, and a weird gurgling came from his throat. Blood came from his mouth in a gush. He relaxed back onto the floor. His chest stopped heaving and his open eyes stared up at the ceiling. But the blood, so much blood, kept on coming out everywhere, all over the floor.

When Grace could stand it no more, she looked back over at Diablo. Her face was wet with tears. He had just been watching her. Perhaps grief and sorrow were emotions alien to him?

"Over there with the others," he said, eventually.

She was forced to step over Serena's body. Diablo simply bent and pulled her out of the way so she topped and tailed with Nicholas.

Grace felt numb. She would wake up and she'd be in her snuggly white fluffy bed, in her girly shabby-chic house, and Dylan would be stirring in the bed next to her. Yes, everything would be right and how it should be. Not this living nightmare she found herself in. It was as though she were an outsider – a voyeur, viewing the scene from a distance.

Diablo was dragging the bodies nearer the front door.

Grace felt a dig in the side of her leg. Trying not to give anything away, she looked sneakily sideways at Cerise.

"We have to rush him," she mouthed.

Grace's eyes widened in horror.

"It's our only chance."

Grace swallowed. Cerise was right, but still, it was suicide. She supposed, even with the gun, he could only kill one of them at a time. That meant if they rushed him as one unit, someone might have a chance. It was time to accept that if they let him carry on his sick game, then he was going to pick them off one by one.

"Then we separate and run like hell."

Grace gave the smallest of nods.

Diablo let go of Nicholas's legs like an old sack of potatoes and stalked back towards them. Then a gust of wind howled through the house from the back door to the front, like a gift from heaven. It opened and slammed doors and rattled windows in their frames as it went and disappeared as suddenly as it came.

Those on the sofa all looked at each other for an explanation. So much about the last few hours defied logic. Diablo, unperturbed, stooped in front of Cerise and put the gun to her head.

Then they were plunged into darkness.

There was a brief moment of inactivity at the sudden piece of luck. Then, "Run!" Cerise shouted.

And Grace did, as fast and as hard as her legs had ever carried her.

.   .   .

Simon had never been so frightened in his life. He ran and ran with no thought to where he was actually going. All that went through his mind was that Nicholas – his friend of several years – was dead, and he must put as much distance between himself and the gun if he didn't want to join him.

He wasn't sure how many miles he ran down the lane when the air hacking in and out of his lungs began to burn and make him sound like a seal. He was forced to slow down to catch his breath. Fitness had never been his strong point.

He huddled in a clump of bushes so he couldn't be seen and poked his head out several times to check whether he had been followed. He caught his breath and relaxed slightly when he was satisfied that he wasn't.

A slight warm glow in the sky meant dawn was approaching, and while he longed for the lifting of his spirits and the warmth it would bring his shivering body, it would also bring light, making him and everyone else easier to spot. Even from his small sanctuary of bushes, he couldn't help noticing that trees were scarce and buildings were nonexistent up here.

He must keep going. There was always a chance that Diablo wouldn't bother with an insignificant geek like him. Then he felt guilty, as that would mean he would be benefiting from someone else getting caught. Especially as it seemed to be the girls that Diablo was particularly interested in.

With his throat sore and dry, but breathing normally again, he set off at a jog. He kept to the rough verge at the edges of the road in the hope that it would make him less noticeable. Eventually, he slowed to a walk; he was just too unfit. Surely he'd got away and out of danger by now.

Something hissed from his pocket. He patted it – his two-way radio. He took it out and held it in front of him, just staring at it. My god, he'd had it all the time. In his blind panic, he'd forgotten all about it. He pressed the button and put it to his mouth. "Anton… is that you?" All he got was a crackle and a hiss of static.

He resumed walking, pressing the button and trying it again every few yards, or so. There was still nothing. He was so busy concentrating on the radio that he didn't see the large lump of flint lying on the grass verge. His foot came down awkwardly on it and his ankle went right over. He gasped in pain and began to hobble. It was badly sprained and it became obvious that he wasn't going to be able to walk it off.

A little way ahead, he came to a dry stone wall. It appeared to go nowhere and was half fallen down. A good place to sit, he lowered himself slowly and examined his ankle. He patted his fingers around the tender flesh on his joint. It was already swollen. *Damn*, this was going to slow him down a lot.

His head was still down by his knee when silent sneakers stopped softly just in front of his eye line.

His heart and his breathing stopped. His eyes slowly followed the line of the fatigue-covered muscular legs and he swallowed hard. He continued up the V of the toned torso to the cruel, handsome face that was watching him quizzically. *Why was he looking at him like that?*

Diablo slowly held out his hand, holding a two-way radio with a look of wonder on his face. He clicked it twice in answer to his confusion, when the radio in Simon's own hand hissed.

Simon sagged, defeated. His own stupidity had just killed him, and that was what had astounded Diablo – that a man such as he was, one of letters, could have made such a funda-mental mistake as to use his radio to lead Diablo right to him. "Why me?" he said, barely a croak. "Out of everyone, why did you follow me?"

Diablo cocked his head to the side as if the question surprised him. Then barked a single blast of laughter that drained instantly from his face. "Nothing personal, Doc... just loose ends."

Simon stared at him for a long moment. His street slang was just a cover. The man was super-intelligent. *For heaven's sake*, the whole evening had come out of his brain. He'd even stupidly carried with him his money and means of escape. *Bloody hell*. No one even knew where he was, to look for him, thanks to his promise to Dylan. He almost smiled in resignation when he watched Diablo's eyes harden and his other hand move to produce the gun that Serena had so kindly brought to him. *Genius!*

It's weird what a man thinks of a second or two before death. All he could think of was that he hadn't written up his notes yet on anything that had happened tonight.

A click, and then a flash blinded him.

ANTON WENT hurtling around the outside of the house, not wanting to be easily seen out in the open. His quick mind was turning over and over; where was the best place to hide? He knew he could never outrun an athlete as fit as Diablo – besides, there was no cover away from the house. Nearby would be too obvious and crowded if everyone had the same idea.

"Aghh!" He tumbled and landed painfully flat on his face. His foot had caught on something soft, like a rolled-up carpet. He spat grass out of his mouth, groaned and rose to his knees. He turned slowly to see what he'd fallen over.

"Shit!" It was one of the bodies. He kept low and in the shadows. He could hear the footfalls of the others, still running and gasping for air. He cursed the madman for reducing him to this, but it was about survival now, each for themselves, and everyone had agreed on it.

A scream galvanised his mind like nothing else. Two bodies were lying side by side on the grass, with the line of cars a few feet away. He shook off any last residue of guilt and pushed his arm between the bodies in the middle and shimmied down between them, making sure the arms and legs covered his own, camouflaging them. Then he lay as still as he could, trying to calm his heart rate and slow down his breathing so that his chest didn't go up and down too obviously. To be hidden in plain sight was the plan, and hope that while Diablo was crafty, he would underestimate him in his choice of hiding place, like the sociopath he was.

Footfalls came nearer and nearer. Anton held his breath. They ran one way, then the other, in panic and indecision. His heart hitched. They sounded light and female. It was either Cerise or Grace. To look, to raise his head and try to help them would be suicide for them both, and so he lay still with his eyes closed and felt ashamed. But still, he closed his eyes and didn't move a muscle.

A car door opened and slammed. *Foolish, foolish girl!* It would be one of the first places Diablo would look. But a few minutes had passed. So long that he was beginning to think Diablo had gone farther afield to search. Someone must have made a run for it. A fatal mistake, as he would run them down like the quarry they were. He only hoped whichever one of the girls had got in the car would realise this and decide to change her hiding place.

Anton lay there puzzling over the way Diablo's mind was working. Surely he would have stayed close and caught the ones nearby easily? His heart sank. Maybe that meant he knew where they all were, and it made more sense to round up the strays. With Nicholas dead, that left Simon and him. If it was Simon who had run, and he guessed it was, then it would be him next.

A shot echoed in the distance. Anton swallowed, but his mouth was too dry. That just left him. Misery and fear swept over him and he cried silently. Two good friends gone; if he came out of this, it would be a miracle. He wasn't sure how he knew it, but he felt positive that Diablo was saving the women till last.

He stiffened. Soft footfalls were coming nearer – stealthy, but definitely male. He heard them easily through the vibrations in the ground. Nearer and nearer they came. He kept his eyes tight shut and concentrated harder than he'd ever done in his life to breathe so shallow that his chest didn't appear to move.

His heart stalled when he heard a snort of air through nostrils in amusement. *Had he spotted him?* He almost opened his eyes to check when he heard the snick of a car door being opened.

Ashamed at the relief he felt at the discovery of someone else, he remained rooted to the spot and awaited the outcome of Diablo's grizzly game of hide and seek.

A squeal. *Cerise... Oh no!*

Every instinct in him was screaming out for him to do the gallant thing and pounce up and shout, 'Leave her alone', but instead, he listened pathetically to the shouts and gasps as she clawed and clung to the seat, the pillar of the car door, and kicked and swore. His sense of self-preservation won through and he remained still, as if playing a sick game of dead soldiers.

"D... D, please!" Cerise was pleading.

Anton heard and felt her being silently dragged from the car and back towards the front door of the house. *Should he run now that Diablo was occupied?*

No, he still felt that was certain death. He had to wait it

out. It was his only chance. However long it took, he had to wait until this whole nightmare was over.

CERISE PUNCHED, kicked, bit and screamed, but mostly she was dragged by her hair back to the house. She fought like a madwoman. The memory of the blows she'd already received from him today was all too clear. If she didn't manage to escape from him quickly, then she was pretty sure she'd be dead this time.

Thrown inside the front door, into the living room, she barely had time to scramble to her feet before she was thrown against the wall, followed with Diablo's forearm painfully wedged across her back making it difficult to breathe. She croaked with pain. He was literally squashing the air out of her.

He eased off slightly, but his body still caged her. He seemed to enjoy rubbing himself up against her to let her know how big and powerful he was. "You're going to die tonight, Cerise," he said, close to her ear so she could feel his hot breath.

Even if she could reply, he was just stating the obvious to scare her. *What did he want, a fucking medal!* But her beautiful children's faces came to her and she stifled a sob. She would never see them again. *Please god, let Fenton be alive to take care of them.*

"Where is she?" he said, pulling her away and bashing her face painfully into the wall again.

"Where's who?" she said, tasting the coppery tang of her blood in her mouth.

"Don't fuck me around, Cerise," he said, slamming her again.

"Aagh!" she moaned. "I don't know… I don't know, okay. We all separated… I don't know where she went."

Diablo was quiet for a few moments. He was either deciding whether to believe her or how he was going to kill her; either way would end up the same. "Why do you have to do this?" she whispered. "You could just go... I won't say anything. Neither would Grace, I promise... the men won't, I'll tell them," she gabbled in the hope he was listening to her.

"Ah, babe," he said softly. "There's only your poncey shrink mate left."

She felt stunned – Simon dead already? Anton was still alive somewhere, though, and so was Grace. "Just like I said, we won't say anything."

He laughed and stood back away from her. "So I just let you go, is that it?

She turned slowly and put the back of her hand to her mouth. Half her face was already swollen and fresh blood now oozed from her lip.

Suddenly, he reached out a hand and made her flinch. But all he did was run a thumb along her lip almost tenderly. He looked regretful. "No one can know what happened here today, or who I was before."

A loud clang echoed from upstairs. Both snapped their head round to the door to the staircase. When Diablo turned back to Cerise, he was smiling. "I wonder which one that is?" He moved next to her and steered her by the elbow. "Shall we go and look?"

As they neared the door, a gust of wind slammed the door shut. Diablo staggered backwards and clutched at his chest for a moment.

Despite him releasing her for a second, Cerise remained paralysed. Her eyes were transfixed by the expressions crossing Diablo's face. They were surprise, confusion, anger and then understanding. The weather up here was freaky, but then again, the whole evening had been surreal. God knew what was going on in that man's head and he terrified her, but she found she couldn't tear herself away to run. "What is it?" she said eventually.

He began to look around the room as if he were trying to see something and couldn't find it. She followed his line of vision, but there was nothing there. Perhaps he was having a psychotic episode, hearing and seeing things she couldn't.

"You are still here!" he said, straightening up and looking flabbergasted. "I don't fucking believe it. He looked up at the ceiling as if he saw the answer there. Then a crafty grin crept over his face. "There ain't nothing you can do – not now."

All Cerise could do was watch in fascination and horror as the man lost his mind and totally went over to madness.

Then he remembered her and grabbed her suddenly by the throat. He squeezed and squeezed. She gurgled and croaked, clawing her fingers into his grip to try to prise his fingers away. But his face was impassive and he appeared oblivious to any pain.

Diablo slowly pulled her closer to his face. "I want Fenton good and angry when I fight him for the last time." And he grit his teeth and hit her and hit her until he released her to the ground, where she lay motionless. She felt nothing after the first couple of blows. It felt like a slow-motion film with the sound turned off. She guessed it was unconsciousness overtaking her, unless this was death. Yes, death. A clang of metal was all she could hear. A death bell sounding, until it receded into the distance.

CHAPTER 37

For the first time, the noises in the house; the constant clanging, like air in the pipes, irked him. It was enough to stop his fist before it connected with her head for a final time. *What was that?* No one was running a tap anywhere. Then it all became clear. He laughed. *Oh yeah, the fucker was definitely still here.*

He straightened up and stepped back from Cerise's lifeless form and reopened the door to the staircase. He nodded to himself. All of it – the wind, the noises, it was all *him*, trying to distract him from whoever he was hurting, *the sap.* "Where are you, you fucker?... I know you're here somewhere."

The clanging continued. It sounded like a spanner hitting a pipe the nearer he got. He looked up the stairs, but he was sure it was coming from the back of the house – probably the kitchen.

He glanced back at Cerise to satisfy himself that she wasn't walking out of there and toyed with where to go next.

"Hanging around like a bad stink as usual, D?"

He paused. An evil smile crept across his face. *Such a thick bastard!* Giving himself and any advantage of surprise away. And all to distract him from beating Cerise to death; he cocked a brow and checked her again. She was as near as damn it. He was so weak, he'd given away that apart from banging, slamming and shooting around like a gust of wind, he wasn't corporeal. In other words, there wasn't a damn thing he could do about anything. He threw his head back and laughed aloud. "Just like when we were kids, D. There weren't nothing you could do then, either." He laughed and shook his head.

The difference this time was that he had no physical body to inhabit and he was forced to wander like some ghost.

The clanging finally stopped. Diablo looked up with his foot on the first stair and narrowed his eyes. "I wonder?" He put his foot on one step, then another. He paused when the clanging started up again. Diablo smiled to himself. *Crafty bastard.* He remembered the loud noise earlier that came from upstairs. He'd done nothing at the time, just made a mental note to check it out later. Now he knew who it was and he was going to find her and teach D a lesson he had been dying to teach him since he was twelve years old. Today was the day he was taking back everything that was his.

Grace sprang forward from the sofa blindly, then made a sharp left. The little logic she had made her change direction at the last minute. The front door was the most obvious direction to run. Catching her arm on the doorframe in panic, she found the door to the stairway and kitchen already open, but ran upwards instead of towards the back door like a woman possessed. Only when she slammed the bathroom door shut behind her and leaned against it gasping for air, did it dawn on her that she'd totally trapped herself. All she knew was she needed to go in a different direction from everyone else if she was to have any kind of chance – panic and the flight reflex did the rest. Her eyes now accustomed to the darkness, she found herself in the bathroom, of all dead-end places. Then, leaping into the bath, she managed to knock a wooden loofer off a hook with a loud metallic clang. Cringing, she pulled the shower curtain across.

Shit! What was she thinking? The shower curtain wasn't going to save her. She'd seen *Psycho*, for fuck's sake.

She held her breath and listened for a second, and when she was satisfied there were no thuds of feet running up the stairs, she climbed out of the bath as silently as she could and stood, frantically surveying the bathroom for another hiding place.

Locking the bathroom door would only buy her a few minutes – If that. She looked at the small frosted window. Even if she could fit through – which she doubted – she was on the first floor. She hated heights.

Get a grip! she told herself. Her mind was racing and the rush of adrenaline was giving her the shakes. She had to think straight if she was ever going to outwit him. She turned to take a more detailed look at the bathroom.

The bath was boxed in next to a cupboard. She opened it and found an airing cupboard containing mainly a hot water tank. She could fit down the side of it, but if he did come in here, the first place he'd look would be behind the shower curtain, and then the airing cupboard.

Wait!

There was about an eighteen-inch gap between the end of the bath and the wall of the cupboard. It was boxed in and tiled. She crouched down and felt it closely. *Yes!* It was a smaller cupboard. *I wonder ... Yes!*

The shelves just slid out on runners. She stopped and listened. Positive she could hear voices coming from down-stairs, she hurriedly re-focused on what she was doing. It wouldn't pay to dwell on who Diablo had caught; empathy was just a weakness he used to his advantage. She carefully began removing all the bottles and cans with chronically shaking hands and stowing them in the airing cupboard next to her; cringing with every clink as they knocked into each other. Taking a deep, fortifying breath, she continued to push them around the side of the tank so they weren't easily seen. Everything inside her was screaming for her to hurry up and sling everything in any old how, but she resisted the urge. Then she slid the shelves out quietly and slowly – whispering, 'more haste less speed' over and over to focus herself, then placed them down the other side of the tank. It seemed to take forever. With her heart still hammering in her chest, she stood and took a quick look around her to make sure she'd hidden everything. As an afterthought, she opened the window wide in the hope he would think she'd escaped, and not look any further than behind the shower curtain and the airing cupboard. Then she backed slowly into the tiny space, praying softly that she'd fit in enough to be able to close the little door.

It was snug, but she managed it. Closing herself in completely with a small click, it was airless, hot and dark. She felt claustrophobic. She struggled to calm herself down and slow her breaths and waited.

What was that clanging in the pipes? Was he trying to terrify her from somewhere? Well, it was working; she felt sick with fear. Her mouth was dry and she was sweating and shivering at the same time. Perhaps he knew exactly where she was and knew hitting the pipes would carry straight to her. *Stop!* Surely he wasn't that clever.

The whooshing of the wind started again. Her fingernails bit into her hand. *It's just the weather,* she repeated over and over. The howling made the house feel desolate and lonely. Just like a horror film where the silly girl goes to the haunted house and you want to shout 'Don't go in!' Where you know she'll be a sitting duck for the monster to come and get her.

The wind was so bad that the doors were rattling in their frames, roaring loudly, so she thought the house might fall down. Grace put her hands over her ears and held her head on her knees, positive the roof would cave in. Nothing would have got her out of that tiny space – not even if the house fell down around her.

Then the wind suddenly stopped. It was the weirdest thing. Her breathing was still ragged and uneven, sweat trickled down her forehead and into her eyes, but she felt ice cold with fear.

The latch on the door clicked. The door opened wide with a creak.

"Angel… I know you're in here."

IT FELT like she hadn't breathed in ages – she daren't. *How did he know she was there? Was he bluffing?* She remained still, her breath came in ragged pants, and the sweat dripped off her.

"He's here, you know," he was saying in a soft sing-songy voice.

The shower curtain was pulled sharply back with a whoosh.

Shit! She held her breath.

"D never left, y'know."

She frowned. *What was he saying?* He was just fucking with her head. Like she was going to rush out from her hiding place to meet him or something.

The hinge on the window frame creaked. He closed it.

A pause.

She wiped the sweat out of her eyes. It was beginning to sting.

The airing cupboard door opened with a click. He was still looking and wasn't buying the escape route.

He laughed like he was having a great time. "He's floating about in the house, Angel, like a ghost."

Then a clank as bottles and cans got knocked over together.

Her heart thumped.

He was rummaging through the toiletries she'd stuffed next to the tank.

Then there seemed to be a long pause. *Had he gone?*

"Can't you feel him, Angel?"

Her heart was beating so wildly. He sounded close and low down, as if he was speaking to her at eye level.

Please god, no!

A sliver of light slowly widened to the left of her face, and her heart plummeted.

"Angel," he smiled, looking delighted to see her. "Out you come," he said, bobbing his head to the side.

She resisted, shaking her head, no – unable to speak with fear.

"Right now, Angel!" he said sternly, like a parent.

There was no point in staying put and risking angering him, so she crawled out of her hiding place until she could kneel, stiffly, on her knees. Everything ached after being so cramped up.

She flinched when he ran his fingers across her brow and down her temples and through the rivulets of sweat. "Such a silly girl," he said, continuing his fingers down her neck, along her collarbone and down to her breast. He took his fingers to his mouth and ran them across his tongue.

She watched in horror. "What do you want?" she croaked. Her mouth was completely dry.

"It's just you and me now," he said with heavy-lidded eyes.

Did that mean everyone else had gone – escaped or dead?

Whatever it was, she was now completely alone and at his mercy, and he appeared to be completely turned on by it. "What is it you want from me?" she said again, trying to keep him talking.

He didn't say anything, but his eyes continued to skate over her, assessing her.

"Are you going to kill me?" she tried again.

He cocked his head to the side in that childlike way that was totally his mannerism and yet so similar to Dylan. "Why would I want to kill you?" he said, smiling slightly as if he was a little surprised by her.

She shook her head like she couldn't believe they were having this conversation. They were sitting on their knees in front of each other, like a pair of kids. The killer in him seemed so absent. She would have thought him actually good-humoured if she hadn't seen his handiwork and knew how unpredictable he could be. "Because you've killed everyone else... and because I know too much," she said finally.

He nodded sagely and put a forefinger to the centre of her forehead. "You're smart... if you play your cards right, I'll let you live."

The arrogance was no surprise to her. She had to tell herself that there was nothing of Dylan in this man in front of her. He was a sadistic sociopath with an enormous ego that needed feeding constantly, and he'd set his mind on her to do it. "What do you mean, play my cards right?"

His hand gripped her shirtfront tightly between her breasts and began to slowly pull her to him. He didn't stop until her face was right up close to his. "You have to please me at all times," he said, seductively, next to her lips.

As he'd pulled her, she'd let her hand drag through the mess of stuff he'd emptied out of the airing cupboard. She gripped a wooden handle that appeared to be heavy at one end – a hammer.

She nipped his lower lip with hers. "How can I please you?" she whispered back. She could have succumbed to him so easily – the similarities to Dylan and the fact that she wanted to live. But her life would be a misery. All the while she mulled it over, she was arranging her grip on the hammer, getting it ready to swing.

He exhaled noisily, "Yeah… I knew it… You're a submissive… I fucking love that!"

Oh no, I'm not! But she kept her eyes riveted to his to keep him from noticing her arm gradually moving.

"I'm gonna love dominating you, Angel." And he began to unbutton her shirt.

Her heart was thumping so loudly and she was running out of time. She had to time this just right; one chance was all she had. If she fucked it up, he would kill her for sure.

"Kneel up, Angel," he was saying.

Slowly, she did as she was asked, making sure she kept the hammer behind her and pushed her breasts forward to keep his eyes where she wanted them. He pulled the cups of her bra down, leaving them under the breasts and pushing them higher and outwards. He kneaded them and ran his thumb over her hard peaks.

"Do you want me to suck them for you, Angel?"

She nodded slowly, trying not to get caught up in the reverent way he was now speaking to her. It was all so confusing. She was becoming agitated. Her heart was banging in her chest. She gripped the handle so tightly.

His eyes narrowed for a second and her heart stopped beating. "What about D… you've forgotten him?"

Fuck! Fuck! Fuck! It was all or nothing. She looked him dead in the eye. "He didn't give it to me like you do."

His hand grabbed her suddenly, between her legs, as if to

test her and massaged her roughly. She groaned and closed her eyes. She must bide her time. She gyrated her hips into his hand, pushing against his fingers.

"Yeah, you want it, don't you… My Angel's a bad girl."

Grace opened her eyes and was surprised to see his eyebrows drawn together in need. He began to dip his head forward slowly to put his lips around the hard pebble of her nipple. She paused for a split second. Her heart was hammering. *Dylan?* She silently cried. Was Dylan locked away in there somewhere? Could she do it?

Then the memory of the massacre downstairs came crashing in – The death of her dear friend Cerise.

Her arm began to move around in an arc, the weight increasing with momentum, until it struck the back of his skull with a dull thud.

She screamed when he almost squashed her, falling forward onto all fours. She wriggled free from underneath him, not sure if he was unconscious or just stunned. She tore out of the room while a roar like a wild beast echoed behind her.

She hadn't killed him; she'd just angered him.

The tiger was loose and after her blood.

CHAPTER 38

Fenton shook his head to get his vision focused on the road ahead. Everything was blurring and moving around where it shouldn't. A pickaxe headache from hell, probably from the cracked skull he'd undoubtedly got from his best friend, was making him drive like he was pissed. *Shit!* At the very least, he was concussed. But being 'laid up' to recover was a luxury he couldn't afford right now; there just wasn't time. They were all up there at the madman's mercy.

Fuck! It didn't bear thinking about. He put his foot down and the car sped up.

Nausea came over him in waves. He wished it would stop. The constant dizziness, pain in his ribs and his leg hindered his breathing and caused his stomach to churn. He'd had to pull over to chuck up twice already, losing valuable minutes.

Nearly there, he told himself. Two more minutes was all. He rounded the last bend.

There it was, the cottage looming on the hillside as spooky as a horror film. Every room was lit up, and the door was left open in eerie invitation. All it needed was a bit of thunder and lightning and a few bats flying around the chimney.

The car shuddered to a halt behind the other cars. It made him wonder why no one had attempted to escape in any of them. It didn't bode well. He reached into the glove compartment for the gun and got out of the car. His head spun and he was forced to lean against the car a moment and spit the excess saliva that was accumulating in his mouth. He swore to himself, straightened up and continued along the line of cars. There was no point going inside all guns blazing until he'd sussed the situation.

His head was light and his heart was fluttering all over the place. He couldn't tell whether it was from fear of what he was walking into or his injuries. He swore to himself again and pugged the gun in the back of his belt, out of sight.

Then he bent down to put his knife down the inside of his sock and had to stifle a groan that escaped his mouth from his complaining knee. He breathed through it while he was still level with the car wheel. He had to get real. The state he was in, Diablo was going to muller him. The only way he could fulfil his promise to Dylan was to get clever. He took some deep breaths, then shuffled a little nearer the wheel and reached his hand as far under the car chassis as he could. *Where the fuck? There...* He gripped the hose. Just loosen it; that was all it needed. He didn't want the brakes to fail straight away – just when he'd picked up some speed on his getaway, preferably round a tight bend that overlooked a ravine. He was sure there was a couple on that poxy road back there.

From his crouch position, he mulled things over. The door was open. The lights were on. And the cars were all still here. *What the fuck went on here?* He prayed that Cerise was okay. He knew Diablo was clever and would know if he came at him again that he wouldn't come empty-handed. He looked around him. He needed a decoy weapon. *The shed.* He needed something that looked as if he'd picked it up on route – something to satisfy Diablo's perception of what he would come at him with, and maybe – just maybe, the last thing he'd think of was a gun.

He rose slowly, allowing his knee to gradually straighten out. The pain threatened to knock him over. Breathing deeply, he made his way over to the shed. The door was left open. He checked quickly over his shoulder and went inside. The gaps between the slats and the lightening sky of dawn approaching gave him enough light to see a bit. *Bingo!* A machete – a bit rusty but just the job. He passed it from hand to hand to feel its weight. This is exactly what Diablo would expect.

A car engine came to life outside. Fenton hobbled out as quickly as he could, just in time to see his car screech backwards, turn and speed back down the lane. All he got was a brief glimpse of the driver. It wasn't Diablo. He was male and blonde – Anton. *Fuck!* Fenton closed his eyes and hoped to god the brakes held long enough for him to get down the lane. He hadn't even looked for who had driven the car in; he must have been scared shitless.

Where did that leave the girls? His blood was beginning to boil. Had he run out on them, or was it too late already? He held the machete in a good, firm grip and stalked as low down as his limp would allow, around the other side of the cars and towards the house.

He paused when he came up to two bodies left side by side on the grass. He heaved and spat again. Swallowing down the bile in his throat, he ventured closer to the house, dreading what horrors he was yet to find. Growing up on Brixton's streets, he'd seen some pretty grizzly sights, and again on the cage-fighting scene, but there was something about the way they'd been laid out so precisely that made it all the more cold, callous and business-like. It had Diablo written all over it. He looked at their faces. One was Nicholas. Terror seized his heart for a second when he saw that the other was female. He crept closer and sagged in relief when he recognised it was Serena. *Poor cow! What the hell was she doing here? What was he up to here tonight?* No Cerise and no Grace, *thank god*. But something else was niggling at him, starting to make him think that a lot more about tonight had been premeditated and planned to the minutest detail – more than Diablo just indulging himself in his madness. Serena, lying there, was testament to that.

He took a deep breath and pressed on towards the front door of the house.

The room had been trashed. He crept in. Even with years of martial arts training, he couldn't help the crunch of glass under his feet. He squinted. *What was that?* He was barely moving.

There was definitely a low moan.

He froze.

"Cerise… Grace?" he whispered.

GRACE RAN SCREAMING and stumbling with her arms and legs flailing. She was so panic-stricken that she overshot the beginning of the staircase and wasted valuable seconds having to double back. Diablo was emerging as she hit the stairs two at a time.

Then everything seemed to happen in a jumble. There was pain in her ankle. A crack and a stumble, making her fall head over heels. She landed with a smack into the wall at the bottom of the stairs. There was no time to scramble to her feet before the large hand landed heavily on her head, gripped her hair and yanked her to her feet.

She howled in pain. Her ankle was badly hurt; it killed her to put any weight on it at all.

"Where d'ya think you're goin'?" Diablo said, throwing her unceremoniously over his shoulder and stomping back up the stairs.

Frantically, she tried to grab hold of something – anything, but the plastered walls on each side of her offered nothing to help. She screamed and shouted and punched his back, but he ignored it, so she resorted to thrashing and wriggling madly like a lunatic.

A SHRILL SCREAM rent the atmosphere in two from upstairs. Fenton's eyes went to the ceiling.

There was the moan again. That was definitely coming from this room.

Stamping footsteps overhead sped him up. Whatever had been going on here was still happening. He circled the room, listening carefully, paying attention to spaces behind the armchairs. He stopped. *There*, a foot just visible from behind the sofa. *Oh no!* He knew that shoe. "Baby?"

He pulled the sofa away from the wall in one wild yank.

A gurgle and another moan escaped her while she tried to bury her face into the skirting board.

"Cerise, baby. It's me, Fenton." He tried to keep it together and keep his voice steady while he rolled her over. She tried to fight him at first and scratched at him wildly. His heart broke and he hugged her to him. The beaten, swollen, almost unrecognisable face was now indelibly printed on his psyche for ever. His blood was rising fast. Her lip was split, one eye was just a slit and the other was closed up completely. Her jaw was all wrong and her cheekbone was twice as wide as it should be. The moaning was because she couldn't form words with a broken jaw.

The only way he kept from going completely berserk was the overriding need to comfort her and let her know she was safe. "Shh, baby… I know. It's me."

She began to cry. It was relief, he was sure. She smelt him close up and knew who he was. He laid her back down gently and fought to control the fury rising up inside him. Trying not to hurt her, he bundled up his jacket and laid it under her head. His gun was now visible, but he didn't give a shit.

She sensed he was going to leave her and became agitated. "Shh, babe. Lie still. I'll be back, I promise."

Her bruised hand reached out to stop him and hung limply on his arm, as she was too weak to grip. An awful wailing seeped from her crooked mouth.

He laid her arm gently on her side. "Please don't worry, baby." His heart was breaking, but the need to calm her down and to end this once and for all were the things that helped him most to keep his temper, because if he lost it, Diablo would plaster the walls with him. No, he needed to be a stone-cold killer just like him, if he was ever to beat him. Seeing Cerise beaten like this, within an inch of her life, was the bitter pill he needed to do the job.

She was quiet now, and he nodded a silent promise to her that he was going to take charge like he always did and make everything better. And despite hating every moment of having to leave her alone, he had to focus, and she had to understand.

He wasn't sure how much she could even see, but she nodded almost imperceptibly back. While he was occupied tamping down his anger and making sure she was as comfortable as possible, he hardly noticed the breeze whipping up around him.

The door to the staircase flew open and banged against the wall. It was as though the very house was growing angry along with him. *And so it fucking should.* He stood, with his eyes still on Cerise, then turned and walked towards the stairs. One foot after another, he slowly climbed. In his head, Dylan's words repeated over and over: "Do this for me, Fent, I'm relying on you to finish it once and for all. Promise me you'll do it, Fent?"

"I will," he muttered while he mounted the stairs with his teeth clenched.

WHEN GRACE next opened her eyes, he'd carried her up to the loft bedroom that she and Dylan shared and thrown her on the bed. She lay out of breath, wild-eyed, and stared up at him.

He put his hand to the back of his head and looked at it. The blood from his head was dripping down his neck and was all over his hand. He narrowed his eyes at her. "Why did you do that?" He looked confounded.

She frowned. *Was he for real?* Did he expect her to answer that? "Wwwhat?" she stammered.

"Why would you want to do something like that to me?" He actually looked a little hurt.

Despite her abject terror, the ridiculousness of his question somehow enabled her to speak. "Because you are a murdering motherfucker!" she blurted, wide-eyed, and bracing herself for the backlash.

Instead, his eyebrows rose, he walked to a pile of fresh towels on the dresser, took one and dabbed the back of his head. "That's no reason to try to bash my brains in, Angel," he said, walking back to face her with the towel held to his head.

She was stunned into silence. Then, "You killed all those people."

He was scrutinising her and nodded, still with the towel pressed to the back of his head. "I had to."

She scrambled backwards up the bed so she could sit up

and feel less vulnerable, with more space between them. "But why… they wouldn't have hurt you?" The enormity of what had happened tonight to the people she had got to know was only just sinking in.

He perched sideways on the edge of the bed, dabbed his head again and faced her. "They all expected D to come out of this," he said flatly.

She stared at him and waited. What could she say; she did too and he knew it.

"I knew… I always knew, if I ever got to do this, then I would win."

She shook her head. That wasn't an explanation. "But why kill everyone?" Nothing was making any sense.

He studied her, making up his mind how much to tell her. Then his look became sardonic. "Come on, Angel, no one must know what went down tonight."

She went to protest, but he held up a hand.

"The scientists were never going to leave it alone… There would be endless tests."

Grace shook her head. "I don't get it. How would they know if it worked or not?"

"With me and D, you mean?"

She nodded.

"I don't think it really mattered to them. What matters was the physics and the rift in the dimensions." He looked intently at her to see if she got it. "It happened exactly at the time and place I said it would."

She remained blank. Then it slowly dawned on her. "They could work out when it could happen again," she said, more to herself.

Diablo nodded. "At the very least, they would have published what they'd proved and never leave me alone."

"And the worst-case scenario?"

"They'd have used it to go there… or got more of the

fuckers over here!" He got up angrily, as the thought pissed him off.

She frowned. "Couldn't you have done it yourself... I mean, you're clever enough?"

He turned and looked surprised for a second. The anger disappeared. He smiled and bobbed his head, accepting the compliment. "You're right, I could've. But I was trapped in my own body, babe, and locked down so tight." He gritted his teeth at the memory.

That was it... It had all been about freedom for him.

Her eyes didn't leave him while she thought deeply about what he'd just said. She hated to admit it, but he was kind of right, in a way. She averted her eyes. "Anton never believed in the whole alien thing," she said, taking a while to meet his gaze again.

He looked at her, now faintly amused – like he didn't give two fucks.

The man was so confusing. Was the whole thing bollocks and he was a talented trickster, good at reading the long-range weather forecast?

He chuffed a single blast of laughter. "Okay, if that's true, do you think he would have let me free after this?" he said, quirking one eyebrow.

He was right about that. The fact was, she didn't know what to think any more. She knew what she had seen with her own eyes, but even after all that, Anton didn't believe it – a man of letters. And now Diablo, sitting there so cruelly handsome, with the face and body of the man she loved more than life itself, was ambiguous at best.

Her heart ached with a longing for Dylan that threatened to tear her in two. But he had gone for ever, whether he'd left or gone completely mad, it made no difference – not really. "No witnesses," she said, aloud. She'd said it to the others earlier, but she'd just been surmising.

"No witnesses," he repeated, nodding at her astuteness.

He could be one of the sharpest minds of their generation and he was determined that no one would ever know. He'd planned everything right down to the smallest detail.

She became aware that his whole demeanour was relaxed around her, as if she hadn't just seriously tried to kill him – that was fucked-up in itself. It somehow gave her the confidence to ask something she just had to know. "You used Serena to bring you the gun?"

He looked pleased with her; apparently, he was assuming the question stemmed from jealousy. Perhaps he was right. "Were you going to run away with her?"

She flinched and stiffened when he put his hands into her hair and gripped her neck, but he simply massaged it hard and shook his head. "No… loose ends."

So he would have killed her anyway. She swallowed hard, and her heart fluttered. *Had he engineered the whole argument, knowing what would happen?* And yet she felt mildly relieved. *Did that make her as sick as he was?* "When did you get a chance to arrange with her to come up here?" It was just killing her when it must have been.

He gripped her neck again. She had to be careful; the sexual tension was building in him, she could feel it. "Back at Oxford. I made a deal behind Dylan's back with the scientist."

Relief swamped her when she remembered Simon's admission in the cellar. *But shit.* The level of his planning was scary, but she had to remember he'd been planning it for years. It brought it home to her that she was the only one left. *Was she a loose end?*

"What now?" she said, suddenly overcome with exhaustion. The orange light of dawn was beginning to trickle in through the small skylight in the roof, reminding her she'd been up all night.

"We'll hold up here, get a couple of hours' sleep."

She sat up straighter, as if doing so would somehow make things easier to understand. "We... I mean... what about the bodies?" *Shit!* He was talking like they were a couple.

He stood up, put his gun on the chair, and pulled his soiled T-shirt off over his head. "You don't need to worry, I'll take care of it."

She swallowed hard, not sure how to play things – or strangely – not sure even if she was playing any more. Then, she convinced herself that going along with him had to be the best course for survival. Everything was so confusing, because despite all the monstrous acts he had committed today, he didn't seem as menacing as he had been before; like now he'd finally got rid of Dylan, the pressure was off him and he assumed they were an item. And if Dylan was still locked somewhere in his psyche, then, of course, he would assume they still belonged together. Her brain rambled on and on. *But what if he wasn't?...* "You want me even though I was his... Dylan's, I mean?" She held her breath and looked down and felt him stalk around the bed, not sure what on earth she was saying any more.

His fingers dragged her chin up so she was forced to look at his piercing brown, crow-like eyes. Then he ran a thumb across her lip. "I was always there." His eyes lowered. "You knew it and you saw me." He arched a brow to remind her. "And you came to me, knowing it would be me." He grabbed her by the throat roughly and pushed her back into the headboard with a smack.

The rough treatment served as a perfect reminder to wake her up out of her wishy-washy weakness. She needed to wise up.

"You wanted me to fuck you. I knew it. You knew it," he went on.

Her mind was now together and she knew, without a doubt, that she had to get away from this man tonight, or die trying. Because if she didn't, she'd never be able to, then he'd own her as his slave to abuse and use at will – and, so help her god, she just might let him, and that would make her no better than he was.

He closed in on her.

"Nooo!" she screamed and ducked under his arm. She went to scramble off the bed.

Laughing, he caught her bad ankle and hefted her right back with one pull. She punched, screamed and bit him while he tried to pin her with his large body. "Yeah, babe. I love it when you fight," he said, biting her back and making her yelp in pain.

Her hand went out and found the lamp. She pulled it across, crashing it into the same place on the back of his head, still oozing blood.

"Bitch!" He leant back and smacked her across the face.

All she could do was gasp. The sting took her breath away, and she knew he wasn't even putting any weight into it. Then she wriggled like an eel to get out from under him, trying to turn her body onto her side. When that didn't work, she went to scratch his eyes, then to bring her knee up into his crotch. But he was just too big, too heavy, with the lightning reflexes of a fighter.

Just as hopelessness threatened to crash down on her with his full weight, a black hand came into her line of vision and grabbed onto Diablo's right shoulder and pulled.

CHAPTER 39

Fenton would have loved to say it was the red mist that came down when he saw Diablo pin Grace down with his weight, but the fact was, he was fully compos mentis – or so he thought.

There had been several severe dizzy spells since he had left Dave; imagined noises, words and gusts of wind, and now a warm glow surrounding the bed like a heat camera. He shook his head to get it back in the game. He had to focus; there could be no sentiment for this man any more. What he'd done to Cerise, was about to do to Grace, and the memory of his friend Dylan, there was no coming back from. It was with that thought that he strode forward and grabbed the bastard by the shoulder, then flipped him around to face him.

There was a quick flash of recognition before Fenton punched him in the jaw. It landed perfectly and Diablo rolled expertly with it, off the bed and onto his feet. He flexed his jaw and bobbed his head in concession for a good shot. He doubted he'd get the chance for many more.

"Are you okay?" Fenton said, flicking his eyes quickly at Grace. He couldn't take his eyes off Diablo for more than a second.

She went to scramble off the bed.

"Stay the fuck where you are!" Diablo ordered.

"You don't need a woman slowing you down, D… Let her go… It's just you and me, like always."

Diablo shot a glance at Grace, who was slowly easing herself off the bed and flattening herself against the wall. The clever girl had gone to the bathroom side of the bed, nearest Diablo and the door, which meant Diablo allowed it and looked back at Fenton with narrowed eyes. A sly grin was creeping across his face when he caught sight of the rusty machete Fenton was carrying. "You brought back-up, I see?" Diablo said, slowly moving away from the bed with his arms wide. "So this is it, Fent. I finally get to see whose side you're on."

Fenton didn't answer. He was only just about keeping a lid on his rage, but that was what Diablo wanted – to rile him up and make him get sloppy with his temper. "Why d'ya do it… Why d'you have to hurt her like that?" It was partly to bide some time, *but fuck!* He really wanted to know. He knew Diablo was a sadistic bastard, but he could never understand it – especially not with someone he knew.

They began to circle each other.

Diablo's eyes were darting over him. *Shit!* He was checking him over for concealed weapons. Then he paused as if he were considering the question.

He really was a fucking lunatic! For a solid moment there, Fenton thought he might genuinely try to answer him – give him some scientific sick answer, but the fucker raised his eyebrows as if the answer should have been obvious. " I love it," he said, goading him and began to circle again. "I love the feel of knuckle on soft, plump skin… the look of fear in their eyes," and he opened his wide to mock him.

They continued to circle.

Fenton was desperately trying to hide the weakness in his leg, so he had to make his move quickly.

"Their eyes change from anger to pleading," he was saying. "There's nothing like it… and there's the blood, Fent. I love to see the blood."

Diablo laughed out loud with Fenton's roar, and the slash of the arm carrying the machete whooshed through the air, just missing Diablo's neck. If he hadn't swayed away at just the right moment, it would have slashed his neck without doubt. But before Fenton could recover his balance, Diablo had bobbed low with a sharp punch to Fenton's ribs. Then, in the same fluid move, he grabbed the still-swinging arm and snapped it at the elbow with the next.

The wind left Fenton's lungs in a rush and the pain almost overwhelmed him in his arm and shoulder. When the machete clunked to the floor, Fenton made a grab for it with his good arm, but Diablo kicked it under the bed. Then his foot connected with the side of Fenton's face, sending him reeling.

As Fenton rolled with the momentum of the kick, he managed to grasp the small gun tucked into the back of his belt. By the time he came out of his roll, he was holding it out in front of him, just as Diablo was round-housing his follow-up kick. He pulled the trigger in that second, without thought.

It felt like slow-motion as he watched the bullet travel and Diablo spin to the side with the impact into his shoulder, but he didn't go down.

Fenton stared in shock while Diablo turned slowly to face him again like the fucking Terminator. He put his fingers to the entry point of the bullet hole and looked at the blood. Then he looked back at Fenton as if he'd truly surprised him. "Fuck!" he said, simply.

Fenton went to fire again, but nothing happened. The gun had jammed.

The look of surprise evaporated from Diablo and turned to malice, then he went to move towards Fenton again, like a footballer taking a penalty. Even shot in the shoulder, he was still in better shape than he was, huddled on the floor as a sitting target.

Diablo's leg came back for the killer strike.

Fenton swallowed hard and looked around him quickly – he caught a glimmer of what looked like the butt of a gun on the chair. But it was touch and go whether he could get to it quickly enough, the state he was in. He guessed he'd always known that Diablo would be the death of him, and this was it.

There was a thud!

Diablo's expression froze with surprise. His leg came down to support him instead of finishing his kick, while he tried to turn around to look behind him. The valuable pause was just enough time for Fenton to come out of his daze, roll and grab the gun and pull the trigger twice. He wasn't a crack shot, but this close up and with D falling towards him, it was hard to miss.

Diablo never got a chance to see who hit him from behind and landed like a felled tree half on top of him. Fenton flinched with the pain but managed to pull himself out of the way so he wasn't completely pinned. Grace stood wide-eyed with terror in the space Diablo had just occupied, with her hand over her mouth. Her eyes were riveted to the machete embedded in his back.

"Grace!" Fenton said to snap her out of it.

They just stared at each other for a long moment, neither quite believing they had actually done it.

Deafening sirens screamed from outside and brought them back to reality.

Fenton looked around, assessing the room. "Go check on Cerise, Grace. She's behind the sofa downstairs," he said, wincing in pain, trying to arrange his limp, broken arm.

Grace nodded and disappeared, still limping.

Car doors were slamming outside. *Dave.* He guessed his hour was up. He shuffled clumsily, scooped up Dave's gun and shoved it back in his waistband. The inevitable questions sure to follow meant he'd have to say he stole it from Dave when he took him to the hospital. Diablo's gun was on full view as the weapon that killed him. He groaned and pulled himself to his feet and stood over the body of the person he'd once loved most in the world (after his family) and the one he most hated. A feeling of absolute desolation came over him. He had done it – carried out his best friend's final wish, even though it was a bit messy, and he'd had help from a woman. He smiled ruefully. It was never going to be straightforward, though, was it?

The nausea was coming over him again. His vision began to blur and go double. There were lights, stars and blobs swimming across his eyes. *Shit*, he thought he might pass out. Guess the concussion was setting in with a vengeance. He slid down onto the floor from the edge of the bed with a curse at the jarring pain. At least it wasn't the full body slam into the floorboards. *Fuck!* Adrenaline and a cracked skull weren't a great combination.

Phew! That breeze felt good. He tipped his head back while it whirred around his hot neck and head. The police must have opened up some more doors and windows.

His vision must be shot now because he could see that glow he'd seen earlier settle all around D's body. He was going to throw up. He kept swallowing until the urge passed. Now he was hearing echoey voices. "Fuck!" He plonked himself down onto his backside and leaned his back against the bed.

I owe you, echoed and ricocheted all over the place.

He leaned his head back on the end of the soft mattress. Shit was definitely getting weird. Unconsciousness was taking him under; nothing to worry about. It was completely normal.

I owe you, man... We did it, we're finally free.

And the world switched off.

DAVE HAD ARRIVED like the cavalry with the police and swarmed the place. Several ambulances came soon after and were needed for the wounded and the dead.

Grace was put on a stretcher, and she welcomed the ability to collapse. The aftermath of what she'd been through, a suspected broken ankle, severe dehydration and the adrenaline, was making her feel the kind of exhausted she'd never felt before. Still, when she saw the body of Nicholas, she felt an overwhelming sadness. He was a good man. At least Anton seemed to have escaped, so their plan had worked for one of them. Fenton and Cerise were to travel together, both critical. She prayed they survived, not just because they were parents, but she'd grown to think of them as her friends.

Barely awake, she was lifted into the ambulance. "Wait!" she cried, realizing that Diablo was being brought out and she just had to have one last look at him. Armed police followed the gurney in with him. *That can't be right?* She felt a sudden chill. "Why does that body need a guard," she kept saying to anyone who'd listen. Everyone was so busy and rushing around.

"Some pretty nasty allegations have been made against him, love," a medic said kindly.

Shit! The guy had completely misunderstood her. She'd meant, why does a dead body need a guard. She now had her answer: he wasn't dead.

She lay back in the ambulance while her head raced. What did this mean for everyone? What did this mean for her? She'd assumed she'd killed him and it was all over. Prison would follow for him but, in all honesty, it shouldn't matter. But it did. Misery swept over her; all she wanted to do was to be left alone to grieve.

The ambulance pulled away and she allowed herself to drift into a troubled dream-filled sleep.

GRACE WAS DISCHARGED after a day or so with her ankle in a lightweight support. Diablo remained in a coma for two weeks, which gave her some breathing space. Anton, she was devastated to learn, had run the car he'd escaped in down a sheer drop and was killed outright. They said his neck was broken. The car had caught light, making determining the time of death difficult, but it was generally accepted that he had died shortly after fleeing the scene.

Dave had come to see her a few times, telling her she had to hurry up and make a statement. He knew she was putting it off. He was not involved in the case so there wasn't a lot he could do but rant at her about Dylan. She ended up promising she would soon. But what could she say exactly? She needed Fenton and Cerise, and soon. The police were pushing her for a statement of what exactly happened that night. There had been no one else left alive or conscious right after, so they'd had to wait a long while and she was the first to come round. *Shit, what did she say? What could she say that they would believe?*

The phone rang and it was the hospital. "Is that Miss Grace Fellows?" a female voice said.

"Yes, speaking."

"Mr O'Shea is conscious and is asking for you."

Grace was stunned into silence.

"Miss Fellows?" the voice repeated.

Her heart was thumping in her chest. One half of her knew she should run a mile from him while she had the chance. She should go to the police and just tell them he'd lost his mind and ran amok, killing everyone on that terrible night. But even that didn't explain what all the scientists were doing up there.

But the other half, the half that still longed for Dylan and wanted to say a proper goodbye, made her want to go and see him one last time.

"Yes… Okay, I'll come," she said quietly. "I'll come before I go to the police station." She replaced the receiver.

THE GUARD in uniform nodded at her as she entered the private hospital room. She was kind of glad he was there, but couldn't see what use he would be outside the room if Diablo decided her number was up. She shrugged. He wouldn't be much use inside the room either, if memory served her right.

A nurse was picking up some medical supplies from the bedside table. She smiled at her and left. Diablo was sitting up in bed, propped up with pillows and plugged into various high-tech-looking machines that bleeped periodically.

"Grace," he said, in a husky whisper.

She stood still. There was something different about him – something off. It was his eyes. She frowned and studied him more closely. Her heart began to thump. *Could it be?*

He remained quiet, still, unblinking and allowed it.

"What? You look like I've grown another head," he said eventually.

"Your eyes," she said, approaching the bed.

He stared back at her with that deep, intense, enigmatic look she'd grown to know and love. Bright-blue eyes, but they were different. Small flecks of brown burst outward from the pupil, but they were blue – deepest blue.

She put her hands to her mouth and a sob escaped her. "Is that you?" She reached out a hand and touched his cheek gently.

He closed his eyes and savoured the touch. "Don't cry," he said softly. "It's me."

"Dylan!" she gasped. Tears streamed down her face.

The door opened suddenly. The policeman looked in. "Everything okay in here?"

Grace turned, nodded and sniffed.

Satisfied, the door closed again.

"I don't understand?" she said, turning back to Dylan.

He held her small hand in his. "I didn't go."

"You mean you were there inside him the whole time?" Her mind was trying to go over all the events rapidly.

He shook his head slowly. "No. When I heard… when he said…" He trailed off.

She closed her eyes in shame. She knew exactly what he was referring to. "I'm so sorry, Dylan."

"The pull was too great," he tried to explain. "I lost it… Then my grip. It pulled me to it."

"The rift, you mean?"

He nodded. "For a second, I was so angry I couldn't think… but I couldn't leave." His eyes were soulful, looking deeply into hers.

"Then how did you?" She gestured her arm up and down his body.

"Get back?"

She nodded, overwhelmed.

I was there the whole time; through all the terrible things…" He looked angry and clenched his jaw. A muscle ticced just beneath the skin. "But I couldn't do anything. I was powerless… I was there, but I couldn't affect anything physical." His look was so helpless. "And when he beat Cerise…" His fingers gripped the bed covers and went white.

"She's alive," she said, animatedly. "I'm going to see her after you."

His face softened. "And Fenton?"

"They were both in a really bad way, but they're gonna be okay."

He bowed his head and pinched his nose. "Thank god, I've been so worried. They wouldn't let me leave the room."

She ran her fingers through the familiar tousled hair.

"What about the kids?"

She squeezed his hand. "They're okay. They're all okay."

He relaxed back into the pillows with relief and winced a little in pain.

All she wanted to do was make him feel better, but everything was different now. She had no clue how Fenton and Cerise would react to him after everything that had happened. "I have to go and make a statement when I leave here. They want me to explain what happened… no one has been able to…" Panic gripped her for a second; she had only just got him back and she would lose him for sure. Although Dylan was innocent, Diablo had committed some heinous crimes. Who would ever believe such a fantastic story? Anyone who could corroborate their story was dead; even if Anton had still been alive to say what really went on that night, he himself didn't believe in travellers from other dimensions.

Looking into those hypnotic blue eyes, did she? Did she think Dylan suffered from Dissociative Personality Disorder? In the end, there was no one left alive to prove anything either way, and dead bodies were dead bodies, whatever way you tried to flower it up.

His intense, strange new eyes waited as if he knew what she was thinking. As if he was allowing her to come to her own conclusions. How ironic it was that Diablo's plan of getting rid of all the witnesses had almost worked, but he hadn't lived to benefit from it. But perhaps he had; after all, Dylan was going to get blamed for the lot. The fact that Anton was killed in a car accident, and Fenton and Cerise were still alive, made little difference.

She shook her head; her mind was running away with her. If Diablo had got rid of everyone, Dylan would have been devastated. The eyes that scrutinised her back were the pure angelic eyes belonging to Dylan, with something extra. "I thought we killed Diablo," she said.

"You did," he said, squeezing her hand again and smiling. "It was then that it became clear to me… when you hit him with the machete, I knew you'd made your choice… Fenton had kept his promise. When I saw his life force leaving his body, and I heard the sirens, I knew I'd timed it just right. I could re-enter it and inhabit it on my own." He smiled weakly, as if he didn't quite believe it himself. "It worked."

Grace thought about it. They would have arrived and resuscitated him just in time, after Diablo had already gone. *But shit!* "What difference does it make, Dylan? They'll lock you up for this and throw away the key."

"Not necessarily."

"What do you mean?"

"I'm going to plead self-defence."

Grace stared at him, stunned. *Did he know – did he see the seven dead bodies?... That was stretching the realms of possibility by anyone's standards.*

"Serena… she tried to shoot him… he took the gun and shot her."

Grace grabbed Dylan's hand and beseeched him with her eyes. "Dylan, seven people died that night."

His eyes looked deeply into hers for a long moment. *Wasn't he aware of all the carnage?*

"Serena shot Nicholas… it was an accident, and so was Anton."

She felt exasperated for a moment. "Yes, but I wasn't even counting Anton. There was Simon, the two medics and the two technicians who all helped with the experiment."

He continued to stare into her eyes with his strange, unblinking gaze. Her heart was breaking for him, as he appeared not to have a clue about the full extent of the killing that night.

"You're sure?" he said, after a while.

She nodded and blinked slowly.

"But Serena and Nicholas were the only bodies they found."

It was Grace's turn to be stunned. She shook her head. "No, I saw them. Well, not Simon, but the others." Then she remembered the spaces of time when Diablo disappeared, then came back dirty and sweating. "He got rid of them," she said, amazed, looking off into the distance.

Dylan didn't appear to hear or take any notice. "Serena came unannounced… she was jealous… of you," he said, evenly.

"Serena…" she said flatly. Even now that the woman was

dead, she still stirred up feelings of jealousy. "No, she didn't, Dylan. She brought him the gun. It was so planned… it was."

His face remained impassive. "She knew he was there with you," he said calmly, lulling, convincing.

She shook her head, as if to break the spell he was pulling her into. "Whatever… it doesn't help explain the others."

He nodded sagely. "He planned the whole thing. There would have been no one left… no evidence. " Then he looked shrewdly at her. "Except you."

"And Fenton and Cerise," she added.

He tipped his head in agreement. "Yeah, lucky for them."

She stared at him slightly in disbelief. "Good men died that night, Dylan. Men with families and loved ones… And, besides, the police will interview Fenton and Cerise. Then they'll know about the others. There'll be missing persons… God, Dylan, we'd never get away with it."

The corners of his mouth began to curl into one of his gorgeous smiles. "We?" he said indulgently. "Looking out for me again, Grace?" And he pulled her in so she had to perch on the bed and hug him. His mouth rested on the top of her head. "Fenton didn't actually see anything."

She pulled away and sat up to look at him again. "That's true." She stayed there, thinking about what he was saying. "But Cerise… she was there for the whole thing and he beat her almost to death."

His face gave nothing away about what he was thinking. "We'll just have to wait and see… a lot will depend on what you say," he said, looking intently at her with meaning.

Grace turned away and looked around her, unsure what to think. "But, Dylan… lying to the police, I'm not a good liar."

He grinned, pulled her back onto the bed with him and stroked the back of her hand. "When you make your statement, just tell them what you *actually* saw."

She frowned. *Could she?* When she racked her brains and thought about it, apart from Serena firing the gun and it hitting Nicholas and Diablo grabbing the gun and shooting her, it was all she actually saw. "What about the other bodies?"

"Until there are bodies, there's no crime. How do you know they didn't just get up and walk off?"

"Trust me, Dylan, I know I'm no expert, but they weren't going anywhere." Something about his whole demeanour was troubling her. He was Dylan, of course he was, but she just hadn't seen this side to him before – a side where he didn't seem to care.

Then she felt guilty. *Bloody hell.* He was fighting for his life. When it came down to it, it still rested on whether or not she believed in the whole two-persons thing.

His eyes locked with hers. Then he slowly closed the gap between them and put his lips to hers, kissing her like she never thought he'd do again.

I suppose it could work... She pulled away from him suddenly. "Suppose they find the bodies... what happens then?"

Dylan pondered her question for a moment. "I guess we'll just have to cross that bridge when we come to it."

"What about you?" she said fearfully. Surely he couldn't escape scot free?

"I was there along with everyone else, Grace, like you... with the level of electricity, the drugs I had to take leading up to it, there was a huge part I can't remember... I'll tell them I was there to help with an experiment that I'd designed to cure my schizophrenia. He touched his chest absently.

It all sounded so plausible – *the maths, it was all there.* It was the small piece of reality that dragged her back from the abyss of indecision and doubt. How could someone who was so clever and knew stuff no human could possibly know be a calculated killer?

"But what about Fenton and Cerise, Dylan… they nearly died?

"I don't know what happened with them, Grace." The look on his face was of total innocence. "With everything else that happened, I'm more surprised they lived."

Everything he was saying was so believable. After all, the whole scientific experiment had happened from what came out of his mind – even Simon and Nicholas had believed in Dylan. That was the reason they had all gone there, and it had worked. She felt ashamed for doubting him.

As always, he seemed to read her so well. "Now come here!" he said, playfully, and held his arms out wide for her to fall into.

He sucked in air through his teeth with pain.

"Sorry," she said, trying to take her weight off him. She'd completely forgotten she had cut his back with the machete.

Dylan wouldn't allow her to pull away and kissed the top of her head and smelt her scent. "We can be together now, Grace… Always."

CHAPTER 41

Fenton stood outside the hospital room door and paused. He didn't know who or what he would find, or how he was going to feel when he met him. *He should be dead, for fuck's sake.* Would he want to hug him or kill him? There was no telling. It had been a couple of weeks since that night, and he just had to come and make sure for himself whether he'd been hallucinating or whether any of it was real. *Fuck! Let's just get this over with.* He knocked with his good arm; the other was in plaster in a sling across his chest.

"You can go in," a nurse said in passing.

Fenton thanked her and cautiously entered the room.

D was lying on his bed, gazing out the window, dressed and ready to go. His head turned towards him as soon as he entered. Their eyes locked for a moment and a slow smile spread across D's face.

Fenton was as struck as he'd been on first meeting the kid with those big baby-blue eyes. Angelic – that's how he looked. The sun even shone on him from the window for effect, making him look like he had a halo all around him. So it had all been true; he hadn't been hallucinating that night.

He approached the bed slowly. "Your eyes... have you seen them?" They were Dylan's, but there was something new – something extra in them, small flecks of dark brown making them look extraordinary.

D nodded and looked as amazed about it as Fenton was. "I suppose he had to leave part of himself behind." Dylan held his arms out wide. "This was his." His fatalistic expression said it all.

Fenton laughed at his joke and couldn't help thinking of the old adage, the eyes being the windows to the soul thing. How much else would he have left behind? Still, it was all so fantastic and there was so much he hadn't had a chance to get his head around. A lot of people died that night – some good guys, and he couldn't let it slide. He had to play devil's advocate. "How d'you do it, D?" There was no police presence around him any more, apart from some pretty heavy question marks; the guy was off scot free. "I'm the one answering charges for stealing a police weapon," he said with a wry smile. And Dave was like a dog with a bone for answers, but thankfully, Scotland was way out of his work remit.

D was still watching him with that enigmatic gaze of his, showing no anger or emotion at all. As usual, he oozed that quiet confidence. "I've been out cold, Fent," he said quietly.

Fenton shook his head, still not fully understanding everything. "I thought you'd go away for that lot, mate, for sure – what about DNA for fuck's sake?"

D continued to study him in that thoughtful, calculating way he had – the Dylan way.

Fenton didn't blame him; he must be as wary of him and whether he could trust him now. A lot of shit went down that night. Stuff even he wasn't sure he could forgive, whoever now inhabited the body.

"He got rid of the bodies... Well, most of them... And you

shot him with the gun Serena brought with her," he said sardonically.

That was true. Dave, first on the scene, had retrieved his gun, but that wasn't the gun that had incapacitated him. Fenton frowned. "But what about Grace? What did she say?" It was weird. Fenton watched his face closely; there wasn't a flicker or a hint of feeling like he'd just got away with the crime of the century.

"How many bodies did you see when you came back?" Dylan threw back at him with the corners of his mouth turning upwards into the smallest of smiles.

Fenton frowned. "Two… Serena and Nicholas."

Dylan nodded slowly. "That's what you told the police?"

He nodded, still frowning.

"Serena killed Nicholas by accident, Diablo took the gun off her and killed her."

"Self-defence," Fenton muttered. *Son of a bitch.*

"What happened to Anton?" Dylan said, "He had nothing to do with that." Dylan pinned him with mischievous eyes as if he saw right through him. Fenton rubbed his forehead. The only person who knew the truth was Cerise, and he'd had to tell her so she didn't incriminate him with her statement. *Fuck.* He pulled his hand away from his face and sighed. "I did it… It was me."

Dylan just watched him and nodded slowly. *He knew… the fucker already knew.* "Look, you have to understand, there was a high chance I wasn't getting out of there alive, and I assumed the next person to get in that car would probably be D in his getaway."

Dylan put his hands up in surrender. "Hey, you won't get any judgment from me."

Fenton sagged in relief, but he still felt bad about the whole thing; after all, Anton had been a good guy. He huffed a mirthless laugh. "Fuck, the sleepless nights I've had over it… not coming clean about the whole thing… I mean, what would be the point? D's gone now."

Dylan was still nodding in that knowing way of his. It wasn't making Fenton feel any better, though. *Shit*, he'd actually ended up helping D eliminate witnesses. Was guilt the real reason he didn't say any more than he did to the police? How he stuck mostly to what he actually saw, and made sure Cerise agreed with him and pleaded amnesia as a result of her injuries?

"I do have you two to thank," Dylan said, pinning him with shrewd eyes and reading him again. "Your injuries… how did you explain them?"

After a moment, Fenton let out a long sigh and looked at him wearily. "I told them the truth as I saw it. That you were under a regime of strong drugs leading up to the experiment… that you lost it, we fought, I got injured. That bloke, Dave, found me and took me to the hospital. By the time I got back after the experiment, I surmised you'd lost the plot, hurt Cerise and were about to hurt Grace in our efforts to restrain you… Serena's gun was on the chair… The gun went off in our scuffle."

Dylan watched him lay out his whole rationale to the bitter end. "And Cerise… she corroborated that?" he said, his face tinged with sadness.

"She didn't remember anything after that," Fenton finished, flatly. The image of Cerise's beaten body was etched into his brain for ever.

As he pinned him with meaning in those last words, Dylan looked genuinely devastated with what he'd done – even though it wasn't him – *Fuck*, a guy could go out of his mind thinking through all this. Imagine if D and Dylan were one person and he'd managed to pull off this whole thing. After all, every witness was dead—well, except him and Cerise, and they'd backed him up, not just to save themselves, but for their belief and love for this man.

At that point, his stomach felt like it fell out of his arse. *Were he and Cerise only alive because he'd killed Anton and kept quiet?* Goose bumps covered him all over and the small hairs stood up on his neck. No. He stopped his train of thought. Even if the whole thing came from Dylan's own mind, it had been his way of working it out and removing his bad side. *Could he return?* He shuddered.

Dylan's face was as angelic as ever. If anything, he watched him inquisitively. *Nah, can't be... could it?*

Dylan broke the gaping great silence: "I wasn't aware Anton's death was anything other than an accident... till today."

The way the guy seemed to know everything he was thinking was unnerving.

"I know everything... now, Fent," he said calmly, proving Fenton right again. "Besides, I was still there a lot of the time, remember?" He looked at him again, waiting for him to fall in with what he meant.

"But there was just nothing I could do physically to affect anything." Dylan pinched the bridge of his nose as if he were in pain at the memory. "I've never felt so useless."

When he looked back at Fenton, he looked ruined.

"All I could do was rattle a few things like a fucking ghost, Fent. But I was there. I saw everything."

Fenton wasn't sure what he thought, but he exhaled loudly and nodded. "So you were... You know, separate?"

D nodded and then looked out of the window, recalling that night. "When it happened, I got wrenched out. I never felt pain like it. Like every part of me was being scalded in a red-hot fire... but then I saw, Fent." His eyes took on a fervent, glazed look.

"Saw what?"

"Everything. Who I really was... Where I'd come from... Who I'd been before I came here." His face looked like he'd had some kind of epiphany or something.

Maybe it was true, all of it. He wanted to believe him, for fuck's sake. "So you know it all?" Fenton said in awe. "A total out-of-body experience?" He was either in the presence of greatness, like a genuine alien/angel or something or, at the very least, he had his dearest friend back. At that moment, he didn't want to think about all the sick crap; he wanted to take him at his word.

Suddenly, he wanted to question him about everything, like, was it heaven where he'd come from, and is it where everyone goes when they die, and shit like that? But he sobered and tamped that part of himself down, the part that remembered exactly what went down that night and what state it had left his wife. The atheist in him, he supposed, just refused to delve any deeper into it. And so he quickly changed the subject. "So you're getting out today?" he said, turning to face the door.

"Yeah," Dylan said, nodding. "Fresh start... I will have to report for some psychiatric evaluations at some point." There was that eerie knowingness again behind those strange eyes, like he knew they'd find him cured, and making a disciple out of him was the last thing he'd do.

Fenton found himself back at the door and stopped and turned. He just had to know. "Why did... Why do you think Diablo left me?" It was the last, fucking million-dollar question.

Dylan's face didn't so much as twitch at the ambiguity in the question. "Let you live, you mean?"

"Yeah. It's been kinda buggin' me." Diablo had left him alive twice on that fateful night, and if he was inside him somewhere now, and if he'd miraculously bumped off every other fucker around, even if he'd unknowingly helped with

Anton, then why had he still let him live now, to be standing like this right in front of him?

Dylan raised his eyebrows, then frowned while he considered the question. "I'm not sure... maybe he just didn't get around to it before..." The idea of Diablo's death was left hanging in the air. "Unless he had an accomplice... maybe he had help that night?"

Was that devilment he saw hiding in Dylan's eyes? *Shit!* He hadn't thought about that angle, that someone could be watching and waiting, just in case. He shivered; that was just the kind of evil shit Diablo would do.

Dylan's lips curled into a slow, charismatic smile. "Or maybe he just thought you'd do the right thing?"

Fenton stared into Dylan's peculiar, hypnotic eyes for quite a few moments with that last flippant comment and if there was any hidden meaning behind it. *Fuck!* He was losing it. But still, was the guy mad? Had his warped mind just pulled off the craziest stunt in history to exorcize his inner demon? "Just a word of warning," Fenton said.

Dylan waited.

"That bloke, Dave. He's a Copper... He won't let this lie.

Dylan nodded slowly. "Thanks, Man."

The sad tone in his words held an inevitability–some innate confidence in what outcome, he didn't know, but Fenton knew it would be the last he'd see of him.

Saddened, he opened the door to leave and took a last look at Dylan, still watching him. The science all over the guy's body was real enough – Fuck knows how he did that. It was enough to get some of the top scientific minds all excited. The only thing he knew for sure was that he'd never really know, not really. There would always be that small niggle.

But maybe, just maybe, it all happened just as he said.

EPILOGUE

Grace waited while Dylan finished pulling his T-shirt on and watched the muscles ripple, bunch and flex under the wings of the eagle on his back. The clean dressing – about four by four inches, was neat and white just below it. Those wings had taken on a new significance now.

He sensed her there and turned around, beaming a smile that changed his face from handsome to butterfly-churning gorgeous. "Come here," he said, bobbing his head backwards to beckon her to him.

She did as he asked and dropped her bag down on the bed. "Are you ready to go?"

He linked his arms around her back and pulled her to him, stirring beneath the waist. Grace couldn't wait to get him out of hospital and alone. It had been so long since they'd made love. He squashed her to him so she could feel him through his jeans and that he felt the same as she did.

She melted as she always did. The feel, the smell, god, *everything* about this man just drove her wild. She touched his face. "Are you sure you're well enough to travel right away... maybe you should rest up a bit?" She was sure that when the doctors gave him the okay to leave, they didn't expect him to be going touring on his bike.

He smoothed the hair away from her face, then closed the gap between them and kissed her deeply. It was done with a promise of what was to come. A blush surged into her cheeks. She was ready right now.

Dylan broke the kiss and grinned. It was uncanny how he always knew his effect on her. It had occurred to her on more than one occasion that technically, he was an alien, so maybe he had some kind of ESP where that was concerned. "I'll be fine," he said. "I want us to get right away... make a new start."

"Where are we going?"

He looked into her eyes, intensely, with his blue ones now flecked with fire. "I thought we'd go across to France, then see where it takes us?"

She felt unsure for a second. It was a big step, one she'd never thought she'd make. Her house was now on the market and her horse with a friend until she could work out what to do with her. This was actually it – the start to a new life with the love she thought she'd lost for ever.

"Are you okay?" Dylan said, touching her lips again to bring her mind back to him.

As if it ever left him, he had her at 'hello'.

"No, it was just that detective bloke, he's been speaking with Dave, and he won't stop asking questions."

The first flicker of doubt she'd seen made him narrow his eyes, then he shook the thoughts away as nothing. "Don't worry about anything, babe."

She nodded and wished she felt as confident. "It's just that Dave has told him he doesn't like or trust you, and that the reason he went tearing up to Scotland was to get me away from you."

"Shh." He ran the pad of his thumb across her bottom lip

and stared into space for a few moments. Then he seemed to shake out any semblance of doubt. "Shh, baby. It's over. It's just you and me. It's going to be how it was meant to be." He held the sides of her face and looked solemnly into her eyes. "It's a miracle we never thought could happen… our chance."

She breathed out a ragged breath and shook off her melancholy. "You're right… let's go!"

"I'll just go and sign out," he said, grinning at her turn-around of mood.

"I need the loo and I'll have a look round – make sure you haven't left anything."

He gave her a last kiss on the mouth and grabbed his holdall. "I'll meet you outside."

She was left alone in the middle of the room. "Okay," she said under her breath and walked into the little bathroom, used the loo and washed her hands, checking herself out in the mirror on the small vanity cupboard. *This is it, girl!* She ran her fingers through her hair, then stopped and looked at the cupboard. Why she needed to, she didn't understand, but she clicked open the door to peer inside. Her heart was thumping, as if another secret was going to jump out at her.

Her breath came out in a rush of relief. *Stupid cow!* It was empty, of course. She laughed at herself, and her mood brightened immediately. It was time to leave all that crap behind now; it was all over. He didn't need medication any longer… *did he?* She frowned.

She was still deep in thought when she came back into the hospital room and jumped out of her skin when she saw a nurse stripping the bed. "Sorry!" came out in a rush without her thinking.

"Oh sorry, love," the nurse said. "I thought you'd already gone."

"I was just having a last check to make sure he hadn't left anything behind." She was almost at the door.

"Oh, love, before I forget. This rolled under the bed. Must have fallen on the floor when I pulled the sheet off."

She handed Grace a tubular plastic container with a blue cap at one end and a white cap at the other. It looked like some kind of medicine dispenser. Her hands were shaking as she took it from her. A feeling of dread began to creep over her. "Is it Dylan's?"

"I guess so."

"What is it, do you know?"

"I wasn't sure at first, but when I took a closer look, I think it's a contact lens case." And she showed her what she meant. It was empty, though.

Grace's world stalled and everything seemed to close in on that single moment in time.

"Does Dylan wear lenses?" The nurse asked.

Grace was totally thrown and became flustered. "Er… um, I'm not sure. I'll ask him if you like?"

The woman looked curiously at her. "Yeah, you take it, love, you can always hand it in at the front desk if it's not his." She carried on remaking the bed for the next occupant.

Grace walked out of the room in a daze. Another woman passed her and went in carrying more bedding supplies. Grace made it to the front of the hospital without any recollection of how she got there.

It was brilliant sunshine after it had rained earlier. A bright new day and there he was, all tall, dark and devastatingly handsome. The angelic, strange little boy he had once been came to her, troubled and achingly lonely. The quietly self-assured, gorgeous bloke who'd swept her off her feet in Covent Garden. The loving, sensual, gentle man she had a deep connection with that she'd never have with another living soul. Everything she'd always dreamt of in a boyfriend – Dylan, her Dylan.

With Diablo gone, did it matter, really? Anton's words echoed.

He beamed that knockout smile as soon as he noticed her standing there watching him. "Come on, sexy," he called.

Two passing girls looked at him and then at her with faces a mixture of lust and jealousy.

Grace took a deep breath, came to an instant decision and walked toward him, tossing the plastic container in the bin as she passed with a clank.

Dylan was already astride his bike. He passed her a helmet, then put on his.

The engine snarled into life.

Could he be any darker or more dangerous?

"Hold on tight," he said, when she got up behind him. "It'll be fast."

Yes it would.

Her stomach flipped when they roared off up the road. She gripped onto him hard, closed her eyes, and trusted in the ride.

Read **The Watchers** next: Here
The second exciting title in the **Dark Valentines Collection**
by T Stedman

Have you tried T's 21st Century Sirens Series? **Soul Breather**
is now absolutely free to download!

To receive your two 21st Century Sirens Novellas, and be the
first to know anything relating to T's books, leave your
details here: https://mailchi.mp/d18c89c14f50/
tstedmannovellas"

Also find her online at:
www.tstedman.com
Facebook
X
TikTok
Books2Read

If you enjoyed this book, please leave a review.

ALSO BY T STEDMAN

21st Century Siren Series

Soul Breather

Blood Sister

Shield Maiden

Tiger Lily

Night Goddess

The Novellas

Protector

Lost Moon

* * *

Non Fiction

My Migraine Story

9 780993 309854